WITCH CROSS INN

LESLEY APPLETON-JONES

A Jakes and Raines Murder Mystery: Book Two

Copyright © 2019 Lesley Appleton-Jones

All Rights Reserved. Witch Cross Inn is a work of fiction. Names, characters, organizations, places, events, and incidents are either products of the author's imagination or are used fictitiously, and any resemblance to actual persons, living or dead, actual events or locales is entirely coincidental.

No part of this publication may be reproduced, scanned, distributed, transferred, stored in a retrieval system, downloaded or transmitted in any form or by any means, including electronic, mechanical, photocopying, recording, or otherwise, without permission of the publisher, except in the case of brief quotations embodied in critical reviews and certain other noncommercial uses permitted by copyright law.

Published by Plumridge Press, LLC
Cover design by Plumridge Press, LLC
www.lesleyappletonjones.com

For my husband, Joe—with love and gratitude

There is no fire like passion, there is no shark like hatred, there is no snare like folly, there is no torrent like greed.

                              Siddhartha Gautama

CHAPTER ONE

Seventeen-year-old Dougie Peterson had a death grip on the steering wheel of his mother's Toyota Sienna. Blasts of icy wind slammed against the minivan, rocking it sideways. Falling snow twisted and corkscrewed in the headlights like an angry tornado.

Until tonight, the vehicle had safely transported him and his three sisters back and forth to elementary, middle and high school for a grand total of two hundred and fifty thousand miles. Hopefully, he thought, it would live to see another fifty. But, as one more gust ripped through Pinkham Notch, creating whiteout conditions, he began to have serious doubts.

In the passenger seat next to him, Laurie Hall, his girlfriend of one week, snapped her gum. She'd been chewing it like a fiend in order to disguise the smell of alcohol. They were heading up the mountain pass that separated New Hampshire's Wildcat Range from the Presidential Range on the way to her father's home in Berlin.

They'd been gaining in elevation for the last ten minutes. On their left was the formidable bulk of Mount Washington, notorious for having some of the worst weather on the planet. On their right, a steep cliff disappeared into the dark.

"Why didn't you tell me you were staying at your dad's tonight?" Dougie asked her, trying to keep both fear and irritation out of his voice.

"I didn't think it was a big deal."

No, he thought, but my mom will if anything happens to the car. If he managed to get Laurie home, he still had to come back, and things were only going to get worse. Besides being one of the deadliest mountains in the U.S., Dougie knew Mount Washington held a world record for wind speed. And it seemed to be setting a new one tonight.

He tightened his grip on the steering wheel until his knuckles ached and dared a glance at Laurie. She seemed clueless to their predicament.

"It's so pretty, Dougie. I love snowstorms. Don't you think they're just so romantic?"

He grunted.

"Don't you think it's pretty?"

Dougie muttered a distracted, "Yeah."

She twirled her hair around her finger. "Do you think Kayla is pretty?"

He craned his neck forward to get a better look out the windshield and grunted another "Yeah."

"Dougie!" she screeched.

Thinking she'd spotted something like a moose or a snowplow heading straight at them, he slammed on the brakes. His father would have been so disappointed to learn that all of his warnings not to hit the brakes in icy, snowy conditions had gone unheeded.

The minivan fishtailed and started to slide sideways toward the drop-off.

Dougie braced himself for the collision, praying they'd hit a tree instead of going over the edge. Forcing himself to take his foot off the brake, he frantically yanked the wheel one way and then the other. Nothing worked. They slid closer to the edge. His leg trembled from the effort of holding his foot high above the brake. They seemed to be going faster now. Fear crawled up his spine and sweat prickled under his arms. Desperate, he slammed his foot back down on the pedal even harder.

The Sienna jerked and spun in the other direction, heading directly for the mountain rockface. Releasing the wheel, he closed his eyes and prayed as he lifted his foot and slammed it down again. He felt the tires jerk and start to veer in the other direction, heading back toward the edge with sickening speed. He forced himself to pump the brake more gently until finally, the minivan responded and slid to a stop.

Opening his eyes, he peered through the windshield. They were inches from the edge of the road. He gulped. If the car had gone over right in that spot, they'd have been lucky to be found by next spring.

"What the hell were you screaming about? We nearly had an accident!" he shouted.

"You think Kayla is prettier than me," she sulked.

"What are you talking about?"

"You just admitted it."

"I was concentrating on the road. I don't know what I said."

"Well, you said it."

"I didn't mean it."

"So, you think I'm prettier than Kayla?"

He sighed. "Of course I do, and you know it." Everyone knew it. Laurie was the prettiest girl in school. Even she knew it. "Now, stop yanking my chain and let me get you home."

She laughed, leaned across the seat and kissed him on the cheek. Despite the fact that they were now parked on the side of a mountain road in a blinding snowstorm, Dougie unbuckled his belt and turned to give her more than a kiss on her cheek, but she pulled away and giggled.

He wondered exactly how much she'd had to drink.

"Dougie?"

"Yeah?"

"I really have to pee."

"You should have gone at the party."

"You know there's no bathroom at that stinky old mill, and I wasn't about to pee in the woods like you guys did." She gave him a well-practiced but still adorable pout and added, "I told you to buy wine coolers instead of beer. Beer always makes me want to pee."

He rolled his eyes. Laurie might have been the prettiest girl at school, but she was definitely high maintenance. "You're such a pain. You know that, don't you?"

She giggled again.

"Can't you hold it until you get home?"

"No," she said, opening the door. The wind was now blowing with such ferocity, it almost ripped the door out of her hand.

Dougie got out with her. The wind howled as it tore down the side of the mountain and blasted snow inside the minivan. He slammed the door shut and yelled, "Where are you going?"

"Just over here a little way so no one will see me."

"Just do it beside the car. No one's coming."

"You'll see me."

"Not from over here I won't."

"No," she said, taking a step closer to the edge.

The next thing he saw was a look of panic flash across her face, right before she disappeared over the edge of the cliff. He heard a scream, then nothing. He ran around the Toyota to the side of the road. There was nothing to see except a landslide of snow, loose gravel and leaves. Beyond that, nothing but blackness.

"Laurie?" he yelled. He listened intently but couldn't hear anything except the moan of the wind.

Rushing back to the car, Dougie frantically searched the floor in the back for a flashlight he knew his mother kept there for emergencies. He found it shoved under the driver's seat and ran back to where Laurie had disappeared. He shone the light down, but he couldn't see her.

Then he heard a sob, followed by a strangled, "Dougie!"

Moving the beam over to the left, he spotted her. Luckily, it wasn't a sheer drop. She was about eight feet below him on a forty-five-degree slope.

"Are you okay?"

"Yes, I think so, but I keep slipping."

Dougie positioned the light beam right in front of her so she could see where she was going. "Try and grab that tree root."

She began to scramble up the slope on all fours. The soil, loose with leaves and debris, gave way, but she managed to snag the root.

"Now grab that boulder," Dougie advised, shining the light a little to her right.

She stretched and hooked her fingers into two crevices on the smooth boulder. Heaving with all her strength, she pulled herself up the slope another foot, but the rock came away in her hand, and she slipped back down into the darkness.

Dougie flicked the beam downward and found her. "What's that you're holding?"

"The rock," she said and looked down. But it wasn't a rock. She was holding a human skull. Her fingers had poked through soft earth packed into the eye sockets, enabling her to get a good grip on it.

Laurie Hall screamed in pure terror.

CHAPTER TWO

Fifteen miles south of Pinkham Notch and at a lower elevation in North Caxton, the snow had turned to rain. Sarah Mooney was unpacking her Christmas nativity set, while Pickles, her Yorkie, was shredding the tissue paper the figurines had been wrapped in.

Sarah placed the baby Jesus in his manger on the mantelpiece and turned to survey the mess. "You are a naughty, naughty little dog," she scolded playfully. "But Mommy still loves you."

Pickles yipped and wagged his tiny tail.

She bent down to scoop him up, but he scampered off. She started to pick up the scraps of paper when he ran back in and tore through the pile. She laughed in delight and threw a handful at him. Watching his crazy runs, or zoomies, as her niece called them, was one of her favorite things. She heard his nails on the kitchen tile and made a mental note to clip them in the morning. Then he shot out of the dining room and back into the living room, circled her legs and took off for the kitchen again, where he stopped to lap up some water.

Stuffing the wrapping into a trash bag, she studied the nativity scene, feeling joy at the sight of it. It had been her mother's.

Suddenly, Pickles started growling and scratching at the back door.

"All right, hold your horses. I'm coming." Sarah dropped the trash next to the kitchen table. "But you just went out less than an hour ago."

In a frenzy now, Pickles clawed even more frantically to get out.

"Stop it. You'll ruin the paint again." She opened the door and cold, damp air hit her.

Pickles tore off across the grass, triggering the security light she'd installed to scare off raccoons. The yard wasn't fenced because her property abutted the forest, and Pickles never strayed far. Until tonight. With a growl, he disappeared into the darkness.

She called him and waited, but he didn't return. Grabbing the flashlight that she kept charging on the wall near the door, she stepped out onto the deck and shone the light into the swath of trees. Something big and furry was running. At first, she thought it was a bear, but she quickly realized it was running like a man. Only it wasn't a man. Her mouth gaped open. It was Bigfoot.

CHAPTER THREE

When dispatch radioed Master Patrol Officer Angel Natale, he was sitting in his cruiser talking to rookie officer Fennis Cooper. They'd parked facing in opposite directions, so their drivers' windows lined up next to each other. Angel, although more experienced, looked just as surprised as Fennis on hearing that a human skull had been found in Pinkham Notch, as well as a report of a Bigfoot sighting right in town.

After confirming that it wasn't a joke, Angel said with a shake of his head, "We're supposed to be gearing up for Christmas, not Halloween."

"Do you want me to respond to the skull?" Fennis asked with eager anticipation.

"No. Take the Bigfoot call. Sarah Mooney called it in. She's a nuisance caller. It's probably nothing more than a moose or a bear scare. After taking her statement, you can head on up to the Notch."

Fennis tried unsuccessfully to hide his disappointment, but he did as he was instructed and pulled into Sarah Mooney's driveway a few minutes later. She came to the front door with a small dog in her arms. The dog growled at him when he stepped into the house. Mustering the respectful attitude he'd been taught in the academy, Fennis listened patiently to her story and, even though it was raining heavily now, he dutifully followed her out back to where she'd spotted Bigfoot.

Sarah stood in the yard watching him as he made his way into the trees, shining his flashlight ahead of him. It was dark, wet and cold, and the forest gave him a creepy feeling, like someone—or something—was watching him. The rain was quickly melting the dusting of snow they'd had earlier that night, creating a spooky fog. It was like a scene out of a horror movie, he thought, and shuddered. He made a cursory search of the area, flicking the flashlight beam here and there, but he found nothing.

"Move to your right," Sarah yelled from the safety of the back porch, which caused the Yorkie to bark as fiercely as a dog at least four times its size.

Fennis jumped at the uproar and nearly dropped the flashlight, but he did as she'd suggested and moved a little more to the right. That's when he spotted a footprint in a dwindling patch of snow. He bent down to take a closer look.

"Well, if that don't beat all," he muttered to himself like an old-timer.

Sarah Mooney started to walk over to him. "Did you find something?"

"Stay back, ma'am. I don't want to disturb the evidence."

"What is it?"

"It's a footprint."

"Is it a footprint or a boot print?"

Fennis shook his head in disbelief. "It looks more like a gorilla print."

CHAPTER FOUR

At the summit of Wildcat Mountain, Holly Jakes skied off the chairlift and bent over to tighten the buckles of her old racing boots. It was her first run of the day, and the conditions couldn't have been better. Blue skies and brilliant sunshine overhead. Underfoot, the snow was perfect: snowcats had groomed all night, leaving trails of fresh corduroy in their wake. Perfect for rocketing down the mountain—her preferred speed. Holly breathed in deeply. Skiing in December didn't get any better than this. And, for a Sunday morning, it wasn't busy yet.

She planned to head straight down the mountain as fast as she could. Expert all the way. Top Cat to Starr Line into the glades and back out onto the Sphynx, which would dump her right back at the lift, so she could do it all over again.

But first, she needed to prepare herself mentally for the run. Clear her mind of all distractions. This wasn't so easy. She'd woken several times in the night from the same recurring nightmare she just couldn't shake. A masked man was shooting at her. When she returned fire, she discovered that the gun wasn't loaded, and no matter how many times she pulled the trigger, nothing happened. Two nights before that, her weapon had been loaded. Trouble was, the bullets kept falling out of the end of the barrel and dropping uselessly to the ground at her feet.

It didn't take a genius to figure out why she had these terrible dreams. Even though she knew that there were plenty of police and military personnel who had the exact same nightmares after a close call, it didn't help. They still kept on coming, like automatic gunfire. Relentless.

If that wasn't distracting enough, she'd just driven past a line of police vehicles on the way up to the mountain. Angel Natale had spotted her and waved her over, practically jumping in front of her

Jeep to get her attention, but she'd ignored him. She couldn't face him. Not yet.

She had no idea what was going on, but it was all hands on deck with multiple law enforcement agencies responding. It would be easy enough to check. Chief Finch had left her a gazillion messages that morning. None of which she'd listened to because she couldn't take another one of his pep talks.

All week he'd been trying to convince her to return to active duty. But how could she do that in good conscience? The chief said she was a great detective. A great detective? Right. Would a great detective have missed the warning signs? No. A great detective would have sensed that something was wrong—had a tingling, a primitive response of some kind, hinting that all was not well in her world. But there had been nothing. *Nothing!* No inkling. Not until it was too late. What made it worse was that she'd been trained to read people. *Trained!* Came in top of her class at the academy. What a joke. She'd missed the warning signs. She had failed to read him.

And yet the chief still wanted her to return to duty. It was pity; she heard it in his voice. But how could she face the department? How could she wear her beautiful gold shield now with any semblance of pride? She couldn't because she didn't deserve it. She was a fraud. Her colleagues knew it. The reporters knew it. People in town knew it. Some of them had even told her. But that was small towns for you.

So, she avoided the supermarket, her parents, and even the local gas station. Skiing was different, though. Her helmet provided her with welcome anonymity.

When the chief's pep talks hadn't worked, he'd switched tactics and tried psychoanalyzing her instead, doling out home truths like he was getting paid for it. Some of them had hit a nerve—a raw nerve. But it didn't matter because she'd made up her mind. She was done. It was time for a new career. That wasn't going to be easy, but she'd done it before when an accident had ended her skiing career.

She sighed and tried to still her mind by focusing on the spectacular view. Across the Notch, snow-covered Mount Washington sparkled like a gemstone in the morning sun. Deep powder filled the Tuckerman and Huntington Ravines. At the base, snow-laden fir trees completed the winter wonderland. Holly had skied all over the world, but this view was hard to beat.

Pulling down the ski goggles from the top of her helmet, she positioned them over her face. The lens was yellow for flat light. Not perfect for a sunny day, but she'd have to make do. She'd left her sunglasses in the Jeep. Next, she looped her hands through the ski pole straps and let her skis rip. She'd force herself to focus by racing to the bottom at breakneck speed.

CHAPTER FIVE

The prison smelled of damp, smelly socks, sweaty bodies, and cleaning chemicals. Detective Cal Raines sat at table twenty in one of four blue plastic chairs arranged around it. The tabletop and chairs were attached to a solid metal frame, which was securely bolted to the floor so no one could pick up a chair and start swinging. Except for the correctional furniture and the prison guards, who stood with their backs to the wall and carefully surveilled the inmates, the visiting room resembled a high school cafeteria. There were even some young faces in the crowd. Some were visiting. Some were not.

One skinny kid, who wore an orange prison uniform and suffered from a bad case of acne, didn't look much older than Raines's fifteen-year-old niece, Abbey. Even though he had barbed wire tattooed across his forehead, it did nothing to age him. He slouched in his seat with the sullenness of a teen who had been grounded for a month, picking at scabs the size of cigarette burns that ran up his left arm.

A heavyset woman, prematurely aged by the smoker's lines around her lips, faced him. Dabbing at her eyes with a crumpled tissue and dressed all in black, she looked like she was attending a funeral. In a way, Raines thought, she was. This is where dreams died, and the person you'd been on the outside ceased to exist. It was depressing.

The fact that Abbey visited her father here every week depressed him even more. This was no place for a kid.

Raines stared coldly at the man sitting across from him.

Nathan Raines said nothing. He just folded his massive arms and stared angrily back at his younger brother. Nate had always been in shape, but now he had a bulked-up prison body: bulging, rock-hard muscles, an intimidating chest, and a thick neck. Raines couldn't remember a time when he'd looked so pale, though. As a high school quarterback and then a football coach after he graduated, Nate had always spent as much time outside as he could and had always sported a tan, even in winter. No sunshine in prison, Raines thought. It had to be hard on him, but he felt no sympathy. In fact, as far as Raines was concerned, his brother hadn't suffered enough. Not for what he'd done to his beautiful, sweet wife, Sherry. It had been over a year since a jury had found him guilty of stabbing her to death, leaving his two daughters, Abbey and Melody, traumatized and without parents to raise them. All they had now was an uncle who knew nothing about teenage girls. And all Raines felt for his brother was loathing. He wanted to grab him by the overalls and make him pay for what he'd done to his family.

"Why are you here, Calvin?" Nate smirked, obviously hoping it would irk Raines if he used his full name. Raines had always gone by Cal.

He didn't take the bait. There were far more important issues to focus on. "I'm here because Abbey wants me here. No other reason."

Nate smirked again. "And I thought you were here because you finally solved the mystery of who killed Sherry, but I guess you didn't care enough about her to do that, did you?"

Raines fought to keep the rage out of his voice. "You, better than anyone, know who killed her. The only mystery left to solve in a case like yours is why you did it, but I don't need to hear your sniveling reasons. I know it was jealousy. What I want to know is why you keep torturing the girls by pretending you're innocent. Tell them the truth. Let them move on."

Nate placed his brawny forearms on the table, laced his fingers together and squeezed them like he wanted to wring his brother's neck. "You don't get to tell me what I say to my girls."

Raines bit back a retort. As their legal guardian, he had the right to stop his nieces from visiting their father, but he hadn't done so. That didn't mean he was comfortable with it. He'd sworn to protect them. Although Nate couldn't hurt them physically, he could mentally. Still, Raines knew in cases like theirs, where the father was convicted of murdering the mother, the horror of essentially losing both parents was often compounded when the children were placed in a tug of war between the two families. Abbey's and Melody's lives had spun horribly out of control. Their father's actions had robbed them of their mother, their futures, and the lives they'd had. Raines wanted to empower them. He believed that even though Melody was only fourteen and Abbey a year older, they were mature enough to decide for themselves if they wanted to see their dad or not. Was it the right decision? He hoped so.

At the moment, Abbey was the only one who visited him, and Raines hadn't missed the toll it took on her. There were dark circles under her eyes from staying up late, pacing back and forth in her room. Not only had she lost weight, but she'd also lost interest in anything other than her horses.

Until recently, she'd been adamant about her father's innocence and furious at his imprisonment, but Raines knew she'd started to have moments of doubt. Seconds, really, of uncertainty. She'd whisper anxiously to him every now and then, "Could Dad have done it?" But in the next breath, she'd squash her doubt with a firm "No." Loyalty and need seemed to be winning out—for now.

Melody, on the other hand, refused to see him. Raines wasn't sure whether Melody believed that her father was guilty or innocent. Although Melody had been there the night her mother was murdered and had found her body, she claimed not to know what had happened. She didn't talk about it, and Raines didn't push her.

The best Raines could do for the girls was to prevent Nate from continuing to poison them with his lies. "Just tell them the truth," he said to him now. "Admit you killed Sherry, and if I know your girls, they'll find a way to forgive you."

Nate's eyes narrowed to slits. "You're a real piece of work. You know that? You have more money than anyone in town, and that's a town stuffed with fat cats from Boston and New York. But you still refused to help pay for a lawyer to defend me. Then you up and buy my house from under me. And to top it off, you're trying to take my girls away from me. Well, you aren't going to win this one. They're my kids," he growled. "And I'll tell them whatever the hell I want to tell them. You'll see. They'll stay loyal to me. No matter how much you try and brainwash them. I'm their dad. I have an appeal coming, and Abbey's going to vouch for me when the time comes."

Raines said nothing for a moment. He simply stared at his brother, surprised to find that Nate could still shock him by how self-absorbed and heartless he was. If their own dad had been alive, would Nate be in here? Or would his calm presence have helped

Nate mature from being the bully he'd been all through school and teach him how to control his anger? Raines didn't know, but he wished his dad were alive now to help him raise Nate's girls.

"You left the girls without a home. You didn't have any equity in the house. In fact, it was in the red. You know this, Nate," he said, keeping his voice level. "The girls were upset that their mother's house was up for auction. They couldn't face living there, but they didn't want to lose that connection with their mother, so I bought it for them and put it in a trust until they're older. Then they get to decide what to do with their mother's house."

"Their *mother's* house? That's it, isn't it? Your refusal to help me is all about Sherry. She was the one thing you couldn't hold on to, and it eats away at you that she dumped you for me. I had Sherry and a family, and all you had were platinum records and a vault-load of cash. Now you have everything you wanted. You wanted my family; now you have it."

Raines stood up. "Sherry wasn't a *thing*," he said, in a voice flat with contempt, "and her girls are not pieces on your chessboard of 'how do I get out of here.'"

Nate's neck turned red, and a vein on his forehead bulged. "They're whatever I say they are."

Raines looked down at him. "I can't believe I expected more from you—a hint of remorse for what you've done to them, to Sherry. But there's nothing there. You're a shell, Nate. Nothing but a damn shell." Raines turned and left the room without looking back.

He headed straight for the car, feeling an intense need to check in on the girls. Prison visitors were not permitted to bring in phones, so when he got to the car, he retrieved his phone from the center console where he'd left it. There were two missed calls from Caxton's police chief and a text. All it said was 911.

CHAPTER SIX

Cal Raines didn't work for the Caxton PD, so an emergency text from Chief Finch was unusual but not unprecedented. They'd worked together before. Raines was head of the Major Crimes Investigative Unit for Kearsarge County. It was a relatively new position, created by the sheriff after a dispute with the state police.

Chief Finch answered on the first ring. "Raines. That you?"

"What's up, Fred?"

"It's Jakes."

A memory of Holly Jakes flashed unbidden into his mind at the mention of her name. She was twelve, and they were playing football in his backyard. She'd just tackled him to the ground and was sitting on top of him, trying to rip the ball out of his hands. She was laughing so hard, tears formed in her eyes. Fear gripped him. "Is she all right?"

"Physically, yeah, but mentally, I don't know." The chief sounded like a worried parent. "She's been cleared to return to duty, but getting her to come back is harder than nailing Jell-O to a wall. And I've just landed the Yorrick case. It's perfect for her."

"Who's Yorrick?"

"A couple of kids found a skull up in Pinkham Notch last night."

Raines grinned. "Was there ever a case more aptly named?"

"What about the Bigfoot case?"

"Bigfoot?"

"Jeez, Raines. Where have you been for the last twenty-four hours? Several people in town called in Bigfoot sightings, and now we have Bigfoot hunters rolling into town hell-bent on snagging one. It's going to be a miracle if one of those idiots doesn't shoot someone by mistake. I'm shorthanded without Jakes. I need her back."

"What did she say?"

"She gave me some baloney about not being up to the job. Can you believe it? Angel's up in the Notch at the scene where they found the skull and saw her drive right by him. Nearly ran him over, for Pete's sake. She had her damn skis strapped to the roof of the Jeep. All hell's breaking loose, and she's skiing at Wildcat. Go talk some sense into her, Raines. Get her back to duty before it's too late. The mayor is hounding me to hire someone else, but I don't want to lose her."

Raines sighed inwardly. There was no way he wanted to get in the middle of it. He'd known Holly since they were kids, and he knew she wouldn't appreciate his involvement. "I'm sure if you tell her you really need her to work the case, she'll come back."

The chief coughed. It sounded like a guilty little breath of air. "Oh, heck. She's mad at me for giving her some unsolicited advice. Says I crossed the line."

"What did you say?"

"That it wasn't her fault she failed to see she wasn't dating Mr. Wonderful."

That was an understatement if Raines had ever heard one. Yet no one had ever suspected Holly's boyfriend could be capable of what he'd done.

"And," the chief continued, "I may have mentioned something along the lines that she's punishing herself—and me, I might add, but I didn't tell her that—because she doesn't feel worthy. She still blames herself for her brother's death, and that's why her choice in men leaves a lot to be desired."

"Oh, boy," muttered Raines.

"I know, I know. It was just some fatherly advice."

"Trouble is you're not her father."

"Don't talk to me about her parents. I bumped into them at church, and they didn't even ask after her. They don't want anything to do with her. Angel overheard them tell someone she's disgraced the family—again. They not only blame her for her brother's death, they still blame her for her accident at the Olympics. Did you know that? And now there's that mess with her boyfriend. She's taking it from all sides over that one, including her parents." His voice sounded husky with emotion. Holly really was like a daughter to him.

Raines knew Holly's parents, and he was fully aware that since the day of Charlie's death in a sledding accident when he was ten, her parents hadn't stopped blaming her. That didn't mean he had the right to interfere now, though. "Fred—" Raines started to protest.

"No. Just listen to me. You have to do it because she trusts you. You guys go back a long way." He sighed, sounding heavy-hearted. "Look, I shouldn't have said those things to her. It was just another blow to her pride. I see that now, but I can't take it back."

Raines thought about his inability to help his nieces; how in the world was he supposed to help Holly if he couldn't get through to them? He wasn't good at the emotional stuff. Never had been. What's more, this was Holly Jakes. She would not appreciate his interference in her life. "She's not going to like it when she finds out we've been talking about her."

"I'll take the hit. Blame it on me. I just don't want to lose Holly. Tempt her back with the Yorrick case. It's something she can sink her teeth into."

Probably right after she sinks them into me, Raines thought.

CHAPTER SEVEN

Cal Raines looked up the mountain. It was below freezing, and the snow guns—strategically spaced all the way up the trail for maximum coverage—blew ice crystals into the cold air, creating a fine powder that drifted like smoke against the cerulean sky.

He watched for a few minutes with his neck tilted back so he could take in the steep incline. How many races had he watched, standing at the bottom of a mountain waiting for Holly, when they were in high school together? Too many to recall.

Suddenly, like an apparition, she appeared, a dark, darting speck against the swirling powder. Then she disappeared back into the billowing snow, only to materialize seconds later, ghostlike and ethereal. She was moving fast. So fast. Raines didn't know how she could see. It had to be whiteout conditions up there. He held his breath and waited as she vanished again.

And then she burst back into view. She was closer now, and Raines knew it was Holly. He'd watched her ski in enough competitions to recognize her aggressive stance: calm upper body, hands forward, weight forward in her boots, driving pressure to the tips of her skis. She carved turns at such a high rate of speed that she had to combat g-forces like a fighter pilot did. This took incredible strength, focus and training. But Holly wasn't carving turns now. She was in a full tuck with her ski poles under her arms, hurtling toward him, attacking the mountain like the champion she was. He shook his head, marveling at her ability. Even though she'd mangled her left leg in an accident at the Olympics that had ended her career, she was still strong enough to ski like a bat out of hell. This made him smile as he remembered how the Meatloaf song of the same name just happened to be her favorite tune when she was training for competitions.

Seconds later, she'd almost reached him. He raised a hand in greeting and knew she'd spotted him because she faltered and caught an edge of her ski. She looked like she was about to wipe out, but she merely balanced on the other leg, lifted the snagged ski, and zoomed right past him, heading straight for the chairlift. Luckily there was a line at the Quad, even in the singles line, which is where she was heading, so he had time to run and catch up with her.

People waiting for the chairlift turned to stare at him, trying to place him. Some got it faster than others and started to nudge one another. He heard someone murmur, "Acid Raines." Someone else said, "Lead singer." A couple of skiers fumbled for their phones to take a photo of him. He ignored them.

"Leave me alone, Raines," Holly muttered as he came up behind her.

"How did you know I was here for you?"

"I like to flatter myself occasionally. No one else will," she said with a wry laugh.

He grinned. He'd been worried that she wouldn't be the same with him after the last case they'd worked, but he could tell from her banter that wasn't going to happen. There would be no awkwardness, no feeling sorry for herself, no emotional outburst, and—thank God—no tears.

As four people got on the chairlift, the line moved forward, and Holly slid up. Raines took a couple of steps and said, "The chief called."

She pulled her hands free from the straps on her ski poles, ready for the chairlift. "I guessed that much. I'm done. Tell him that."

He leaned closer to her so people wouldn't hear what he was saying. "You're not a quitter, Holly. You're a fighter."

"It doesn't matter how many nouns you have up your sleeve, Raines. I'm not going back."

He saw the stubborn tilt to her chin. A look he'd seen many times before. "You can't tell me you're not interested in what's going on in the Notch."

"Curiosity doesn't make you good at your job," she muttered, more to herself than to him.

He frowned. "That's a cop-out. You know you're good at your job."

She said nothing.

Raines took a few more steps to keep up with her. They were close to the front of the line now. "The chief's calling it the Yorrick case."

Sliding her goggles up on to the front of her helmet, she turned to look at him. With her skis and bindings, she was almost as tall as him. He stood over six feet two in his boots. "What? Like in Hamlet?" she asked.

"Exactly like in Hamlet," he said. "Some kids found a skull. There's nothing to identify it. The chief says the case is yours if you come back."

Her eyes widened with excitement. In the bright sunlight, they were the blue-green of an ocean, he thought.

She shrugged, tamping down her eagerness. "It's probably just a missing hiker. Besides, I have other things lined up."

"Like what?"

"Ski instructor."

"As noble as teaching is, you'll miss the hunt."

The line of skiers moved. She slid forward again, nearing the front of the line. She looked at his feet. "You need skis to ride the chair, Raines."

This wasn't going to work. He needed more time to convince her. He had to come up with another plan. "Are you going to the benefit on Friday night?"

"What benefit?"

"There's a plot of land available next to the high school, and Principal Donaldson is raising funds to buy it for a pollinator park. The plan is to teach the kids about flowers and bees."

"That should be interesting when all they're thinking about is the birds and the bees," she said.

They were first in line now. The lift attendant checked the front row for tickets. "Why don't you come?" he suggested.

"Are you singing?"

"No, but I'm donating a guitar for the auction."

"I'll come if you sing," she said with a sly smile. She knew he didn't perform anymore.

He didn't hesitate, though. "If you show up, I'll sing."

She laughed and skied off to the chairlift.

CHAPTER EIGHT

The scar from Jimmy Turner's decompressive craniectomy was gruesome. The right side of his skull had been removed to relieve pressure on his brain after he'd suffered a brutal attack and head injury several months earlier. Once the swelling had subsided, the doctors reimplanted the bone flap, which had been removed and cryopreserved. Then they closed his scalp with more than fifty surgical staples. Because Jimmy's hair had not grown out yet, the vicious wound was clearly visible.

This was his first day back at school. His mother had chosen Friday so he could ease his way into a full schedule. She'd requested that he join the art class because she thought that it would be good therapy for him. Before the surgery, Jimmy Turner would not have taken art. Before the surgery, Jimmy Turner would have bullied the kids in art class instead.

Melody Raines sat behind him. She couldn't take her eyes off the huge "C" that had been carved into the side of his big fat head. It was like the doctors had given him his own personal scarlet letter, she thought. Only it was a "C" for cocky instead of an "A" for adulteress. But Jimmy wasn't cocky anymore. He wasn't much of anything. He just sat there in class with a pencil in his hand doing nothing, looking at no one, while the kids whispered "Frankenstein" and "freak." For once, she was not the focus of the class's attention. Jimmy now had that honor, for which she was so very grateful. It was a relief not to be the only freak in class.

With the focus on her unfortunate classmate, Melody found herself relaxing a little—until Mrs. Lucas began to discuss their next project. She opened a box on her workbench and pulled out a clay reindeer.

"For the rest of the quarter, you are to create a multicultural winter holiday gift for your parents. You can choose from

Christmas, Hanukkah, Kwanzaa, the winter solstice, or the Chinese New Year. Whatever you think your parents would like."

If Mrs. Lucas had slapped Melody across the face, the shock wouldn't have come anywhere near the painful memory that hit her at the mention of Christmas. Her mother had loved the holidays. They had made cookies together, shopped, wrapped gifts and decorated the tree. All Melody could see now was the image of her mother's dead, bloody body on the kitchen floor.

Melody would not make anything for Christmas in art class because Christmas was not something she wanted to think about. She would never celebrate Christmas again. Not without her mother. It was too painful. It had been a special time. But no more.

Last year, she'd told her Uncle Cal she didn't want to celebrate the holiday. He'd understood, and so there were no presents, no Skiers' French Toast for breakfast, no turkey dinner, no tree, and no decorations.

If she could lock herself in her bedroom until the holidays were over, that would be perfect. She hated the thought of Christmas Eve. Christmas morning. Christmas Day. But she couldn't escape it. It was everywhere. Even in art class. If only she could hide somewhere. If only she could forget that terrifying image of her mother. But she couldn't. There was no forgetting. No escape.

As Mrs. Lucas spoke, she glanced around the class, looking for positive reactions. When her eyes met Melody's, though, she must have remembered that Melody did not have parents at home to make a gift for, because Melody could see a flutter of panic cross her teacher's face. Then she watched, squirming, as Mrs. Lucas proceeded to make it much worse by trying, somewhat awkwardly, to amend what she'd said.

"What I, um, mean, is that it doesn't have to be your parents. No. The gift can be for anyone special in your life. Your uncle, for example. Or, um, your grandparents." Flustered and red in the face, she patted her clay reindeer. "Yes. It can be for anyone, absolutely anyone."

Stricken, Melody looked down at her desk, but not before she saw all eyes turn in her direction.

Then the whispers started. "Can prisoners even have Christmas decorations?"

A few girls up front giggled, and someone near her snorted.

"Does she get strip-searched when she visits her daddy?" a husky voice asked.

Someone else sniggered and added, "I'd pay to see that."

Melody wanted to point at Jimmy Turner's head and say something—anything—to get them to look away from her. Why had she come to class? Could she pack up her things and go? No. They would know why she was leaving. She had to sit there and wait for the bell. But tears started to fill her eyes, and her hands began to shake. She had to get out of there fast. There were two doors in the classroom, one in the front and one in the back, which was closest to her.

She stuffed her drawing pad and pencils into her bag, stood up and grabbed her coat off the back of her chair.

Mrs. Lucas looked at her and frowned. Melody held her breath and silently pleaded that she wouldn't stop her from leaving. As if hearing her silent plea, Mrs. Lucas gave a slight nod of consent, and Melody made a beeline for the door while Mrs. Lucas drew the teenagers' attention to the front of the class.

In the hallway, Melody pulled on her coat and headed for the side exit, which led to the parking lot. She had no idea where she was going but didn't care. She just had to get out of there.

Standing outside in the bright sunshine, she looked around, unsure of where to go, or what to do. Melody didn't want to call her uncle, or Po, their six-foot-four, tattooed nanny.

A voice behind her said, "Hey. Aren't you Abbey Raines's sister?"

Melody glanced around and spotted a leggy redhead with wide green eyes and a pouty mouth. She was leaning against Zack Blackthorn's silver BMW.

"Leave her alone, Kayla. Let's go," Luke Johnson called out from the passenger side of the vehicle. Luke and Zack were seniors and had been voted the most eligible bachelors in high school by the cheerleaders.

"Just wait a second, Luke," the girl snapped, and walked over to Melody.

She was tall and wore black leggings with a purple miniskirt and a skintight green sweater. A purple ski coat was folded over her arms. Her skin was creamy white with a smattering of freckles, but they didn't make her look younger. There was something sexy about them, Melody decided, and wished she had freckles like that. She didn't recognize her, which was no surprise. These days, she didn't pay much attention to anything at school. Plus, this girl looked old enough to be a senior. Melody was a freshman.

"I'm right, aren't I? You *are* Abbey's sister?"

Abbey didn't have many friends. Neither of them did since her mother's death, and Melody knew all of her sister's friends. Besides, Abbey was only sixteen. At least a year younger, if not more, than this girl. So why the interest in her sister?

"Are you all right, kid?" Kayla asked. "You looked like you'd seen a ghost when you came out of school."

Melody just stared at her.

"Are you skipping school?"

Melody shrugged.

"Why don't you come with us?"

"Kayla! No way. She's too young. She's just a kid," Zack Blackthorn protested.

"Oh, shut up! She'll be fine. Come on. I'm Kayla Jenkins."

"I'm Melody Raines."

The older girl looked her up and down and said, "Oh, I know exactly who you are."

CHAPTER NINE

Melody Raines got into the back of Zack Blackthorn's SUV with Kayla. "Where are we going?"

"Verity Falls," Kayla told her with a gleeful smile.

"But that place is deserted. There's nothing out there," Melody mumbled.

"I know. It's a ghost town," she said.

"Wooooo, wooooo!" Luke Johnson moaned playfully in a creepy ghost voice.

Kayla laughed and slapped the back of the headrest.

He turned to them and grinned, his smile almost as big as a jack-o'-lantern's, Melody noted. His blond hair was short on top and buzzed even shorter on the sides, making his ears look like satellite dishes. She knew who he was because he played football, and it was practically impossible not to know who played for Caxton High. Zack played, too.

"Why are you guys going to Verity Falls?" she asked them.

"You'll see when we get there," Luke told her, and turned to face the front again.

Melody glanced behind her over the seat and spotted a cooler. She could guess what they had planned. She didn't party, but if she didn't go, there was a good chance she'd have to go back to school. Anything was better than that.

Zack looked at her in the rearview mirror, squinting his brown eyes like he was thinking about something important. Zack Blackthorn was a confident kid who oozed wealth with about as much subtlety as an oil rig. He drove a brand-new BMW SUV, all his clothes had fancy logos on them, and his teeth were perfect. The kind of perfect that expensive dental work gets you. The Blackthorn family was well known in the area—well known for being loaded.

"Are you sure you want to come with us?" he asked.

Melody nodded. What did she have to lose?

Zack put the vehicle into drive and pulled out of the parking lot. She had a vague idea of where the abandoned town was. Still, she was surprised when he headed north toward Crawford Notch instead of south to the Kancamagus Highway, which is how she thought they would get there.

Kayla turned toward her. "So, your sister is into horses, right?"

"Yep."

"What's she like?"

Melody glanced at her. Why all the interest in Abbey? "She's okay."

"I hear she can be a pain."

Kayla was right. Abbey could be a major pain, but Melody wasn't about to admit it to a stranger. "Who did you hear that from?"

Kayla squinted at her. It was a hard squint, the kind that made her look much older and meaner. "People."

"She's my big sister. You know how they can be."

"Not really. I don't have a sister."

Melody looked away from her, out the window at the passing town full of ski shops and restaurants, outlet stores and gift boutiques. Most of them were there to serve the million or so tourists who passed through the valley each year, rather than the locals. After a few minutes, they reached the intersection where you could make a right to head up through Pinkham Notch, past Mount Washington, but they didn't turn. Instead, they headed straight on Route 302. Leaving town, they entered the glacier-carved Crawford Notch with its steep, craggy cliffs, frozen cascades and the hardwood forest that was famed for its fall colors.

Eight miles further on, Zack started to slow down. Melody craned her neck to see the road. She spotted an entrance on the left that appeared to be nothing more than a logging track. Zack turned in, and the SUV bounced up and down on the rough, unpaved road for about another mile. Snow covered the frozen ground, but it wasn't deep enough to fill in the deep ruts, which looked like they'd been made by heavy trucks. A startled snowshoe hare hopped quickly off the road, its distinct large hind feet propelling it to safety.

They were in the middle of the Pemigewasset Wilderness, deep in the heart of the White Mountains, surrounded by trees and granite. Melody checked her phone.

Kayla noticed. "There's no signal out here. None for miles."

Did she sound more sinister now, or was it Melody's imagination? "Is this the only road to Verity Falls?"

"No," Zack told her. "This was the lumber railroad for steam engines. There were several of them in the Notch to move logs. Have you ever taken a ride on the Mount Washington Cog Railway?"

She nodded.

"The steam engine here was just like that. Very cool. Verity Falls is an old logging town. I think the original road became overgrown, or we haven't found it yet. There's another logging road off the Kancamagus Highway, but it's barely a trail."

"Does the tourist train that goes through the Notch from North Caxton run on the tracks of an old lumber railroad?" Melody asked. She'd been on that one, too. Her dad loved trains.

"Yes." Zack turned a corner into a large clearing.

On their left, brick foundations were just visible in the thick brush. Ahead of them was a narrow path that appeared to have been used recently. To their right was a two-story derelict sawmill. Its corrugated roof had rusted, and some of the wooden planks had rotted away. The building had many windows. This was probably because the old mill didn't have electricity and they had needed light to work, Melody thought; only a few glass panes had survived. A stream trickled alongside the mill and flowed into a large log pond behind the structure. Flooding had damaged the foundation so much that the building sagged in the middle. A rickety wooden log chute lolled out of the back into the pond like a giant tongue. A sign with "Blackthorn Lumber" stenciled on it hung at a precarious angle above the main doors.

Zack drove into a small clearing to the right of the mill that was not much wider than his BMW. As he pulled forward, Melody realized that it was a good hiding place for the SUV. The narrow opening in the trees was just wide enough for the vehicle, and it was angled behind overgrown bushes.

"So, this is your family's place, Zack?" Melody asked.

He said nothing, just opened the door and got out. Luke and Kayla followed. Luke retrieved the cooler from the back as well as a small gas can.

Melody stared at the gas can. What were they planning on doing with *that*?

Heading for the old mill, Kayla called over her shoulder, "Come on, Melody. Wait until you see inside."

Melody opened her car door and eyed the dilapidated building with skepticism. "It's not safe."

Kayla laughed. "Don't be a chicken."

CHAPTER TEN

Deciding that she'd look like a fool if she stayed in the SUV, Melody Raines followed the little group over to the mill. Zack gave the door a tug. It moved far more easily than she expected given the age of the building. The interior was a surprise. A large canvas canopy occupied the far-left corner of the building. From where Melody stood, it looked as if lights were strung up around it, and she could see two camp beds and two camping chairs were under it. The walls of the building itself were made of rough-sawn planks that had grayed with age. Old train tracks ran down the center of the mill, and a railroad dolly stood at the end of the tracks. She assumed it had been used to move logs past the saw. An ancient steam engine was located to the left of a rusted saw. Next to that was a newer-looking saw. Melody thought the mill would smell musty, because of the damp and rot, but it still smelled of pine. Sawdust covered most of the surfaces.

Melody followed the boys and Kayla to the tent. Luke started to lift several planks of wood that were leaning against the wall. Behind them, Melody saw a small generator and a box that appeared to contain camping supplies, plastic cups, plates, and tinned food. Next to that was a 3D printer that was similar to the one they had at school. Melody picked up one of the plastic cups and examined it. It was lime green.

"Did you make this with the printer?"

"Sure did," Luke said proudly. "And the plates."

Kayla sat down on one of the camping beds. Zack sat opposite her, while Melody sat in one of the chairs.

Luke opened the cooler. "If we'd known we were having company, we'd have made more cups."

"What did you manage to get?" Zack asked.

Luke held up a bottle of champagne and a six-pack of beer from Hurricane Mountain Brewery, which was located not too far from where Melody lived.

"Champagne?" Zack asked, raising his eyebrows.

"Mom just had a bunch delivered for an event tonight. It's the one thing she won't miss."

"I'll take a beer," Zack said. "Let the girls have the champagne in the cups."

"So fancy," Kayla gushed.

Melody had never had champagne before. For that matter, she'd never had any alcohol.

Luke ripped off the foil and aimed the bottle up at the rafters before popping the cork with great fanfare. They all cheered. He filled the cups for the girls and handed them out. Then he tossed a beer over to Zack, grabbed one for himself and sat down next to Melody.

Kayla took a big gulp of champagne and giggled. "This is so good."

Luke looked over at Melody, who was just holding her cup. "You're not going to waste that, are you?"

She didn't want it, but they were all looking at her with assessing eyes, waiting for her to prove she was unworthy to be there with them. She took a sip. It was fizzy like soda, except more bitter. Bubbles shot up her nose, making her eyes water a little. "So, do you guys come here a lot?"

"It's our home away from home," Zack told her with a proud grin. He pulled the ring on his can, and beer foamed out of the top. He slurped it up fast. "Next time, Luke, just hand me the beer. If I wasn't so fast, I'd have wasted a mouthful."

"Just keeping you on your toes," came Luke's response.

Melody took another sip of her champagne. It wasn't as bad as she thought it would be. In fact, she liked it.

Zack gestured to her with his beer can. "What's it like living with a rock legend?"

It surprised her that he knew who she was, but it shouldn't have. Her family had been front-page news all over the world. "It's okay."

"It's got to be more than okay. Is your uncle a wild man? I picture him like he was on the cover of *Hard Raines*. He looked crazy."

"That album came out a long time ago. Uncle Cal's mellowed since then."

"I hear you have a male nanny who's just as psycho," Luke added.

Melody laughed. She could see how Po would appear like that to people. He was a big, burly, tattooed biker, but he was a sweetheart. He'd worked for the DEA before retiring, which was where he'd met her uncle, who had worked undercover to bust some drug dealers. Po had been shot protecting her uncle, and he'd come to live with them when her uncle had returned home to look after them.

"Po's cool." She took another sip of her champagne. She could already feel it in her legs. They felt a little like jelly, strangely free from tension. Better still, the hard, painful memories that were her constant companions began to smooth out and flow away from her, leaving softer, gentler thoughts in their wake. She drank some more, seeking a deeper peace.

Kayla pulled a sleeping bag over her legs and scowled at Zack. "It's cold in here. Why didn't you bring a heater?"

"I'll warm you up if you'd like," Zack offered, grinning.

Kayla held up a warning hand. "You stay right where you are, Zack Blackthorn. I'm here for the champagne, not you."

"You're breaking my heart, Kayla."

"It can stand some breaking."

Luke laughed, and Melody emptied her cup. Luke reached over and refilled it and handed another beer to Zack. The boys began to talk football, and Kayla pulled out her phone and began to take photos of them. Melody drank and listened. After a few minutes, Kayla stood up and started taking pictures of the mill.

Then Kayla got right up close to Luke and snapped a photo of him taking a swig of beer. "That's for blackmail, Luke Johnson. If you don't do exactly what I say, I'm going to show your mommy."

"Oh, yeah. What exactly do you want me to do?"

"I haven't decided yet, but I'll be sure to let you know." She sat back down on the camp bed.

He reached out a hand to grab her. "Don't leave me hanging."

She laughed and sidled away from him. "Perhaps I'll do a project about this old mill for history class."

"You could, but then we'd have to kill you," Luke said, and laughed. "We don't want anyone to know about this place, do we, Zack?"

Zack nodded. "That's right. Consider yourselves lucky that you're even here."

Luke looked over at Melody. "Speaking of killing, what was it like finding your mom murdered?"

Melody was so stunned that her mind went blank. She didn't even experience the usual flashback that came whenever anyone asked her about her mom.

Kayla jumped up off the bed and stood next to Melody. "How could you, Luke! What a dumb question. Look what you've done to the kid. She's as white as a sheet." Kayla put a comforting hand on Melody's shoulder. "Don't pay him any mind. He's a jerk."

Melody just sat there frozen as the memories raced back. If her legs hadn't felt so wobbly, she would have stood up and marched right out of the mill.

"I didn't mean anything by it," Luke said. "I was just making small talk. I'm sorry, Melody. Here—have another drink." He leaned over and poured more champagne into her cup.

"I don't want another drink," she told him, but he kept pouring anyway.

Zack looked over at the door. "You hear that?"

"What?" Luke asked.

"It sounds like an engine."

"It's a motorbike," Kayla said, putting her cup down on the floor. "That's my ride."

"You told someone about this place?" Zack asked, sounding annoyed.

She had the good manners to look a little guilty. "The last time I was here, I may have mentioned it to someone. Anyway, I've gotta run."

Melody stood up on shaky legs. Her head spun, and she felt sick. "I have to go, too."

Kayla pointed at the boys. "You two dorks make sure the kid gets home okay, or there'll be hell to pay."

"I can walk," Melody said.

"No, you can't. It's more than ten miles," Kayla told her.

"Don't worry. We'll take you home," Zack said.

"Yeah," Luke added. "I need to get going anyway. My mom is forcing me to work the event tonight."

Kayla walked over to the door and looked back at Melody. "You take it easy, now," she told her as she pushed the door open and walked out into the daylight.

Melody looked past Kayla to the guy on the motorcycle. It was Jesse Keegan. Her sister's boyfriend.

CHAPTER ELEVEN

When Cal Raines arrived at the Witch Cross Inn on Friday night, the parking lot was already full, so he drove around back and found a space. Carrying his guitar case, he strolled around the building to the front door, taking the time to admire the old house. It was a center-chimney Colonial, and although he was interested in architecture, he had not been there before.

The ell that extended from the back of the building where he parked appeared to have been turned into a kitchen. As he came around the side of the inn, he noticed that the windows were double-hung with nine-over-six panes. Wreaths with red bows on them hung from every window, and Christmas lights twinkled in the neatly trimmed rhododendron, azalea and holly bushes that surrounded the house. The cranberry-painted front door also had a wreath on it. Before opening the door, Raines took a moment to admire the door handle, which the inn was famous for.

The wrought iron handle had two saltire crosses engraved on it and set between parallel lines that looked like Roman numerals: IXXI. These were apotropaic marks, or hex marks, used to ward off witches and evil spirits in Colonial times. Although the inn didn't date back to 1692 and the era of the Salem witch trials, there had still been plenty of superstitious people in 1775 when it was built, according to the plaque on the wall near the door.

Since high school, Raines had been fascinated by mythology, folklore and superstition. As a songwriter, he'd studied universal themes and archetypes in order to better communicate with an international audience. While touring the world with his band, he'd seen many protection symbols. The Irish, for example, placed St. Brigid's crosses over doors. In England, he'd seen overlapping circles carved into stone walls, scratches in wood lintels above fireplaces to confuse demons, and intertwined VV's gouged into support beams to represent the Virgin Mary as the protector. In the

U.S., the pointed stars and compass rose designs found in Pennsylvania Dutch country folk art were familiar examples. And then there was the *wedjat* eye of Egypt, and the palm-shaped Hamsa from the Middle East and Africa. One of his favorites, though, was the troll cross of Sweden and Norway. But none of them were as meaningful to him as this New England hex on the door of the Witch Cross Inn.

Entering the inn, he found that it was packed. A couple of men in camouflage gear were checking in at a desk next to a flight of carpeted stairs. They had a metal detector with them that had cameras attached to the base. Odd, he thought. Just as odd was the ruddy-faced man behind the front desk checking them in. He had on a sailor's cap and wore a navy and white striped sailor's sweater.

Chief Finch sat in an armchair in the lobby next to a marble fireplace talking to Olivia May. In the room on his left, Principal Donaldson stood next to a table loaded with items for the auction. He was surrounded by a group of people, fielding questions about the event. Raines headed in Olivia's direction but was intercepted by a young man wearing a U.S. Forest Service uniform. He had curly, sandy hair, brown eyes, and an eager smile.

The man extended a hand to Raines, which he shook. "I'm Justin Jarvis, Mr. Raines. I couldn't believe it when Principal Donaldson told me that you're donating a guitar for the cause."

"You're part of the fundraiser?" Raines asked.

"Yes, sir. I went to Caxton High and can't think of a better project to be involved in. My aunt and uncle are helping coordinate the effort."

That helped Raines place his name. "Your aunt is Bliss Jarvis? The Senior Assistant Attorney General?"

"That's right. Do you know her?"

"Yes. I've had the pleasure of working with her."

Justin nodded in the direction of a table in the dining room off the lobby. The room had double doors that were open so people could mingle more easily. Bliss Jarvis sat in there with an older, stocky, gray-haired man. "My uncle is from Caxton originally—Judge Jarvis. He's a Supreme Court Justice in Concord now, but they have a home in North Caxton and are active in the community. He knows Chief Finch, which is lucky because the chief knows you. He asked him to approach you for your help. We're all so excited about the guitar, and of course very grateful. We've had several calls about it."

Raines held up the case.

"Awesome," Justin exclaimed. "We have a spot right over here for it."

Raines followed him to one of two tables set up in the dining room for the donated items, placed the guitar case on it, and opened the lid.

"Wow. That's a beauty. Is that a rosewood fretboard?"

"Yes."

"You know rosewood is on the protected species list, right?"

"I do. But I purchased this one in the nineties, and it's made of Indian rosewood, not Brazilian. I have the documentation required to donate it."

"That's great. But I'm surprised you want to give it away. I heard from one of my friends who plays that the sound is warmer with a rosewood neck."

"I have a lot of guitars and not much time to play them. It's wasting away. I hope some kid gets to enjoy it as much as I did."

"But the rosewood guitars are not as easy to come by now," Justin argued, giving Raines an out if he wanted to reconsider donating it.

Raines smiled to himself. The kid clearly wasn't a sales guy. "I have others," he said. "I read a report that the rosewood trafficking from Africa to China is almost as bad as drug trafficking."

Out of the corner of his eye, Raines spotted a woman with a tray of champagne glasses walking in their direction. She came up and stood beside them, politely waiting for them to finish their conversation.

"It's a real shame," Justin continued. "People don't realize how bad illegal logging has become. Forests are being decimated."

Raines turned to the woman with the tray. She was a plump woman, probably in her mid-forties, with rosy cheeks and a kind smile.

"I didn't want to interrupt you while you were talking shop," she said, offering him a drink.

Raines took a glass and thanked her.

The woman asked, "How about you, Justin?"

"No thanks, Christine. But I'll take a glass of milk when you get the chance."

She laughed. "Still drinking the hard stuff?"

"You bet."

"Mr. Raines, this is Christine Johnson, the owner of the inn," Justin told him.

"I'm honored that you came, Mr. Raines."

"Please, call me Cal."

"Cal it is, then."

"You have a beautiful building. Did you restore it yourself?"

"Why, yes, I did. A few years ago, now. As you can see, we kept all of the original features." She pointed to the exposed beams and the built-in corner cabinet, which appeared to house memorabilia as opposed to china. "But we installed a new kitchen, updated the bathrooms and had the roof replaced."

"It's a grand old building," Justin added. "And it was part of the Underground Railroad."

Christine laughed. "That's just talk, Justin. There's no proof."

"But there's a secret passage here. Mom told me about it." He turned to Raines. "My mom used to work here when she was in high school, and someone told her about the passage."

"She must be talking about the servants' stairs," Christine told him. "I think they were removed to add more bathrooms for the guest bedrooms years ago." As she finished, a burly teenage boy walked into the room. "Luke, darling," she called, motioning him over. "Will you fetch Justin a glass of milk?"

The boy gave her a sullen look, then noticed Raines. He looked away immediately and eyed the room nervously before hurrying off in the direction of the kitchen.

Strange, Raines thought.

"That's my son," Christine explained. "He's usually not so shy. He's a football star, you know, and is used to attention, but sometimes he's too exhausted after practice to help around here. I hope you'll forgive his lack of manners."

Raines smiled. "Of course. I was a teenager once myself, you know. Has the inn been in your family long?" he asked, deftly changing the subject.

"Why, yes. One of my ancestors built it in the late seventeen-hundreds as a wedding present for his daughter, but it was sold decades ago and turned into an inn."

She glanced up at a painting on the wall above the fireplace. Raines followed her gaze. It was an old painting of a woman, at least several hundred years old, he thought. She had long brown hair that was pulled back off her forehead and pinned behind her neck. She wore a luxurious blue silk gown with sleeve ruffles at her elbows. The plaque on the bottom of the frame read, "Verity Caxton."

"You're a descendant of the Caxtons who founded the town?" he asked, intrigued.

"The very same. I felt so fortunate when the inn became available. I just had to bring it back into the family fold, so to speak. After all, with a family history like ours, it's so important to maintain it for future generations. Something to be proud of. Besides, once Luke became busy with school and football, I needed something to occupy my time. What could be more wonderful than restoring your ancestors' home to its former glory?"

Just then, a man called out to her. "Christine, the champagne is getting warm over there by the fire."

Christine rolled her eyes. "Thaddeus is only here for the free drinks."

Raines turned to look at the man. He was tall and thin, and although he was probably in his late forties, he dressed like a prep school boy in khakis and a blue blazer with a button-down pink shirt. The woman standing next to him was both beautiful and elegant in cream pants, a navy blouse, and pearls. She had a patrician nose, arched eyebrows, full red lips, and looked like money.

"Excuse me, Mr. Raines," Christine said. "I should hand out the drinks."

As she left, Olivia wandered over to Raines. He hadn't seen her in over a week and was pleased she was there. Raines had first met her when she had assisted Holly and him with an arson-homicide case several months earlier. She was a psychiatrist with a law enforcement background, and had adopted Abbey's boyfriend, Jesse Keegan. Although Raines wasn't thrilled about the fact that Jesse and Abbey were seeing each other, he'd managed to maintain a good relationship with Olivia.

"Hello there," she said, and smiled.

"Long time no see," he responded.

She let out a breathy laugh and flipped her glossy chestnut hair over her shoulder. She was five foot nothing, had impeccable taste, and was one of the smartest women Raines knew. "How did it go with your brother?" she asked with a concerned look.

"About as well as I expected. Abbey wasn't happy to hear that we didn't hug and make up."

Olivia nodded. "She told me she was disappointed it didn't go better."

Several months ago, Abbey had agreed to meet with Olivia once a week to help her learn how to cope with her mother's death and her father's imprisonment, but it was on the condition that Raines visit his brother. Raines suspected that Jesse was also a major factor in Abbey's decision to go to therapy, because she'd get to see him when she was at Olivia's. As long as she was finally getting professional help, though, he didn't care about her motives.

Raines shook his head. "Our relationship is mercurial. The best analogy I can think of is that it's like the ocean. Some days we have calm seas; the next it's hundred-foot waves, and I'm frantically searching for my life vest."

She laughed and placed a supportive hand on his arm. "It's a process, Cal," she said gently. "Just give it time and keep listening to her. Let her talk. You'll find the way. You love her, and she loves you."

He smiled and nodded, and then his breath caught in his throat as, over Olivia's shoulder, he saw Holly Jakes stroll through the front door. She wore a tight black ski sweater with equally tight black leggings. There was a lump under her sweater at her hip that he knew was her weapon. Her hair was down, which was rare. Department regulations required her to keep it up off her shoulders. The honey-soft curls shone in the overhead lights, and the skiing had given her cheeks a healthy glow. Raines sensed the other men in the room turning their attention to her.

Holly glanced around the lobby and then spotted Raines in the dining room. She smiled and started to walk over to him, but then she noticed Olivia, who stood with her back to Holly. Olivia still had a hand on his arm. Holly nodded to Raines and turned to head in the other direction.

CHAPTER TWELVE

Seeing Raines and Olivia together confirmed Holly's suspicions: they were dating. Two weeks ago, she'd spotted them in the Sweet Cakes Bakery drinking coffee and chatting, all warm and cozy. Now they were at the auction together. Not wishing to interrupt the lovebirds, she carefully maneuvered her way through the throng of people who had congregated in the lobby area to enjoy cocktails in front of a roaring fire. She spotted the chief in what appeared to be a serious conversation with Bliss Jarvis and her husband Elliot, whom the locals referred to as the "Judge."

Holly wasn't up for another lecture from the chief about returning to work. Nor did she want to talk to Bliss who, as the head of all criminal prosecutions for the state, had been responsible for the investigation into Holly's officer-involved shooting. That was the last thing Holly wanted to discuss. In fact, the last thing she wanted right now was to be here at all, she thought glumly. Leaving was out of the question, though, so she skirted the lobby, avoiding eye contact, and made for the second set of doors that led into the far end of the dining room.

The room was filled with tables and chairs. Holly recognized a few people, who turned to stare at her. She ignored them but didn't fail to notice that they bent their heads closer together so they could whisper to one another. She didn't need to guess whom they were talking about as their eyes didn't leave her.

Keeping to the back of the room, Holly made her way over to a corner cabinet, which was filled with memorabilia. As she perused the knick-knacks, she heard someone complain that the inn was filled with Bigfoot hunters. Another whispered something about Cal Raines that she couldn't catch. He and Olivia had entered the auction room now and stood together at the far end, near a table with a guitar on it.

To avoid making contact with anyone, she turned her back to the room and gave her full attention to the items inside the glass-fronted cabinet. On the bottom shelf, the inn's original door handle was proudly displayed in a royal-blue velvet box. She bent closer and saw that the handle had witches' crosses hammered into it. Like almost everyone else in town, Holly knew that the handle on the inn's front door was a replica. Someone had stolen the real one—this one—years ago, long before she worked for the department. Luckily, the chief had recovered it and returned it to its rightful owner, who had kept it safe in this display case ever since.

There were also photos of the inn through the generations, as well as several photos of a lumber mill with an old man in a three-piece suit standing in front of it. There was one of him on board a steam engine grinning like a kid, and some more recent family photos with North Caxton as the scenic backdrop. Several polished tennis cups occupied the top shelf. North Caxton hosted a tennis tournament every year, and the dates on the trophies were from forty years ago. Eaton Blackthorn had been quite a player, Holly thought. There was also a sailing trophy from Boston, with the name of Skip Johnson, the inn's owner, engraved on it. How had an avid sailor ended up in the White Mountains, Holly wondered? There were several marksmanship trophies for someone named Cricket Blackthorn, and in 1976, someone called Judy Dane had won a beautiful cut-glass vase for her roses.

A male voice to her right said, "Looking at that hoard could put your family to shame."

Holly turned to the man. Although she recognized him, it took a moment for her to remember his name. "Phil Montague, right?" He was the director of operations for Blackthorn Timber. She'd met him several times because the company sponsored an annual ski race at Hurricane Mountain, and he occasionally handed out the winning prizes.

"You have a great memory for names."

She smiled. "It comes with the job." Phil had a rugged frame and straight black hair that was brushed back off his broad forehead.

"Are you entering the race this year, or are you going to give someone else a chance to win the cup?" he asked her good-naturedly.

She laughed. "We'll have to see." She looked at him expectantly, recognizing that he had sought her out for a reason.

He nodded and said, "Olivia May mentioned that you know Cal Raines."

She hadn't expected that. She'd thought Phil had wanted her to volunteer at the race. "How do you know Olivia?"

"We're trying to purchase a plot of land she owns so we can construct a small wind turbine farm, but she's not interested."

"So, how does Raines fit in?"

"My boss's kid would love his guitar, and if Raines would autograph it, that would be even better. If I manage to win it in the auction, do you think he'd sign it?"

"You'd need to ask him, but I don't see why not."

"How about you put in a good word for me?"

They were interrupted by Christine Johnson, who walked over to them with a plate of canapés. She offered one to Holly, then turned to Phil. "I'd like to introduce you to someone who's thinking of putting a wind turbine on his property. He needs some advice."

"Sure," Phil told her. He nodded in Raines's direction and then looked back at Holly. "Don't forget to ask about that signature."

"I won't," Holly responded, and glanced over at Raines. He was looking right at her, so she turned her attention back to the trophy case.

In the reflection in the glass cabinet doors, she watched him move across the room toward her. Several people stopped him. At least two people asked for his autograph, which made her smile. It was no wonder the sheriff had hired him over her. The locals loved him, and he would undoubtedly bring in the votes for Sheriff Cleghorn at the next election.

Holly turned to watch him squat down so he could talk to a white-haired old lady in a wheelchair. Holly realized it was their middle school librarian. He laughed with ease at something she said and kissed her on the cheek.

Finally, he stood and made his way over to Holly. As he came up to her, he muttered, "Enjoying yourself, Jakes?"

"Just waiting to hear you sing, Raines. See if you still have it."

"Oh, I still have it, Jakes, and I'm willing to prove it to you."

In this light, his gray eyes were the color of steel, and she knew he used them to slice right through many a woman's resolve, which she'd long since taken to heart as a cautionary tale. "I'll have to take your word for it, Raines, because I don't want you to strain," she paused for effect, "your voice."

A gunshot muffled his amused chuckle.

Then a woman screamed.

CHAPTER THIRTEEN

As Chief Finch yelled for everyone to stay where they were, Holly and Raines ran out the front door. Phil Montague was already ahead of them.

Outside, the first thing they saw was a smashed widescreen TV on the ground. Next to it lay Justin Jarvis. Blood pooled around his body, and Bliss knelt beside him performing chest compressions. Tears ran down her cheeks as she murmured, "Come on, Justin. Come on, honey."

The Judge was on the phone to 911. His breath was rapid and shallow from shock, and he looked like he'd aged ten years.

"Where's the shooter?" Raines asked, drawing his Sig Sauer as he scanned the parking lot.

"I don't know," yelled Bliss. "It seemed to come from nowhere."

Holly glanced down at the forest ranger on the ground. He had a chest wound on his right side. "Bliss, we need to stop the chest compressions. It's pumping the blood out of him faster."

"But I don't think he's breathing."

Holly felt his neck. "There's a weak pulse. We need to keep as much blood in him as we can by applying pressure."

Bliss put her hands over the wound, applied pressure and looked pleadingly up at Holly. Her pupils were dilated, and her eyes were wide with fear and shock as Justin's blood seeped between her fingers. Both she and Holly knew he didn't have long.

"Who has an emergency kit?" Holly called out.

"I do," Chief Finch said, coming up behind her. He looked down at Justin. "Holy Mother of God!" he muttered and crossed himself automatically. "My kit isn't good enough to help him. We don't have time to hang around. It has to be a scoop and run, or the kid's not going to make it." He raised his voice. "Raines, Elliot," he called, "help me lift him to my car while Bliss tries to keep pressure on the wound. Holly, I want you to secure the scene and get everyone here. And I mean everyone."

Just as they were about to pick Justin up, they heard sirens. Seconds later, an ambulance, which had just left a house call down the road, screamed into the parking lot, followed by Fennis Cooper and Angel Natale in their cruisers.

The paramedics moved quickly, applying dressings to Justin's wound and bundling him into the ambulance; his only chance of survival was rapid transport to the emergency room. Bliss and the Judge insisted on going with him. Fennis took the lead with his cruiser's lights on and sirens wailing.

As the cruiser's taillights disappeared down the drive, the chief took charge. He told Phil Montague to get back inside the inn because the scene wasn't secure. He watched the man scurry through the front door, and once he was inside, he turned to Holly, Raines and Angel. "That kid is one of ours. And nobody messes with one of ours. Nobody. I want the shooter caught yesterday. Are you armed, Holly?"

She nodded and removed a compact Glock 26 from her inside-the-waistband holster.

"Good. Angel, set up a roadblock," he ordered. "Jakes and Raines, you two search the parking lot while I make some calls to get everyone rolling."

CHAPTER FOURTEEN

The following morning, Chief Finch had called a meeting in his conference room. He sat at the head of the long wooden table. Holly, Raines and Bliss Jarvis were on his right and Lieutenant Gustafson, Caxton PD's second in command, and Lieutenant Dennis Hendricks, of the state police, on his left. FBI Agent Brady Coles sat facing Chief Finch at the opposite end of the table. Holly knew Brady Coles; he was in his forties, a devoted dad and husband who worked out of the FBI's resident agency in Portsmouth, New Hampshire. They'd been on a task force together, and Brady would sometimes call her looking for information on a suspect. He was a thoughtful guy, polite and always willing to help.

It was a somber gathering. Justin Jarvis had died in surgery. His uncle, the Judge, was with his sister and family. His aunt Bliss, however, was in full battle mode; not only was she the Senior Assistant Attorney General, but she served as the chief of New Hampshire's Criminal Justice Bureau. Although only five feet when not in her customary stiletto heels, her self-confidence, poise, razor-sharp intellect and no-nonsense approach made her a formidable force.

Bliss's face was tight and pale, now, with a "heads are about to roll" demeanor to it. So far, the crime scene techs had found very little. They had established the trajectory of the bullet. The shooter had been in the trees at the back of the parking lot to the right of the building. Eighty percent of New Hampshire was forested, and North Caxton was even more so, providing excellent coverage for a shooter.

Everyone at the inn had been interviewed. This had taken all night because so many people had attended the auction. They were also unusually busy with guests who were staying there because they'd heard about the Bigfoot sightings.

The only people who had left the auction early were Thaddeus Blackthorn and his wife, Lilly. Everyone else appeared to have been inside at the time of the shooting, except for Bliss, the Judge and Justin.

Lieutenant Gustafson had interviewed the Blackthorns at their home earlier that morning. He reported that the Blackthorns had left early because their son, Zack, had been in an accident while tubing at the Hurricane Mountain Snow Park. It turned out that he hadn't suffered any serious injuries, but Gustafson learned that Thaddeus had not actually gone to the snow park with his wife. Nor had he gone with her when she'd taken Zack to Caxton Memorial to get him checked out. Thaddeus himself claimed to have stayed home all night.

When he'd finished speaking, Bliss cleared her throat. Although the chief sat at the head of the conference table, she was running the show. "Justin is twenty-three." Her voice caught, and she paused for a moment, looking down at the papers on the table as she struggled to regain her composure. "Justin was only twenty-three, and he'd just finished training with the U.S. Forest Service. He's a good kid without any enemies that we're aware of, so we can't rule out that the intended target was the Judge or me. I've instructed my team to investigate cases that I've prosecuted recently. Lieutenant Hendricks has agreed to investigate any controversial decisions my husband may have presided over on the Supreme Court." She looked around at their faces without really seeing them. "Because Justin worked for the Forest Service, the FBI will take the lead on his case."

Brady Coles, the FBI Special Agent, took his cue. "I've spoken with Justin's parents. They're not aware of any issues that would make him a target. He was a good kid. Outdoorsy and environmentally minded for years. He was a hard-working student, not top of his class, but a solid student. He didn't have a lot of friends, but he was part of a close-knit group of good kids his parents had known for years. He had a girlfriend in his sophomore year of college, but none since, or nothing serious because he didn't mention anyone to his parents, and they were very close. They said his idea of a wild weekend was backpacking into the wilderness to see if he could spot some rare bird or count frogs at a pond."

Bliss wiped a stray tear away with a tissue, and Brady paused, but she nodded for him to continue.

"They gave me a list of his friends, whom I'll follow up with later today. I've had a brief conversation with Justin's supervisor, who says he doesn't believe that this is related to his job. Justin was fresh out of training and hadn't been assigned anything significant. Still, I plan to swing by his office after this meeting to review everything he was involved in."

Bliss thanked him, then glanced over at Raines and gave him a nod to proceed.

"I interviewed Skip Johnson, who told me that Justin was staying at the inn. I'm curious to know why he wasn't staying with you, Bliss. After all, you do have a place in town."

She didn't take offense. "Justin was a history buff. History and the environment were his favorite topics. Years ago, when his mother was in high school, she worked at the inn. She told Justin stories about the old place, and he was fascinated by it. When the Judge and I realized the auction would be there, we bought him a gift certificate for a couple of nights as an advanced Christmas gift." She choked up and cleared her throat again before adding softly, "We thought it would be fun for him."

They were all quiet for a moment, respectful of her grief.

The chief asked, "I'm curious why there was a TV on the ground next to him."

Bliss fingered the papers in front of her. "I'd asked him to help his uncle carry it in for the auction. We were donating it, you see, and the auction was just about to start."

"Okay. And who knew Justin was going to be there?" Finch asked, keeping his voice gentle.

"His parents," she responded. "His supervisor. Maybe his friends. Principal Donaldson and the rest of the team at the high school organizing the auction. He was close to Principal Donaldson all through school. They shared many of the same interests—history and nature. The environment and pollination. Donaldson is a beekeeper, and all through high school, Justin helped him maintain his hives."

"Who knew that you and your husband would attend the auction?" Lieutenant Dennis Hendricks asked. He was a serious man, with a take-no-guff attitude. He wore a white button-down shirt under a gray sweater with a black jacket that had a State Police badge on the left side. Holly and Raines knew him from the last case they'd worked together, although he had a closer working relationship with Gustafson.

"My staff knew," Bliss said. "As well as a few friends and family members. The same goes for my husband."

Bliss turned to Chief Finch. "Fred, I want your team to follow up with any leads here, review the interview notes, follow up with Principal Donaldson again. He was in a state of shock last night." She gathered her papers together on the desk. "Let's hope the crime scene techs come up with something fast. We'll plan on meeting at the end of the day, sooner if something comes up. You have my number. Don't hesitate to contact me."

Bliss, Dennis Hendricks, and Brady Coles stood.

After they'd left, the chief sat in silence for a moment, rocking back and forth in his chair while tapping his stomach with his fingers like he was playing the drums. Holly recognized this as his thinking posture. For the first time, she noticed the age spots on his big hands. He was looking old, she thought. When had the strong, fit man begun to age and sag? He'd always been on the heavy side for as long as she could remember, but he'd still appeared strong and commanding. Now his face was lined, and his hair was almost white. She felt a pang of sadness at how the job was aging him, and she wondered how much longer he'd continue to work.

"Raines," Finch said, "I'd like you to head back to the inn. Check out Justin's room. Make sure we didn't miss anything. Gus, I want you to re-interview Thaddeus Blackthorn, his wife and his son. I want the exact times his wife left Thaddeus alone at home. Follow up with the hospital to confirm their story. Then have a talk with Principal Donaldson. See if he remembers anything. Bliss was right: he was in a deep state of shock last night. He may remember something now. I'll have Angel and Fennis continue canvassing the area. Make sure they've knocked on every door."

Holly sat waiting for her assignment with anticipation. She was back to duty with a passion. Any thought of quitting had died with Justin Jarvis. There wasn't a law enforcement officer in the whole

Witch Cross Inn

country who didn't want to avenge his death. He was part of the Brotherhood.

"Holly, I need you to work the Yorrick case."

"Chief! With all due respect—"

The chief held up his hand to cut off any argument. "When you say that, I can just feel the serving of disrespect coming. I said I need you to do it. We don't have anyone else to cover it. I also need you to follow up on these Bigfoot sightings."

Gustafson guffawed at that, and Holly shot him a look. She knew she was not his favorite, and over the years, he'd made no secret that he didn't think she was up to the job. He wanted her out of the department.

She felt an angry blush rise up her neck. What the hell was going on? *Bigfoot!* She wanted in on the shooting. Was Finch trying to get her to resign? What an insult. She should be investigating Justin's death like the rest of them.

"Bigfoot hunters are arriving in droves," Finch continued, as if he couldn't tell she was silently fuming. "The inn was full of them last night. Who knows? Sarah Mooney's place is only two houses away from the inn. Maybe one of them was out in the woods looking for Bigfoot and shot at something and missed. For all we know, it could have been a stray bullet that hit Justin. I need someone I trust to handle both the Yorrick case and the Bigfoot case without me having to look over your shoulder. Just get it done, so I don't have to worry about either of them."

He had a good point, Holly conceded grudgingly. Could it be a coincidence that there were two cases on the same street in the same week? Perhaps Sarah Mooney knew something about the Justin Jarvis case.

She heard a muffled snort and realized Gustafson was laughing at her.

"What's so amusing?" she snapped.

"Just taking in that Mr. Perfect," he said, referring to Raines, "gets a juicy assignment, while Miss Wholly Inadequate gets the crazy case. Seems appropriate. Or at the very least, justified."

"Thank you, Gus," Chief Finch said, sounding more caustic than usual. "That will be enough."

CHAPTER FIFTEEN

The state police had closed the street leading to the Witch Cross Inn to all traffic, with the exception of residents. Reporters milled about at the end of Elm Road taking photos and talking on their phones. A trooper had to clear a path for Holly to drive through the throng. On the way to Sarah Mooney's house, Holly passed the inn's parking lot, which had been taped off to traffic. The only vehicles parked there were a crime scene truck, Angel Natale's Ford Explorer and a run-down, beige cargo van that had "Bigfoot Investigations" painted on it.

Sarah Mooney lived two doors down from the inn at the end of the street. Beyond her house lay the White Mountain National Forest. Fennis Cooper was parked in her driveway and standing beside his cruiser, looking somewhat perplexed.

Holly pulled over at the curb and got out. "What's going on, Fennis?"

He greeted her with a big smile. "Hey, Sarge. Glad you're back." He gave her a friendly salute.

She grinned and walked over to him. "So, you pulled traffic duty?"

"No, Sarge. Sarah Mooney called this morning claiming two men were trespassing behind her house. She's pretty freaked out about it. First of all, she spots Bigfoot, and then we had the shooting last night. She's worried they're going to shoot her. Anyway, she called it in as soon as she spotted them, but when I got here, they were nowhere to be found. She says she saw them take off when I pulled up, but from where they were at the back of her house, you can't see me coming down the street. It's like they have a cruiser alarm system or something. Anyway, she's driving me nuts. I need to be out canvassing. That's more important, but she insists I stay here until I find them." He glanced around to make sure they couldn't be overheard and lowered his voice conspiratorially. "Personally, I think she's losing it."

Holly knew Sarah from her numerous nuisance calls over the years. She called about anything and everything. There were at least eight public intoxication calls that usually coincided with a wedding party at the inn, and the time someone smashed a glass bottle near her driveway. She'd called to report a man lurking around there late at night and creeping into the inn. Couples making out in their parked cars always warranted a call, as did any squirrel, raccoon or rabbit that looked like it was rabid and might chase her precious Pickles around the yard.

"At least she wasn't calling in to complain that she got the wrong size fries with her fast food meal," Holly told him.

"That really happened?"

"Sure did."

"I thought that was an urban legend," Fennis said, shaking his head. "So, are you here because you're working the Bigfoot case, Sarge?"

"Yep. I read your report. It was well written, with plenty of detail."

"Thanks, Sarge." He puffed out his chest the way he did when he was proud. Report writing hadn't come easily to him, and he'd taken a lot of grief over it.

Holly studied Fennis. The rookie still looked shiny, new and eager to please, with an air of innocence about him that he'd probably lose with another year on patrol. His big round face and smile the size of Texas made him appear like an easy mark, and it encouraged some of the less savory characters in town to give him a hard time.

"That photo you took of the footprint came out great," she told him, "and your idea to put your boot print next to it, so we had something to compare the size with before the snow melted, was a really good call."

"It was?"

"Yes."

He looked so appreciative she worried that he was about to get all sloppy.

"Well, Sarge. I'm learning from the best."

She winked and pointed a finger at him. "You got that right, Coop."

He gave her a big, cheesy smile. "The chief hoped you'd come back and take the case."

"He told you that?" Chief Finch was the rookie's uncle. Some claimed Fennis had got the job with the department because of nepotism, but Holly knew for a fact that the chief hadn't wanted him to join. He often mumbled that he'd pay good money to find out who'd helped Fennis pass the psych exam.

Fennis nodded eagerly. "He came over for dinner a few nights back. He always comes when Mom makes pot roast. It's one of his favorites. He claims no one makes a pot roast like his sister. Anyways, we started talking about the footprint. It was the darnedest thing we'd ever seen. You know what he said?"

"I have no idea."

"He said, 'Fennis, what we need is Holly. She has a nose like a bloodhound and will sniff out this business in no time.'"

That certainly sounded like Finch, who had a fondness for similes and metaphors. She smiled. "How about before I do that, I give you a hand catching those two hiding out back?"

"How are we going to do that? I searched, and they're long gone."

"Grab the megaphone you have in the trunk, and I'll show you."

As Fennis opened the trunk, Sarah Mooney opened the front door. She was cuddling Pickles. "I thought that was you, Detective Jakes."

Holly walked over to her. "How have you been, Ms. Mooney?"

"Not so good. I'm stressed out of my mind. First, I have Bigfoot running across my property, almost eating my dog, and then there's the shooting at the inn. We heard the shot, didn't we Pickles?" She lifted the little dog up to face her. "We were so scared, weren't we? I knew it wasn't a hunter because it was too late and far too close to the houses. I thought maybe Bigfoot had come back to get us, but that was just crazy thinking. Bigfoot wouldn't have a gun. He'd just use his bare hands to strangle us, wouldn't he?"

Pickles' only response was to lick her on the mouth, which made Holly feel queasy. She had a problem with germs, and although Pickles was one clean little Yorkie, she doubted that he flossed. "Did you see anything last night either before or after you heard the shot?"

"Hmm. Let me think." She cradled Pickles to her chest again and furrowed her brow in thought. "Before the shooting, I was quilting in my study. Pickles was watching TV. He likes the Animal Channel. And after the shooting, I am sorry to say that I was too scared to look out the window. I grabbed my phone and Pickles, and we hid in the closet in the guestroom until I heard the police sirens. I didn't see anything last night, but I did see something today—two figures in my backyard. They were sneaking around out there. I thought North Caxton was a safe place, but this is terrifying."

"Did you recognize them?"

Fennis came over with the megaphone and listened intently to Holly's questions. He was still eager to learn.

"No," Sarah responded.

"Could you identify them?"

She shook her head. "I didn't get a good look at their faces, but one of them was skinny and tall. The other one was big and fat. I told Officer Cooper they reminded me of Laurel and Hardy. They didn't have the top hats and canes, of course, but they were holding something that looked like a gun. What are you going to do about it?"

"Why don't you go inside, and I'll see what I can do."

"Officer Cooper didn't have any luck catching them, did you, Officer Cooper?"

Fennis looked a little sheepish and shook his head.

"Time for you to head back inside, Ms. Mooney," said Holly, more firmly this time. "Lock your doors and keep Pickles safe. If you see anything else or think of anything strange that happened other than Bigfoot, give me a call."

She looked worried. "If Bigfoot comes back, should I call you or Animal Control?"

It took Holly a moment to answer for fear she'd start laughing. "Why don't you call us both. I may need backup to handle that particular call."

"Okay. I have both of your numbers. Just be careful, Detective Jakes. I don't want you getting hurt out there," she said, before stepping back into the house.

Holly heard the click of the door lock, followed by the thud of the deadbolt.

"She's right. I never have any luck." Fennis sounded discouraged.

"We don't need luck, Fennis. Just a megaphone and my phone."

"How are you going to catch them with a megaphone? I don't think they'll come if you ask them."

"I could ask them nicely, but there's no fun in that," she told him, and started to walk around the side of Sarah's house while checking something on her phone.

"What are you looking up, Sarge?"

"You'll see."

Around back, Holly checked the surroundings. There was a patchy lawn full of crabgrass, and a worn shed at the end of the yard on the left. Beyond that was all forest. Although there were plenty of trees, there was not much undergrowth, which made traveling through the woods on foot relatively easy here. Holly headed for the left side of the shed. Trees shaded that area and provided excellent cover.

Leaning against the wall, she waited for a video to load on her phone. "Have you ever heard the Bigfoot mating call before?" she asked, staring at the title of the video.

His eyes widened. "No, Sarge. What does it sound like?"

"How the hell would I know? There's no such thing as Bigfoot, Fennis."

"But the print, Sarge. There's no getting around that print. Even the chief thought it looked real. You've heard about Occam's razor, right? I learned about it in a movie. It means that the simplest explanation is most likely the right answer."

Holly suppressed a smile. She knew the movie. Contact. It was one of her favorites. Wasn't there also a movie quote about a little information being a dangerous thing? "Look, Fennis. If we find a Bigfoot out here, I promise you I'll shave it with Occam's razor. How about that? Now give me that megaphone and let's get busy."

He turned it on and handed it to her. She held up her phone to the mouthpiece and hit the play button on the video. Loud, guttural moans and groans started to rumble out of the other end of the megaphone, filling the forest with the sounds courtesy of a group called Bigfoot Lurkers.

Fennis looked at her quizzically.

"The power of the internet," Holly whispered as she replayed the footage. "It's supposed to be the creature's mating call."

She played it again, and they waited in silence. A few moments later, they heard rustling. Fennis looked at her a little nervously and opened his mouth to say something, but she held a finger up to her lips, then unholstered her weapon and waited for whatever was heading their way.

CHAPTER SIXTEEN

Holly switched off the megaphone and placed it on the ground. They heard more rustling, followed seconds later by heavy, fast footsteps. They held their position behind the shed. She could hear Fennis breathing heavily from the excitement. He reached to unholster his weapon, but she shook her head. "Go less lethal," she whispered.

Fennis nodded and removed his taser.

Holly heard crashing and a branch snap. She held her breath. They were close now. Suddenly, two men ran past the shed, coming from the right of the property.

One of the men was armed with a shotgun.

"Police!" Holly yelled. "Drop your weapons."

Startled, they pulled up short and spun around to face her. As they did, the tall man swung his gun in her direction.

"I said drop your weapon," Holly yelled again, stepping away from the shed with her Glock pointed directly at him. Skilled at analyzing situations quickly, Holly observed, with some surprise and confusion, that the man had a jetpack on his back. Wires ran from the bottom of it, up under his arm and along the barrel of the gun. Attached to the end of it was a device that looked an awful lot like a motion detector and a light that would be used on the side of a house to scare racoons.

The shorter, fatter man was holding what appeared to have once been a metal detector. A black cylinder, which had multiple camera lenses screwed around it, had replaced the search coil used to wand over the sand. He also had a jetpack strapped to his back, but the wires ran out from the top of it, over his shoulder and down his arm to the detector.

"Lower your weapons," Holly told them again, keeping her gun trained on the man with the shotgun.

"This isn't a weapon," the tall man squeaked.

"Whatever it is, lower it."

He complied.

As Holly walked over to him, Fennis covered her. Both men wore lightweight harnesses in front of them, outfitted with flaps that lay open like the tables on the back of an airplane chair. On top of both flaps were small computer screens. The devices looked like something out of a sci-fi movie.

"What is that?" she asked, pointing to the tall man's shotgun.

"This is a Bigfoot motion detector. It's not loaded. It detects movement. Stubby," he said, nodding in the direction of the shorter, heavier man, "has a Bigfoot heat sensor. It can track a Bigfoot's trail by heat signature. It uses FLIR thermal cameras similar to the ones used in search and rescue missions."

Holly fought the eye roll. "You're trespassing."

"We thought this was part of the National Forest."

"No. You're on private property."

The tall one shifted uneasily. "We didn't realize."

Holly gave them a hard stare. "The shed, the lawn, and the house should have been a clue."

"But we didn't walk on the grass. That's where we thought the property ended," the short one explained.

Holly squinted at them. "The property extends into the forest."

"How far?" he asked.

"Way back."

"How far is 'way back'?" He sounded annoyed.

"Way back yonder, that's how far."

"That's not helpful, Officer."

"It's Detective, and I'm not in the customer service business. Now, what are your names?"

"I'm Sticks, and this is Stubby."

Recalling the beat-up van in the parking lot of the Witch Cross Inn, Holly said, "Let me guess. You're with Bigfoot Investigations."

Their eyes rounded with surprise, and they smiled with delight. "You've heard of us? Wow! What an honor."

"No. I saw your truck parked at the inn."

Their looks of pleasure turned to disappointment.

"What are your real names? Let's see some ID."

"We don't carry ID when we're hunting the Bigfoot."

"Names!" she snapped.

"I'm Frank Stanko, and Stubby is Kenny Fritz." Frank Stanko had dark hair, dark bushy eyebrows and acne-scarred cheeks. He had to be somewhere in his early thirties, Holly surmised. Kenny Fritz was about the same age and had a pear-shaped face with close-set brown eyes. They both wore camo jackets and pants with hiking boots and camo gaiters.

"Where are you from?"

"Lancaster, New Hampshire," Kenny Fritz told them.

Lancaster was over an hour's ride away, on the other side of the White Mountains near the Vermont border. "What brings you here?"

"We heard that Bigfoot was spotted in town, so we packed up our stuff and headed right over."

"I mean what brings you here to this house?"

"We heard a rumor that someone found a Bigfoot footprint here."

Good grief, Holly thought. If Sarah Mooney were smart, she'd start selling tickets. "And you're staying at the Witch Cross Inn?"

"Yes."

"You checked in last night?"

"How did you know that?"

Holly had seen the men in the lobby during the auction, but she wasn't about to let on. "We know everything that happens in our town because the Caxton Police Department has the latest detection grid technology available to law enforcement. We even use it to track how many Canadians are crossing the border to shop at our outlets."

"Really?" Frank Stanko, the tall one, questioned, but he looked like he was buying it. His eyes were bugging out a little.

"Yep. The Canadians already get tax-free shopping here, but we're thinking of giving them extra discounts for being so nice. And if they're with the Mounties, they even get a free dinner."

"Are you shooting me straight?" Stubby asked, clearly amazed.

Holly nodded. "I'm about as straight as a gun barrel."

Behind her, she heard Fennis suck in air in an effort to stifle a laugh, and she had to fight really hard not to crack a smile. "Now, where did you go after you checked in? And remember, good police work means we know the answer to the question before we ask it."

The men looked at each other and shifted nervously. Sticks said, "We were out with the detectors, seeing what we could detect. We heard there was a sighting a few miles out of town on the way to

Crawford Notch. It's long been believed that Bigfoot travels through the notches and the Pemigewasset Wilderness to get from one side of the state to the other. We met up with someone who told us about the footprint someone found here, so we came back to town only to discover that the inn was on lockdown. At first, we thought someone had captured Bigfoot, but then we heard a forest ranger got shot."

"What time did you get back?"

"Well after two this morning. It started to get really cold."

"Did you see anything?"

"Nope."

"Did someone take your statements already?"

"Yes. Lieutenant Gustafson did when we arrived back at the inn. He's a real ball breaker. He messed around with our equipment. Could have broken it, too, but he didn't care."

If they had a problem with Gustafson, maybe they weren't so bad, Holly decided as she assessed their equipment. "What do you do for a living?" They had to be computer geeks.

"We own a comic store with a bunch of Bigfoot memorabilia."

"So, you don't work for NASA?"

They guffawed at that. "Nah."

"If that equipment works the way you think it does, maybe you should consider a change of careers." She'd probably hear that they'd become billionaires in a couple of years, she thought wryly.

"So, Detective. Maybe you could help us out. Have you seen anything around these parts?"

"What? Like something seven feet tall and super hairy?" she asked.

"Exactly like that."

"Sorry to disappoint, but I've seen nothing except bears and moose."

"You haven't heard about any other sightings in town?"

"None. Now, what I want you to do is to give this place a wide berth. Okay? I'm letting you off with a warning. But wherever you go, make sure you're not on someone's property. With all of the Bigfoot sightings and the shooting last night, people will have itchy trigger fingers. If you plan to be in the woods, wear an orange vest. You're from the North Country. You guys should know better."

"Okay, Detective," Kenny Fritz said.

Holly pulled out a business card from her pocket. "If you see anything suspicious, or remember anything, give me a call."

Frank Stanko studied the card. "Will do, Detective Jakes."

Fennis and Holly watched them amble off in the direction of the Witch Cross Inn.

Once they were out of sight, Holly asked Fennis to show her where he'd seen the footprint. He walked about twenty-five feet to the right of Sarah's property, heading away from the Witch Cross Inn, deeper into the woods where Sticks and Stubby had come from.

"It was right here, Sarge. Next to this maple tree. There weren't any others because the ground was frozen and there's lots of pine needles. Ms. Mooney said Bigfoot was heading in that direction." He pointed into the forest at a forty-five-degree angle.

Holly walked off in that direction, glad of the lack of vegetation to obstruct her passage. The canopy overhead was thick, though, and gray clouds heavy with snow dimmed the sunlight. Holly turned on her flashlight.

Fennis followed right behind her, practically breathing down her neck but remaining silent as she searched the area. Finding nothing, she turned around to head back to her vehicle and spotted a long hair snagged on a branch.

She shone the light on it, and Fennis muttered, "Well, would you look at that."

CHAPTER SEVENTEEN

Police everywhere had mastered the information superhighway long before computer scientists had ever dreamed of the internet. Good policing required a steady source of reliable information. It helped if you worked in the town where you grew up because you knew a lot of people—their family histories, the grudges, the marriages, the divorces. You also knew those individuals with unique skills and interests and those with criminal inclinations and shady pasts.

Developing new relationships was critical. So, too, was building a cache of favors owed to you. Holly often gave someone a break for a minor incident if she thought they could be useful at a later date. And because they lived in a small town, she could always find them when she wanted to cash in that favor.

Unfortunately, Scotty Pepper didn't owe her any favors. Still, he was a knowledgeable outdoorsman, had a military background, and was just the person she needed to help her with the hunch she had about the hair she'd found in the woods. Holly would send it to the crime lab later that day, but first, she wanted a quick answer as to whether the hair was synthetic or not. Although there were several easy ways to test for that, she didn't have a microscope and performing a burn test to see if it was synthetic or not would destroy the evidence.

Policing in your hometown also came with some significant disadvantages. She'd once been on friendly terms with Scotty, but that had changed when she'd interrogated him about Sherry Raines's murder two years earlier. She felt bad about it, but policing in a small town inevitably led to damaging some relationships. Knowing your neighbor's sordid little secrets, seeing your friends at their weakest, or their drunkest, or in the middle of an argument with their husband when you were called to a domestic disturbance, didn't endear you to them. Over time, many friends had stopped inviting Holly to their parties because people were uncomfortable with her there, even when she was off duty.

Being a good detective required coping with uncomfortable situations. She'd questioned plenty of people who wanted nothing more than to take a swipe at her, but couldn't because they were handcuffed to a table. So, Scotty's dislike of her wasn't a deterrent. As she pulled into his driveway, he was chopping wood. Even though it was cold enough to snow, all he had on was a t-shirt, jeans and boots. She noticed the ax hover momentarily above his head when he heard her Jeep, but then he swung it down with full force and split the log. He bent over, picked up another log, placed it on the block and struck it just as hard.

She climbed out of her Jeep, leaned against the side of it and folded her arms, waiting for him to acknowledge her. He chopped up another six logs, pretending she wasn't there, but his natural rhythm was off. He was working really hard not to look at her. Finally, he swung the ax down and buried it in the chopping block.

Turning to her, he wiped his brow with his forearm. He wore an Acid Raines concert t-shirt. It was from the *Spiral Galaxies* album tour. A patchwork of scars ran up his right arm, under his sleeve and up the side of his neck.

"Can my day get any better?" he muttered.

"I could invite myself over for dinner instead of just stopping by long enough to pump you for some information."

"You're worse than a recurring nightmare, Jakes. At least nightmares end when you wake up," he grumbled.

Holly thought about the recurring nightmares she'd been having, then tried to force them out of her mind.

She must have made some kind of expression because his body language changed. It softened and relaxed. She pretended not to notice. "Scotty, don't tell me you haven't had rougher times than going a few rounds with me in the interview room. I thought you lived by the motto that the only easy day was yesterday?"

"That's the Navy Seals' motto, Jakes."

"What's Special Forces', then?"

"'Live free or die.'"

She squinted at him. "Very funny. That's New Hampshire's state motto."

"True, but ain't it grand?" He yanked the ax back out of the wood and slapped the side of the head against his palm and asked, "So, what do you want? I have wood to cut."

"I'm investigating the Bigfoot sightings."

At first, he just stared blankly at her for a moment, then he started to laugh so hard she could see a shine of tears in his eyes. "Tell me you're kidding. Bigfoot? Really?"

She nodded slowly, knowing that she should feel shame about being assigned such a fluff case, but she was surprised to find herself laughing, too. It had been a long time since that had happened, and it felt good.

Scotty managed to regain his composure. "They must really love you to give you that assignment."

"Yeah. Well. What can I say?"

That sobered him a little. He knew Holly had been involved in an officer shooting. Everyone in town knew it. She'd been raked over the coals by reporters, and by many of the locals, even a couple of fellow officers.

"Look. For once, I'd be willing to help you, but I don't know any Bigfeet." There was a glint in his damp eyes.

Holly pulled out the plastic bag from her pocket. "I want to ask you about this."

"What is it?"

She walked over to him and handed over the bag. "It's a hair."

He held it up to get a closer look. "What about it?"

"I can't test it to see if it's synthetic or real hair because I'll damage it, but do you think this could have come from a ghillie suit?"

He looked interested and studied the hair.

She'd come to him because of his experience in the military and in hunting. They use ghillie suits in both fields.

"So, you're thinking it's not Bigfoot running around town, but a hunter in camo?" he asked.

"Could be," she said, but failed to mention the footprint. She was actually thinking Halloween costume and hoax.

"Traditional ghillie suits were made of jute that comes in one-pound bundles," he told her. "It's rougher, smells like burlap gunnysack and comes in twenty-four-inch-long fibers. On the other hand, synthetic ultra-light fibers are common now. They weigh less, come in half-pound bundles, and the fibers are eighteen inches long. This looks about eighteen inches to me." He held it up to the light. "It's brown. Could be dyed, but it's hard to say." He handed it back to her.

"Great. Thanks, Scotty."

"You owe me, Jakes." He sounded serious. Then he added with a grin, "Make sure I'm the first one you call when you bag the beast. I want a photo."

His laughter followed her all the way back to her Jeep. As she reversed out of his driveway, her phone rang. It was the Medical Examiner. They'd found more human remains up in Pinkham Notch.

CHAPTER EIGHTEEN

Snow started to fall as Holly drove toward Pinkham Notch. The temperature hovered just below freezing. She hadn't checked the weather report, but from the look of the low, heavy clouds, they were in for a good dumping. The snow gods had looked favorably on the White Mountains, Holly thought as she made a right turn. The ski resorts could really use it, especially with Christmas right around the corner, which was one of their busiest weeks. She felt a familiar buzz of excitement at the prospect of a good storm.

On the opposite side of the road, a state police crime scene truck, followed at a safe braking distance by a Medical Examiner's van, passed her, heading south. Holly checked the vehicles but couldn't see the ME in either of them. The weather must have forced them to pack up early.

As she gained in elevation, the snow fell harder and started to settle on the road, but her Jeep could handle far worse conditions. She flicked the wipers on full bore to keep up with the faster-falling flakes and gripped the steering wheel a little tighter as high winds buffeted the ten-year-old Wrangler. The hard, glacier-scoured land was strewn with car-sized boulders, and bordered by steep, unforgiving headwalls and slopes of treacherous scree that slipped and slid underfoot. She thought about whoever had been found up here and wondered how long they'd lain there waiting to be discovered. It had been a lonely, silent grave except for the howling winds and the passing traffic.

Nearing where the crime scene trucks had been parked the weekend before, Holly glanced up to her left. Tuckerman's Ravine was hidden by the thick cloud cover, but she could sense its bulk. She'd hiked Mount Washington in winter with skis strapped to her back just to ski the bowl-shaped headwall. It hadn't been easy, but it had been worth it every time.

Fifty feet further on, the ME's vehicle was parked on the side of the road under the fir trees. When Holly pulled in behind her, Margaret Macquarie got out and hurried toward her. She wore a black hat with flaps that covered her ears, snow boots laced up to her knees, and a padded goose-down parka that reached down to the tops of her boots.

She was holding something in a plastic bag. Opening Holly's passenger door, she hopped in. Cold air followed her. It felt at least ten degrees cooler up here with the wind chill.

Although well into her fifties, Macquarie had the physical fitness of a twenty-year-old. Mac was a vegetarian who shied away from tofu in favor of bread, soup and cheese. She hiked and ran the trails with her pack of dogs in summer. In winter, she snowshoed and skied, both cross-country and downhill. Not only did she and Holly know each other through work, they'd also skied together.

Mac's weather-beaten face was usually tanned, even at this time of year, but it was as gray as the storm clouds now.

"Are you all right?" Holly asked.

Mac sighed wearily.

Holly glanced towards where the skull had been found. "Is it that bad?"

"It's not this case. I had two more fentanyl overdoses this week. It's rough going. It was a relief to get out of the office for a while."

Holly nodded her understanding. Overdoses depressed her, too. Unbidden, the image of a fifteen-year-old girl dead in her bed flashed into her mind. She'd been covered all the way up to her chin by a pink fluffy comforter sprinkled with silver shooting stars. It had happened in August, on the hottest day of the year. Holly remembered the sobbing mother telling her that she'd come home from work to find the sink still full of dishes and her daughter in bed asleep. She'd shaken her shoulder a little harder than she should have because she'd been annoyed that she'd slept all day. She repeated over and over again that she'd shaken her too hard. As the mother spoke, she gripped the wrist of her right hand tightly with her left. Holding the offending hand up, she presented it to Holly as if it were evidence of wrongdoing. It had been heartbreaking.

Feeling as flat as Mac looked, Holly asked, "So, what did you find?"

"Something interesting," Mac said, perking up a little. "In addition to a couple of vertebrae and an ulna bone, we found this." She held up a bag so Holly could clearly see the contents.

She took the plastic bag to get a closer look. "Is that a German Iron Cross?"

Mac nodded. "Looks like it, but I've never seen one up close before. I tried to check it out online, but I don't have a signal up here."

Holly studied it through the clear plastic. It was caked with mud, but she could see a small swastika in the center of the cross with "1939" engraved below it. "Did you find it with the body?"

"It was a few feet from the vertebrae."

"That's interesting," said Holly. "Can you tell me how long the body was here?"

"All I can tell you is that this level of skeletonization takes at least a year, but it's difficult to nail down a more precise time of death if it's not recent or ancient. Anything in between is tricky, but I'll consult with a forensic anthropologist I know who specializes in bone weathering to see what he can tell us. He's one of the best and, lucky for us, works in Boston. Although he's busy, he agreed to travel up to Concord tomorrow to take a look for me."

"So," Holly said, "the skull could have been from World War Two?"

"It's a possibility. I was hoping to narrow down the time period through dental work, but the teeth exhibit no major procedures to date the remains. In fact, they are beautiful teeth. Straight and well cared for. I only wish my teeth were half as good. That in and of itself causes me to gravitate toward this being more recent."

"How about the skull?" Holly asked. "Is it male or female?"

"Because it's larger and heavier than a typical female's skull, has squarer eye sockets, a prominent supraorbital ridge, and a square chin, I'd say it's male—an adult male. Females tend to have more rounded foreheads, rounder eye sockets, and pointed chins."

Still studying the Iron Cross, Holly said, "A male skull fits with the medal."

Instead of answering, Mac barked a dry cough. Holly eyed her with concern. The last thing she needed was a cold.

Mac caught her look of concern and wheezed, "Don't worry. It's the dry air. Nothing a cup of coffee wouldn't fix."

"How about a bottle of water?"

Mac coughed again, and Holly reached behind her seat to retrieve one from a pack she kept on the floor for emergencies.

Mac opened it and took several big gulps. "Thanks. I had a thermos of tea, but I finished that hours ago."

"What else can you tell me?"

Mac didn't answer right away, and Holly glanced at her, expecting to see her drinking more water. She wasn't. Her lips were so tightly compressed that a single drop of water wouldn't have been able to pass between them. Holly knew that look. She'd seen it in plenty of suspects who were trying not to reveal their secrets. Some even went so far as to cover their mouths with their hands, physically restraining themselves from uttering a word.

"You found something else, didn't you?"

The ME said nothing.

"Come on, Mac. Spill the beans." Holly's tone was buoyant with anticipation.

Mac gave her a long, considering look. "I need to examine the bones under a microscope before I make an official statement."

Holly shifted in her seat to face Mac more squarely, excitement charging through her at the prospect of her case turning out to be something more than a mere hiking accident. "My lips are sealed until you make it official," she said, while thinking that the buzz she felt at someone else's misfortune would surely leave a black mark on her soul.

"We found three cervical vertebrae. The C1, which is the topmost vertebra that sits just below the skull, the C2 and the C3. We also found a section of ulna bone. All four bones show signs of chop marks from a heavy, sharp tool."

"What kind of tool?"

Mac shrugged. "Something like a cleaver, ax or machete."

"You've got to be kidding!" Holly muttered.

"I wish I were."

"That's crazy. Will you be able to narrow the weapon down?"

"The ulna has been crushed, which could indicate an ax was used, but I need to look at it under the microscope. A machete or cleaver would leave thinner lines than an ax with less crushing-type injuries."

"We're not dealing with a hiking accident, then?"

Mac shook her head. "The ulna has a nightstick fracture to the midsection of the shaft. We often see this in defensive injuries when someone raises their arms to protect the head."

Holly slipped the Iron Cross into her pocket. "Do the cuts to the side of the neck show similar injuries to the ulna?"

"Yes."

"Which side of the neck took the blow?"

"The left."

"Okay," Holly mumbled thoughtfully, picturing the attack. "Based on the defensive injury to the ulna bone, I assume the killer was facing the victim?"

"That's my reading of the evidence right now," Mac confirmed. "The marks to the vertebrae show damage to the front and side of the neck."

"What a way to go," Holly muttered. Her earlier spurt of excitement vanished as the reality of the brutal attack hit her.

"If it's any comfort, the chop to the neck most likely severed the carotid artery as well as the vertebral artery. He wouldn't have suffered for long."

"Let's hope not." In her rearview mirror, Holly spotted a semi slowly creeping up the mountain road. She waited for it to pass before continuing. "And there's no chance it's a hiker who broke his arm and neck in a fall?"

"It's a homicide, Holly. However, do me a favor and wait until I've wrapped up my examination before you tell anyone," Mac asked her as she reached for the door handle. "I can't deal with a late-night call from Mayor Randolph. He's not going to want to hear that we're dealing with another homicide."

"You got it. I'm going to take the cross to a local historian I know in town to see if he has any idea why a German war medal was found here. Feel like coming with me and then grabbing something to eat?"

"I wish I could. I'd rather be out investigating with you than returning to the morgue, but the bodies are piling up." With a sigh, Mac opened the Jeep door and stepped back out into the cold.

CHAPTER NINETEEN

Holly followed Mac back down the Notch heading south. Once they reached Route 302, Mac made a right to cut through Crawford Notch, either heading for her home in Bethlehem or taking a long route to the highway, while Holly made a left and headed back to town.

She glanced at the medal on the seat beside her, wondering if she should go back to Scotty's. Although he knew more about the military than probably anyone else in town, she needed someone who knew the history of the town's people.

Even though it was snowing, North Caxton was full of Christmas shoppers taking advantage of tax-free gifts. There were so many cars parked along Main Street, there wasn't an empty space.

Lights twinkled from storefronts and from the trees in the park. Hotel owners had created fairytale wonderlands on their grounds, some with sparkling reindeer and sleighs and others with contingents of brightly colored nutcrackers. Tinsel decorations shaped like candles and stars adorned the old-fashioned gaslights that lined the street.

On Holly's right were the tourist train depot, an ice rink, and a bandstand where the kids would line up later in the week to see Santa. It was a closely guarded secret in town that Chief Finch played jolly old Saint Nick himself.

Just before reaching Caxton, Holly pulled into a gravel parking lot on the right. The Greek Revival–style building facing her had been painted a rustic red with white trim. It had a front-gable orientation with a porch that spanned the width of the house. On top of the porch stretched a long, white rectangular sign with "The Best of the Wurst" painted in bold black letters on it. The building had once been a general store, but now it was a sausage shop with a home on the second floor.

Opening the door, Holly smelled nutmeg and caraway seed, coriander and garlic.

Karl Hoffman stood behind an immaculately clean glass-fronted cabinet that ran the length of the shop. His butcher's apron was as spotless as the rest of the place. The stainless-steel counter and sink behind him gleamed like they were brand new, and the walls were a bright white.

He made all of the traditional German sausages. Holly feasted her eyes on the pork and veal bratwurst, and the parsley-flavored bockwurst, which was a perfect complement to bock beer. There were short, thick knockwurst, and milder, white Bavarian weisswurst. These were made from veal and back bacon, and they were traditionally eaten before noon. And of course, there was the ancestor of the great American hotdog—pork frankfurters.

German sausages were not the only type for sale. Karl was a true connoisseur, and The Best of the Wurst was the melting pot of the sausage world. He made Polish kielbasa, sweet and hot Italian sausages, English bangers, Irish breakfast sausages, and plump chicken and turkey links. For the local hunters, he ground their bear and venison meat into sausages.

He was ruddy-cheeked with thinning brown hair and fingers as fat as his sausages. "Hello, Holly," he boomed. "Is it letting up any?"

"No, Karl. Looks like it's going to snow all night."

"That's what they said on the radio, but I never trust the weather report. The snow is good for business, but my back needs a break from shoveling." For emphasis, he pushed his fists into his lower back. "I just finished making those chicken and garlic sausages you like so much."

"Unfortunately, I'm not here for the sausages."

Karl looked down at the case. "Turkey sausages, then?"

"No. I'm here about this." Holly held up the plastic bag containing the Iron Cross.

"What have you got there?" he asked, pulling his glasses from his pocket and putting them on.

"It's an Iron Cross," she told him. "Or at least I think it is."

"May I?" He held out his hand.

She passed it to him over the counter. "We have to leave it in the bag."

He nodded and studied it for a moment, his eyes narrowing with interest. "This is definitely an Iron Cross. Where did you get it?"

"We found it up near Mount Washington in the Notch."

Recognition hit him. "Was it with the body they found up there?"

"We believe so. What can you tell me about the Cross?"

"It was awarded for valor during World War Two."

"I thought so, but I'm trying to figure out how it got up there. We didn't have any plane crashes that I am aware of. That's why I thought I'd check with you. If I remember correctly, you help run the Caxton Historical Society."

"You have a good memory, Holly, which makes you such a good cop. You're just like Columbo—only prettier." He winked at her before looking back down at the medal. "Have you ever been to Stark?"

"What? Stark, New Hampshire?" she asked.

"That's right," he said.

Holly nodded. "I've passed through it a few times." Although Stark was only about a forty-minute drive west of Caxton, it wasn't on one of the routes she typically took.

"During World War Two, Stark had a prisoner of war camp. It was the only one in New Hampshire."

"Really?"

"Yes. German POWs were brought there to help in the logging industry. Timber was in great demand during the war, and there weren't enough young men left here to do the work, so they brought in POWs. There's a great book written about it by Allen Koop called *Stark Decency*. You should check it out. They have a copy at the library."

"Interesting. I'll take a look at it."

"Anyway," he continued, "some of the POWs and guards became friends. After the war, not all of the men returned to Germany. Some of them stayed here; some moved to Canada. Maybe this belonged to someone who stayed on after the war. Or perhaps it belonged to someone who escaped. The men were in the forest cutting down trees, so it wasn't difficult to get away. Could be someone escaped and died in the Notch. There's a family in town you should talk to, the Langs. They had a relative in the camp."

"I don't know them," Holly said.

"They own Blackthorn Timber."

"I thought Thaddeus Blackthorn owned it."

He shook his head. "That's another interesting piece of local history."

At that moment, a woman entered the shop. Holly glanced out of the window and saw a car full of people, probably tourists. She'd been so wrapped up in Karl's story, she hadn't heard them pull in. The woman ordered three pounds of bratwurst, some of Karl's homemade mustard that he was also famous for, as well as a jar of his homemade sauerkraut. Holly tried not to look impatient as the woman added a pound of frankfurters to her order before paying and leaving.

"Blackthorn's was started by Thaddeus's great-great-grandfather," Karl went on after the door had closed. "The first Thaddeus Blackthorn married Verity Caxton, who was the closest this town came to having royalty. Her family founded the town. Anyway, he was the one who started the logging business."

"Is that where Verity Falls got its name? From his wife?" Holly asked, thinking about the logging town in Crawford Notch that was now a ghost town.

"Yes. That's right. The Blackthorns had a sawmill there and even a railroad. They logged thousands of acres. Blackthorn bought up a lot of land around here. Anyway, old man Blackthorn had a son, who in turn had two sons and a daughter: Thaddeus the Third, Zacharias, and Patience. Zacharias died in World War Two, but his oldest son, Thaddeus the Third, didn't fight. He accidentally," Karl used his fingers to emphasize *accidentally*, "shot himself in the foot and stayed home. He was supposed to help run the business, but by all accounts, he preferred spending his family's money and partying. Rumor had it that he threw lavish parties."

While he talked, he started to clean the counter where he'd wrapped the sausages for his last customer.

"During the war," he continued, "Blackthorn needed help logging to meet the government's demand. Helmut Lang was a POW in the Stark camp. He was a strong young man by all accounts and a hard worker. I met him when he was much older, over at the German club. He loved my sausages; said they were better than the ones he'd had at home. Anyway, Helmut worked hard for the Blackthorn family and fell in love with Patience Blackthorn and married her. She was a lovely woman. So kind and generous. As you may have guessed, Helmut made a fine son-in-law. He had a head for business, and the old man left the majority of the company, including Verity Falls and all the land, to him and his daughter.

"Helmut's grandson lives up on Hurricane Mountain in one of those new big houses. Helmut loved to tell stories, especially the old stories about the camp."

"Thanks, Karl. This is really helpful. I'll see if I can find the Langs. Do you know his first name?"

"It's been a while since Helmut died. He was the only one who came in here." He thought for a moment. "Stefan. I believe it was Stefan. I'm sorry, I can't remember the wife's name, though."

CHAPTER TWENTY

When Cal Raines pulled into the Witch Cross Inn parking lot, Angel Natale was standing next to a beat-up van talking to the two men who'd checked in during the auction. They were loading bulky backpacks into the back of the truck, as well as the odd-looking metal detector he'd seen the night before. The vehicle had a "Bigfoot Investigations" decal on the side, which helped explain the unusual equipment. Angel raised a hand as he drove past, and Raines nodded. The crime scene techs had finished. Raines parked and got out. He walked up to the inn's front door, reached out for the handle, and noticed the hex marks. So much for warding off evil, he thought.

Inside, he found Skip Johnson sitting on the couch in the foyer, staring into the cold fireplace. He didn't even look up when Raines entered. On the wall behind him were photos of him sailing in races. The pictures were all similar, featuring big blue skies and deep blue oceans, a white-hulled sailboat with a rainbow-colored jib, and Skip Johnson at the helm, tanned and smiling.

The man before him bore little resemblance to that sailor. His slumped shoulders, rumpled clothes, bloodshot eyes, and red, blotchy face screamed "hangover." It was late morning, and he already had a glass of whiskey in his hand. He looked like a man without a purpose, adrift in despair. A man at the mercy of his thoughts. As Skip raised the glass to his lips, his hand shook. In a single gulp, he drained the contents and then pressed the empty glass against his forehead.

Raines studied him. Could the death of a guest, even one as young as Justin, cause such devastation? Or was Skip drinking to forget something he'd done?

At the time of the shooting, Skip claimed he'd gone upstairs to find an aspirin for a headache and had lain down for a few minutes. No one had seen him, though, meaning he'd had the time to leave the building and shoot Justin.

Skip said nothing as Raines walked past him, heading for the stairs. Justin's room was on the second floor. He found the door open and fingerprint powder all over the handle.

He stood there for a moment on the threshold, looking into the bedroom. Christine Johnson had created a shrine to Colonial living that was authentic and tastefully done. Still, it wasn't the kind of room he pictured Justin choosing to stay in. An ornate four-poster bed dominated the space. Raines couldn't tell if it was an original or a reproduction, but it looked as if it was made out of mahogany and expensive. Along the far wall, there was a matching dresser. An embroidered alphabet sampler in a wood and gold frame hung above it. A washstand with a small, antique mirror stood in the corner; a pitcher and basin sat on top of it.

Justin's overnight bag was still there on a fan-back Windsor chair. Even though it was probably in keeping with the period of the house, it looked like it would be uncomfortable to sit on for any length of time. Not the best chair for guests who wanted to spend time in their room, Raines thought. He always noticed furniture. After spending years in hotel rooms while touring with his band, comfortable beds and seating were a top priority. So, too, were blackout shades. Typically, he performed at night and slept late into the day. Gone were the days when bands trashed hotel rooms. Most of them made their money touring. They couldn't afford either the legal costs associated with wrecking a place or the bad reputation they'd earn with hotel management.

Sitting on the edge of the bed, Raines surveyed the room for anything out of place. It didn't appear as if Justin had taken the time to unpack anything except his toothbrush and toothpaste, which Raines could see on the sink in the small bathroom that adjoined the room. It was an old-fashioned bathroom, complete with a clawfoot tub. The bedroom windows overlooked the back of the property. The bed was covered with a handsewn quilt in browns, reds, and creams. It hadn't been slept in because Justin had died before he'd had the chance.

Raines was overcome by a wave of sadness. A little over twelve hours ago, he'd been talking to Justin about his rosewood guitar, and now he was gone.

Raines sighed and ran a hand through his hair. What a terrible waste. Justin had been so full of life, so full of promise. Now all that remained was a bag of clothes, a toothbrush and toothpaste. And another family left to cope with the loss of a loved one.

Justin would be missed. In the short time Raines had known him, he'd come across as friendly and conscientious, with one of those personalities that would have made him the heart of the family.

It was inevitable that Raines's thoughts turned from Justin to his nieces and their mother, because he reminded him of Sherry. She'd been sweet, kind, and a loving mom. Losing someone so special felt physical—like a fist driven into your gut so hard you couldn't catch your breath. And that shortness of breath came back with the memories, a permanent reminder of the loss.

Raines sighed again. Winter storm clouds passed across the watery sun, darkening the room. God, he felt old.

Leaning forward, he rested his arms on his knees and looked down at the rug. It was a round, braided wool rug in reds and greens. Staring at the pattern, he followed the spiral coil outwards from the center. His mind drifted. Cases worked like that, spiraling out from the victim, but what if Justin hadn't been the intended target? Wasn't it far more likely the bullet had been meant for Bliss or the Judge? Both worked high-profile cases. What could someone have against Justin Jarvis? There had been an honest goodness about him, with his eager, ready smile and kind eyes.

Who had known Justin would be at the Witch Cross Inn? Bliss and the Judge had given him the room as a gift for Christmas, but who else had known he would be there? And how long had they been waiting outside? If Justin hadn't left the building to help bring in the TV, there was a high probability that he'd have stayed inside the inn all night.

What if the Jarvises were not the target at all? What if the shooting had simply been a random act? Or a hunter's stray shot? Or even someone on the prowl for Bigfoot?

His eyes wandered across the painted pine floorboards. Over by the wall, he noticed faint scratches in the wood, like a door had been opened there. But there wasn't a door. Curious, Raines stood. A white chair rail ran around the room, separating the dark green–painted beadboard below it from the white beadboard above it.

He studied the wall. There was a gap in the chair rail that lined up perfectly with the groove in the beadboard. Pushing against the wall, he checked to see if there was a pressure spring. It didn't move.

Next, he studied the chair rail, which had a rounded edge that protruded nearly an inch. He ran his fingers under the lip and felt a button. As he pressed it, a door swung back, revealing a dark space.

Raines stepped into the gloom, but he couldn't see anything. Heading back into the bedroom, he unplugged one of the bedside lamps and moved it to the outlet closest to the secret door. Switching it on, he stepped back into the concealed room. Only it wasn't a room. It was a narrow landing with a flight of stairs going down. At the auction, Christine Johnson had mentioned she believed the inn had had servant stairs at one time. These certainly looked like servant stairs to him.

Had Justin found the passage? Was that why he'd brought up the Underground Railway and the secret passage? But if he'd found it, why hadn't he said so last night? If for no other reason than to prove his mom had been right about it.

Raines squinted down the stairs as his eyes adjusted to the gloom. The staircase was steep and narrow, with rough stone walls. Footprints were clearly visible in the dust, and they looked fresh, but there were a lot of them, and in the poor light, he wasn't sure they were good enough for a match. Someone had walked up and down the stairs more than once. Raines followed them down the staircase, careful to keep to the edge so he could preserve what evidence remained, which wasn't easy given the tight space. The old wooden stairs creaked, and he wondered if they were safe. How long had they been boarded up?

Perhaps the poor condition of the stairs was the reason Justin hadn't wanted Christine to know he'd found them. It would be an insurance risk if they hadn't been maintained, and she may have stopped him from using them.

Halfway down, Raines found the light too dim to see where he was stepping. That's when he remembered the light on his phone, which, he told himself, would have been the smartest and fastest thing to use in the beginning. Switching it on, Raines could now see the whole staircase without a problem. He reached the bottom without disturbing the footprints on the stairs, but on the ground floor, someone had milled around, because there was no dust left.

Unlike upstairs, the door and handle to exit the staircase had not been disguised. Raines cracked the door open and peered out. It was the dining room where they'd congregated for the auction. Everything was still there, even his rosewood guitar.

Raines stepped into the empty dining room and closed the secret door, which was located to the left of the fireplace. Wide wood panels and a chair rail similar to the one upstairs cleverly disguised the door. Raines ran his fingers under the rail and found a button that released a latch.

It was too early in the investigation to know the significance of any piece of information. Yet, someone had clearly been creeping around the inn. Had they seen something? Had Justin?

He walked out into the lobby. Skip Johnson was still there, sitting in the same spot. The only difference was that his glass was full again.

He looked up in surprise as Raines walked out of the dining room. "I thought you were upstairs."

"I was up in Justin's room."

"I didn't see you come back down the stairs."

"I came down another way."

"Oh," came the vague response. He turned back to the empty fireplace.

"Did you know about the staircase in the dining room, Mr. Johnson?"

With some effort, Skip refocused his attention on Raines. "What staircase?"

"I just came down a hidden staircase that connects Justin's room to the dining room."

Skip shrugged, not even mildly interested.

"Your wife never mentioned it?"

"No."

"Are you sure?"

He gave a weary sigh. "Look around you. My wife is into family history. And let me tell you something, it's an expensive hobby. Believe me, if she'd known about a secret staircase, she would have mentioned it to anyone willing to listen. And, for that matter, she would have been sure to use it when marketing the inn, as she did with that hex mark on the door handle. In fact, if I know my wife, she would have charged extra for staying in that room."

"Is she here?"

"No. Christine is out with our son." Skip rose unsteadily to his feet. "Can I fix you a drink?"

"No, thanks. I'm good," Raines said, walking to the front door.

Raines drove slowly out of the parking lot, unsure of where he was heading. He needed a lead, something to keep him moving forward. He switched on the radio, and Led Zeppelin's legendary guitar riff from "Whole Lotta Love" thumped from the speakers. As the lyrics started to tell the story of a casino fire in the Swiss town of Montreux, Raines mulled over the case, looking for an angle.

Justin had worked for the U.S. Forest Service, and the Blackthorns owned a timber company. Thaddeus Blackthorn had been at the auction, but he'd left early. Christine Johnson claimed that Thaddeus had only attended the function for the free drinks, but maybe he'd been there for something else. His alibi for the rest of the evening was weak. The problem was that he couldn't interview Thaddeus because the chief had asked Gustafson to follow up with him, and Gustafson would blow his top if he learned Raines had been to see him. The lead wasn't worth risking a jurisdictional confrontation. Although Raines wasn't concerned in the least about upsetting Gustafson, this lead wasn't worth jeopardizing the effective collaboration of the multijurisdictional task force.

But there was a workaround. Raines knew that Phil Montague worked for Blackthorn Timber, and after witnessing what had happened to Justin, he suspected the man would probably be willing to answer a few questions—even some regarding Thaddeus Blackthorn.

CHAPTER TWENTY-ONE

Holly was familiar with Hurricane Mountain Road. It was home to some of the most luxurious slope-side vacation properties in North Caxton. Many of them were gated, and all had expensive landscaping with big boulders and mature trees planted to provide privacy. Most had electronic surveillance, some had intercoms at the gates, and there was at least one house with a helicopter pad.

The Lang property was no different. Black wrought iron gates and a granite wall bordered the property. The gates were already open, so Holly headed up the steep, curving driveway. Although it had been snowing steadily for several hours, there wasn't a flake on the tarmac. Probably heated, she guessed. That was one home improvement she wished she could afford.

A row of magnificent blue spruces, too perfect and too evenly spaced to have been part of the natural landscape, ran all the way up to a post-and-beam house. Although that style of architecture heralded back to the more modest origins of a log cabin, there wasn't anything humble about this residence. It looked more like a grand mountain resort in the Colorado Rockies than a home. It had to be at least five thousand square feet, Holly estimated. River rocks formed the base of the structure, with log walls above the stone foundation. The green metal roof and a wide portico supported by massive gnarled tree trunks added to the American West feel. Beyond the house, Holly spotted a four-car garage. One of the doors was open, and two snowmobiles were inside. Everything reeked of wealth and grandiosity.

Phil Montague stood under the portico talking to a younger man. In contrast to Phil's dark hair and short, burly build, the younger man's hair was so blond it looked almost white in the flat gray light, and he was at least six inches taller than Phil and slim. He appeared Swedish or Danish, she thought. He had the tell-tale raccoon eyes in a suntanned face common to skiers, who wore sunglasses on the sunny slopes. He wore a green turtleneck and faded jeans.

Holly pulled up behind a black pickup, which had the Blackthorn Timber logo painted in white on the doors. The portico was nice on a day like today, providing plenty of protection from the elements.

Both men watched her with puzzled expressions as she approached them.

"Hi, Holly," Phil said, extending his hand, which she shook. Then he introduced Andreas Lang.

Up close, Andreas looked younger. Maybe seventeen or eighteen, she surmised.

Phil continued, "Are you here to see me about what happened last night? I heard Justin didn't make it. It's so sad."

"Did you know him?"

"No, I met him last night. We were both admiring Cal Raines's guitar."

With keen interest, Andreas cut in, "You saw Cal Raines's guitar?"

"It was up for auction."

The teenager's eyes widened slightly. "I wish I'd known that, Phil. I'd love to get my hands on one of his guitars."

Holly remembered that Phil told her he wanted the guitar for his boss's son. This must have been the kid he was talking about. Karl Hoffman had said that Blackthorn's was owned by the Langs.

Phil looked at her expectantly, waiting for her to tell them why she was there.

"I'm here to see Mrs. Lang. Is she home?"

Andreas nodded. "She's inside. We've just finished a business meeting."

To confirm the information Karl had given her, she asked, "You work for the Langs?"

"Yes. They own Blackthorn Timber. It confuses a lot of people in town, who think Thaddeus is the owner."

"I see."

He waited a moment for her to say something else, then said, "I'll let you head in to see Helga. That's Mrs. Lang." He placed a hand on Andreas's shoulder. "Will you show Detective Jakes in?"

"Sure. Please follow me."

Holly heard Phil get into his truck and drive off as she entered the house. She rubbed her boots vigorously on the mat at the door and looked around. The interior was as impressive as the exterior. A vaulted foyer featured exposed log beams, skylights and an immaculate flagstone floor.

As she followed Andreas, they entered an open-plan, lodge-style room. What struck her first was the incredible view. The house was situated on one of the best runs on the mountain, and the floor-to-ceiling windows overlooked it. From here, the Langs could either ski down to the main chairs at the base, or they could cut across to the mid-mountain chairlift and catch a ride to the top. Outside, the tails of several sets of skis were embedded in a snowbank, awaiting another run. If she lived here, she would never leave, she thought.

Dragging her gaze away from the view, she admired the stone fireplace. It was two-sided, like the one Raines had. A mound of logs burned on a cast-iron grate.

"Mother, we have a visitor," Andreas said to a woman seated on an overstuffed leather couch by the fire. "Detective Jakes, please meet my mother, Helga Lang."

He was so formal and polite that it threw Holly for a moment. Although only a teenager, there was a maturity to him, a composure she didn't see in many boys his age.

As Helga stood to greet Holly, the fire cast a warm glow over her features. She was wearing a Dale of Norway ski sweater that Holly would have loved but couldn't afford. From Helga's looks, it was apparent that she was Andreas's mother. She was as tall as her son, and they had the same Nordic coloring, with white-blonde hair and glacier-blue eyes. Although the laugh lines around her eyes showed her age, her body was lithe and youthful.

She indicated for Holly to sit on the couch opposite her, while Andreas sat in an armchair.

Business papers were stacked on the coffee table between them.

"Is this about the shooting last night? So tragic. Phil told us he was there, but you just missed him."

Helga's voice was modulated, cultured, and she had an accent. Scandinavian, Holly decided. Not German. She'd met many Norwegians, Swedes, Austrians and Germans on the ski circuit.

"No. I'm here about another case. My friend Karl Hoffman said that you may be able to answer a few questions. He owns the

German sausage shop in town and told me that one of your relatives was encamped at Stark during World War Two."

Helga and her son both looked surprised.

Andreas leaned forward, interested. "That's correct. My great-grandfather Helmut was there during the war. He worked for the Blackthorns."

"I see," said Holly. "And Helmut married into the family?"

Andreas nodded. "Correct again."

Holly retrieved the plastic bag from her pocket and held it up. "I realize this was a long time ago, but perhaps you know if your great-grandfather ever mentioned knowing someone who had an Iron Cross at the camp?"

Andreas stood up abruptly and held out his hand.

She gave it to him. "Please don't remove it from the bag."

He studied it intently. "Where did you get this?" He walked over to his mother and showed it to her.

Helga's gasp was audible from where Holly sat. She watched her place a hand at her throat.

"You recognize it?"

Andreas sank down on the couch next to his mother. He looked dazed. "Yes. Of course," he mumbled. "It's my father's."

Holly couldn't keep the surprise out of her voice. "It's your father's medal?"

Andreas nodded. "My great-grandfather, Helmut, gave it to him. It was his medal. It was awarded for valor months before his plane was shot down and he was taken prisoner."

"How can you be so sure it's his?"

"There's a nick on it, right here." He pointed to it. "And a scratch on the back."

Helga sat staring at the medal. Holly noticed how pale she'd become. "May I speak to your husband?"

Helga looked up at her. "He's not here."

"When do you expect him?"

"He's in Germany."

"For how long?"

Helga glanced nervously at Andreas and murmured, "I don't know."

Andreas held up the bag. "My father always keeps this with him. Where did you find it?"

Holly ignored the question and asked Helga another one. "Where in Germany is he? I'd like to talk to him about this."

"I don't know where he is."

Andreas placed a protective arm around his mother's shoulders. "My father left us two years ago, Detective."

"Do you have a number where I can reach him?"

Helga shook her head wearily.

"Have you had any contact with him in the last two years?" This time they both shook their heads. That was strange, Holly thought. Who doesn't speak to their husband and father for two years?

"Where did you find the medal?" Andreas asked again.

"We found it today in Pinkham Notch."

Helga covered her mouth with her hand.

Holly continued, "I'm afraid we found it near human remains."

"You think it's Stefan?" Helga's modulated tone was gone. She sounded nervous, agitated.

"We don't know. We're trying to figure that out."

"But the Cross. It's his. It has to be him."

"There could be another explanation as to why it was there," Holly told them, but she was beginning to think that she'd just identified the remains. "Is there anyone who knows where your husband is staying in Germany?"

Helga looked blankly at her for a moment before responding. "No."

"Since he's been gone, have you tried to find him?"

"No."

"Why not?"

"We had our differences. We grew apart."

Andreas snorted. "You mean he grew apart with someone he met in Germany when he was there on business."

"Those are nothing but rumors, Andreas," she snapped.

He recoiled slightly as if she'd slapped him, but he didn't remove his arm from around her shoulders.

She softened her tone. "They are nothing but nasty rumors." She clasped the hand Andreas had draped around her shoulders and patted it gently. "Two years have gone by so very quickly. I always thought he would come home to me. To us."

Mother and son looked down at the Iron Cross in the palm of Andreas's other hand.

Neither said anything. Holly waited, letting the silence continue.

Finally, Helga looked back up at her. "Stefan would never have left the medal behind. He adored his grandfather. He'd earned the cross for saving several planes and crew in his *Staffel*, his squadron. They'd taken heavy fire, and they were in trouble. Helmut flew in front of the English Spitfires, drawing and returning their fire. He was shot down over the ocean, but a battleship was there and rescued him. The medal was supposed to be passed down through the generations. Stefan would have left it to Andreas." She fell silent.

Holly watched Andreas rub his thumb over the plastic covering the medal. She waited a moment before continuing with her questions. "Who has been running the company since he's been gone?"

"I have, with Phil's help, and now Andreas is learning about the company."

"What about money? Your husband would have needed money."

"We have many bank accounts. Some business, some personal. I have several in Sweden. He had multiple accounts in Germany. I assumed he was using those funds." Helga looked away from Holly to stare out of the window. "I thought he'd had enough of the family business. He wanted to race cars. He loves speed and the Autobahn. He has family near Munich."

"And you never called them?"

"No."

Holly looked at Andreas. He was as pale as his mother and sat staring at the medal in his hand.

"How did you know he was going to Germany?"

"It was a planned trip. He traveled there several times a year."

"We will need his dental records. Can you get them?"

Helga looked over at her. "I have Stefan's power of attorney. I'll contact the dentist."

Now that's interesting, Holly thought. Having her husband's power of attorney would enable Helga to take over the business and keep all of the money. "Thank you," she said with a nod of her head. "That would be very helpful."

CHAPTER TWENTY-TWO

Barreling down Helga Lang's driveway, Holly nearly collided with a Chevy Suburban that was just about to pass through the gates. Cal Raines sat behind the wheel with an amused expression on his face. He reversed so Holly could get out. She pulled up alongside him and rolled down her window. He did the same.

"What are you doing here, Raines?"

"Someone at Blackthorn Timber told me Phil Montague was here."

"You missed him. He left nearly an hour ago."

Casually, he rested a wrist on the steering wheel like he wasn't in a hurry to leave. "Why are you here, Holly?"

"I'm here about the human remains found up in the Notch." Holly couldn't bring herself to think of it as the Yorrick case anymore. She had a name now, and that name was associated with a teenage boy whose father had left home two years ago and hadn't been seen since.

"What are the odds that we'd end up at the same place even though we're investigating two different cases?" Raines mused.

"Slightly better than me seeing a penguin on the ski slopes this year."

Raines chuckled.

Although it was only four thirty in the afternoon, it was dark. Snow still fell, and the wind had picked up, driving flakes in through his open window.

"Do you want to get something to eat and discuss our cases?" he asked.

Did she want to have dinner with Cal Raines? Not particularly, Holly concluded, but she was interested in how the Justin Jarvis case was progressing, and she was starving since she'd missed breakfast and lunch. "Sure. Where do you want to go?"

"How about the Paw?" he suggested.

"Fine with me."
"I'll meet you there."

Several hours beyond hungry, Holly was thankful to be heading to The Muddy Paw. It was one of those restaurants that offered something for everyone: steak and burgers, chicken, seafood, pasta dishes, vegetarian meals, and a vast selection of après-ski appetizers to satisfy even the hungriest mountain-goer. It happened to be one of Holly's favorite places and was owned by Frannie LaCroix, who was a good friend to both Holly and Raines and was the love of Po's life, except he hadn't plucked up the courage to tell her yet.

Holly's taste buds had lit up like a Christmas tree at the prospect of one of Frannie's chubby burgers. Or perhaps she'd have the Buffalo wings, which were absolutely exquisite. By some cooking miracle Holly would never understand, the skin remained crispy even after the wings were drenched in sauce.

It was relatively quiet when they arrived; the whole place smelled delicious, like grilled steak and onions. Her stomach rumbled so loudly that Cal raised an eyebrow and glanced at her. She ignored him.

As they headed over to the bar, Frannie looked up and greeted them with a sad smile. Holly guessed that Justin's death had been the main topic of conversation all day. She'd tied her bleached blonde hair back in a loose ponytail and was wearing a lime-green, skintight, long-sleeved t-shirt with a Muddy Paw logo on it and pawprints running across her chest. Holly had no doubt that Frannie's wardrobe was one of the reasons the restaurant did so well.

Turning her attention back to her task, Frannie poured sweet vermouth, bourbon, and bitters into a glass. She finished it off with a couple of ice cubes and placed the Manhattan in front of a customer.

Holly scooped up a handful of pretzels from a bowl on the bar and crunched down on them with satisfaction.

Frannie poured a beer and served it before making her way over to them. She wiped the bar in front of them, and by reflex, placed a couple of new drink mats down on the clean countertop. "It's terrible what happened over at the Witch Cross Inn." She shook her head sadly.

"Did you know Justin?" Holly asked. Frannie was a good source of information. She knew a lot of people in town, and although tourists liked to eat at the Paw, it was also a favorite with the locals.

"No, but I do know Christine Johnson."

"How do you know her?" Raines asked.

"I know most of the restaurant owners in town. And I know this is going to hurt her business; I'm sure of it. I really feel for her. It's a shame this happened so close to Christmas. We all count on the holiday shoppers to give us an extra boost at this time of year. We're so lucky people are still willing to drive up here for the outlets and tax-free shopping. God forbid they change the law. A sales tax would ruin a lot of businesses around here."

Raines nodded and continued with his questions. "How about her husband, Skip? Do you know him?"

"The Sailor." It wasn't a question, and they could tell from her dismissive tone that she wasn't impressed with him. "I don't know how Christine puts up with him. I guess it's the money."

"He's wealthy, then?"

Holly listened to Raines ask questions while she munched on the pretzels. She hadn't thought much of Skip when she'd met him the night before, either.

"Skip's family comes from the North Shore of Massachusetts," Frannie explained. "A big sailing family I hear. He had the money to buy the inn and fix up the place, but boy does he drink and flirt with the waitresses."

Three college-aged guys came in and sat down at the stools next to them. Two of them were teasing the third about a girl named Star.

"Can we get a table with some privacy?" Raines asked.

"Take the corner booth. Do you know what you want to eat, or do you need menus?"

"I'll take Buffalo wings and a blue cheeseburger, medium rare," Holly replied without hesitating.

Raines gave her a questioning look.

She grinned at him, not caring what he thought. "The body needs fuel."

"Yeah, but not rocket fuel," came his response.

"And we'll take a salad for Raines. He doesn't want to ruin his wispy figure."

He laughed. "Add a steak on the rare side to that salad."

"Any dressing?"

"Nope."

Holly grinned. "See what I mean?" She was still smirking when she slid into the booth at the far end of the dining room. It was the smallest booth in the restaurant but also the most private. A perfect spot for a romantic dinner for two, or a discussion about a homicide case.

As Cal sat down opposite her, his knee brushed hers under the table. Heat raced through her body, which she didn't care for in the least. Luckily, Raines didn't seem to notice that anything was amiss, even though she was sure her cheeks had darkened to a deep burgundy.

Holly remembered feeling that same heat when she'd kissed him all those years ago on the night of the prom. She'd been drunk on Peach Schnapps and was hobbling around on a broken leg when she'd bumped into him. He'd stopped her from toppling over and making a fool of herself in front of the whole senior class, and then she'd done the craziest thing she'd ever done in her life. She'd reached up and kissed him right on the lips. She tried to stop herself thinking about it, but failed miserably. To avoid his eyes, she glanced around the room.

There were only two couples. All four of them looked well over sixty and were probably taking advantage of the early-bird specials.

Raines draped an arm over the back of the bench and sat in silence for a moment studying the wall behind her.

She knew there was a vintage photo of people skiing down Tuckerman's Ravine on the wall. She marveled every time she saw it, wondering how they hadn't killed themselves skiing on the stiff old wooden boards.

"That's an interesting shade of red Frannie selected for the wall. It adds a warm glow to your skin tone," he teased, unable to keep the amusement out of his voice.

Holly squinted at him, trying to come up with something witty. Luckily, she spied Frannie walking over to their table with a basket full of her famous bread rolls. She placed them on the table along with a small dish of butter and a couple of plates.

"Let me know if you want more," she told Holly, and gave her a sly wink.

A waitress followed with tall glasses of ice water.

Holly flipped back the white napkin covering the rolls and grabbed one. They were still warm. Tearing it open, she inhaled the yeasty aroma as if she hadn't eaten in days. She peeled back the golden wrapper that protected the butter and spread a thick layer of it on a hunk of bread. It started to melt into the dough immediately. She loved Frannie's rolls. Crisp and flaky on the outside, soft on the inside, they were definitely the best in town, and she'd been known to eat a basket of them after a day of skiing. She bit into the crusty bread and sighed with pleasure at the taste of the salty butter.

Raines watched in mock horror as she devoured the rest of the roll.

She didn't care what he thought. It tasted divine. She finished it and eyed the breadbasket longingly but managed to control herself. "Is Skip a solid suspect?" she asked him, forcing herself to focus on the case rather than on Frannie's tempting baked goods.

Raines nodded. "He doesn't have an alibi for last night, and when I saw him today, he sure as hell looked worried about something—could have been guilt." Then he told her about the secret staircase he'd found.

At the mention of a secret staircase, Holly's hunger evaporated. "You're kidding."

He shook his head.

"I'm beginning to feel like I'm in a Twilight Zone episode," she said. "First, we get a call about a Bigfoot sighting, then a couple of kids find a human skull, and now you found a secret passage. What next?"

"I shudder to think," Raines responded.

Holly smiled. "So, the stairs led from Justin's room down to the dining room, but you're not sure he knew about it?"

"No. The stairs are being processed right now, but there were so many prints, the techies are not sure there's one good enough to match with Justin's boots."

"Did Skip know about it?"

"He didn't seem to, and he claimed his wife didn't know either. It's his opinion that if she had known, she'd have monopolized on it to make some money. The night of the auction, Justin mentioned a secret passage and the inn being part of the Underground Railroad while Christine and I were with him. She denied it and seemed to believe that the stairs were for the servants and had been removed years ago during a remodel." He paused for a moment to consider. "The staircase probably has nothing to do with the shooting. It's not as if the shooter ran inside or outside the building via those stairs. We were in the dining room," Raines said.

"Still," Holly added. "It's something. So, how come you wanted to talk to Phil Montague? How does he fit? He can't be a suspect. He was with us at the time of the shooting."

"Thaddeus Blackthorn doesn't have a solid alibi for the time of the shooting, but I can't question him because Gustafson has been tasked with that. You know better than I do, he won't appreciate anyone butting in on his investigation. I thought that if Justin was the intended target, the issues of timber and forestry connected him to Thaddeus Blackthorn. I knew Phil Montague worked for the Blackthorns, so I wanted to ask him if Blackthorn knew Justin. When I called the office at the lumber mill, though, I discovered that the Langs actually own the business and have for decades. Thaddeus Blackthorn doesn't have anything to do with the company."

"Which means," Holly said, "if Thaddeus Blackthorn isn't involved in the timber business, there's no connection to Justin."

"True, but I still thought it was worth following up with Montague. After all, Thaddeus is a Blackthorn. If he's not connected to the business now, perhaps he was in the past. At the very least, I thought there was a good chance that Montague knows him."

They stopped talking as Frannie came over with a mound of Buffalo wings.

Placing them on the table in front of Holly, she warned, "Watch it. The wings are piping hot."

The aroma of hot sauce and a hint of garlic wafted up from the plate. Holly waited a moment for them to cool down before dunking a wing into the blue cheese. Frannie's wings were the best, and she sighed with pleasure. It was the honey Frannie added to the recipe to sweeten them just a little that made them so great.

"So," Raines said, after she'd polished off a few wings and licked her fingers with satisfaction. "Why were you at the Langs'?"

Holly told him about the Iron Cross the ME had found and her subsequent visit to Karl Hoffman. Raines was intrigued to learn about the prisoner of war camp at Stark and the connection to the Langs.

"How likely is it that the remains are Stefan Lang?" he asked, once she'd finished summing up her visit with Helga and Andreas.

"I could tell that they were convinced it was his cross. Helga had a strong physical reaction when I showed it to her. There is a nick and a scratch on it that they identified as being on Stefan's cross. It was an important family heirloom, and Stefan always carried it with him."

"What did you make of Helga?" he asked.

"Her reaction could have been grief, guilt or even fear now that the body has been discovered. She was hard to read, but what rang my alarm bell was the fact that she's had no contact with her husband for two years. Her story seems to be that he walked out on the family, and she was too proud to chase him. Who does that?" Suddenly remembering that Raines's mother had walked out on him when he was just a kid and his father had done nothing to bring her home, she hesitated for a moment.

Back then, Raines hadn't wanted to talk about it, and Holly had respected that. There had been things in her life that she hadn't wanted to discuss either. This didn't mean that they hadn't acknowledged or understood what each other had been through; they just didn't need to talk about it. A meaningful look had been enough to offer support when the other was feeling down, or an apology for a careless word instantly regretted. At the time, they'd found solidarity in that ability to silently communicate.

That felt like a lifetime ago. Now Holly found she couldn't look at him that way. It was too intimate—too awkward. Unsure of what to say, she decided to ignore it and plow on with her analysis instead. "I find it hard to believe that Stefan just up and left for Germany, with or without a girlfriend, and Helga never heard from him again. That's more than a little fishy, unless you look at what she gains with him out of the picture. She gets the business and his money, and that's a whole lot of motive. You should see their house. She even has a heated driveway. I'd kill for one of those."

His eyes crinkled in a genuine smile. "I don't doubt it. You never liked shoveling."

Relieved to see that he wasn't bothered by her comments, she picked up another wing and pointed it at him. "You want to know something really intriguing, Raines?"

His smile deepened. "When you put it like that, it's hard to say no."

"Last night, Montague told me that he wanted to buy your guitar for his boss's son, and he wanted me to ask you if you'd sign it. Now that we know he works for the Langs, I assume he meant it for Andreas. Who buys their boss's son such an expensive guitar?"

"So, you think he's in a relationship with Helga?"

"I didn't see Helga and Phil together, but he certainly was friendly with Andreas." She took a bite out of the wing and swallowed a mouthful of chicken. Licking the sauce off her fingers, she thought about the way Phil had placed his hand on Andreas's shoulder. "He was more than friendly. He was paternal."

As Raines watched her lick her fingers, he unconsciously picked up one of the small packets containing a wet paper towel, ripped it open, and handed it to her like he would do for one of his nieces. "What we do know is that Montague has been helping Helga run the timber business since Stefan disappeared two years ago."

Holly nodded, wiped her fingers on the moist napkin, and studied his face as he stared at the wall above her head. His brow was furrowed in thought. He had a five o'clock shadow that looked more like the designer stubble favored by actors seeking a slightly scruffy style that was both cool and sexy. It suited him, she thought, and wondered how it would feel against her skin, then immediately gave herself a mental slap back into reality. "What are you thinking about, Raines?"

"I had been developing Thaddeus Blackthorn as a potential suspect in Justin's homicide because he ran a timber empire and Justin was a forest ranger. It was the best lead I could come up with. Only now we discover that it's the Langs who actually own Blackthorn Timber, which seriously weakens that theory. But, if the skull turns out to be Stefan Lang's, then forestry connects your case with mine."

She looked doubtful. "I don't know. It's a stretch. When Stefan disappeared two years ago, Justin was in college."

"It's a possibility, though. Could be forestry related."

"You're going out on a really thin limb," she said, and smirked at her own joke.

"That's real funny, Jakes."

"Hey, I impress myself sometimes—what can I say? But seriously, neither the chief nor the mayor will want to hear that you're trying to connect the cases. The last thing they'll want is for it to get out that we think a lone suspect is responsible for two murders. When they hit the roof, make sure you tell them it's all your idea."

"Who said anything about telling them? We could work the angles together to see if they're connected before we tell anyone," he suggested.

"And then there's the Bigfoot case," she muttered.

"That has to be a hoax," Raines said.

"A hoax that happened just two houses away from the inn."

"But not on the same night as the shooting. That was a week before Justin was shot; the same night the skull was found."

"True, but Bigfoot was seen running from the direction of the inn. Perhaps it was a dry run and the shooter was wearing a ghillie suit to disguise himself."

His face registered surprise. Obviously, he hadn't thought of that angle. "That's a good idea, but what about the Bigfoot print Fennis found? Do you really think a shooter is going to slow himself down with fake feet?"

Raines had hit the issue Holly had been struggling with right on the head. If the killer was worried about leaving boot print evidence, there were better options than running around in fake rubber feet. Simply buying a pair of new boots a size bigger and throwing them away after committing the crime would have made far more sense.

CHAPTER TWENTY-THREE

Frank Stanko and Kenny Fritz, aka Sticks and Stubby, sat in their Bigfoot Investigation van and watched a detective leave the Witch Cross Inn.

Stubby pointed a fat finger at the passing SUV. "Where do you suppose he's off to?"

"How should I know?" Sticks responded glumly. His mood had gone from bad to worse after their run-in with Detective Jakes, and a confrontation minutes later with an Officer Natale when they'd attempted to enter the inn.

Sticks wanted to remain there, at the heart of the Bigfoot action. Sticks had argued, and they'd been informed that no one was permitted to stay at the inn for the foreseeable future. Sticks had tried pleading then, but Officer Natale had been unsympathetic and had moved them on.

"It's just like Roswell," he muttered. "The federal government is shutting us down, and we are so close, oh so close, to revealing the truth. I could smell him out there, Stubby. We're that close."

His best friend looked crushed. "What are we going to do now? We're not going home, are we?"

"No way! We're not going to let a bunch of Feds stop us," Sticks almost shouted.

Stubby looked confused. "I thought they were local cops, not the FBI."

"How many times do I have to warn you about this? They want you to think they're local, just like they wanted us to believe it was a weather balloon that crashed in Roswell instead of a UFO. But we're no fools. We're onto something. Otherwise, they'd leave us alone."

"But you seemed to like that female cop…uh…I mean FBI agent."

Sticks turned to him. "I was playing her. You got to let them think you're not a threat. Get me?"

Stubby nodded. "You had me fooled, for sure. So now what?"

Sticks scratched his pockmarked cheek with a dirty fingernail. "Remember that story I told you about those loggers who disappeared in Verity Falls at the turn of the last century?"

Stubby nodded. "Yeah. The Legend of Verity Falls. I remember. They were never found. Most people think it was Bigfoot, but you reckon the aliens took them for research."

"What if it wasn't aliens? What if it was Bigfoot all along? Probably makes more sense when I think about it." Sticks stuck a finger in his ear, waggled it about before adding, "We know Bigfoot runs through the notches and must live in the wilderness, right?" He didn't wait for Stubby to acknowledge it. "What if everyone got it wrong, and the Legend of Verity Falls was all about *Bigfoots*, plural, instead of Bigfoot?"

Stubby whistled. "What? Like there was more than one?"

"Yes. There could have been a den right there, right smack in the heart of Verity Falls before it was even Verity Falls. Think about it. It was in the middle of nowhere. A river runs through the Notch, so they'd have access to water. And there's plenty of wildlife for food. Plus, no people. Nothing except wilderness. Made for a nice place to settle. Then when the loggers showed up, the Bigfoots had to kill them to protect their home. That's probably the real, true legend, but nobody figured it out until us."

"You think?" Stubby asked a little breathless from excitement.

"Yeah. It's a ghost town for a reason. The loggers heard loud moans in the night. I remember reading that."

Sticks reached across Stubby, who was in the passenger seat, and opened the glove compartment. He rummaged around until he found what he was looking for. It was a map of the White Mountains. Opening it, he draped it over his steering wheel, studied it for a couple seconds before placing a finger approximately where the Witch Cross Inn was located. From that point, he ran his finger right across the map. He traced a route to Sarah Mooney's house, out through the green forest area behind her place, all the way through the White Mountains to Verity Falls. He whispered with reverence, "I think we've hit the jackpot. It's a straight shot from here to Verity Falls."

Stubby giggled and slapped Sticks on the shoulder.

Sticks grinned at him. "We need to go to Verity Falls. Bigfoot isn't hanging around here. I bet he was just dumpster diving at the Witch Cross Inn. They can probably smell a steak frying twenty miles away. I bet dollars to donuts that's where they get their food in winter. And there's so many restaurants both sides of the White Mountains, they must make the rounds like raccoons. They hit the dumpsters and vanish back into the wilderness. Dammit! We should have been staking out the dumpsters all along." He peered at the map and pointed at a spot marked Verity Falls. "There it is."

Stubby craned his neck to get a good look. "But there's no road on the map. How are we going to find it?"

"Easy. See this old landmark cabin?"

Stubby bent closer. "The Jeremiah Pitt house?"

"That's the one. If we check out that area, we're bound to find an old road. Luckily, there's not much snow, but there's enough for us to track their footprints."

"You think there's still a den of them out there?" Stubby asked.

"I'll bet you a C-note they're there."

Stubby shifted nervously in his seat. "Should we tell that detective about it so she can check it out? I mean, one Bigfoot we could probably handle, but what if there's a whole gang of them?"

"No way! We're not letting the government anywhere near this. This is *our* find. We're going to be famous, Stubby. Famous! And all the doubters will have to eat crow."

CHAPTER TWENTY-FOUR

Monroe Podell yelled up the stairs to Melody. "I made you a grilled cheese sandwich."

She closed her notebook that contained her song lyrics and rolled over on her bed. She wasn't hungry, but Po would worry about her if she didn't eat anything. She'd managed to skip breakfast because he'd left early with Abbey. Abbey visited their father in prison practically every Sunday morning. Because her uncle was working a case, Po had taken her. They'd just returned, and as was his custom, Po had fixed them lunch.

Melody walked into the kitchen and found Abbey sitting with her feet up on the breakfast nook bench with her chin resting on her knees. Her arms were wrapped tightly around her legs. It only took one look at her sister for Melody to realize that she should have stayed up in her room. Abbey looked pissed. More than pissed. She was fuming. Had Jesse broken up with her so he could date Kayla? she wondered.

Memphis, their Chocolate Lab, wagged his tail at her. He was lying near Po, waiting for him to drop something. She scooted down and gave him a kiss on the head.

Po placed a plate loaded with potato chips as well as a bulging grilled cheese sandwich on the counter in front of Melody.

"Eat all of it," he said, giving her a playful glare.

"That's enough for a week," she protested.

"Eat it all up like a good girl," he teased.

She rolled her eyes as she swung her leg up and over the saddle that had been turned into a counter stool.

Po turned to leave.

"Aren't you eating with us?" Melody asked, wanting him to stay so he could fend off Abbey.

"I ate while Abbey was visiting your dad. I'm behind on that paint job for the sixty-six Mustang. Call me if you need anything, though."

Po lived in an apartment above their garages and ran a restoration business from home when he wasn't looking after them.

Melody waited for Po to leave before hopping off the stool and picking up her plate. Time to get out of Dodge, she thought. She looked down at Memphis and nodded her head in the direction of the stairs.

Memphis got up. He would follow a sandwich to the ends of the earth.

As she turned to leave for the safety of her bedroom, Abbey said, "Dad thinks Uncle Cal is stopping you from visiting him."

Melody's stomach clenched at the mention of her dad. She stood still, with her back to her sister.

"Dad's not happy," Abbey went on. "He thinks you love Uncle Cal more than him."

Was she for real? Melody wondered bitterly.

"Why won't you let him explain what happened with his lawyers? He didn't want them to point the finger at you. It was just a tactic they used to create reasonable doubt."

Melody shivered. She felt like someone had just walked over her grave. She spun around to face her sister, and her potato chips and the sandwich went flying.

Memphis scrambled and slipped in his desperate rush to get to the food before it was scooped up.

Melody opened her mouth. She was going to tell Abbey the truth. All of it. The secrets she'd been keeping so she could protect her. She wanted to yell it at her. Get her to shut up once and for all. But it would destroy her sister, and she couldn't do that, could she? Deflecting, she snapped, "So, you're not in a bad mood about Jesse, then?"

Surprise registered on Abbey's face. "Why would I be in a bad mood about Jesse?"

Melody pressed her lips together and said nothing.

"What is it, you little sneak?"

Melody couldn't take it anymore. She yelled, "You're so blind. You don't see anything, do you? Go ask Jesse who he was with yesterday."

Abbey paled. "Who was it?"

"That's for me to know and you to find out." After what had happened to their mother, trust was something that would never come easily to either sister again. Melody instantly felt mean for hurting her sister, playing on her insecurities, but her sister was relentless.

"You little beast," Abbey hissed. "You're jealous that I have a boyfriend and you don't."

"Keep telling yourself that, Abbey, and see how far it gets you. I see things way more clearly than you. You've always been so blind to anything other than what you want to see."

"What's that supposed to mean?" Abbey was yelling now.

"You've got your head buried so far down in the sand, you don't see anything that goes on around you. And you never listen to anybody." Melody itched to throw something at her. "You only care about yourself and what you want. It's always Abbey, Abbey, Abbey!"

By now, Memphis had wolfed down Melody's lunch and started to whine.

"It's okay, boy," Melody said as she ran out of the room. He ran after her to the front door. "No, boy. You can't come with me this time." She grabbed her coat, hat and mitts off the stand, slipped on a pair of boots that turned out to be Abbey's, and opened the front door. She stalked over to the garage, hauled out her bike and started pedaling down the driveway. The snow was falling, and her bike slipped so much she had to get off and push it until she got to the road, which had been plowed. The temperature was dropping, but Melody was so angry she didn't feel it. She was out of there, and she was not coming back.

CHAPTER TWENTY-FIVE

Melody pedaled furiously down the road, heading in the opposite direction of town. She was crying, and her nose was running. Wiping it with the back of her glove, she swerved and nearly fell off the bike. Even though the road had been plowed, there was still slush and the ongoing storm to battle. Fighting against the wind and driving snow, she leaned into the handlebars and pushed harder.

Next time, she thought, she would tell Abbey everything and see how she liked it. *If* there ever was a next time.

She pedaled for fifteen minutes, battling the wind and snow. She wished she'd taken the time to grab her goggles because the snow was icy and pricked at her eyes. She tucked her head down and pumped hard. Reaching the main road, she turned left, heading into Crawford Notch. She was relieved to find the wind behind her now, because she had nearly seven miles to go.

The roads were deserted, but a couple of miles further on, she heard the sound of an engine coming up behind her. She heard it slow and a voice yell out something. Glancing over her shoulder, she saw a van. She pedaled harder, but the van pulled up alongside her.

A dark-haired man rolled down his window. "Hey. Kid. Where are you going? There's nothing out here for miles."

"Leave me alone."

"We can't leave you out here. Why don't we put your bike in the back and take you home?"

"You freak. Go away," she yelled. "Or I'll call the police."

"We're only trying to help."

"I don't want your help."

He drove alongside her for a moment, and she fumbled in her pocket, pretending she was getting her phone. "I'm going to call now."

The other man in the passenger seat looked worried and said something Melody couldn't hear.

"You shouldn't be out here, kid." With that parting comment, he buzzed up his window and continued down the road.

"Freaks," she muttered.

She slowed until they were out of sight, and then she resumed her fast pace. A few minutes later, another car stopped, and this time a white-haired man offered her a ride, which she again refused. Thankfully, he left her alone without another word. Next time, she thought, she might not be so lucky. After cycling hard for a couple more minutes, she heard a truck coming. Hopping off her bike, she dragged it into the bushes and hid behind a big boulder until it had passed.

Ten minutes or so later, she reached the gap in the trees and the dirt road where Zack had turned off. She sighed with relief. Her face was wet, and she couldn't feel her nose. The rough trail leading up to the mill made it too difficult to ride her bike, so she got off and pushed it, lifting it in areas where the snow or the ruts were too deep.

There were patches of bare ground where the dense trees sheltered parts of the road. It looked like a big truck had recently gouged uneven ruts in the dirt.

Nearing the mill, she heard another engine, but she couldn't tell from which direction it was coming. She lifted her bike off the road again and hid behind a tree, waiting for it to pass, shivering from the cold and damp that had penetrated her winter coat. Her teeth started to chatter. She waited for a couple of minutes, but nothing came. Instead, the sound of the engine seemed to stay at the same distance, so she decided to keep on going. As she neared the mill, though, the engine grew louder. She stopped again, listening. It didn't sound like a car, she thought, so she inched her way further up the trail.

In amongst the trees, she spotted the old mill. It looked like something out of a fairytale, with snow bowing tree limbs and covering the old tin roof. A glimmer of light glinted out through the cracks in the mill's old wooden walls.

Zack Blackthorn's BMW was tucked away in the hideaway parking spot he used to the right of the building. The big doors were shut, and it looked like no one was there. Because the doors were far too heavy for her to open, Melody pushed her bike around back, ducking under what was left of the rotting ramp that lead down to the pond, which was used to store logs. Coming out the other side, she spotted the generator, which she realized had been the engine she'd heard running. A power cable ran through a crack in the wall. It amazed her what a great setup the boys had out here.

As she leaned her bike against the side of the mill, she noticed the back door had been nailed shut. Fortunately, there was a narrow gap in the wall just a few feet beyond the door, so she squeezed in through it.

Luke and Zack sat huddled in blankets on camping chairs, drinking beer out of cans. On one of the camping beds, Kayla sat zipped up in a sleeping bag with a bottle of champagne in one hand; her other hand was tucked into the sleeping bag. Strings of lights shaped like red chili peppers and white snowballs hung from the canopy over their heads. Even though the mill wasn't heated, it looked warm, cozy and inviting.

"Hello," she whispered.

Kayla screamed, Luke dropped his beer can, and Zack's mouth fell open.

Melody grinned for the first time that day.

"Holy crapola," Luke sputtered. "You look like a damn ghost."

Melody looked down at her coat and realized that she was covered in wet snow.

"Girl, whatcha doing here?" Kayla stood up in her sleeping bag and jumped like a kangaroo towards her. "How did you get here?"

"I rode my bike."

"*What*? Are you crazy? In this weather?" Zack said, shaking his head at her like a worried parent.

Melody just shrugged, but she liked the way his concern made her feel like one of them.

Then Luke ruined it by giving her an accusing look. "You didn't happen to tell anyone about this place, did you?"

"No."

"You sure?"

"Yes."

"Well, someone's been here in a truck and took stuff."

She glanced around. Everything appeared to be there—the tent, two chairs, two beds, the small camping stove. Thinking about the hidden printer, she asked, "Did they get the stuff in the wall?"

"No. They took the big saw that was over there." Zack pointed to the middle of the mill.

"That's weird," she said.

"No kidding," mumbled Luke as he dug around in his cooler for another beer. "It couldn't have been easy to get that thing out of here."

Zack stood up, walked over to where they stored stuff in the wall, and removed the planks. "We didn't think to check and see if everything was here. Come to think of it, we should take this stuff home now that we know someone has been here." He began to pull items out, piling them to one side.

"Come and sit over here with me," Kayla instructed. "Take that coat and those boots off and get into the other sleeping bag."

Melody did as she was instructed. She was shivering violently now, and her nose was stinging.

Luke lit the camp stove and placed a pan on it. Next, he dug around in a backpack and pulled out a half-full bottle of rum. He poured it into the pan and got up. Keeping the blanket wrapped around himself, he shuffled over to a box that hadn't been there before and retrieved three tin mugs.

Soon she smelled spices that made her think of Christmas. She squeezed her eyes shut. Christmas was the last thing she wanted to be reminded of. There was no escaping it. Not even here in the middle of nowhere.

"Here. Drink this," Luke said, stretching out a tin mug to her. "It will warm you up."

She was going to refuse, but Kayla said, "Drink it. You're freezing to death."

She took it. The mug was nearly full and felt wonderfully warm in her cold hands. Raising it to her lips, she sipped tentatively in fear that it was too hot. It wasn't. It was just warm enough to drink. Swallowing another mouthful, she felt a warmth rush through her. It felt good. She sat there in the sleeping bag, sipping at the rum and listening to Luke tease Kayla.

"So, why won't you go out with Zack? Is it because you secretly want me?"

"Get over yourself, Luke Johnson. I told you I don't date boys my own age."

He flashed her a big, cheesy smile. "You don't know what you're missing."

Kayla laughed and took another swig from the champagne bottle.

Zack drained his can of beer and crushed it between his hands. "Okay, it's time to tell your deepest, darkest secrets. Let's start with you, Melody."

She looked up, startled. "Me?"

"Yes. We're all dying to know if your dad did it. Abbey tells everyone he's innocent," Zack said.

Fear flooded through her as she once again felt the big hand on the back of her head, and the way the fingers had clenched her skull with the strength of a vice, right before the hand had slammed her head against the counter. She shuddered and stared at Zack without really seeing him.

"Hey, stop looking at me like that. You're creeping me out."

"What the hell is wrong with you boys?" Kayla snarled. "Can't you leave her alone?"

"We're just interested in what happened that night."

"Why? So you can pretend to know what it feels like to lose your family, and tell everyone how tough you would have been dealing with it?" Kayla vented, raising the champagne bottle up high like she was going to throw it at him. She pointed it at him accusingly instead. "It would have crushed you, Zack Blackthorn—*that's* how you would have felt."

Melody glanced over at Kayla. Their eyes met and held as they silently communicated with each other, each recognizing the other's agonizing pain. The abyss of loss. It was written across Kayla's face and mirrored on her own. At that moment, Melody realized Kayla was letting her in.

Kayla took another swig from her bottle and wiped her mouth with the back of her hand. "You want to know what it's like to walk home from school on a beautiful sunny afternoon, when the little kids are playing in the yard, and the dogs are barking at the hose, and dads are on vacation cutting the grass, and moms…" Her voice caught, and she swallowed some more champagne.

Melody wanted her to stop talking, but she couldn't say anything. She drank her rum instead but didn't feel the warmth now.

Kayla continued. "And the moms—the moms are hanging your sheets out to dry because you love the smell of fresh air on them.

Then you walk into your kitchen, expecting to see your mom there. But she's not where she should be. You sense something is wrong. At first you wonder, *Where is she? Why isn't she baking cookies for me?* You listen for her. Then a horrible tingling starts to run through your body because your body knows before your mind does that something is seriously wrong. Your body wants you to run, but you can't. You strain to hear her, but there is no sound. You realize that the house doesn't feel right. In fact, it feels really weird. You want to yell out and tell her you're home and hear her call out, 'Okay, honey. I'll be right down.' But you don't call out because you're frozen now. You *know*. And then your brother is there, and it takes you a moment to realize that he's holding a knife. It's one of your mom's knives from her butcher block. And then you know for sure. You try to run, but it's too late. He's on you, stabbing and stabbing until he leaves you for dead. Just like he did your mom."

Kayla was crying now. Luke and Zack sat rigid, shocked into silence.

"My brother was a scary kid," Kayla said, struggling to keep her voice level. "When he turned twelve, he started to like to hurt people. My parents tried to get him help. They took him to therapy. When that didn't help, they went to the police. They did nothing until he beat me the first time. Then they put him in an institution for a while, and everything was okay. Then the doctors decided he was all fixed and released him. Only he wasn't. He would stand behind the door and step out and grab me or Mom. Then Dad took off. He couldn't deal with it. Blamed my mom. Mom was so scared, she started hiding the knives. Then my brother went back into the institution for a while, and when he came home, he seemed good. But he'd just learned to hide the evil. And then in a split second, the world as you know it ends. You have no future. It's all gone."

"Why didn't you go to your dad's instead of into foster care?" Luke asked, his voice uneven with emotion.

"My dad has a new family. He doesn't even know me. I'm damaged goods, a reminder of his failure. I'm not bright and shiny like his new kids."

She stared at Luke and Zack with a hard, worn look, like she'd been fighting through decades of war. "You want to know what really sucks?"

They nodded apprehensively.

"People try to comfort you with words like 'I'm sorry,' but what are they sorry for? They didn't do it."

Melody couldn't breathe. Her head was spinning, and her hands started to tremble so hard rum sloshed over the rim, ran down her hand to her wrist and soaked the cuff of her sweater.

"People say stupid stuff like 'This will make you stronger.' Oh, and here's my favorite: 'We're only given what we can handle.' But they've been through nothing. They have no idea what it's like, but they're willing to give you all kinds of advice, like they know what they're talking about."

Melody wanted her to stop; she couldn't take any more. But Kayla didn't stop. In fact, she sounded like she couldn't stop.

"After a few months, people start telling you it's time to move on. They don't get how there's no moving on. There will never be any moving on with your life because the life you had is over. They don't get how much you want things to go back to how they were. How you don't want to live in that moment forever. They refuse to see that you can't climb out of that moment. You're stuck down in that hole. You just have to learn to live in the dark." Then suddenly she seemed to run out of steam. Tears she'd been holding back suddenly spilled down her cheeks. She swiped at them with her free hand and then slumped over like an old woman—spent and exhausted.

Melody sat stock still, hardly daring to breathe. Kayla's story had stirred up the nightmarish memories again, the sounds and smells and images that she tried to keep buried. *Light from the hall outside her bedroom crept across the wall as her door was slowly opened.* She squeezed her eyes shut, trying to stop the images from coming, but it was too late. Something had snapped inside her as she listened to Kayla. It was as though a dam had been breached, and she stood powerless, watching the memories churning through the gap.

"I can't remember my mom any other way than what she looked like that night," she said, sitting forward. Her voice sounded tiny; she could see her breath in the air. "You want to know what it feels like? I'll tell you. I feel like I died that night, too. I wish I had died that night, because then it would all be over, and I'd be with my mom. That's how it feels, Zack Blackthorn." She looked up and met his eyes. "It feels like I'm dead inside. And I don't want to feel anything ever again because it hurts too much."

There was a long silence. Melody took a sip of her rum. It was barely warm now.

Then Luke cleared his throat. "I think my parents are broke," he said. "As in, they don't have two nickels to rub together broke."

Melody and Kayla stared at him, their brows furrowed. He began to squirm. Melody could see that he was trying to come up with something worse now.

Then Zack piped up, "My dad is an angry little troll."

Melody glanced at Kayla, who had opened her mouth to say something and then suddenly burst out laughing.

Melody listened as Kayla's laughter grew to a feverish pitch and felt a giggle build in her. It burst forth like lava, releasing the tension. She didn't know if it was Kayla or Zack or the alcohol that had done it, but once she started to laugh, she couldn't stop. She set down her mug and clutched her midriff, gasping for air and worrying she would wet herself, and that made her laugh even harder.

Suddenly, in the distance, they heard a gunshot, followed seconds later by another.

Their laughter died instantly, as they looked at each other for confirmation of what they'd just heard.

Kayla was the first to react. She jumped up, letting the sleeping bag fall at her feet. "We have to get out of here," she hissed. No one moved. "Now!" she commanded.

"What about all of our stuff?" Luke asked.

"Leave it. We've got to go."

Melody stood up, swaying a little from the alcohol, and stumbled out of the sleeping bag into Kayla, who steadied her.

As the boys and Kayla headed for the front doors where Zack had parked his car, Melody turned, stomped her feet back into her boots, picked up her coat, and staggered towards the back of the mill.

"Come with us," Kayla ordered, keeping her voice low.

Melody shook her head as she struggled to get her wet coat on. "I can't. My bike's out back."

"Forget the damn bike."

"I can't. It was a gift from my uncle." Squeezing back through the gap in the wall, she tripped and fell over a plank. Dazed, she lay there for a moment, trying to get her bearings. Her head spun, and she felt sick from the rum. Then she heard Zack's SUV start. He revved the engine twice, and then there was the sound of tires spinning on gravel as the vehicle sped away into the distance. She wanted to yell for them to come back, but she was too scared to make a sound.

Then, from out of the dark, came a guttural scream that sent a shiver up her spine.

It was time to get out of there. Stumbling to her feet, she used the wall for balance. It had stopped snowing now and the moon was out, but visibility wasn't good, and she almost tripped over her bike. As she steadied herself against the wall, she listened for anyone approaching before she started pushing her bike around to the front of the mill.

She'd just made it under the log ramp when, from deep in the woods behind the mill, she heard another blast from a gun. Wobbling, she fell against the bike and started to slide down the edge of the pond toward the water.

CHAPTER TWENTY-SIX

Abbey Raines stood staring out of the kitchen window. The snow had begun to taper off, so she could now see the driveway, but there was no sign of Melody. She bit her lip. *Where had the little fool gone?* She'd left hours ago, and the temperature had started to drop. She'd texted her, even tried calling her, but she hadn't responded. Out of desperation, she'd called Skeeter Parrish, who was about Melody's only friend, but he hadn't seen her. She tried the library, but it hadn't opened because of the storm.

She wanted to call Jesse and have him come over to keep her company until Melody got home. She couldn't, though, not after calling him earlier and accusing him of betraying her. They'd argued, and it hadn't ended well. He'd hung up on her and hadn't responded to her texts, either.

Hearing the front door open, she felt relief flood through her, and she ran to confront her sister. Unfortunately, it was just Po, who stood there, shaking snow off his coat. It took him less than a second to realize something was wrong.

"What is it, Abbey? Did you and Melody have another argument?"

Abbey bit her lip again. "We may have got into it a while ago."

Memphis moseyed over to him and sniffed his pant leg. "How long ago did this happen?"

"Lunchtime."

Po bent down to pat Memphis on the head. "Is she okay?"

Abbey couldn't meet his eyes.

"Abbey?" There was a warning tone to his voice.

"She's not here, okay? She threw a hissy fit and took off on her bike."

"What? In this weather? How long has she been gone?"

"Just after you left to fix the Mustang."

"That was hours ago. It's dark out, and it's been snowing all afternoon. Did you try calling her?"

"Yes, but the brat isn't answering. I tried Skeeter Parrish, too, and the library. No luck."

"Did you call your uncle?"

"No." Abbey stared at the floor, not meeting his eyes.

"Abbey. You should have told me as soon as she took off."

"I realize that now. But what are we going to do?"

CHAPTER TWENTY-SEVEN

Cal Raines was parked outside Holly's home. They were on the way to interview Phil Montague and had dropped off her Jeep on the way. Raines was waiting for Holly to come out of the house when his phone rang. It was Po.

"Hey, buddy," he said.

Po dispensed with pleasantries. "Have you heard from Melody?"

Instantly alerted by the tone of Po's voice, Raines tried to keep calm but failed. "No. Why? What's going on?"

"Abbey and Melody had an argument at lunch, and Melody took off on her bike hours ago. We've tried Skeet and the library. She's not there."

Raines's stomach dropped. He clenched the steering wheel. "I'm on my way over. Call me if she shows up."

Heart pounding with fear, he disconnected, slammed the Suburban into drive, and cranked the wheel hard to begin a three-point turn.

Holly was heading down the driveway and ran into the road to stop him. "Raines!" she yelled, waving her arms.

He stopped long enough for her to open the passenger door and hop in.

Buckling her seatbelt, she turned to him. "What the hell is going on?"

Finishing the three-point turn, he stamped on the accelerator. The tires chirped as he headed for home. "Po just called. Melody is missing."

"What happened?"

He told her as much as he knew, and they both fell silent. When Raines started to make a right at the end of her street instead of the left he needed to take to head toward his house, she placed a hand on his arm.

"Where are you going?"

He glanced at her. "I just realized. She could be at school."

"It's closed, Raines. It's Saturday night. Are you sure you should be driving?"

He braked hard, swung the SUV to the left, and gunned it towards his house.

Holly braced herself by holding onto the grab handle above her door. "Have they called her friends?"

"She doesn't have many. Skeet is about the only one she has—or the only one I'm aware of. They've called his place. She's not there."

Hearing Skeeter Parrish's name brought back painful memories for Holly, but she ignored them. No time to dwell on history. "Where else would she be?"

"I have no idea," Raines muttered. And then, "I'm not up to this, Holly."

"Up to what?"

"Raising the girls. I don't know what the hell I'm doing. I don't know the right things to say to help them, and they're starting to run wild. I'm losing them."

"You love them. Just keep on doing that, and you'll make it."

He shook his head. "I visited Nate this week."

"Why did you do that?"

"I promised Abbey. What a disaster it was. I'm sure the kids' argument has something to do with Nate. Abbey still holds out hope that he's innocent. It's a mess, and I don't know what to do about it."

Holly looked at his big, strong, capable hands gripping the steering wheel, and her mind flashed back to a time she wanted to forget forever. It was twenty-five years ago, the night of her brother's sledding accident. She'd refused to leave the scene where Charlie's sled had plummeted off the trail, taking him with it and crashing three hundred feet below her. Police Chief Jim Raines, Cal's dad, had scooped her up, carried her all the way down the mountain to the backseat of his cruiser, covered her with his jacket and driven her home. She remembered watching his big strong hands on the steering wheel; they had been so gentle and kind when he'd picked her up and tucked the jacket around her.

Cal Raines had sat beside her in the backseat that night, waiting with her while his dad went up to her house to break the news of Charlie's death to her parents. They could hear her mother's screams from inside the cruiser, and Raines, just a few months older than her, had slipped his hand through hers and waited for his dad to return. For the first time, she realized his hands were just like his father's.

"You're a good man, Raines," she said gently. "Just like your dad was. You'll find a way to help the girls. I know it."

"But what if something has happened to Melody? What then?"

CHAPTER TWENTY-EIGHT

Melody felt someone pulling at her coat, dragging her up the slope. She batted at the hands and felt herself slip further down toward the pond. Drowning was better than getting shot, she decided.

"Melody," someone yelled above her. "What are you doing? Let me help you."

She twisted around and found Jesse Keegan on his knees in the snow reaching for her. He looked freaked out.

"Give me your hand."

She raised her hands to him, and he took them, pulling her towards him. She pushed with her feet, and he stood, keeping a firm grip on her bare hands as he walked backward up the slope. She tried to scramble to her feet, but her coordination was off.

Panting heavily, he managed to drag her to the top of the pond and sank down next to her. His blond hair flopped into his eyes. He brushed it back.

A car was running a few feet away, its headlights on.

"Are you hurt?" he asked, sounding concerned.

"No."

"Did you fall off your bike?"

"Must have."

"You shouldn't be out here. It's too cold. How long have you been down there?"

"Not long." She was shivering. She had no idea how long it had been, because she'd either bumped her head or passed out.

Jesse stood up and held his hand out to her. "Let's get you into the warm car."

She took it, and he pulled her up. Feeling woozy, she held onto his arm for a moment. Her sister's boyfriend was tall and slim, but he was strong.

"Are you sure you're okay?"

"Yes. Anyway, why are you here?"

"I'm looking for someone and spotted your bike." He pointed to it. The pedal was dug into the snow and the forks were twisted, making the wheel stick up at an odd angle.

He walked her over to the car. It was Olivia's Volvo SUV. She got in, and he retrieved her bike and stuck it in the back of the vehicle.

Getting into the driver's seat, he put on his seatbelt, told her to buckle hers, and put the car in gear, slowly backing the Volvo up, turning as he did. The tires slipped in the snow, but he kept up a steady pressure, and they managed to get rolling.

"Why were you out here, Melody?"

Still shivering, she muttered, "I needed to get out of the house for a while." No way was she going to mention Kayla and the boys. He'd tell Abbey, and Abbey would tell her uncle.

He turned up the heat full blast. "What happened?"

"The usual."

"You argued with Abbey?"

"You got it in one." The heat started to feel good on her face, and she held out her hands to the vent.

"I need to get you home so you can change. Your coat is soaking wet."

"I'm not going home."

He glanced at her. "You've been drinking, haven't you?"

She shrugged but said nothing.

"What were you thinking? It's dangerous being out here on your own in the middle of nowhere, especially when you're drinking. Were you meeting someone?"

"No." It wasn't a lie. She hadn't planned to meet Kayla and the boys.

"You have to go home, Melody. They'll be worried about you."

"I'm not going home! I'll jump out of the car if I have to. I mean it, Jesse."

"What is it with you Raines girls?"

She glared at him. "Don't act so high and mighty with me. I'm not the one cheating on my sister."

He shot her a sideways glance and then looked back at the road. "Is that where Abbey heard it?"

"Don't deny it. I saw you with Kayla Jenkins."

"You think I'm cheating on Abbey with *Kayla*?"

Melody frowned. "Look, I don't blame you. Abbey is a nightmare, but you should have just dumped her first. I never pegged you as a liar."

"Don't you trust me?"

"I don't trust anyone, least of all a lying cheat who's going to hurt my sister."

"I'm not dating Kayla Jenkins." His voice was hard and cold now.

"Sure looked that way when she was all snuggly and squeezy with you on the back of your bike."

"When was this?"

"When you picked her up from the mill."

"You're so wrong."

"Sure I am."

The SUV fishtailed on a patch of icy snow, but he steered expertly into the skid and pulled the vehicle back out on to the main road. "Kayla is living with me and my mom. She's in foster care, you nitwit."

Melody's mouth dropped open. *Foster care.* It made sense now. Especially after hearing Kayla's story, and knowing that Olivia May took in foster kids. Jesse himself had been one until she'd adopted him. That had happened only a few weeks ago. Afterward, she, Uncle Cal, Po, and Abbey had been invited to join Olivia and Jesse for dinner at the Hemlock Inn to celebrate. She started to feel sick, and the rum began to burn the back of her throat. "Pull over," she mumbled.

"You're not getting out. I told you that I'm taking you home."

"I'm going to be sick in your mom's car if you don't pull over."

Jesse swerved to the side of the road just in time for Melody to open the door and vomit. He yanked a bunch of tissues out of the box Olivia kept on the center console and handed them to her so she could wipe her mouth. "What were you drinking?"

"Rum."

"Oh, boy. Your uncle is going to be p.o.'d—big time!"

"You're not going to tell him."

"I won't have to. He'll smell it. He's a cop, for Chrissakes."

"Can't you just take me to Olivia's?" she pleaded.

CHAPTER TWENTY-NINE

Melody sat on Olivia May's couch, wrapped in a blanket, drinking hot chocolate and thawing out in front of a blazing fire. Although Melody had begged her not to call her Uncle Cal, Olivia had told her it wasn't an option. What Olivia did agree to do, however, was to ask Cal to allow Melody a little time with her before he came over to pick her up. Reluctantly, he'd agreed to it.

As soon as Jesse had dropped her off, he'd gone back out again to find Kayla. They were worried because she'd been out all day. Melody wanted to tell them she'd been with Kayla but wasn't sure if that was the right thing to do. So, she said nothing.

Olivia came back and sat down in an armchair next to her. "Are you warm enough?"

Melody nodded.

"That's good."

Her brown eyes were gentle, and she gave her a reassuring smile, but Melody could tell she was concerned about her. Melody had met her several times since Abbey had started dating Jesse. What really intrigued her, though, was the fact that Olivia was not only Abbey's therapist, but she'd worked for the FBI as a forensic psychiatrist. She must be smart, she supposed, because the FBI took only the brightest. Melody wondered what Abbey talked to her about, and how a forensic psychiatrist would analyze her. What would she see in her sister? And could Olivia really fix her?

Melody glanced at her before turning back to face the fire.

They sat like that for a while, neither one talking, as Olivia gave her space to consider the situation.

Melody sipped her cocoa and let the silence stretch on. She glanced over at Olivia again. Dressed in a black wraparound sweater fitted over loose, flowing, winter-white pants and high-heeled black boots, Olivia looked like a runway model for sophistication. But she had the calm presence of an ancient Zen master. It radiated out from her, seeming to cross time and space to touch Melody.

Something had snapped inside Melody when Kayla had told her story at the mill. She seemed so strong and brave. Had Olivia helped her deal with all that had happened to her? Could Olivia help *her*? Could Olivia convince Abbey to stop hounding her about *that* night? Make her stop insisting that she visit their dad? The idea of talking to Olivia was tempting. Her nightmares were not getting any better. In fact, they were getting worse. And they were so terrifying, so real, she was scared to fall asleep at night. But she couldn't talk about her mother. She shuddered even thinking about it. And what about her secret? Could she trust Olivia not to tell Uncle Cal and Abbey? It was such a massive secret. Wouldn't an adult feel like they had to interfere—to set things right? But then hadn't Olivia sworn some sort of sacred oath as a therapist not to reveal secrets?

Finishing the hot chocolate, Melody placed the cup carefully on the side table and started twisting the blanket's fringe. "What has Abbey told you about me?"

Olivia gave her a kind smile. "Why don't we focus our time together on you?"

"Abbey won't leave *it* alone. Did she tell you that? She keeps forcing me to remember."

Olivia said, "I'm sure you've heard the expression, 'What happens in Vegas, stays in Vegas.'"

That made Melody smile, amused for a moment by the modern reference. They were sitting in a massive, square room lined with bookcases that were filled with old leather books in an enormous stone mansion that had gargoyles on the roof and big oak doors. Even though Olivia must have been around her uncle's age, Melody thought, the old place suited her because she had an old soul.

"Well," Olivia continued, "what we discuss here, stays here. It's between us."

Her softly spoken words gave Melody the confidence that whatever she told her, Olivia wouldn't betray her and tell Abbey the secret.

Olivia continued. "Are you curious about therapy?"

Melody stiffened. "I can't talk about what happened."

"I see," Olivia said. Slowly, she lifted her hands from her lap where they had been resting palms up, as if she were meditating.

Fascinated, Melody watched her open her hands in a graceful, calm way like she was spreading her wings. Then Olivia rested her hands, palms down, on the chair's arms.

"Would it be okay with you if I described one of the methods that I have used to help people who have experienced a traumatic event?" Again, she spoke slowly and softly, almost hypnotically.

Melody looked at her questioningly. A prickle of fear made her heart beat a little faster, but she nodded.

"It's called Prolonged Exposure Therapy. It involves repeatedly confronting those thoughts you fear most by talking about it until you are able to gain control over the fear and reduce your anxiety."

Instantly, Melody's heartbeat quickened, and her body started to tense. "I can't talk about *that*. Not *that!* So, you can't help me?"

"There are other ways to help. Sometimes, when the event is too traumatic to talk about, you can just think about it while I simply sit here next to you, just like this. You just think about it in a safe environment. You wouldn't have to tell me. Thinking about it is the challenge. Still, the act of making yourself think about the trauma, or scary thought, or frightening image, over and over again can help you gain control of your fear. So, too, can writing or drawing about it. I know you are an artist and a musician. Do you write your own lyrics?"

Melody nodded. "They're not very good. Not like Uncle Cal's."

"Writing about it can help."

Melody plucked at the blanket.

Olivia went on, "When something so traumatic happens, some people avoid thinking about the event to protect themselves. They don't want to recall the sights and sounds of what happened. At first, in the short term, avoiding these memories can reduce your fear. However, researchers have found that avoidance maintains the post-traumatic stress associated with the event. People don't process what happened. Some even develop distorted beliefs. For example, they may come to believe that the whole world is a very dangerous place, or even that they are to blame for what happened."

Melody continued to pick at the blanket.

"Would it help if I gave you an example?"

Melody nodded.

"A man was in an explosion. He survived, but some people didn't. He saw terrible things and didn't want to think about it.

Afterward, the sound of fireworks and thunder, or any sudden, loud noise made him feel like he was right back in that moment. He had heart palpitations and chest pains so severe he thought he was having a heart attack. His muscles would tense, and he would start to sweat. He developed the belief that all loud noises were dangerous.

"What I do to help is explain that his reaction to loud noises is a fear response. The explosion is not actually happening again. His physical symptoms of a rapid heartbeat and muscle tension mean that he is afraid. It does not mean that he is dying. He is not in physical danger at that moment. Over time, he will gain control of his fear."

Melody was on a cliff. Her mouth was dry, her legs shaky. Could she do it? Dare she try? She couldn't talk about *that* night, but could she tell Olivia the secret? That way Olivia would understand why she needed to tell Abbey to stop tormenting her for answers so much.

"Something happened before…" she began, wanting to tell her, but as soon as she started, the memories came. The unwanted ones. She closed her eyes as her bedroom door opened. Then in a flash, she was standing in the blood. And her mother was on the floor in all of the blood. Melody shuddered. And that smell of rust… The smell of rust filled her nose, and she could taste it. And then she felt it again. The hand on the back of her head. And she knew she was going to die.

Her heart raced, and her throat tightened, choking her. She clutched at her throat, panicking.

"Melody. Focus on my voice. You are safe here. Safe with me. Your thoughts can't physically hurt you. You're not choking. You're experiencing a fear response. You are having a panic attack, Melody. Focus on my voice, sweetheart. This is your body's reaction to your scary thoughts, but you are safe with me in my home. I want you to take a deep, slow breath for me. Just breathe in slowly through your nose. Come on. Take a deep breath. That's it. Now focus on your breath. Feel it fill your lungs as you breathe in. And hold it, Melody. Hold it. Now exhale, releasing it slowly through your mouth. Let your muscles relax. Feel your face begin to go slack, and now your shoulders. Let them slump down."

They sat there for a few minutes, just breathing together, until Melody felt calmer. She opened her eyes and tried again.

"Something happened before… before my mom died."

Olivia nodded.

"I heard my parents arguing." She paused. Was she really going to do this?

Then she heard a gentle, "Go on if you're comfortable."

Melody coughed to clear her throat. Her palms were sweating, and she felt a little dizzy, but she pushed on. "They argued about my Uncle Cal."

Melody watched Olivia for any sign of shock. There was none, just a calm, relaxed expression on her face. "My dad claimed that my mom had an affair with Uncle Cal and…" She covered her face with her hands and mumbled, "My dad said Abbey was Uncle Cal's daughter, not his."

Olivia didn't react. "And," she prompted.

"And my mother didn't deny it. She said nothing at all, which if it's true, means it's not only a motive for Dad to do what he did, it's…" Melody paused.

Olivia nodded for her to continue.

"It's going to destroy Abbey if she finds out. She'll lose both parents. She'll lose more than me. She's clinging to the belief that Dad is innocent. It keeps her going, but what if she finds out he's not even her dad? And what will her memory be of Mom?" She drew in a ragged breath.

"Have you spoken to your uncle about this?"

"No!" she burst out, clearly agitated. "And you *can't* tell him. He'd feel like it was his duty to tell Abbey. He may even want to. Dad told us that Mom and Uncle Cal dated in high school, but she broke up with him because she fell in love with Dad, who was a star quarterback.

"When they were fighting, Dad claimed that Uncle Cal was still in love with my mother all these years, and that Uncle Cal had never got over losing her. I know he was trying to make Uncle Cal look guilty. He even sold the story to the tabloids. Uncle Cal had an alibi, of course. He was on stage singing in front of thousands of people, but my dad suggested he'd hired a hitman.

"What my dad didn't know was that I'd found one of my mom's diaries hidden up in the attic not too long before… You know, before *it* happened."

Olivia sat up straighter, interested.

Melody twisted her hair around her finger and stroked it in a soothing, pacifying way. "The diary was one she'd been writing in right before she died. About a month before that night, Mom, Abbey and I went down to Boston for one of Uncle Cal's concerts. Dad refused to go. He said he was sick, but I know it was because he was jealous. Anyway, we got to hang out backstage and then go out to eat with Uncle Cal afterward. It was a good night. The four of us were all so happy."

Melody's thoughts drifted then to her mom's smiling face, and to them all singing her uncle's songs out loud at the concert and laughing and laughing. That memory felt so good, but the loss was there, knifing into that perfect bubble of time. There was no escaping the reality that there would never be another night like that again.

Olivia said nothing as the minutes passed, and Melody became aware that she'd stopped talking.

She sniffed. "Mom wrote about the concert in her diary. I feel guilty telling you about her private thoughts, but I don't know what else to do. Mom wrote that she wished Uncle Cal had been in love with her because all of their lives would have been different. You see, it was Uncle Cal who broke up with *her*."

She stopped to give Olivia a meaningful look. "Mom went on to write how she'd tried to get back together with Uncle Cal after they graduated, which was when she was with Dad. It didn't work out because he was in love with someone else from high school. She also wrote about regretting that she tried to make Uncle Cal jealous by dating Dad because it ended up ruining their lives."

Melody tossed the blanket to the end of the couch. "So, there is a possibility that Abbey is Uncle Cal's daughter." She let out a big sigh and took a deep breath. "My sister is convinced that I know something that will prove my dad is innocent."

"Do you believe he is innocent?" Olivia asked quietly.

Melody thought about her bedroom door, and the familiar way it had opened that night: slowly and deliberately. Light spilled from the hall across her bedroom wall, stopping just before it hit the poster near her window. It was her favorite poster. It was from one of her uncle's concerts. And then her thoughts flashed down to the kitchen, to that hand on the back of her head. The way the fingers had spread around her skull. Familiar. So familiar.

Melody said nothing. She just pressed her fingers hard against her eyes.

"It's okay, Melody. You don't need to answer that."

From behind her hands, she mumbled, "All I want... All I want is for you..." She paused and looked up at Olivia with beseeching eyes, but she couldn't say it.

"What would you like me to do?"

"If you could somehow... If Abbey would just leave me alone, let me forget... But she won't. And now Christmas is coming."

"Christmas triggers the bad memories?" Olivia asked.

"Yes."

"Is that why you drank today?"

"It helped make it all stop for a while."

"Alcohol is a way people suffering from trauma self-medicate, but it's not the answer. You are just masking the problem, and soon it develops into a whole other problem. Have you been drinking for long?"

"No. Just twice."

"When you feel like you need to drink, will you come here? Come to see me?"

Melody nodded, and she thought about Kayla. Kayla got it. Got *her*. If she came over to see Olivia, maybe she'd get to see her again. She wondered where her room was in the huge house and if she liked living there with strangers. At least she'd had Uncle Cal after it happened. Kayla had had no one. Then she wondered where Luke and Zack had taken her after they'd left the mill. She wanted to ask Olivia about her, but if she did, she'd have to explain how she'd met her. And that could get Kayla into trouble for being at the mill. No, she'd have to keep it a secret. Kayla was in foster care. If Olivia found out—or worse her uncle, who was a cop—it could result in Kayla being placed somewhere else.

Suddenly, she realized that Olivia was talking to her.

"Christmas, holidays and birthdays can all be trauma-related triggers. Does your uncle know that Christmas is a difficult time for you?"

Melody nodded again.

"Does he know about the diary?"

Fear stabbed at her heart. "No! I don't want anyone to know about it."

"Okay," came the calm response. "Perhaps you would come back to see me next week so we can talk some more?"

"It's so hard."

"Just think about it. And maybe think about writing a song about how you feel."

"I'll try." But she didn't sound convincing, even to herself.

CHAPTER THIRTY

Raines poured himself a cup of coffee and headed to his studio. He always thought best in there. It was the soundproofing. The utter silence. And he had a lot on his mind. Chiefly, Melody. The night before when he'd arrived at Olivia's, she'd cautioned him to respond instead of reacting to what Melody had done. Her words seemed to echo his martial arts teacher from years ago. He'd practiced mindful meditation for over a decade, but it failed him now.

How could he not react? He'd been terrified, but Olivia stressed remaining calm, supportive and loving while establishing new boundaries. *Calm!* This wasn't karate. Melody had been drinking. Anything could have happened to her, and he had to remain calm. On top of that, Melody had point blank refused to tell him who she had been with, where she'd got the alcohol, and where she'd been.

He'd never felt so ill-equipped to handle a situation as he did now, parenting the girls. He'd never been challenged like this, and he'd spent a good part of the night on the internet looking for videos to help him. Most of the good ones echoed Olivia's advice: respond, don't react. He groaned inwardly; how the hell were the girls going to make it if their uncle, who was raising them, had to turn to the internet for advice? he wondered with a shake of his head.

As Raines walked through the living room, heading for the ell that connected the main house to the barn, which he'd converted into an office and his studio, he heard strains of a strumming guitar. Then the music stopped. Nearing the studio, he heard the strumming resume, followed by Melody's sweet voice as she began to sing unfamiliar lyrics.

He walked through the control room where his mixing console and speakers were and leaned against the studio's doorjamb to listen.

Melody sat on a stool with her back to him, head bent forward, and her brown hair falling about her face.

She sang only a few words before choking up and stopping. Clearing her throat, she sat up tall on the stool and started over. Her voice was softer this time, just above a whisper, and Raines had to strain to hear her.

Sunshine, don't let it rain
I want to see her
Coming down the lane

Thunder, stop your growling
So I can hear her
Calling out my name

Snow, stop falling so hard
On that mountain pass
Let her come on home
Need her to come home
Please come on home

She paused and sniffed.

He swallowed, feeling the familiar anger and hopelessness that were always there because there wasn't a damn thing he could do to take away her pain.

Sensing him, she glanced over her shoulder and gave him a watery smile.

"That's beautiful, honey. Did you write it?"

She shrugged. "It's okay. It's not finished yet."

As a kid, she'd been cute, happy and impish, reminding him of a little pixie, but the tragedy had changed her, changed everything. Her once-chubby cheeks were now thin and pale. Her shoulders drooped, and her clothes were baggy on her slender frame. She had let her hair grow long so it could cover her face.

"Are you recording it?"

"No."

She got up and followed him, guitar in hand, into the control room, flopping down on the denim-covered couch that stood against the back wall.

He sat down next to her. "The song is about your mom, isn't it?"

Her only response was to stare at him.

He had no idea what she was thinking, but he noticed the circles under her eyes were darker than usual, and he felt his heart break all over again.

As she lowered her head to pluck at the guitar strings, her shoulders started to tremble.

He wrapped his arms around both her and the guitar, and just held her. She slid the guitar out of the way and clung to him.

Her thin, bony frame shook as she sobbed. She felt so delicate, like she would crack if he squeezed her too hard. She wouldn't loosen her grip, though, so Raines hugged her tightly and found himself humming "Brahms' Lullaby." After a while, her sobs subsided, and he kissed the top of her head.

"I'm sorry," she mumbled, sniffing loudly and pulling away from him. "I'm sorry I freaked you out yesterday. I didn't mean to scare you and Po."

Genuine relief flooded through him at her sincerity. "I'm just thankful you're okay." He felt himself start to choke up and found he couldn't say anything else.

She gave him another squeeze. She felt as fragile as a little bird. Then she settled back against the cushions, lifting her feet up and crossing her bony ankles.

"All night I've been wondering if I should tell you where I was, but I'm worried you'll get mad."

He thought: respond, don't react. It was going to become his mantra; he could see that clearly now. "I will not get mad. I promise. But knowing what you were doing will stop me from imagining all kinds of crazy things."

She told him about meeting Kayla and what she'd been through and how she'd connected with her. She told him about the mill, about Luke, Zack, and the alcohol, and at the end, she told him about the gunshots, which she now thought might have been fireworks.

Most probably a hunter, he theorized, and his mind immediately drifted to Justin Jarvis, whose death could have been a hunting accident. That could have been Melody, too. His breath caught at the thought of a stray bullet hitting her. Raines realized that when it came to raising kids, it wasn't merely a matter of not reacting. It was learning how to not *overreact* when one of the people you loved most placed themselves in incredible danger.

As he sat there thinking of an appropriate response, she said, "I promise not to do it again, and I promise not to go back to the mill."

When he said nothing, she jumped up nervously and paced around the small room for a moment before settling on the arm of the couch with her bare feet on the cushion. She started to pull at the threads on her ripped jeans. "It's okay, Uncle Cal. I don't want you to worry. I'm going to talk to Olivia when I feel like doing crazy things."

Thank God for Olivia, he thought. "Okay. But you can tell me, too, if you want. I did some pretty crazy things myself when I was younger."

She giggled at that and added, "Olivia told me writing and singing could help me. I'm just having a hard time getting through the song because it's about *that* night. The song's not right. And I can't get the rhyme scheme right."

He smiled at her. "It's a process. Usually, it takes a lot of work to craft the lyrics just the way you want them."

"And I'm pitchy. How did it sound to you?"

"You have a beautiful voice."

She frowned. "Come on. Tell me the truth. I sounded too breathy, and I kept missing notes."

"Sometimes, especially when you are singing about something as painful as what happened to your mom, you put a wall up to protect yourself. The trick is to let go of the emotion. Feel it. Your song is about the death of your mom. To express what you're feeling must be terrifying, but use that emotion. The more you sing it, the more control you'll have. Don't suppress it: let that emotion guide you to the right pitch. Just remember, the best singing comes from the heart. Letting your audience feel what you have gone through is what will help them connect to you."

She pursed her lips, thinking. "But I'm having a hard time just getting the words out, so it sounds how I want it to sound. I don't want it to be so breathy. I don't always sound like that. Do you know what I mean?"

He nodded. "A lot of things can cause that. In this case, I think singing about your mother's death as you fight to control your emotions is causing your muscles to tense. You're jutting your head forward, straining your neck and shoulders. I know it's difficult, but try to align your neck and head. Focus on relaxing your shoulders.

You'll get it. Give it time. The more you sing it, the more control you will have."

They sat there for a few minutes in companionable silence. She plucked at the guitar strings while he sipped his coffee. He began to relax, and was starting to feel the effects of a sleepless night when Melody asked, "Don't you miss it?"

"What?"

"Writing and performing."

"Sometimes."

"Are you miserably unhappy about having to leave it all behind you to be here with us?"

"There is nowhere I'd rather be than here with you and Abbey. You two are my life."

She gave him a tentative smile. "But it must be hard. Sometimes you must want to get back to the life you had. It was so glamorous and fun."

His thoughts drifted to Jenny Hargrave, a talented singer and his one-time girlfriend, who'd struggled with insecurity and many other demons. Heroin had been on top of the list. She'd been clean while they were dating, but one night, she couldn't resist it, and Jenny had died of an overdose. Although that had been years ago, he still felt the loss keenly. It had changed his life, and it had ultimately led him to law enforcement.

"Uncle Cal?" Melody queried, sounding a little insecure—and a lot like Jenny. "Should I not have said that?"

He realized he'd fallen silent. "It's okay, honey. I was just thinking of someone."

"Was it someone you met in high school?"

He frowned. "No. This happened much later." He paused for a moment. "I met someone when I was touring with my band. We were in love, but she died from a drug overdose."

"That's so sad."

"Yes. It is, and losing her changed me, altered my course."

"Like how I am after Mom?"

"Yes, honey. Exactly like that. When Jenny died, I was no longer the same person. My music, all of the ideas I had, all the notebooks full of future song lyrics and words, meant nothing to me. It was as if a stranger had written them. The way I felt about life changed. I had a new purpose. I worked with the DEA to help track down her dealer because I had to do something, or I would have gone crazy. Now, there is nothing more important to me as being here with you and Abbey."

She sighed and reached out a hand to him, which he clasped in his.

"I want to tell you a secret," she whispered.

CHAPTER THIRTY-ONE

Hyperalert at the mention of a secret, Raines struggled to keep his eagerness from showing. He didn't want to divert Melody in any way from what it was she needed to tell him. He felt it was important not to push her. She hadn't been able to talk about either Sherry's murder or Nate's actions since that traumatic night. He needed to be patient and let her tell him in her own time.

Wondering if the secret had something to do with his brother, he raised an eyebrow to express interest in what she had to say but waited for her to continue. Seconds passed, and the tension built in the small control room.

Finally, she mumbled, "Did Mom and..." She wrung her hands together and gave a slight shake of her head. "Umm. Mom told me that she thought your voice was a gift from God."

He suspected, from her body language and tone of voice, that this wasn't what she really wanted to say, but he could have been wrong. It had been a stressful night, and she was nervous. He swallowed hard as he thought about Sherry. He could almost hear her say it. "She did?"

"She loved to hear you sing and must have gone to all your concerts."

He smiled, remembering. "Almost all of them. Boy, how she loved music—all kinds of music. In high school, she forced me to listen to musicians most teenage boys would never admit to listening to."

"Like who?"

"Neil Diamond."

"Oh, she was so crazy about him." Her eyes brightened with the memory. "Do you think she called me Melody because she loved music so much?"

"I'm sure she did, sweetheart." His heart throbbed against his ribs. He didn't want to think about Sherry and how much Melody must miss her. "Your mom would be so proud of you."

She looked down and started picking at the skin around her thumbnail. "You think she would have liked the song?"

"Like it? She would have loved it!" He grabbed her guitar and strummed the notes she'd been playing. "Your mother always judged a singer by their ability to give her goosebumps."

Melody looked up at him. "I didn't know that."

"Did you know that when she found a song that gave her goosebumps, she'd play it over and over until I was ready to scream?"

Melody laughed. "She did that with us, too."

He played the G major chord. "Do you want to know a secret?"

"Sure." She sounded eager.

"I get goosebumps whenever I hear *you* sing," he told her.

"Really?" Her voice quavered. She bit her thumbnail again, this time drawing blood at the quick of the nail. "I miss her so much."

Cal covered her hand with his. It broke his heart to see her little red fingers all picked and chewed. "I know you do."

"I wish it hadn't happened."

"Me, too." He wanted to say the right thing so he could make it better for her, but there was nothing he could say or do to achieve that. And that inability to do something tore at him. He rubbed his eyes and sighed. He felt a hundred years old.

"Uncle Cal?" she whispered.

"Yes?"

"Can I ask you something personal?"

This was the secret she'd wanted to tell him all along. "Yes."

"You have to promise not to tell anyone, okay?"

He looked her right in the eye. "I promise."

"Are you Abbey's dad?"

If she'd said she wanted to go to the moon, he couldn't have been more shocked. He was speechless.

She went on, covering the silence. "It's just that Dad accused Mom of it before, you know, before that night."

He thought about all of the ramifications. "I wish you were my kids. You are amazing people, and I love you both very much, but Abbey isn't my daughter."

She let out a big sigh of relief. "I've been really worried about it, and how Abbey would feel if she knew the truth."

"What truth?" asked a voice at the door.

It was Abbey. She was still in her pajamas.

Raines noticed there were Labradors all over the fabric. She looked so young and innocent. "It's nothing, honey. We were having a private conversation."

"About me. What are you telling him, you little sneak?" Abbey pointed at her sister.

Raines heard Melody draw in a deep breath. All he had time to do was think "Uh-oh" before she let Abbey have it with both barrels.

"You've hounded me for the truth until I thought I'd go mad. Now I can tell you because I now know that Uncle Cal is not your dad."

Abbey looked stunned. "What are you talking about?"

"Dad accused Mom of having an affair with Uncle Cal, and he claimed you were a result of that affair."

"That's... That's crazy."

"Yeah. Well. Consider the source."

Abbey paled. "What's that supposed to mean?"

"When are you going to accept the fact that Dad killed Mom and tried to kill me?"

Abbey held up a hand as if to stop the words. "You! You slipped in Mom's blood and hit your head running for the phone."

"Melody," Raines cautioned. "Abbey's not ready to hear this."

"She needs to hear it, Uncle Cal," Melody said softly. She turned back to Abbey, her voice surprisingly calm and even as she began to tell her sister what she'd been unable to say for more than a year. "It took me a while to figure it out because of my head injury," she explained, "but the pieces of the puzzle are all there now. I've remembered things, things I didn't want to think about."

Instinctively, Abbey backed up a step. Melody could see the start of panic in her sister's face, but it was time she knew everything, especially since she now knew Uncle Cal wasn't Abbey's dad.

"Dad came home that night from the party. I know it was him because he came upstairs like he always did and opened my bedroom door like he always did, just wide enough for him to glance in to make sure I was tucked up in bed. The light from the hall always stopped in the exact same place. It did that night, too. He never liked that poster I had on my wall of Uncle Cal's concert.

"I was mad at Dad because he'd been arguing with Mom, so I didn't say goodnight. I felt guilty about it after a while and went down to kiss them both goodnight." She drew in a ragged breath.

Abbey stood stock still as if she were unable to move.

Tears started to stream down Melody's face. "When I walked into the kitchen, I saw Mom on the floor, and all the blood. I stepped in it with my bare feet. And it felt warm. And for a split second, I wondered why there was warm water all over the floor. Then I heard him behind me. Heard him breathing hard like he did after a workout." She paused long enough to wipe her nose on the back of her sleeve. "Then he put his hand over my head like he'd been doing since I was a kid and slammed my head down against the counter. I was knocked out. When I woke up, he was gone, and I ran to the phone, and *that's* when I slipped in Mom's blood."

Melody fell silent, her shoulders slumping in exhaustion.

Abbey opened her mouth to speak, and then closed it, turned and ran.

CHAPTER THIRTY-TWO

Raines sat at a stop sign, lost in thought. After Melody's revelation, Abbey had shut herself in her room and refused to talk to either Melody or him. After a while, Melody had crept up the stairs and knocked tentatively, trying to connect with her sister. She'd been wrong about Jesse, she said through the door. He hadn't been cheating on her. Abbey had yelled back that she was wrong about their dad, too, and there was a heavy thud like a book being thrown against the door. Melody had given up at that point and stalked off with Memphis, who barked every time either one of them shouted.

About an hour later, Abbey had yanked open her door, stormed down the stairs and informed Raines that she was riding over to see Jesse and Olivia.

Someone honked behind him, and he continued on to his office at the sheriff's department. As he reached town, traffic slowed and came to a standstill as someone attempted to parallel park and took up both lanes. Waiting, he glanced in a store window that advertised guns and ammo and thought about the gunshots Melody had heard at Verity Falls. Verity Falls was an old logging town, and Melody had been partying in an abandoned sawmill. There were several connections to make with the Justin Jarvis case, he thought.

First, the ghost town was named after Verity Caxton. Christine Johnson, the owner of the Witch Cross Inn, had told him at the auction that Verity Caxton was related to her. And then there was the fact that it was an old logging town. Justin was a forest ranger. Could there be a connection? No. He shook his head. That was too much of a stretch. Still, he wondered, could it hurt to check it out?

The man trying to parallel park gave up and moved on to find a more accessible spot. Raines pulled forward. As he neared the Caxton PD, he spotted Holly's Jeep there. He pulled into the parking lot and called her.

"Do you want to go on a scavenger hunt?" he asked when she answered the phone.

Holly lowered her voice. "Does it involve treasure?"

"It could if we get lucky."

"Where are you?" she asked.

Again, she kept her voice low, and it gave him the chills. She had the sexiest voice he'd ever heard. "Outside in the parking lot."

"Give me a second to wrap up with the chief, and I'll be right out."

When she said "second," she meant it. She hadn't even taken the time to put on her jacket as she hurried out of the building and climbed up into his SUV. She tossed her coat in the back.

"What's up?" she asked.

She looked hopeful and seriously gorgeous in her white cotton blouse and black pants, he thought. "Melody told me something. It may be nothing, but it's worth checking out."

"What is it?"

As he drove toward Verity Falls, he told her everything that had happened since he'd dropped her off at home last night before heading over to Olivia's. After Melody had told Abbey the truth, Melody said she was glad that it was no longer a secret. Secrets were dangerous things, she'd told him. She'd cried and said that if only her mom had told her dad the truth—that she hadn't slept with him—she might still have been alive.

Holly whistled. "And Abbey? How is she doing? She was so convinced Nate is innocent."

Raines looked drawn. "She's with Olivia and Jesse. Olivia called to say that she's safe and is processing the information now. Abbey asked to sleep over there, and I agreed. I can't imagine the psychological pain she's in right now, but if anyone can help her, it's Olivia."

"You're lucky you met Olivia," Holly told him, suddenly feeling flat. She should be happy for Raines. Olivia was perfect for him. In fact, she didn't know any person better suited to help Raines raise the girls than Olivia. She turned and stared glumly out of the window, trying to figure out her emotions. Was she jealous that he'd found someone so right for him when she hadn't? Her list of failed relationships was growing, and she was heading for spinsterdom at a rapid pace. And now the holidays were coming. She'd spend

Christmas with Angel and his family, and they would all try to act like it was normal that she was on her own—again. It was all too depressing to think about.

He glanced at her. "Yes. That's true. Olivia's great."

Holly hesitated before continuing, trying to snap out of her doldrums. After all, was there anything worse than feeling sorry for yourself? Yes, she determined. But it had to include some dire medical emergency, or the total destruction of your home, or at the very least, a run-in with the IRS. She was lucky she had Angel. Lucky to have her job. Lucky to have her cute cabin. Okay, she told herself. That was quite enough counting her blessings for one day. "And Melody?" she asked, forcing herself to perk up. "How's she coping?"

"She's gone for a drive with Po in a Mustang he's restoring. He promised her ice cream."

"You think ice cream will help?"

He glanced at her with a worried frown. "It's all we could think of to make her feel better."

She cracked a smile. "Ice cream is good. So, you think the mill is connected to the Jarvis case?"

"Who knows? My mind is all over the place, but it's worth checking out."

"It sure is," she agreed. "What's more, my friend Karl Hoffman—"

Raines interrupted. "The guy from the sausage shop?"

"Yes. He told me that the Langs own Verity Falls. The fact that Zack Blackthorn was there is interesting. If circumstances had been different, Thaddeus Blackthorn would have owned it."

Raines nodded. "And Luke Johnson was there, too, which is another connection to the Witch Cross Inn."

Holly looked at him. "But how does it all tie together?"

"I have no idea, but let's hope we find something useful. Anything happening on your case?" he asked.

"The ME called. After reviewing the dental records, she's positively identified the skull as Stefan Lang. The chief and Gustafson want to break the news to the family."

"But it's your case," Raines noted.

She shrugged. "Death notifications are the worst, and his son is going to take it hard. He's been angry with his father for two years, and now he's about to find out that anger was misplaced.

"Once they've seen Helga, we're supposed to reconvene for yet another meeting. Stefan Lang was a high-profile resident, and Gustafson wants more visibility on the case."

"You okay with that?"

"No, but I'm not worried about the competition." She grinned at him. "Besides, if I'm not there, they can't reassign me."

Raines laughed.

CHAPTER THIRTY-THREE

Although Raines hadn't known exactly where the entrance to Verity Falls was located, he spotted it easily. The snow and mud had been churned up from numerous vehicles turning in and out of the road.

His Chevy Suburban plowed up the road to the sawmill without a problem.

"For a ghost town, there's been a lot of heavy traffic up here," he observed.

Holly pointed to some fresh tracks. "And some of them are recent."

Raines parked in front of the old mill, and they got out and began to walk towards the front doors. "I had no idea this place existed," he said.

"I came here a few times when I was in high school," Holly told him. "There's a great swimming hole not too far from here."

"How come you never took me with you?"

"You think I wanted to risk you skinny-dipping again?" she said. "You would have scarred me for life."

"That was one time, Jakes. One photo," he said, referring to a photo one of the kids had taken of him in high school and sold later when Acid Raines had hit number one.

"Well, it was priceless. And when I feel like I've made a real fool of myself, I just pull that old tabloid out of the closet, take a good long look at you running butt naked into Echo Lake for all the world to see, and then I don't feel so bad."

"So, you've kept photos of me and my butt? That warms my heart. I could give you a few more if you'd like?"

"Only if you sign them, so I can sell them."

"You're killing me, Jakes."

"Just open the mill door, Raines, and do something useful."

He laughed but complied, pushing on the left-side door. They stepped inside and waited until their eyes adjusted to the gloom.

"It's the perfect place for teenagers to hang out," Raines said, pointing to the tent and camping equipment at the far end. Then his eyes widened. "Tell me that's not a camping bed," he said, gaping.

"It's not. It's two camping beds."

"You don't think…?"

"What?"

"Melody?"

"No, Raines. I don't think that. All she did was drink with them."

"That's bad enough. God, I'm starting to feel like an old man."

"Now that you mention it, you *are* starting to gray at the temples."

"Holly! I have two girls in my life who are about to send me over the edge, and now my oldest friend has a hand on my back ready to give me a good shove."

Holly laughed and headed for the party area. Halfway across the mill floor, she stopped and sniffed.

"What is it? You're not all emotional because you hurt my feelings, are you?" Raines joked.

"Not exactly. For an abandoned mill, it sure smells of fresh sawdust."

Raines squatted, brushed some sawdust off the ground. "It looks like there was some sort of machinery here not too long ago."

Holly brushed off another area. "It looks like it was long and heavy, and given the amount of sawdust, I'd guess it was a saw of some sort."

"That's interesting," Raines noted. "At the auction, Justin Jarvis and I were discussing illegal logging. He knew a lot about it, and even expressed concern that I was giving away a rosewood guitar. He knew that it would be difficult to replace because most rosewood species are protected now. Mine is old, purchased long before the new laws, and I have the necessary documentation to prove it, but it's an interesting angle. Is there a better place to cut up illegal logs than an abandoned sawmill? Perhaps Justin stumbled on to something without being aware of it. He could have been in the forest and seen something he wasn't supposed to see. It's a possible motive."

Holly stuck her hands in her pockets. It was cold inside the mill. "It would be interesting to find out if this area was part of Justin's patrol. It's out of the way, and it would make a good hiding place for just about anything. The mill is practically big enough to house a cruise ship. Those marks could be some other type of equipment, and the sawdust nothing more than teenagers cutting up logs to start a fire. Do you see a chainsaw around?"

"No, but the kids may know something. It looks like they've been coming here for a while. We need to talk to them," he said. "Then we need to have a conversation with Helga Lang and Phil Montague. It could just be that the Blackthorns have resumed logging here."

Then something caught Holly's eye at the back of the mill, beside the makeshift camping area. She walked over to it and called over to him. "Look at this, Raines. Is this a 3D printer?"

Raines stepped up beside her. "Looks like it."

"What's it doing at an abandoned sawmill?"

Raines picked up a plastic cup on the floor next to a camping chair and sniffed it. "Seems like the boys made cups with it." He noticed a power cord and followed it to the wall. Peering out through a gap, he shook his head. "The power cord runs to a generator out back. Looks like the kids really knew what they were doing. They were prepared for anything, even manufacturing what they needed to stay here. Cups for parties, plates, bottle openers, cable drums," he said, pointing to a plastic device. This had another power cord wrapped around it, which sat on top of a small space heater. "People have even used them to make guns."

"I heard about that," she responded. "Terrifying."

Raines picked up a spool of beige filament. "I read an article about how 3D printers are changing the face of prosthetics."

Holly nodded and took a good look at the printer. "Do you think that's big enough to print a couple of Bigfoot feet?" she asked with a hint of excitement.

Raines smiled. "No, but they could print them in pieces and glue them together."

Holly rubbed her hands together to warm them. "And Luke just happens to live at the Witch Cross Inn, which is practically next door to Sarah Mooney and Pickles. I think we need to have a talk with Zack and Luke."

"At least it appears we've solved one case," Raines said. "Let's go and have a conversation with the boys."

As they were heading for the door, a car horn honked.

"Did you hear that?" she asked.

"Hard not to."

Stepping outside, they looked around.

The horn sounded again, for longer this time.

Raines pointed to a narrower trail they'd spotted when they'd arrived, which cut through the forest off to the left. "It's coming from that direction." He strode off toward it, and Holly had to lengthen her stride to keep up.

Following the trail, they passed the crumbled remains of a brick wall on their left, which was partially hidden by the thicket. Trees arched above them, overgrown and forming a tunnel. Several limbs had been snapped and bent backward; a couple of smaller branches lay on the ground on top of the snow.

"Looks like something big came through here," Raines observed.

Holly lifted one of the branches. "Check this out."

Raines looked down. There was a large print in the snow.

"Fennis said the print he found at Sarah Mooney's looked like a gorilla footprint. His photo didn't do it justice. This looks like something bigger than an ape has been here," she said.

Raines grinned. "The primitive teenage primate."

She laughed, and they continued to follow tire tracks and more of the scattered footprints that hadn't been run over for about two hundred yards further down the trail until they reached a clearing. There, they discovered an old brick building about the size of a garage. It had an old rusted, corrugated tin roof, but there was a new door with a brand-new padlock. A few cracked logs were scattered to the right of the building.

As Holly examined the padlock, the horn honked again. It was close now. Exchanging a glance, she and Raines ran behind the building and spotted the Bigfoot Investigations van. It was rammed headfirst into a tree trunk.

The horn sounded again. Sprinting over to the van, Raines saw that it was riddled with holes from shotgun blasts. Peering inside, he saw Sticks first. He was still buckled into the driver's seat, and he was clearly dead. It looked as if he'd taken a shotgun blast to the side of his head.

From the passenger seat, they heard a feeble, "Help."

It was Stubby. He had a scalp wound and soft tissue swelling on his forehead. The collar of his heavy camo jacket had soaked up the blood from the head wound. His nose looked broken and had bled profusely. Dried blood ran down over his lips and dripped thickly from under his chin. One of his eyes was swollen shut, but he looked at them with his other one.

"Help Sticks," he managed to croak, before passing out.

CHAPTER THIRTY-FOUR

Worried that Stubby might have a spinal injury, Raines and Holly decided not to move him. They were in the heart of Crawford Notch, and neither of them had a cell signal. While Holly stayed with Stubby, Raines ran to his SUV. Spinning his tires, he sped down the road until he could call it in. Once dispatch confirmed that help was on the way, he returned just as fast, stopping only long enough to sprint into the mill to retrieve the sleeping bags he'd seen there. They needed to keep Stubby warm.

It took a little over fifteen minutes for help to arrive. Stubby was still alive but had not regained consciousness. After the paramedics had stabilized him, loaded him into the ambulance and left, sirens blaring, Raines and Holly decided to check out what was in the brick building while they waited for the chief.

They didn't want to tamper with the new lock, so Raines pulled out his multipurpose pocketknife like he was still in the Boy Scouts and removed the screws attaching the lock to the door. The building was empty, but there had been signs of recent activity. There were fresh scratch marks on the concrete floor, and some chips of wood.

They searched the area and took photos of the different tire tracks that had been left in the snow. Then Raines went back to the mill to conduct a more thorough search while Holly waited for Chief Finch.

He showed up fifteen minutes later with Lieutenant Gustafson; they'd been with Helga Lang and her son. Holly briefed them about what she and Raines had found at the mill. Then Finch told her about what had happened at the Langs', where he and Gustafson had officially notified Helga and her son that the remains found were indeed those of Stefan Lang.

"Helga and Andreas took the news hard," the chief told them. "Their reactions seemed genuine, but when I tried to question Helga about her husband's disappearance, she was vague, started acting like she had something to hide. Then Phil Montague showed up, took one look at her and decided she wasn't up to answering any more questions at that time. He shut us down fast." The chief pressed his lips together in frustration.

"Did you get the vibe that Helga and Phil were in a relationship?" Holly asked.

"He certainly comes across as overprotective, but he didn't touch her, and she didn't so much as glance at him in any way that would suggest they're intimate. He did put an arm around Andreas to comfort the kid, but it was a quick hug of support, nothing more. I'm more interested in Helga. There's something not right about her. What do you think, Gus?"

From the look of his deep-furrowed frown, Gus wasn't happy that he was expected to share his observations with Holly and Raines. "That was my reading of the situation. She's a cold, hard woman. Tough as nails. I could see her whacking her husband with an ax for just telling her she'd overcooked the steaks. She's not bad looking, but she's not somebody who's going to warm your bed at night."

Holly gave a mental sigh. She really had to send some of his DNA into the Neanderthal genome project. They'd probably discover a major curveball to the theory of evolution.

Holly didn't catch Finch's reaction to that comment because he'd turned to glance around the clearing where they were standing, his eyes pausing to look at the van. Sticks' body was still there and would be until the Medical Examiner arrived. "So," he said, turning to face Holly and Raines, "do you think the kids are involved in the shooting?"

Holly rubbed her forehead. She needed coffee in the worst way. "No. Melody told Raines that she was with the boys when they heard the shots. I don't think Melody would lie about that."

Finch nodded in agreement.

"How about we give the Langs a little time to themselves while I interview Luke Johnson and Zack Blackthorn?" Holly suggested. "After I finish talking to them, I'll head over to question Helga and Andreas. I need to notify them that there's been a death on their property, and I need to find out if they are aware that the mill has been used."

Gustafson cut in. "Not only are we dealing with one of the wealthiest families in town, but they're also one of the oldest. They'll expect to deal with us, not a sergeant."

Dammit, not this again, she thought. She could feel the case slipping away from her. Gustafson was a master at pulling the best cases right from under her, but this time she wasn't going to go down without fighting for it. "Andreas Lang is a huge fan of Acid Raines, so I could bring Raines with me. He may be able to get him to talk. You could update Bliss Jarvis, while Lieutenant Gustafson handles the media," Holly suggested. She could hear the hope in her voice.

Chief Finch gave her an assessing look. He knew when he was being manipulated. He was no fool, but his ruddy, stern face cracked into the slightest of smiles.

Gustafson didn't miss his response. "Look, Fred. This isn't the right time to bring this up, but based on Jakes's last case, her evaluation skills and ability to read the situation are shaky at best. Her reputation has been damaged. We can't have someone with a black mark against her working such a prominent case. Think of your position in the community. I'll handle the Langs," Gustafson said forcefully.

The chief said nothing for a moment, and Holly's temper started to raise its hot head.

"Now, Gus. Don't get your dander up," Finch said at last. "In little more than a New York minute, Holly got us what we needed to ID a skull that could have taken us years to do—if ever. At the same time, it appears she's cracked the mystery of the Bigfoot sightings. She's earned this. You'll keep working the Jarvis case. And I'll handle the media. Holly gets to run with the Lang case."

Gustafson glared at Holly, who fought back a grin of delight.

"There's nothing happening with the Jarvis case. No new leads," Gustafson complained.

"Then get out and make something happen," the chief growled.

Gustafson stared hard at Fred Finch as if preparing to tell him exactly what he thought about his command. The chief puffed out his considerable chest, squared his shoulders and looked him right in the eye.

Gustafson shook his head in disgust and turned on his heel.

Finch turned to Holly. "Give Helga and Andreas some time to process what happened to Stefan Lang before you head over there. Interview the kids first. See if they've seen anyone here."

"Right, Chief."

"And Jakes?"

"Yes, Chief?"

"You know what's at stake here. Gustafson is watching you, and he has the ear of the mayor. Don't let me down."

"I won't, Chief," she said, sounding far more confident than she felt.

CHAPTER THIRTY-FIVE

Raines and Holly sat in the warm dining room at the Witch Cross Inn. A fire blazed, and Christine Johnson brought them over coffee and a plate of ham sandwiches, insisting they eat them while they waited for Luke. She'd called her son and asked him to come home, but she hadn't told him why, just insisted that he get home now.

On a typical Sunday lunchtime, the room would have been packed with diners, but the place was deserted because the inn had remained closed.

As they tucked into their sandwiches, Luke Johnson barged in through the front door and yelled for his mother. He didn't sound like a happy camper, Holly decided.

"We're in here, Luke," his mother called sweetly.

"Zack and I were in the middle of an awesome game. What do you wa—" He stopped dead in his tracks when he spotted Raines. He swallowed and turned to leave.

Christine patted the seat beside her. "I want you to come and sit down next to me and tell me what you've been up to."

"I haven't been up to anything," he said, not meeting her eyes.

"Then why do these detectives want to talk with you?"

"You know mindreading isn't a school requirement, right?" He scoffed as he shifted his weight. He still had his parka on and looked like he might bolt at any second.

"Sit down. Now!" came the sharp command from his mother.

Luke rolled his eyes. He was clearly not too intimidated, but he complied.

"So, Detectives. What's going on?" Christine asked them.

"We'd like to know where Luke was last Saturday night between nine and midnight," Holly said.

While Holly asked the questions, Raines had agreed to sit there and look fierce. He didn't have to try hard. His cold gray eyes bored into Luke Johnson like a dentist's drill.

Luke fidgeted nervously, and they watched him try to force his features into a blank expression as he strove to look innocent. He failed. Raines, on the other hand, was utterly convincing when he scowled at him as if he wanted to tear him apart limb by limb.

Luke swallowed hard and tried to brazen his way out of trouble. "You mean last night?"

Holly tilted her head to one side as if she was really considering it. "You raise a good point, Luke. To avoid any confusion, why don't you tell us where you were both last night and a week ago last night."

"Don't you mean Friday night, the night of the shooting?" he asked.

"No. I'm interested in what you were doing the last two Saturday nights."

His guilty expression told them he'd been made, and Holly could almost hear his panicky inner voice yelling, 'They know! They know!'

But the kid was a fighter. "I was with my cousin, Zack. You can confirm my alibi with him."

"Alibi? That's an interesting choice of words," Holly went on, as Raines continued to drill him with his eyes. "Why would you need an alibi? I'm not accusing you of doing anything. Normally, people only offer up an alibi when something terrible has happened, and they're considered a suspect. Were you involved in something last night that would require you to need an alibi?"

He flushed at that, and his jaw tightened.

If she kept pushing, she could get him to snap. He had one of those tempers.

He shrugged. "It's a figure of speech. Cops don't just question you for no reason. Something had to have happened for you to show up here, asking me questions. Doesn't mean I know anything about anything."

Christine looked from Holly to Luke and back to Holly. "Will you please just tell me what's going on?"

"Luke and Zack have been running around town in a Bigfoot suit, terrifying the neighborhood and trespassing," Holly told her.

"What?" Genuine shock registered on Christine's face. "You mean the Bigfoot that Sarah Mooney reported seeing? The one that nearly killed Pickles?"

"That's the one," Holly confirmed.

Christine turned to her son. "Luke?"

Luke hung his head. Guilty as charged, Holly thought.

"Why on earth would you want to run around as Bigfoot, scaring women and dogs? Especially Sarah Mooney, after what she's been through," his mother asked, sounding bewildered.

"We meant no harm by it, Mom. And I did nothing to that yappy little dog. I swear on my life. The idea came to us one night when me and Zack—"

"Zack and I," Christine corrected automatically.

"When Zack and I were telling ghost stories. Zack remembered the Legend of Verity Falls, which is about a Bigfoot attacking a bunch of loggers. Anyway, I thought it would be a good way to drum up some business."

His mom gave him a quizzical look. "What do you mean by drum up business?"

"I thought it would bring in a lot of guests for the inn if there was a Bigfoot sighting. It would have worked, too, if someone hadn't shot that guy."

In a voice that suddenly rose several octaves, she screeched, "That's ridiculous. The Blackthorns have never needed to drum up business."

"We're Johnsons, Mom, not Blackthorns. Zack is a Blackthorn."

Christine straightened her plump figure, breasts and stomach straining against her blouse, and said rather loftily, "I am a Blackthorn, as are you. What's more, you're the spitting image of your great-great-granddaddy, Thaddeus the First. You're nothing like your father's side of the family."

He sighed as though he'd heard this a thousand times already. "Just saying, Mom. Zack is a real Blackthorn."

"Zack looks nothing like the family. He's his mother's son through and through."

Luke looked a little sulky now. "That's good, because he's going to inherit her money through and through." He turned his attention to Holly. "It's not a crime to dress up like Bigfoot."

"What about serving alcohol to a minor? Melody Raines is only fourteen."

Luke glanced at Raines and slid his chair a little closer to his mother's. "She drank that all on her own. With absolutely no pressure at all from us. Poor kid. We wouldn't have let anything happen to her. She's cool."

"If you go near her again, I'll make you wish you lived in the outer reaches of Mongolia," Raines rasped with enough cold anger to make even Holly believe he was serious.

"Our only crime was trespassing at the mill, and our family owns Verity Falls, so that's not a problem."

"Verity Falls!" Christine screeched. "You were at Verity Falls?"

"Jeez, Mom. It's not a big deal. Aunt Helga won't mind."

"Helga is not your aunt."

"Whatever. She'll let it slide. I'll square it with Andreas."

"You're related to the Langs, Christine?" Holly asked, even though she already knew the answer.

"Yes. Stefan was my cousin."

Holly picked up on the past tense. "You heard about his death?"

She nodded, and Holly noted that the news hadn't appeared to upset her.

"How did you hear about it?"

"Over the phone. Andreas called. He wanted to tell Luke."

"What happened?" Luke asked.

"Stefan Lang's body was found in Pinkham Notch," Holly explained.

He leaned forward. "Does Andreas know?"

"Of course he knows," Christine said. "I just told you he called here looking for you."

"But Andreas said his dad has been in Germany for two years. When did he get back?" Luke asked.

"We don't believe he ever left for Germany," Holly told him.

"Wow!" came his reply. "Andreas must be freaked out."

"I'm sure he is." Holly turned to Christine. "And Thaddeus Blackthorn is your brother?"

"That's right."

"And he has no ownership of Verity Falls or Blackthorn Timber?"

She pressed her lips together in annoyance and shook her head.

"And you have no ownership, either?"

Another annoyed shake of the head.

Holly turned her focus back to the teenager. "When you were at the mill, did you ever see anyone?"

"No."

"How about trucks?"

"I didn't see any, but there have been trucks out there. Lots of tracks on the road. It's weird. It's supposed to be a ghost town, but someone has definitely been in the mill."

"How do you know that?"

"There was a saw in there, but it's gone now."

"Was it an old saw?"

"No. It looked portable—it had wheels and stuff—but it was big and painted red. Looked fairly new. After that, we were worried about leaving our stuff there, and last night we were planning to bring it home, but someone started shooting."

Christine gasped and covered her mouth with her hand.

"When you heard the shooting, what did you do?" Holly continued to prod.

"What do you think we did? We got the hell out of there."

"Luke!" his mother snapped.

"Sorry, Mom. We piled into Zack's Beemer and took off."

"And you left Melody there on her own," Raines snarled.

Luke looked like Raines had actually tried to take a bite out of him. "She wouldn't come with us, Mr. Raines. I swear. She had her bike there."

"What happened next?" Holly asked.

"Nothing. We drove home."

"Did you see anything as you left?"

"Nope."

"And the generator and 3D printer are yours?"

"No. That stuff belongs to Zack. The camping gear is mine, and I need it back."

Holly stood. "That could take a while. It's part of a crime scene."

"Trespassing's not that big a deal," he muttered.

Standing, Raines looked down at the kid. "No, but murder is."

"Murder? We had nothing to do with a murder."

"Someone was shot close to the mill," he explained. "You, Melody and Zack were lucky you weren't hurt."

"What time did you get home?"

"Midnight. I went to Zack's after leaving the mill."

"What time did you get to Zack's?" Raines asked.

"Sometime after nine, probably closer to ten."

"Okay, I think that's all for now," Holly said, getting to her feet alongside Raines. She thanked Christine for the sandwiches and was about to leave when she remembered something. "What was it exactly that Sarah Mooney went through?" she asked her.

"Oh, that. I was talking about something that happened to her a long time ago."

"What was it?" Holly pressed.

"I found this out by accident and haven't discussed it with her, so I don't know how true it is," Christine said, lowering her voice as though she might be overheard. "One summer, a friend of Sarah's came to visit her, but she was allergic to dogs, so she stayed here instead. Late one night, she sat by the fire with a glass of wine and told me that Sarah had once lived in Massachusetts. Her neighbor there was single, a lovely woman with a young son. Sarah can't have children of her own, and so, as you can imagine, she became very attached to the child.

"One day, she saw a stranger in their neighborhood, sitting in a parked car a few houses away from her. The next day, he was there again, sitting in his car across the street from her neighbor's house. Sarah thought it was odd, but she didn't report it. This went on for a few days. She watched him, but he did nothing. Turns out he was stalking her neighbor and ended up killing the woman and child. The whole thing really messed Sarah up. She had to move, and she came up here where she thought it would be safe."

And, Holly thought, that explains why Sarah Mooney reports everything now.

CHAPTER THIRTY-SIX

Thaddeus Blackthorn's house wasn't as spectacular as Helga Lang's mountain retreat, but it was beautiful, nonetheless. It was a three-story, pale yellow Georgian Colonial with a wraparound porch that was situated on the outskirts of the picturesque village of Liberty. The village was accessed via a red covered bridge and was home to seven hundred and fifty residents. The gift shops, bakery, florist, cross-country skiing center, and the prestigious Hemlock Inn & Spa, though, catered more to the year-round tourists.

Thaddeus opened the front door just as Holly, with Raines beside her, was about to knock. He was dressed in black, stretchy cross-country ski pants and a lightweight red jacket. Under that, he wore a black silk turtleneck. It was apparent that he was heading out to ski. Liberty was famed for its groomed cross-country trails.

Holly made the introductions, and Thaddeus turned to Raines curiously.

"You were talking to my sister the night of the auction. I didn't realize you were with the police. Someone told me you were a singer."

"I was. Now I'm not."

Thaddeus gave him a dismissive glance, as if only a failed musician would have to work for the police, and he didn't have time for either. "Lieutenant Gustafson has already interviewed me *ad infinitum*. I have nothing left to say, and I have an appointment."

"We're here to talk to your son."

"Zack? Whatever for?"

Raines didn't answer his question. "Is he home?"

"Yes," Thaddeus said, stepping back into his house.

Not waiting for an invitation, they followed. The entrance hall was spacious, with a red and blue paisley-patterned oriental rug, a chandelier, and a curving staircase made out of rich, warm oak.

"Zack!" he yelled up the stairs.

"What?" a voice shouted, coming from the left, startling all three of them.

They turned to see a teenager slouched on a leather couch. His brown hair looked like he'd run his fingers through it about fifty times. Holly couldn't tell if it was supposed to look that way, or if he'd been too lazy to brush it. His steady brown eyes assessed the three adults before he returned his attention to his phone.

They entered the living room and stood before him. With an annoyed sigh, Zack looked up at them, uninterested, and Holly suspected that he had known they were coming. Luke had probably called him the moment they'd left the inn.

Confirming her suspicions, Zack didn't wait for their questions. "I'm not sorry for trespassing at the mill."

"What mill?" Thaddeus asked, obviously hearing this for the first time.

As Raines explained how the kids partied at the mill, serving minors alcohol, and cavorted around town dressed as Bigfoot scaring people, he didn't even attempt to keep the anger out of his voice.

Zack did not appear intimidated in the slightest. He was one of those cocky kids who never worried about getting into trouble, because their parents always bailed them out. He looked up at Raines from where he sat slouched on the couch with a smug expression on his face. "I'm not to blame for your niece drinking. She did that all on her own without any encouragement from us."

Holly noticed that Raines clenched his jaw so tightly that it must have hurt.

"What were you thinking?" Thaddeus muttered before Raines could respond. "You need to stop hanging around with Luke. He has no prospects. It doesn't matter if he gets into trouble. They can't afford even community college, but not you. We have plans for you."

That interested Holly. "If your sister doesn't have the funds for college, how did she afford to buy the inn?" she asked Thaddeus.

He shrugged. "Who knows? She could have had money back then. Skip is an excellent sailor, and he won many of the top yacht races. You had to have seen all of the trophies and photos at the inn. Christine loves displaying them for all to see. I presume he had winnings from the races, and from what I hear, he's no stranger to

Vegas. He's quite the poker player, which…" he said, turning to his son and pointing at him, "will be about the only way you'll be able to make a living if you end up with a record. The Langs could easily press charges."

The teen rolled his eyes. "They won't press charges, Dad. Not after what they did."

"We'll talk about this later."

"No. Tell them what Stefan Lang did to us."

"I said we'll discuss it later."

"What did they do?" Raines asked Zack so fast, and with such a hard edge to his voice, that the teenager responded before thinking about it.

"They stole our land."

"How so?"

"They won't let Dad cross their land to get to ours."

Raines looked over at Thaddeus for an explanation.

At first, Thaddeus said nothing, just blinked a few times. "It's a long story."

"We have plenty of time," Holly told him.

Stalling, he glanced at his watch. "I need to be somewhere."

Raines folded his arms and stared down at the man. "That's fine, but on the way there, you can stop in at the station and answer our questions officially."

"Fine," Thaddeus muttered in exasperation. "It's nothing significant. I discovered that we own a parcel of old-growth forest that is surrounded by Lang land."

"You mean you can't access any part of the forest unless you cross land owned by the Langs?" Holly clarified. When he nodded, she asked the most obvious question. "How did that happen?"

"As far as I can tell, a mistake was made with my great-grandfather's will. At that time, he left most of his empire to his daughter Patience and her husband Helmut. Although he left some money as well as property and land to my grandfather, it was nominal in comparison to what the Langs inherited. My grandfather did not have a good relationship with his father, who doted on his only daughter."

Recalling the story Karl Hoffman had told her about Thaddeus's grandfather, Holly almost smiled when she realized he'd neglected to mention that his grandfather had been a draft dodger.

Thaddeus continued, "Anyway, he left a plot of forest to my grandfather, which was smack dab in the middle of land he left to the Langs."

"When did you learn about the land?"

"After my father died, and once my mother retired to Florida, my sister, Christine, became obsessed with her ancestry. She completed our family tree, bought that old inn, which had once been in the family, and started to chronicle all of the family exploits, photos, and memorabilia. You've seen the inn. It's crammed full of slices of our history. She insisted that I go through all the boxes my mother left with me when she moved, and I found a stack of letters between my grandfather and Helmut Lang."

Zack interrupted him. "Can I read them, Dad?"

"Maybe. Anyway, in the letters, my grandfather asked permission to cross Lang land so that he could log the acreage. He was desperate for money because some of his business ventures had failed. Helmut Lang refused. After this, my grandfather asked for a legal right of way, so he could sell the land. Helmut refused again, although he did permit him access to the land for any other purposes. He even offered to buy it, claiming in one letter that he wished to preserve the old-growth forest, as there was very little old growth left in the White Mountains after all the logging. My grandfather believed Helmut wanted the land so he could log it himself, and he refused to sell it to him. Over time, it was forgotten—that is, until I read those letters."

Zack piped up. "Don't forget to tell them that Stefan was no better than his grandfather Helmut when you tried to gain access to the land."

Thaddeus glared at his son, clearly understanding the implications this could have in a murder investigation.

Slowly, Zack appeared to glom onto the idea, and his mouth made the 'oh' shape of a light-bulb moment.

"You learned about the land before Stefan's disappearance?" Holly confirmed.

Thaddeus nodded reluctantly.

"And you've heard that Stefan Lang is dead?"

"Who hasn't at this point? It's a small village full of big gossips."

"You don't appear too upset by his death."

"He was a bastard. Go and ask Phil Montague about how nice my cousin was."

"What did he do?"

"At first, he offered to give me a right of way on to our land or to buy it from us at a good price, but then he changed his mind when he realized that it was an old-growth area. He claimed he agreed with his grandfather that old-growth trees should be protected. Phil Montague told me that Stefan commented to him one day that he didn't need to buy the land to protect it because we couldn't reach it."

"And you didn't want us to know about it because it gives you a motive for killing your cousin?" Holly asked.

He nodded. "I'm not a fool, but I had nothing to do with what happened to Stefan."

Holly's eyes remained fixed on Thaddeus's face for a few seconds. He didn't look away. "Thank you. I think that will be all for now," Holly said. They shook Thaddeus's hand, and then as they were leaving, Raines turned back to Zack.

"What time did you get home last night?"

The teenager tilted his head up, looking at the ceiling for a moment as if he was deep in thought. His sly smile, though, broadcast to the detectives that he knew this question was coming, and he'd already prepared an answer. "Must have been somewhere around ten, maybe before that."

"And what time did you hear the gunshot?" Raines asked.

"Around nine, but you can ask your niece about it. She was there, too. And if we get in trouble, so does she."

CHAPTER THIRTY-SEVEN

Snow had started to fall while they were talking with Thaddeus and Zack. Holly sat quietly in the passenger seat as Raines drove back to North Caxton, staring out the window. It wasn't a driving snow. The flakes were big and fluffy, and she could see each one drift gently to the ground. This was her favorite kind of snow. It made her feel dreamy and yearn for a roaring fire, hot cocoa and someone to share it with.

The tires thumped rapidly as Raines drove the heavy SUV over the covered wooden bridge. "I once dated someone from Nunavik," he said, startling her out of her reverie.

"Where's that?"

"Northern Québec. She taught me the Inuit word for falling snow: '*qaniy*.'"

"That's a beautiful word, Raines. What happened to her?"

"Her high school love traveled thousands of miles to find her, and she realized that she'd seen enough of the world to know her home would always be with him in the Arctic."

She grinned. "That's either a testament that living with you is so difficult that she'd rather be in the Artic, or it's really romantic." Then she remembered his song "Snow Star." She glanced over at him. "Didn't you write a song about them on your *Spiral Galaxies* album?"

"Yes. Their story inspired me."

Holly fell silent again, returning her gaze to the falling snow. She could feel Raines beside her, his presence calm and thoughtful, too. They were deep in it now, she thought, the pieces of the puzzle falling like the snow around them. They just had to make sense of it.

As if reading her mind, Raines said, "Forestry connects all three homicides. Justin Jarvis was a forest ranger. Stefan Lang owned Blackthorn Timber and the land surrounding Thaddeus Blackthorn's old-growth forest. Even Frank Stanko, our Bigfoot hunter, could be connected. He was killed at Verity Falls, a logging ghost town."

"And," Holly said, holding up a piece of paper, "the copy of the old map Thaddeus found with his grandfather's letters locates the old-growth forest within a few miles of Verity Falls." She folded the map Thaddeus had given them and put it back in her pocket. "The challenge is finding a suspect with a motive to kill all three of the victims. There's a clear motive for Thaddeus Blackthorn in Stefan Lang's death. He wanted his land, and Stefan refused to let him get to it. He didn't have a strong alibi for Justin's shooting, but why would he want to kill him? And why would he kill Sticks?"

Raines slowed for a red light. "Perhaps Thaddeus Blackthorn was using Verity Falls to log his land. The map he gave you shows the best access to it is through Verity Falls. He could have then used the mill to process the timber."

Holly watched a middle-aged man in a green pickup brake too late for the red light and slide through the intersection. "But what's his motive for Justin's death?"

Their light turned green, and Raines made a left heading south toward Blackthorn Timber. Holly had called Phil Montague, and he'd agreed to meet with them at the lumber yard in town. "Skip Johnson didn't have an alibi for Justin's death. He said he was upstairs lying down, but no one saw him. He appears deeply troubled, but that could simply be because they've had to turn guests away from the inn. I can't see why he would want to damage his business by shooting Justin at the Witch Cross Inn, especially since we know things aren't going so well. That's why Luke ran around dressed as Bigfoot. He was trying to drum up business for his parents."

Holly nodded. "I think Luke and Zack were telling the truth. They're not involved in the homicides, but Helga Lang has a motive. She benefitted financially from Stefan's death, but why would she shoot Justin Jarvis or Sticks?"

The windshield wipers automatically picked up speed as the snow began to fall harder. Raines mused, "Phil Montague could be having an affair with Helga, but he was right there with us when Justin was shot."

"We need to take a look at that old-growth forest," she said.

The windshield started to fog, so Raines put on the front defroster. "That's not going to be easy from the look of the map."

Holly glanced at the clock on the dash. "It's two o'clock. We only have daylight for another couple of hours. It's too late to go now. After we talk to Phil Montague, let's head over to interview Helga. We've given her time now to grieve with Andreas. We'll have to head out first thing in the morning to take a look at the forest, but we're going to need snowmobiles. We're getting eight inches of fresh snow tonight."

"I have snowmobiles and a suit you can borrow, but I don't have boots that will fit," Raines offered.

"I have boots," she said.

Raines slowed to make a left onto Mill Creek Road. Half a mile from there, he made a right into Blackthorn Timber. Situated on twenty acres, the log cabin–style office was the first building they saw as they passed through the gates. Beyond that sat the sawmill and the log yard, which was full of stacked, raw timber. There were smaller piles of logs laid out, waiting for evaluation. Over on the right were ten large water-based kilns for drying the wood, and massive storage sheds for the finished products. As they watched, fascinated, a log loader with four monstrous fangs scooped up a pile of logs, closed its jaws around them and trundled from the log stack toward the sawmill. Trucks full of raw trees waited to be unloaded, and a backhoe with forklifts was moving the pallets of milled, finished planks toward a storage building. An excavator fitted with a grapple saw attached to its long arm, and another backhoe with chains dangling from the bucket, stood idle in the busy yard.

Raines pulled up in front of the office and turned to her. "What do you think?"

She smiled. "You bring me to the best places."

"Interesting," he said. "I didn't know you had a thing for timber."

She shook her head. "Excavators and backhoes."

His gray eyes lingered on her face, making her pulse skip. She squinted at him.

He grinned. "I was wondering if we were going to give Montague a rough ride to see what we can shake loose."

"Easy ride for now. I know Phil."

Raines raised an eyebrow. "As in the biblical sense?"

"Well, there was this one time…"

"Okay, okay. I don't need to hear the gory details."

Holly continued. "Phil gave me…" She paused for effect. "…a check from Blackthorn Timber for winning a ski race they sponsor every year at Hurricane Mountain."

Raines chuckled. "Maybe I should start sponsoring a few races to see if I can meet any agile skiers."

"Stick with the singing, Raines. You're already spreading yourself way too thin," she advised, thinking of Olivia May, who had the gamine charm of Audrey Hepburn. Oh yes. Raines had plenty to keep himself busy with the elegant Olivia.

Raines laughed. "Are you ever going to give me an easy ride?"

She poked him in the arm. "I could try scooping you up in one of those backhoes, but I doubt the bucket is big enough to fit that massive ego of yours."

At that moment, Phil Montague opened the office door.

"Showtime," Holly muttered under her breath. She and Raines stepped out of the SUV and walked up to the office.

Holly exchanged pleasantries with Phil and then listened as he fawned over Raines and his music for a couple of minutes, referencing his favorite songs and asking about his guitar influences. When Holly could see that Raines had had enough, she said, "Unfortunately, we have some bad news, Phil."

He ran a hand through his hair and sighed. "I heard about Stefan. That came as a shock. We all thought he was in Germany."

"We're here about what happened in Verity Falls."

"What? The kids partying in the old mill? Andreas told me about that. I don't think Helga wants to press charges."

"No. Someone was shot and killed close to the mill today." Holly watched for a reaction. Although his eyes widened slightly, his face didn't seem to register too much surprise. "Who was it?"

"Frank Stanko."

"I don't know him. What was he doing out there?"

"Searching for Bigfoot."

"Are you serious?"

"Yes."

Phil put his hands in his pockets. "I heard about the Bigfoot sighting in town, but I didn't think much of it. What happened?"

"We're trying to figure that out. Has Blackthorns been operating at Verity Falls?" she asked.

"No. It's been abandoned for decades."

"So, you don't know anyone who has been using the site?"

"No. There's nothing out there except run-down old buildings."

"Have you been out there recently?"

"No."

Holly rubbed her hands together. It was cold, and she'd left her gloves in the SUV. "Before Stefan disappeared, Thaddeus told us that he was in discussions with him about a parcel of land he'd inherited. Do you know anything about that?"

"I'm familiar with the situation. Stefan owned the land surrounding his property."

"Can you tell us what happened?" Raines asked.

"What did Thaddeus tell you?"

"We'd like to hear what you know."

"There's not much to tell, really. I know that Thaddeus discovered he owned the acreage after reading his grandfather's letters to Stefan's grandfather, Helmut. He wanted access to the land to either log it or sell it. Thaddeus wanted the same. Early on in his discussion with Thaddeus, Stefan seemed sympathetic, but he had a change of heart. He wanted to honor Helmut's wishes that the old-growth forest be preserved for future generations. As you can imagine, this did not sit well with Thaddeus, but there is nothing I can do to help him."

"Thaddeus found an old map showing where the parcel of land is," Holly told him, pulling out the copy from her pocket. "The forest appears to be close to Verity Falls. We'd like to cross the Langs' land to check out the area indicated on the map."

"You'll need permission from either Helga or Andreas. It's not my land. With everything that's happened, they'll need to make the decision. They have their family reputation to think about." He glanced at the clock on the wall. "I have a shipment I need to take care of for tomorrow."

"When was the last time you saw Stefan?" Raines asked.

That seemed to bring Phil up short. "It was right before he left for Germany." He thought about it for a moment. "Actually, it was soon after he refused to let Thaddeus have access to the land."

"Did Stefan tell you he was going to Germany?"

"He mentioned something about it. It was a planned trip. He visited there often on business and to see family."

CHAPTER THIRTY-EIGHT

It was the winter solstice and the darkest day of the year. As Raines turned on the headlights and drove away from Blackthorn's at four fifteen, Holly pulled out her phone and checked her messages. There were two from Fennis Cooper, and as she scrolled down the screen, she felt her blood pressure hit boiling point.

Fennis Cooper was at the hospital, he'd written, guarding Kenny Fritz, aka Stubby, in case the shooter tried to take another shot at him. Gustafson had shown up and was waiting to interview him. Fennis knew it was her case and wanted to give her a heads-up. A short time after that, he'd messaged again, informing her that Stubby was awake. Gustafson was still in the cafeteria eating an early dinner. He'd told Fennis to let him know when Stubby woke up, but Fennis, loyal guy that he was, wasn't going to let Gustafson highjack her interview.

Scowling, Holly shoved her phone into her coat pocket. "We need to stop by the hospital on the way to Helga's. Stubby is awake."

"You don't sound happy about it." Raines shot her a look.

"It's not that. Fennis texted me and told me that Gustafson is at the hospital waiting to talk to Stubby. Fennis is trying to stall him until I get there, but if Gustafson finds out what he's doing, he'll make Fennis pay for his loyalty to me."

Raines flipped on the lights and stepped on the accelerator. "I thought the chief was letting you handle it?"

"Gustafson has never let that stop him before."

Raines pulled into Caxton Memorial Hospital four minutes later. He dropped Holly off at the doors and went to park.

Besides the morgue, Holly's least favorite place was the hospital. She knew people who loved going to visit patients there. She even knew a couple who enjoyed spending their date nights in the cafeteria. After all, they'd explained to her, it was a beautiful New England cottage hospital with views of the mountains. But Holly had spent a lot of time in hospitals recovering from skiing injuries and avoided them whenever she could. She entered through the emergency room doors, wryly thinking that they were in the right place if there was going to be a showdown.

Gustafson had been a thorn in her side since she'd started working at the Caxton PD, and a poisonous one at that. Seeing her as a threat to his dream of becoming the police chief, he'd gone out of his way to make her life miserable. What infuriated her more was that she'd almost let him win. Over the last couple of months, he'd made it clear to anyone who would listen to him—including the press—that he didn't think Holly was up to the job.

Since returning to duty, she'd realized how much she loved being a detective, and she wasn't about to let a knuckle-dragger like him beat her. She just had to prove she was up to the job and solve the case before he did.

To save her more time, Fennis had thoughtfully texted her the room number. He waited outside the door, still resolutely guarding the patient. Holly felt a swell of affection for the kid. He was wearing a perfectly starched uniform that his mom had probably cleaned for him, and he stood to attention outside the room like he was in a military parade.

"Hey, Coop. Thanks for the heads-up."

He gave her a mock salute. "You bet, Sarge. He's awake. I heard him in there. He seems pretty cut up over losing his friend."

She nodded. "If the Lieutenant shows up, you didn't call me. Okay? I showed up. Technically, that's not a lie, as you texted me."

"Got it, Sarge."

Holly knocked and entered the room.

Kenny Fritz lay in bed, his head and torso partly elevated, white hospital sheets and a blue cotton blanket pulled up over his round belly. He was in the bed next to the window. The other bed was empty.

He had two swollen, black eyes. The right side of his head had been partially shaved, and there were stitches in his scalp. His eyes were bloodshot, and his cheeks were damp from crying.

"You've already heard about Frank?" she asked.

He tried to nod but flinched in pain. "Yes. I can't believe Sticks is gone."

"I'm sorry, Kenny."

"Call me Stubby. Kenny reminds me of my dad."

"Okay, Stubby. Sticks seemed like he was a great friend."

"He was the best. We grew up together. I don't know what I'm going to tell his family."

Holly walked over to the side of his bed and leaned back against the windowsill. "The official notifications have been made."

"Yeah, but... I still have to make an unofficial one." He looked crestfallen. "What am I going to tell them?"

"You'll find the words. Most of the time, I find that people want details. They want to know exactly what happened. You just have to figure out how much detail they really need to know. Most of them really just want to know that their loved one didn't suffer."

"Sounds like it's going to be tough." He wiped tears away with his knuckles, and Holly handed him a box of tissues from the bedside table.

"It won't be easy," she told him. "It's the worst part of my job, but you were the last one with him, and it will help them to be with you."

He coughed. "That's what I figured."

"So," she said, "do you feel up to telling me what happened? How did you end up at Verity Falls?"

"Have you heard about the Legend of Verity Falls?"

Holly nodded, thinking about Luke and Zack. They'd been inspired by the legend to dress up as Bigfoot. "Is it the story where loggers disappeared, and Bigfoot was the suspect?"

Stubby's eyes rounded. "That's the one. I didn't realize the police had investigated it."

"We didn't. 'Suspect' is just cop talk."

"Oh. That's too bad. An official investigation would give us all the validation we need. Sticks would have loved that." A tear ran down his chubby cheek. "Oh, boy. Am I going to miss that guy." Although Stubby was a grown man somewhere in his thirties, there was something childlike and innocent about him.

"Can you tell me what happened after you left Sarah Mooney's house?"

"That's the lady with the dog?"

"That's right."

He smoothed the blanket up over his chest. "Sticks remembered the legend and that Bigfoot was responsible for the missing lumberjacks all those years ago. He hadn't believed it. He'd always suspected that it was aliens who had taken them. Then his thinking got turned around when he realized it wasn't aliens or a single Bigfoot, but rather a whole gang of Bigfoots." He took a quick breath. "And Sticks decided we needed to go check it out. I told him we should call you. I was scared we'd run into a den of them. But he refused. Anyway, we knew roughly where Verity Falls was and decided to drive through Crawford Notch looking for trails into the area. We spotted a road with several tire tracks leading into the forest, but we didn't have time to slow down for it and missed it. Then, a little ways down the road, we found another way in. It looked like a better road. It was flatter and wider. Our van's not great in the snow."

That interested Holly. By taking the second road, they would have missed the mill.

He went on, "Even so, we had a hard time getting the van up the track. It was rough going. Our van isn't made for that kind of terrain. Then we reached a clearing, and the going was easier. We found an old brick building there, and we got out to take a look around. I found the ruins of another building deeper in the woods. Sticks spotted another path and walked down it. Next thing I knew, I heard him yelling. He scared the hell out of me when he came running back toward me. I thought Bigfoot was chasing him." Remembering, he gripped the blanket.

"What was it?" she asked.

"It seems he'd found some Bigfoot prints heading off down a narrower path. Anyways, Sticks yelled for me to get back in the van because he'd picked up their trail. He drove slowly, so I could hop out and take pictures of the prints. Got some good ones too. Just need my phone back to upload them. Do you have it?"

"I don't. It was collected as evidence. We'll get it back to you soon."

"Good."

"What happened next?"

"We ended up following the prints to the back of this old, run-down mill, but when we went inside, we didn't find them. We did find a bunch of camping equipment there, and we knew we'd struck pay dirt. We'd just discovered that Bigfoot had become smart enough to steal camping beds and chairs. They have it all set up there—you should see it! I think the species must be evolving. They even had a cooler and beer! Can you believe that?"

Holly looked straight into his bruised and bloodshot eyes and felt a sincere sympathy for him. She didn't have the heart to tell him that they'd stumbled on a teenage hideaway. He'd had enough bad news for one day. "That's hard to believe," she mumbled.

"Don't worry, Detective. I got photos. Anyways, Sticks goes out back to secure our surroundings."

Holly frowned. They'd had weapons? "Were you armed?"

"Not with guns, but we do have Bigfoot sensors that will tell us when they're coming. They work kind of like garage door sensors. There's a red trip beam. If it's tripped, my phone bleeps, and we have time to set up the video recording devices and hide until we can figure out if they're friendly or not. Only then will we decide if we should try talking to them."

Oh, boy, Holly thought. "Then what happened?"

"Well, we realized that we'd left the sensors at home. From where we were in the Notch, it was only about a forty-five-minute drive home. So, we left everything as it was—we didn't want to spook them—and we headed home to pick up the stuff. On the drive, we decided that we would make the old brick building we'd found in the clearing our base. We could hide the van in there and set up camera surveillance."

He broke off and looked down at his hands, which were clutching the bedclothes. "Anyways…" His voice was quieter now, drained of its prior animation. "As we drove back to the clearing and the brick building, we saw a big truck heading right for us. Sticks swerved to miss it, but we hit a tree, and then someone started shooting at us." He swallowed. "And that's when Sticks got hit."

"Did you see the driver?"

He thought about it. "No. The sun was on the windshield."

"What about the truck? Was it a semi?"

"It had a big grille, but I don't think it was the size of a semi. I remember it was painted dark red. It looked old, and as we passed it, I remember seeing out of the corner of my eye that it had a flatbed with some kind of red frame on it."

"Could the frame have been a portable sawmill?"

"It could have been. I didn't get a really good look at it before we hit the tree and the shooting started, but yeah. It could have been."

"Was it the driver who shot at you?"

Stubby rubbed his chin. "No. Couldn't have been. There wasn't enough time. It all happened so fast. We saw the truck gunning for us. Sticks swerved, hit the tree, and right away someone started shooting at us."

"Did you see the shooter?"

"No. I'm hazy on what happened. I remember trying to duck, but I think I passed out for a while."

That was all Stubby knew. After he'd finished, Holly knew that she needed to tell him the truth. She didn't want to risk him putting himself in danger anymore. It was an unpleasant task, but she explained as gently as she could about the Bigfoot hoax, the 3D printer that had been used to make fake Bigfoot feet, and that it was actually teenagers using the mill and not a Bigfoot gang.

Stubby was polite, and nodded solemnly as if agreeing with her, but she could tell he wasn't buying a word of what she was saying. Holly suspected that he'd upload his photos to the internet as soon as he got his hands on his phone.

As she left the room, she thanked Fennis again before heading for the parking lot. She was about to sigh with relief, as she'd nearly cleared the hospital without bumping into Gustafson, but she wasn't that lucky.

"Jakes," he bellowed from an adjoining corridor she'd just passed.

She ignored him and kept on going. The hospital doors swished open as she approached.

He was right behind her. "Jakes!" His voice was stern and strained with anger.

She turned to face him, saying nothing, just staring at his red, blotchy face. He had a broad forehead, small mean eyes, and droopy cheeks.

"What are you doing here?" he growled.

She kept it simple. "Interviewing Kenny Fritz."

"He isn't awake yet."

"That's odd. I just finished talking to him. He sure does an outstanding job of talking in his sleep."

He took a step closer to her, getting right in her face. He was so close, she smelled tuna fish and onion on his breath. He made her skin crawl. She wanted to take a step backward, but she knew he'd take that as a sign of weakness.

"Your days are numbered here, Jakes. You should think about quitting before you screw up again and get fired."

She leaned into him, so that they were almost nose to nose now. "I'm not going anywhere."

"That's right. Be selfish. It's not just your career you're damaging, it's Finch's." He pointed a finger at her. "And he's going to go down with you."

Gustafson's words struck a nerve. She knew that the chief had stuck his neck out for her, and her stomach twisted uneasily at the thought of damaging his reputation. She steeled herself and forced herself not to look away. "And you're going to make sure of it, aren't you?"

He leaned his face forward a few more inches. "I won't have to; the mayor is ready to step in and do it."

As he breathed into her face, she knew it would be a long time before she'd be able to enjoy another tuna fish sandwich again. "And you'll be in the wings ready to assume the position."

He squinted his beady little eyes at her. "What's that supposed to mean?"

"You can take it whatever way you want."

His nose twitched with contempt. "You're such a smart aleck, but just wait. We're all waiting for you to screw up. It's only a matter of time."

A horn sounded, and Gustafson jumped.

They were standing near the sensor to the sliding glass doors, which were still open. Holly turned to see Raines, who was sitting in his SUV. He pulled over to the curb and rolled down his window.

"Jakes, we've got to roll," he shouted. "I have a hot tip."

"What tip is that?" Gustafson called out to him.

"Sorry, Gus," Raines said, looking like he was on to a serious lead. "Don't have time to talk."

Holly was already heading for the Suburban.

"Jakes!" Gustafson bit out, sounding like he was about to pass a kidney stone. "You'd better call me and let me know what the hell is going on."

"You bet..." she called out, waiting to finish her sentence until she'd hopped in and slammed the door. "...You better not count on it." She turned to Raines. "Thanks. I owe you one. What's the hot tip?"

"There isn't one."

"I'm so relieved to be away from that jerk, I'm not even disappointed."

He nodded knowingly. "How did it go with Stubby?"

"We're looking for two people and a red truck with a flatbed. Stubby thought it could be carrying a portable saw. I need to call in a BOLO," she told him and filled him in on the rest of her conversation with Stubby.

When she'd finished, and Raines had said nothing, she took a good look at him. "What's going on with you? You look like you just went twenty rounds with Gustafson instead of me."

"It's girl trouble."

She immediately thought of Olivia. Had they broken up? "That's a first," Holly said.

"Not that kind of girl trouble. I mean Abbey. She's having a difficult time accepting what Melody told her about Nate. She's lost hope in his innocence. God, Holly. It was awful to see her face. She's devastated. If I could get my hands on Nate, I think I'd kill him.

"Abbey has refused to come home and wants to stay with Olivia, and I'm tempted to let her, but there's only so much I can ask of Olivia—or should ask of her. She says she's fine with Abbey staying over, but I don't know. I'm just worried if Abbey comes home, there will be another argument, and then God knows what will happen. The showdown between Melody and Abbey came at a bad time. Christmas is only a few days away, and that's hard enough for them to cope with."

"Perhaps Christmas is what triggered Melody," Holly suggested. "She's been shut down for so long, trying to control her emotions. The holidays must be a nightmare for them after what happened to their mom. It may have all become too much for her."

Raines gave her a sideways glance. For once, she could read what he was thinking. He knew that after her brother Charlie had died, her parents had never celebrated Christmas, or any holiday, for that matter. Not even her birthday. From the age of nine, her life had had little joy in it.

"The things we do to each other," was all he said.

Holly pushed the thought of Charlie out of her mind. "I'm sure Olivia won't mind. It's not like she's hurting for room."

"Let's hope not."

"Why don't you head over to see Abbey. I can interview Helga. I'll let you know how it goes."

"Unfortunately, Abbey doesn't want to see me, and I don't want to pressure her."

They fell silent after that.

"Where are you heading, Raines?" Holly said at length.

"You look like you could use a sub before we head over to Helga Lang's place," he told her.

"So long as it's not tuna."

He glanced at her.

"You don't want to know, Raines."

CHAPTER THIRTY-NINE

Holly felt an ache of sympathy as Andreas Lang opened the front door. His grief was heartrending. He was pale, his nose was red, and his eyes were swollen from crying.

His face lit up briefly as he saw Raines standing beside her.

Raines held out his hand and introduced himself.

Andreas gaped at him for a moment before taking his hand and bowing over it in devotion, as if Raines were a holy man.

"I'm a huge fan, Mr. Raines." He smiled bravely. "And a fan of your band, of course. I have all of your music. Amazing stuff. Really amazing."

"Thank you."

"I even saw you play once, in Massachusetts. The *Hard Raines* tour. Absolutely incredible. I still have the t-shirt. My dad took me to the concert." As he remembered his father, his face fell, and the spark of happiness vanished.

"I'm sorry about your dad, Andreas."

He nodded and swallowed.

"We're here to see your mom. Is she in?"

They found Helga on the back patio. She sat in an Adirondack chair with her back to them, wrapped up in a blanket and lost in thought. Silver moonlight glimmered on the ski trail in front of her, and the fir trees swayed in the wind. The air was crisp and cold enough to keep the decent base they had on the slopes from melting, Holly noted. A fire roared in a stone-walled pit, and the glass of wine resting on the arm of Helga's chair glowed a warm ruby red, illuminated by the flames behind it.

Holly walked around to the other side of the fire. As she passed Helga, she noticed that her skin looked almost translucent in the light. She wore a thick, baggy white turtleneck sweater, warm black pants, and fur-lined boots.

"Mrs. Lang?"

Helga started and looked at Holly in confusion. Holly wondered if she was intoxicated, but her eyes weren't glassy or bloodshot. Perhaps it was the fog of grief, or maybe worry and guilt? Whatever was troubling her, there wasn't any evidence of the coldness or hardness Gustafson had used to describe her.

"I'm sorry for your loss, Mrs. Lang," she said. "This is my colleague, Detective Raines."

Helga nodded slowly and motioned for them to take a seat. "Chief Finch came over earlier today to confirm that the dental records were a match with my husband."

Andreas stood behind his mother with his hands resting on the back of her chair.

"Unfortunately," Holly began, "we have some more bad news."

Helga tensed and leaned forward. "What is it?" She sounded fearful—almost as if they were about to arrest her for killing Stefan, Holly thought.

"Someone was shot at Verity Falls today."

Helga slumped back in her chair again and looked at them wordlessly.

"What happened?" Andreas asked.

"A man called Frank Stanko and his friend Kenny Fritz were in the vicinity of the abandoned mill. Frank Stanko was shot and killed there."

Andreas opened his mouth, but nothing came out.

Helga recoiled. "What were they doing there?"

Holly explained quickly.

"They were searching for *Bigfoot*?" Helga said in astonishment. "Why, that's ridiculous. You can't be serious."

"I am. They'd heard about the Bigfoot sighting in town."

Helga frowned. "That had to be someone in a Halloween costume, surely?"

Holly ignored the question. "Do either of you know if the mill at Verity Falls has been used recently?"

Andreas shook his head. "No. It was abandoned a few years after World War Two. I could call Phil Montague to confirm it, but I remember my grandfather, Helmut, talking about it. He worked out there during the war."

"That's okay. We talked to Phil earlier about it."

"Then why ask us?" Helga said, sounding annoyed.

"You own the property. You may know more about what it's being used for than your employee does."

She gave a slight nod, conceding Holly's point.

"How long has Phil worked for you?"

"He worked for my husband, not me. He joined the company about four years ago."

Holly changed tack now. "Were you aware that Luke Johnson and Zack Blackthorn had been using the old mill as a campsite?"

"Of course not! What were they doing out there, anyway? It seems like that would be a dangerous place for teenagers to spend time," Helga said, looking at Holly for confirmation.

The air felt cold on Holly's back, but her face was warm from the fire. "You've never been out there?"

"Why would I?"

Raines stretched out his legs and crossed his ankles. "How about you, Andreas? Have you been out there?"

"When I was a kid, I went with my grandfather and my father. It was exciting. I swam in the river and hunted for treasure, but that was a long time ago."

Holly then told them about Luke and Zack's escapades as Bigfoot and the prints they'd left there.

"I had no idea they were doing that," Andreas blurted.

"Are you close with them?" Raines asked.

"Well, I wouldn't say 'close.' But even though Luke and Zack's grandparents didn't like mine, and our families have never been friendly, we get on fine. I go to school with them."

From the trees on her left, Holly heard the beat of wings and watched as a barred owl flew over them, off to hunt. "Do you want to press charges?" she asked, turning back to Helga.

Helga shook her head. "No. I'm sure they did no harm. I'm just relieved they didn't get hurt." She frowned. "You don't think they had anything to do with the shooting, do you?"

"At this point, we don't believe so, but there were at least two other people out there."

"Who?" Andreas looked interested.

"We don't know, but we suspect that someone was using the mill to cut up timber. Kenny Fritz told us that he saw a truck towing a portable saw on a flatbed. There's also relatively fresh sawdust in the mill."

"I'm not aware of any logging going on over there. How about you, Andreas?" Helga asked her son. "Do you know anything about that?"

"Nothing, and if our company were logging there, I would know. Since my father left...uh...died, I've been involved in the operations. Mom handles the financial side of things."

"What do you know about Thaddeus Blackthorn's land?" Holly asked them.

"What land?" Andreas sounded perplexed.

Holly explained about Thaddeus's land and his disagreement with Stefan. "Can you think of a reason why Stefan would say that he intended to grant Thaddeus access, only to deny it later?"

Helga pulled the blanket more tightly around her body and seemed to shrink back against the chair. She shook her head stiffly but said nothing.

"That doesn't sound like my dad," Andreas said, with the earnestness of a loving son. "If you'd asked me a week ago, I probably would have said it was possible, because I thought he'd abandoned us, and for the last two years, I believed he was a changed man. Now we know he's been dead all this time, though, and that he hadn't actually changed, I would say no.

"My father was not a cruel man. He was thoughtful, and not a person to say one thing one day and change his mind the next. You had to know him." Andreas touched his mother lightly on the shoulder. "Tell them, Mom. Dad wouldn't be so cruel to Zack's dad. We're all family in the end. That's what Luke, Zack and I think, anyway."

"I'm sure your father had his reasons," Helga said quietly.

Raines held his hands out to the fire. His jacket was lighter weight compared to Holly's ski parka. "Do you think it would have made a difference to him if he'd known that it was an old-growth forest?"

Andreas perked up at that. "Primeval forest would be of interest to many people, my dad included. It's so rare to find land here that hasn't been logged. Do you know for sure it's old growth? There are hardly any old trees left in the White Mountains.

"I plan to study forestry at university," he told them, his face lighting up. "I'm interested in restoring forests to their pre-logged state. My grandfather had the same interest. As he aged, he began focusing on preserving old-growth areas and learning from them.

He'd seen the landscape change so much from logging, and it made him angry and sad. My father was influenced by him, of course, and he would have wanted to try and save it too. Where exactly does Thaddeus claim the land is?"

Holly stood up and handed him the printout of the map Thaddeus had given her.

Andreas used the flashlight on his cell phone to look at it. "It's not a huge parcel of land—maybe sixty acres, maybe eighty. From this map, it looks like it's on higher terrain, which is probably why it wasn't logged. It was too difficult to reach with logging equipment. If you're right, and this is undisturbed forest, it's going to cause a stir. We'll need to think about keeping it a secret to protect it."

"Can you see how to get there?" Holly asked, looking over his shoulder.

He pointed to a spot on the map. "This is where the mill is. This square was the engine house, and back here was housing. The loggers had homes there at one time. Right here," he ran his finger along a line, "is the old railroad. The train ran right through Verity Falls. It's abandoned now, and the train tracks are probably completely overgrown, but if you can find the tracks, they'll take you fairly close. They run close to the river right here. That's where you'll need to turn away from the train route and follow the river until you see this ridge. A couple of miles from that point and you should be in the area, but you'll need snowmobiles."

"And we have your permission to cross your land?"

Helga stood up to face them, rewrapping the blanket around her like a shawl. "Why do you need to see it? It's just forest. What if something happens to you? We'd be responsible."

"We're police officers," Holly told her. "We can take care of ourselves."

Helga looked at Andreas. There was such love on her face for him that it made Holly wonder what it was like to love someone like that, and she felt a sudden pang of loss for something she'd never had.

"What do you think, Andreas?" Helga asked softly.

"I say yes, and I'd like to go with them. Could you imagine what's been hiding there all this time?"

"We need to do this on our own," Raines told him. "But we'll let you know what we find."

Disappointment flashed across Andreas's face, but he nodded.

Helga walked past them, heading indoors. They followed her, and she led them to the front door. Andreas stayed outside, tending to the fire.

As they were about to leave, Holly said, "How did you know Stefan had left for Germany?"

"It was a planned trip. Stefan traveled there several times a year on business and to see family."

"We're trying to put a timeline together of the days before your husband disappeared. How did you know he was gone?"

"He'd packed his bags and left."

"Did you see him pack them?"

"No, but that wasn't unusual. I didn't spend time watching him pack."

"Did he say he was leaving for Germany?"

"No."

"Then how did you know?"

She said nothing.

"Did you have a fight?"

Helga opened the door and held it as if she needed support. "I don't recall the exact details. It was a long time ago. Now, please go, if you don't mind. I'm exhausted." She said nothing more and stood there waiting for them to leave.

CHAPTER FORTY

Although it was still dark when Holly woke at five fifteen the next morning, it wasn't as dark as it should have been. Dawn was more than an hour away, but snow light from the moon reflecting off the fresh powder cast its magic glow into her room. Pushing back the covers, she hopped excitedly out of bed to take a look, just as she'd done in her days as an Olympic skier. Another couple of inches had fallen while she slept. With delight, she remembered that she was going to spend the day outside in the woods instead of sitting at her desk.

Her eagerness was somewhat diminished when she remembered she'd be spending the day with Raines, but he had the snowmobiles.

Before the prom, she would have jumped at the chance of going snowmobiling with him. They'd been best friends as kids, and sometimes when she was with him now, she found the years slipping away, taking them back to that easy relationship they'd enjoyed growing up.

Then there were those moments that left her feeling as awkward as she had the night she'd kissed him so long ago. She'd lain in bed that night thinking about all the ways she could avoid seeing him again. There had been death, the convent, or even a job on a cruise ship folding towels into cute animals.

Fortunately, she hadn't needed to resort to any of those drastic measures because he'd left town a week later to form his rock band, Acid Raines. For years, she hadn't had to worry about him or how good his lips had felt pressed against hers. But now, unfortunately, he'd given that life up and returned home, upsetting her applecart by swooping in and complicating her life in ways she hadn't imagined.

Holly had arranged to meet him at his place at nine thirty, which gave her plenty of time to catch up with her reports and fill the chief in on what they planned to do later that day.

The coffee pot finished sputtering, and she filled her largest mug to the brim. Sniffing it with pure delight, she switched on the radio for company and sat down at the kitchen table. She lived in a small two-bedroom ski cabin on a wooded, one-acre lot. The kitchen and dining area were at one end of the cabin and opened onto a knotty pine–paneled living room. A vintage pair of skis hung on the wall above the fireplace, and old trapper snowshoes had been nailed to the opposite wall. The bedrooms and bathroom were at the far end of the cabin.

Picking up her pen, she started making notes. With the exception of death notifications, report writing was her least favorite activity. She reminded herself to be precise and concise—a little mantra that helped her focus. As she sat sipping coffee and outlining the main events, she nearly missed the weather update on the radio. More snow was expected in the early afternoon, and there was a high-wind advisory for the White Mountains.

She glanced up at the clock. Six ten. They should leave now for Blackthorn's land. Snow was one thing, but snow and wind in the forest were dangerous. Was it too early to call Raines? Probably not. It was Monday morning and a school day. She decided to call him and let him know she was heading over now. By the time they reached the mill, it would be light. Besides, the snowmobiles had lights.

She picked up her phone and pressed his number, hoping he wasn't still in bed. He didn't answer, so it was a possibility. She left a message about the weather forecast and said that she was on her way over. In ten minutes, she was bundled up in warm layers; gulping her last sip of coffee, she grabbed her snow boots and headed out, then groaned as she saw her driveway. It was almost completely drifted in. She hadn't taken the time to shovel it last night when she'd got home and didn't have time to do it now. Thank God for four-wheel drive, she thought as she tossed her bag into the back of her Jeep and started the engine.

It was still dark when she turned onto Raines's driveway, which someone had taken the time to plow last night—probably Po, who did a lot of work around the place for Raines.

The lights were on in the house when she pulled up. Raines lived in a nineteenth-century farmhouse; it had several smaller structures attached to it that had once comprised the kitchen, a shed for wood, and storage for carriages. The buildings were connected to each other in a row and attached to the side of the huge barn. On the far side of the barn were buildings originally used for the cows and pigs. From the outside, the architecture had not changed. Inside, though, the farmhouse had been modernized to provide open-plan living.

Walking up the steps to the front door, Holly felt a shudder of apprehension; she was glad Abbey Raines was staying with Olivia. After Sherry Raines's death, Holly had used information Abbey had confided to her as evidence to help convict Nate of his wife's murder. Unfortunately, that evidence had consisted of letters that had been placed in Sherry Raines's coffin with her. To the horror of the girls, it had been necessary to exhume her body to retrieve them. Abbey would never forgive Holly for exhuming her mother's body, or for being instrumental in her father's imprisonment. Perhaps that would change now Abbey knew her father was guilty, Holly thought, but she wasn't hopeful.

She knocked on the door and soon heard footsteps, but the tread was too soft to be Raines. Must be Melody, she concluded.

The door opened and Abbey stood there, her expression changing from puzzlement to recognition to outrage in a matter of seconds.

"I thought you were at Olivia's," Holly mumbled. She ached to apologize to the girl for being there, for reminding her of the worst day of her life—and so close to Christmas. Not that there was ever a day when Abbey probably didn't think of it, she thought unhappily. "I'm here to see Raines," she said lamely. "I mean, your Uncle Cal."

"You're not welcome here," Abbey sputtered. She turned on her heel and slammed the door in Holly's face.

Holly jerked back instinctively. She stood there for a moment before deciding to wait for Raines in her Jeep. If he'd somehow failed to hear the door slam, she'd call him in a couple of minutes.

As she was going down the steps, the door opened again. She turned, expecting to see Raines, but it was Melody. She looked like a lost waif, bone thin with hair falling across her brown, expressive eyes.

"Uncle Cal is in the gym," she said softly. "I can show you the way if you'd like."

Holly turned and walked back up the stone steps. He couldn't have got her message if he was working out. Melody said nothing further as Holly followed her through the house. As they passed the kitchen, Holly caught a glimpse of Abbey sitting rigidly with her back to them in one of the saddle stools specially designed for her. They crossed the expansive living room, where a ski lift chair hung from the beams, and walked through double French doors to an area of the house she hadn't been in before. They passed an office and what appeared to be a recording studio.

Melody pointed to a set of floor-to-ceiling glass doors ahead of them. "Uncle Cal is through there. I have to get ready for school."

"They didn't cancel because of the snow, then?" Holly asked.

"I wish," she said, then turned and headed back to the main house.

Holly pushed open the glass doors and entered a bright atrium that housed an indoor swimming pool. The magnificent room had once been the carriage house. A few years before Raines bought the property, it had been converted into a conservatory with a pool in the center. It felt like a tropical paradise in the snow-covered mountains. The air was hot and humid. There were potted palms, hibiscus, lemon, lime and orange trees, and many more lush plants Holly couldn't name. They surrounded the pool, creating an oasis. The wall on her left held glass sliding doors that led out to a patio and fields. To her right, a wall of glass overlooked the end of the driveway and the horses' paddocks. The roof also had glass panels, and in the center of the room was a saltwater swimming pool. The right edge of it, near her, had a concrete beach sloping gradually into the water. Memphis, the family's Chocolate Lab lay there, wet and content, basking in a sunny spot under the glass roof. He raised his head to look at her and then settled back with a satisfied groan.

There was a splashing sound, and she spotted Raines. He was at the far end of the pool, making a turn under the water to come back to her end. He swam with grace and speed, his hands and arms slicing through the water like a cutting machine, his powerful shoulders propelling him toward her.

She stood at the edge of the pool, watching him, feeling hot in her winter clothes.

As he turned his head to breathe, he must have noticed her because he stopped, treaded water and lifted his goggles. "What's happened?"

"Nothing bad. There's a storm coming this afternoon, so we need to head out now."

He swam over to the slope and walked out.

He reminded her of Colin Firth in *Pride and Prejudice*, only in a lot less clothing. No foofy shirt and long pants for him; instead, he wore navy board shorts that were laced up and snug on his toned thighs.

Water gleamed on his lean, muscled body, and she suddenly felt even hotter. She had to get out of the room before she needed to take off her sweater. She feared it would send the wrong signal. "I left you a message."

"I didn't get it."

"Obviously."

He lifted both hands to run them through his wet hair, and his swimming trunks slipped a little.

"Jeez, Raines. Put some clothes on." At least he wasn't wearing a skintight Speedo. That would have been just a little too much for a Monday morning.

"You really know how to crush a man's ego, Jakes."

"I think you can handle it. Now let's get going."

Memphis stood up and followed Raines to a chair where there was a stack of towels. He picked one up, and Holly hoped he'd wrap it around his body, but he began rubbing the dog with it instead. And Memphis loved it. His tail wagged, his body wriggled, and he lifted his head in pleasure.

After Raines had taken care of his dog, he wrapped a clean towel around his waist, and they all headed back to the main house so he could shower and change.

He suggested that Holly grab a coffee while he got ready.

As they stepped into the kitchen, Holly was relieved to find that the girls had left for school, because she didn't want to upset Abbey again.

The coffee smelled amazing. Raines probably roasted his own beans, she thought. As good and tempting as the aromas were, though, she didn't take a cup. They would be out in the woods together with no bathroom.

Ten minutes later, Raines strolled back into the kitchen.

Holly took one look at him and laughed. He was wearing a snowmobile suit that had to be three sizes too big for him.

"You can laugh, Jakes, but wait until I see you in this." He held up another suit.

"Whose is that?"

"It's mine. I'm wearing Po's."

"That's just great."

He grinned. "I haven't got to the good part yet."

"I can hardly wait."

"You have to share a snowmobile with me."

"What! You said you had 'snowmobiles.' That's plural, Raines."

"I do, but I didn't realize that Po had stripped the engine of one of them to get it ready for winter."

"You discovered this when?"

"Last night."

"And you didn't think to call me so I could arrange to have my own?"

"I didn't think you'd mind riding with me." He flashed her a faux sheepish grin.

"It's my second worst nightmare," she snapped.

He quirked an eyebrow. It was one of his unique talents, that ability to quirk a single eyebrow. When they were eight, he'd shown her that he could also wiggle his ears. "So, what's your worst nightmare?"

She didn't hesitate. "Spending the day with you and having to wear your clothes." She pointed to the snowmobile suit he was holding.

He laughed hard but showed no sympathy for her plight.

CHAPTER FORTY-ONE

Raines's pickup struggled to get up the road to Verity Falls in the fresh snow, even with the added weight of the snowmobile in the bed of it. Deciding to stop at the mill instead of pushing on to where they'd found Stubby, Raines hooked up the ramp to the back of the truck, climbed up, started the engine and reversed the snowmobile down it.

Holly felt ridiculous wearing his suit, but she knew the bulk of it would keep her warm. She had the map spread out on the hood of the pickup and was examining their route.

Raines rumbled up beside her.

Before putting on her gloves, she showed him the map. "We need to keep the sun to our right."

"What sun?" he said, glancing up at the overcast sky.

She put the map back in her pocket and zipped it up. "Let's cut up through where we found Stubby, then try to find the old railroad track through the trees and head west until we hit the river. Then we'll head north for about two miles."

He nodded, and then, grinning, jerked his thumb toward the back of the machine. "All aboard the fun train."

And to think, she thought, Angel had given her the chance to buy his old snowmobile a couple of years ago at a reasonable price. Worried about spending the money, she'd declined his offer. If only she'd had the power of foresight, she'd have bought a brand-new one just so she didn't have to ride behind Raines now.

He handed her his helmet, which was smaller than Po's. Sliding it on, she buckled it and noted that it smelled faintly of citrus trees and cedarwood. She wrinkled her nose. It wasn't an unpleasant scent. It just felt like Raines was all over her.

Reluctantly, she climbed onto the snowmobile. Next time Angel offers you a sled, *take it*, she admonished herself.

Her knees slid down around Raines's hips, which fortunately were particularly well padded by Po's monosuit, so although she could smell him, she couldn't feel him. Well, not too much, anyway.

Then he patted her knee to indicate that he was ready to go. A thrill of excitement shot through her, which she decided to put down to the fact that she was on the hunt for a killer, rather than the feel of his hand on her knee.

Raines revved the engine, and they were off. Holly leaned against the backrest and held on to the grab strap. She watched the passing trees along the road they'd walked down just the day before when they'd found the Bigfoot prints, and then Sticks and Stubby. An image of Sticks's face, destroyed by a gunshot, flashed into her mind. Such a terrible waste. More images followed—of broken bodies, of people left to die in pain, of her brother's small body as rescue workers recovered him from the bottom of the mountain. Despite the beautiful landscape and the soothing rumble of the engine, she could feel depression creeping up on her, lurking behind her like a creature in the snow. She wanted to yell at Raines to go faster, fast enough to outrun the memories. But there was no escaping; she knew that from bitter experience. She drew in a breath, and suddenly felt as though the helmet were suffocating her, as if the images were trapped in there, pressing in on her. She wanted to rip the helmet off and let the icy wind rip the thoughts away. She closed her eyes, willing her heart to stop pounding.

She felt the snowmobile slowing, heard the high whine of the engine dwindle to a stutter, and opened her eyes. They had reached the brick building and the clearing where Sticks had been shot.

Raines turned his head this way and that, scanning the area. He pointed off to the right where some trees had been cleared. The space was almost overgrown with young beech and hemlock trees, ferns and bunchberry dogwood, but it looked like a trail.

That must be the old train track Andreas had shown them on the map, Holly decided. She tapped him on the shoulder and gave him the thumbs up to indicate that she agreed, and he drove forward.

The trail was bumpy now. The forest undergrowth, hiding fallen branches and rotted stumps, made for a rough and treacherous ride. Raines wrestled the handlebars like he had a bull by the horns, and they kept going, bouncing up and down, heading deeper into the woods.

The snow wasn't too deep because it was only December, but fresh powder plumed up around them, and tree limbs bowed under the weight of the snow. If it hadn't been for the loud *braaap* of the engine that sounded like a million angry bees, it would have been magical.

Eventually, they reached the river. Snow was mounded on boulders by its edge, but the water hadn't frozen. It was shallow here and rocky, and the water ran fast. Standing on either side of the river were the remains of a low bridge that had been washed away decades ago. Not too far downstream from there was the swimming hole she'd visited in high school.

Raines twisted the handlebars and turned the machine away from the train tracks toward the river. They ran along the riverbank now, weaving in and out of trees and shrubs. At one point, they had to head further into the forest as large boulders the size of small houses blocked their route, and they discovered a road that hadn't been on the map. Then, all of a sudden, the forest ended. Before them, acres of trees had been clear cut. Some of the cleared land was on a steep ridge.

Raines stopped the snowmobile, and Holly slipped off the sled to survey the devastation. It looked war-torn, as if bombs had been dropped in the middle of the mountains. Only stumps remained; some were enormous platforms that looked big enough for a helicopter to land on. A few trees of lower value had been left standing, ones that were either diseased or crooked. Deep gouges in the earth from heavy-duty logging vehicles that had worked the land were visible, even though snow covered the ground.

Holly removed her helmet and was greeted by the terrible silence of a land laid to waste. On this stripped land, there would be no "who-cooks-for-you" call of the barred owl, no forest for peregrine falcons to hunt in. There were fewer trees near the river now for nesting bald eagles, and less habitat for moose to feed on leaves, buds, and twigs. Before them lay the evidence of greed with no thought for either the forest's vulnerable residents or the trees' regeneration.

Holly felt sick to her stomach.

Raines came to stand by her. "Unfortunately, we have our answer," he said quietly. "Someone has been logging on Thaddeus Blackthorn's land."

"Thaddeus could have done this," Holly mused aloud. "And killed Stefan because he tried to stop him."

Raines lifted his visor. "It's a possibility."

"It's got to be better odds than a possibility, Raines; I'm thinking it's a likelihood. And somehow Justin stumbled onto it. As a forest ranger, he could have been out in the area and spotted logging trucks."

Raines shook his head. "This clearing doesn't look recent. Justin has only been working for the Forest Service for six months."

Holly watched the wind pick up and blow snow across the barren land. "There's another way to look at it. Stefan could have logged it illegally, and Thaddeus found out."

"That would mean your friend Phil Montague had to know about it. He's the operations manager for the timber company, but he was right there with us when Justin was shot," Raines pointed out.

Holly stamped her feet. The temperature was dropping. She was glad she had on Raines's monosuit. "Stubby told me that we're looking for two people. Thaddeus didn't have an alibi for Justin's shooting, and he would need equipment to log his land. With Stefan out of the way, Thaddeus and Phil would be free to use Blackthorn Timber's equipment to do it. I don't think Helga or Andreas are involved enough in the operations of the company to know if the machines are not where they should be."

"What about Helga?" Raines said. "You said that Montague was tight with her and Andreas. She had plenty of motive to get Stefan out of the way. The money and business are hers now. Plus, she didn't strike me as someone who wouldn't know what was going on, either. It could be Helga and Montague. Helga wasn't at the auction, so no one checked her alibi. She could have shot Justin. And neither Montague nor Helga were keen on us coming out here."

Holly shrugged noncommittally. "She's hiding something, but is she a killer?"

Gray clouds drifted low, colliding with the distant mountain range. The wind started to pick up as the first flakes began to fall.

Holly put her helmet back on to protect her from the wind and cold and smelled Raines all over again. She flipped up the visor. "Storm's coming in earlier than they predicted."

Raines took out his phone and snapped a few photos. "I've seen enough. Let's head back and interview Montague and Blackthorn, find out where they were when Sticks was shot."

The ride back was easier because they had a route to follow, but Holly was glad to reach the mill. Riding off-trail was bumpy and hard on the back.

Holly got off the sled so Raines could load it. He stood, revved the engine and rode the machine up the ramp into the truck bed. As he switched it off, Holly removed her helmet and tossed it into the pickup.

Turning to Raines, Holly felt something slam into her. Confused, thinking the snowmobile had fallen off the truck, she opened her mouth to shout. Then she heard the distinct metallic racking of a bolt-action rifle, followed by the whip-crack of a supersonic bullet as it passed her ear and slammed into the snowmobile just above her head. Then the pain hit her.

CHAPTER FORTY-TWO

Holly dropped to the ground, rolled under the pickup, and groaned in pain. Her left side felt as if it was on fire.

She scrambled out the other side of Raines's truck as another bullet whined off the metal above her.

"Raines!" she yelled, terrified he'd been hit.

He jumped down off the back of the truck, landing in a squat a few feet away from her before falling back on his butt.

"Are you hit?" she yelled.

"No," he yelled back as he started struggling with his snowmobile suit. "Are you okay?"

"I'm fine," she said even though she knew that she'd been hit. She looked down at her own suit but couldn't see anything. The suit was big and billowed out around her. She ripped off her glove to touch her side. It didn't feel wet, but she checked her fingers. No blood. That was a good sign. The searing pain in her side, though, told her at least part of a bullet had nicked her.

Another shot hit with a thud in the dirt near her feet. She coiled herself as tightly as she could behind the wheel rim and started unzipping her suit to get at her gun. White-hot pain seared through her left side as she moved, and a wave of nausea and dizziness struck her. She sucked in air to steady herself.

Raines managed to yank out his Sig Sauer from its shoulder holster just as another bullet hit a rock no more than six inches from him. He returned fire, but he was out in the open.

"Get over here," she hissed, unholstering her weapon.

He crawled to her, keeping low, and took cover behind the pickup's other rim. It offered the best protection from rifle fire. A bullet could punch a hole right through the skin of his truck and hit him, but the rims had steel in them.

Holly started to feel shaky. "Can you see where the shooter is?"

"Somewhere in the trees on the path to the clearing."

"We're pinned down here," Holly hissed. "The shooter could move through the woods and come up behind us. We're sitting ducks. We need to get into the mill."

"How about I lay down some cover while you run for it?"

In the distance, they heard a snowmobile start and rev. Raines stood up, resting his hands on the hood of his pickup to steady his aim, but the snowmobile was moving away from them.

Raines climbed back up into the bed of his truck and jumped on to his snowmobile. When he turned the ignition switch, nothing happened. He examined the sled and then swore. "It's been hit. The engine has had it."

Holly stood and felt like her side was on fire. Through gritted teeth, she muttered, "We can't go after them in the pickup. We need to call it in."

"There's no cell signal here. We need to get going." He strapped down the sled, jumped back out of the truck bed, yanked off the ramp and loaded it beside the snowmobile, and headed for the driver's door. Holly groaned as she tried to step up into the pickup. It hurt like hell when she stretched.

Raines looked at her. "What's wrong?"

"I've been hit."

"*Jesus!* No! You said you were okay."

"I am okay."

He ran around to her side and moved her hand to look at her left side. "There's a bullet hole in the suit."

"Yeah. Kind of figured that, Raines." She saw panic rising on his face. "I'm fine. Let's get moving. I want to call it in."

"Not until I take a look. Let's take the suit off so we can see what's going on." He took hold of the collar, carefully unzipped the suit all the way down, and let it drop to her feet.

She stepped out of it, wincing.

"No blood," he told her, carefully lifting her layers of sweaters. "You're lucky you had on my suit. If it had been tighter, the shooter would have had a better target to aim at."

She tried to look down but couldn't see anything. His fingers brushed the skin on her stomach. Luckily, the pain from the wound helped to keep her mind off how good his hands felt on her body.

He crouched down to get a better look. "The bullet has grazed your side."

"It feels like they hit me with a blowtorch."

Raines nodded. "It looks like a big oven burn. We need to get you to the hospital."

"I'm fine," she muttered, but didn't feel it. "We need to get moving and call in that BOLO."

"We can call it in on the way to the hospital."

"Raines—"

"Just get in the truck, Jakes, or I'll leave you here."

"You wouldn't dare."

"I thought you knew me better than that," he said. "Now get in."

Holly hoisted herself carefully up onto the seat, butt first, and slowly repositioned herself. "I don't want to go to the hospital. I have a first aid kit at home," she muttered.

Raines put the truck in drive and headed down the bumpy trail as fast as he could without making her wince in pain. He glanced at her. "I never realized how bad your hospital phobia is."

"I don't have a phobia."

"Oh, yeah? Could have fooled me."

She'd spent many painful months in hospitals around the world, recovering from her various skiing injuries, and any kind of medical facility creeped her out completely now. She could walk through the woods in the middle of the night without a care in the world, but walking down a hospital corridor was a whole other matter.

"I just don't like the smell," she said testily. "It's that combination of disinfecting chemicals, bodily fluids and food left on trays."

"I could find you a nose clip if that would help."

"Very funny, Raines."

She winced as he hit a pothole.

He grimaced. "Sorry."

"Just drive, Raines. There's a chance we can catch the shooter if we can call in a roadblock."

He reached the main road, took a right and tore down it, heading for town.

A few minutes later, as Holly lay back on an exam table letting a doctor tend to her injury, she could hear the chief arrive at the nurses' station. She heard his voice rise and fall, sounding strained with worry, then she heard Raines tell him everything was going to be okay. When the doctor left the examination room, Holly sat up gingerly, pulled on her shirt and sweater as carefully as she could and walked out to meet them. The chief, his face pale, hurried over to her.

"How are you?"

"I'm fine."

"Don't pee on my leg and tell me it's raining, Jakes. You look like someone dragged you through a hedge backward."

"Oh, gee. Thanks a lot."

He squinted at her. "Working with you is going to give me a heart attack."

"I'm okay. Really. The bullet barely grazed me." It was throbbing like hell, but he didn't need to know that.

"Raines can take you home, and I'll call you in the morning."

"I'm not going home. We're on to something, or they wouldn't have taken the risk of shooting at us. And it's my case. I'm not losing it to Gustafson."

The chief grunted. "That's Lieutenant Gustafson."

"Chief, I have to see this through."

"You're injured and you can't shoot."

"First, it's my left side that's hurt, and I shoot with my right hand. Second, I can move just fine." She raised her left arm for emphasis and had to fight not to groan.

Chief Finch grunted again and scowled dubiously.

Raines gave Holly a look that seemed to say, Good luck on getting the chief to agree with you.

"Let's go to the cafeteria and get some food," Finch said at length. "You look hungry. You can fill me in on what you know so far, and after I've seen you eat, I'll decide."

That was fine with her. She was starving, and for once, didn't mind hanging around the hospital.

Holly sat at the table and finished off the last bite of her egg salad sandwich, which, she had to admit, wasn't actually all that bad. It didn't have too much mayo, and there was just enough onion to flavor it, not overpower it. Even the cafeteria was pleasant, she noted with surprise. It was located on the ground floor, in a wing at the end of the hospital that was more like a combination sunroom and café, and it overlooked the forest and mountains. There was no sun now, though; the wind was blowing the snow sideways across the winter landscape.

All Raines had eaten was yogurt and a banana, and he'd finished fast. While Holly had tucked into her sandwich, he'd told Finch about the shooting and the logging, and that they wanted to interview Phil Montague, Thaddeus Blackthorn and Helga Lang. They now had two incidents where they needed alibis: Sticks' shooting, and now Holly's.

The chief asked, "Who out of those three knew you were heading out there today?"

"All three of them," Holly said, and sipped her hot chocolate. The chief had insisted she order it because it was good for shock, he'd told her. She never turned down hot chocolate, and surprisingly, she felt calmer drinking it.

The chief pushed his plate to the side. "I can't see Helga Lang taking an ax to her husband."

"No, but if she's having an affair with Phil Montague, or just working with him, he could have done it. He worked at the lumber yard with Stefan, and Stefan is not going to be suspicious if there's an ax laying around. All he has to do is wait for Stefan to turn his back, and it's *whack*." Holly hit the table with her palm, making the chief jump.

"Okay, Jakes. Enough of the theatrics. Go talk to Blackthorn first. See if he looks guilty as hell when you start talking about how all his old-growth trees are gone."

She beamed at him.

"And keep Raines with you. You work this together. No flying solo. Got me? We don't know who took a shot at you. I need to call Bliss Jarvis and give her an update. She'll probably want to start redirecting resources here. She's not finding much on her end of things, and neither are the state police or the FBI. Justin's boss, the Judge, and his sister have all gone over his movements for the last month and can't find anything suspicious. They interviewed a bunch of people, but no one has raised an alarm. It's been over forty-eight hours now, and the only hot leads we have are coming from your end of the investigation. The more I look at it, the more I think you're on to something."

CHAPTER FORTY-THREE

Although Holly wasn't keen to let Raines tag along with her, she wasn't so sure she could drive by herself. She knew she couldn't turn a steering wheel without causing herself more pain. She sighed and got to her feet. If they didn't get moving, there was a big chance she'd be pushed into the backseat of her investigation. There were too many investigators and too few leads.

"Let's get out of here," she said to Raines, reaching to pick up the chocolate chip cookie the chief had also bought her.

She needed to change, so they headed over to her house first and talked suspects and strategy on the way. They didn't come up with anything better than what they had, which was to interview Thaddeus Blackthorn, followed by Phil Montague and finish with Helga Lang. At that point, they would reassess the case.

Raines pulled into her driveway, which now had over a foot of snow covering it. He pulled up as close as he could to the front door for her.

As she got out, he asked, "Do you need help undressing?"

She craned her head around to get a good look at him, to see if he was serious or not.

His eyes glinted in the low light, but his face was unreadable—or had she seen a muscle twitch at the corner of his mouth?

"I'd rather be shot again." She slammed the door and stomped off—or tried to. Her side hurt too much to do it properly. But in her mind, she stomped all the way into the house, huffing and puffing like a big bad wolf at the sound of his laughter behind her, which was far too deep and rich and way too sexy.

Holly undressed slowly, removing the right side of each layer of clothing first. That way, she could just slip all of them over her head at once and let them slide down her left arm without having to lift it. The wound was beginning to feel stiff and really sore.

She examined her sweaters. She'd worn three layers to go snowmobiling that morning. Layering was an old skiing habit. First layer: thermals. Second layer: turtleneck. Third layer: sweater. She stuck a finger right through the holes where the bullet had slashed all three layers. It struck her then just how lucky she'd been, and her legs went a little weak.

After she'd changed, they headed over to Raines's place to switch vehicles. He parked his pickup, leaving the snowmobile on it, and ran in to check on Abbey and Melody. Then he let Po know what was happening so that he could keep an eye on the girls that night.

Holly sat in his Suburban, waiting for it to warm up while he was inside. She had elected to stay here, not wanting to see Abbey again and upset her. The wind was howling now, with gusts that even managed to rock the massive SUV a little. This was the worst December Holly could remember in a long time, but she loved it.

Raines came back looking glum.

"What happened?"

"The girls aren't talking to each other, and Abbey isn't talking to me."

"They'll get over it."

"I'm not so convinced."

Holly wasn't convinced, either. She'd witnessed too many family feuds take a turn for the worst, and knew that many people never, in fact, got over it. "Time will help," she said, knowing that this, too, was not always the case. She just hoped for all of their sakes that it was true.

Raines didn't comment any further as he put the truck in gear and headed back to town.

Holly decided to change the topic. "How much do you think Thaddeus Blackthorn would make from the timber?"

"Why?"

"You saw his house. The guy is loaded. Did he really need the money?"

"You can look like you have money but be mortgaged up to the hilt," he told her. "He could really need the money. I own a lot of land, and I've been offered anywhere from eight hundred dollars an acre to two thousand here in North Caxton by loggers, but none of the land has old-growth trees on it."

"Okay. Let's say Thaddeus has sixty acres and all of that is logged at two thousand an acre," Holly theorized. "That's only one-hundred and twenty thousand, minus the expense of logging it and transporting it. It's not worth it."

Raines shook his head. "Old growth is worth a lot more. I own land out west that has a handful of old, magnificent redwood trees on it. I also have some land in Virginia with a couple of acres of old beech, oaks, hickories, and white pine on it. In Alaska, I have old cedar, spruce, and hemlock. These trees are worth more because there's not much old growth left in the country."

Sometimes it took Holly by surprise that Raines had so much money and land. When they were growing up, his dad had been the police chief in town; his mom had been a homemaker until she'd taken off for the lights of Hollywood, never to be seen again. "I didn't know you had a thing for trees, Raines."

"It's called asset diversification. One of my brokers is big on buying land. A lot of it is undeveloped forest." He continued, "I've been aware of illegal logging for a long time now. Even old trees protected in national forests aren't safe. Individual trees are targeted by thieves and sell for tens of thousands of dollars. Poachers will even hack off burls from ancient redwood trees to sell to specialized markets. Some experts estimate that illegal logging is a hundred-billion-dollar business.

"But it's not just illegal loggers taking the old trees. Right now, timber companies—and even people in our government—are pushing to log eight-hundred-year-old trees in Alaska's Tongass National Forest. It's a tragedy, especially when there are plenty of second-generation trees available."

"It's depressing," was all Holly could think of to say, and she did feel depressed. She looked out of the window but saw nothing except snow. She had grown up in the mountains surrounded by beautiful forest, clean running rivers, and eagles soaring overhead. She couldn't imagine it stripped bare. "*If* the trees on Thaddeus Blackthorn's land were old growth, how much could he make?"

"They could make over ten thousand a tree, even more."

"You know a lot about it."

"Musicians are aware of the problem because some of our instruments were made out of wood that was illegally logged. Back in 2012, musicians released a statement in support of the Lacey Act, which helps make sure the wood used in our instruments, and in other industries, is legally sourced."

"And you talked to Justin Jarvis about this the night of the auction?"

"We discussed the fretboard on my guitar. It's made of rosewood, which is protected, but there's still widespread trafficking depleting resources. Justin was curious whether I knew about the law."

"It's interesting that logging connects all four deaths."

Raines said nothing as he drove through the covered bridge and pulled up in front of Thaddeus Blackthorn's house.

Thaddeus answered their knock and showed them to the living room where Zack had been sitting the day before. He seemed eager to hear what they had found. He sat in a leather armchair near the wide, cut-stone fireplace that had a thick, three-foot log burning in it. Raines and Holly took the couch, and Raines proceeded to tell him about the clear-cutting.

"Stefan was a real bastard," he said, looking genuinely angry. "I went to him about the land, and he used it against me."

"Where were you this morning?"

"Here. I've been here all day."

"And Saturday evening from six until ten? Where were you then?"

"Here. At home."

"And was anyone with you either of those days?"

"Zack was here on Saturday."

Raines shook his head. "Zack was at the mill over in Verity Falls Saturday night until around nine and didn't get home until ten, according to his statement."

Thaddeus said nothing.

"How about this morning?"

"I was at home."

"Was your wife with you?"

"No."

"Where is she?"

"Zack and Lilly are in Boston. Zack had an interview at a couple of universities today. Why do you need to speak to her? She already gave the police a statement after the shooting at the Witch Cross Inn."

Raines ignored the question. "When is she returning?"

"They'll be home tomorrow morning. Look, you can't possibly consider me a suspect. It was *my* land that was robbed."

"How do we know you didn't log it yourself, and Stefan caught you?"

He stood up in agitation. "That's crazy. Consider it for a minute. All I'd be in trouble for was trespassing over Stefan's land. I own the trees. I wouldn't kill Stefan over that. Besides, look around you." He held his arms out wide. "Does it look like I need the money?"

"What happened the last time you saw Stefan?"

"I already told you."

"Tell us again."

"I met with Stefan to discuss access to my land. At first, he was sympathetic and said he'd either give me access to the land or buy it from me. Then he changed his mind."

"Did he change his mind right then and there?" Holly asked.

"No. It was later."

"What happened in that meeting?"

"Well, we didn't actually meet. Stefan sent Phil Montague to inform me that he had changed his mind and wanted to honor his grandfather's wishes that the trees be preserved. Phil let it slip that Stefan had also commented that he didn't need to buy the land to protect it because I couldn't reach it without his permission."

"Did you see Stefan at any time after that?"

"No."

"Are you sure?"

"Yes. I even went to Blackthorn's to look for him. I had something to tell him."

"What was that?"

He hesitated. "I wanted to tell him to go to hell."

They fell silent for a moment. Raines and Holly let the silence stretch on to see what he'd say. It was a common police tactic and very effective.

Thaddeus hunched his shoulders defensively. "Look. I know that sounds like I had a motive, but the money wouldn't have been worth it."

"You were angry with him, though. And there was bad blood in the family. You could have snapped," Raines said.

"I didn't snap," Thaddeus roared, his temper exploding. Then, with a look of realization that he'd just snapped in front of them, he dropped back down into his chair. "I didn't do it, and I'd like you to leave now."

CHAPTER FORTY-FOUR

The wind had died down while they were inside, but the snow was falling more heavily now. Raines brushed snow off the windshield on the driver's side of the SUV, and Holly did the same. Brushing snow off their coats, they got in.

Raines started the engine and ran the defrost. "He wasn't telling us everything," he said, looking up at the house. Thaddeus stood in the window watching them.

"You picked up on that, too? I wonder what it was he really wanted to tell Stefan when he went to look for him."

"I don't know, but he looked surprised when we told him about the clear-cutting."

"True," Holly said, "But he knew we were coming out here, which gave him plenty of time to practice his outrage."

The windshield cleared and Raines flipped the ventilation system over to floor heat and reversed down the driveway. "Let's say we believe Thaddeus. What's interesting is it was Montague who told him that Stefan had reneged on the deal, not Stefan—which means Stefan could already have been dead at that point."

"Yes. Thaddeus may not have needed the money from the trees, but Montague is just a manager. The money could be more appealing to him, and he had access to all of the equipment needed to do it, especially once Stefan was out of the way. We know Stefan was probably murdered with an ax. And where are you going to find an ax?" she asked.

"A lumber yard," Raines responded.

"Right, and it would be easy for Montague to kill an unsuspecting Stefan," Holly continued. "After all, he wouldn't be suspicious if he saw an ax in Montague's hands. Not surrounded by all that timber."

"And then there's Helga," Raines said thoughtfully. "She wouldn't tell us how she knew that Stefan had left for Germany.

She's been vague about it. Perhaps Montague and Helga are in on it together?"

Holly unzipped her coat. "Assuming that Justin's case is related to Stefan's, Phil Montague was right there with us when Justin was shot. We know there was at least one other person involved in Sticks's death because Stubby said someone was driving the truck while whoever it was shot at them. That means, if Helga was working with Montague, she shot Justin."

"Hmm. I'm not sure about that."

"Nobody checked her alibi that night because she wasn't even on the radar."

Raines shook his head. "I like Thaddeus and Montague working as a team better than Helga and Montague."

"Why? Because she's a woman?"

"No. It's because Helga didn't strike me as someone who would gun down a twenty-three-year-old."

"Okay," she said. "What if we take Justin out of the equation, and it's just Stefan and Sticks?"

"Why would Thaddeus drop Montague in it if he was working with him?"

"Who knows? Either way, Montague knew about the land, and he had access to the equipment and the expertise to pull it off. We can make an argument for the second person being either Thaddeus or Helga or even someone else we don't know about. But Montague fits."

CHAPTER FORTY-FIVE

It was six fifteen Monday night, and they both decided the most likely place to find Montague was at Blackthorn Timber. The yard hadn't been plowed yet, but Raines pulled into the same spot they'd parked in the day before without a problem. There was only one other vehicle there, a black pickup with a Blackthorn Timber decal on the door. Lights were on in the office, and although the yard looked empty, the floodlights were still on. Holly watched snow eddy in the wind.

They entered the office, but Montague wasn't there. They heard the low rumble of an engine. It sounded like a piece of heavy equipment moving slowly.

They headed back outside, and in the distance, near the sawmill, they spotted a massive wheel loader moving toward them. Attached to it was a grapple arm, with jaws that opened to scoop and lift logs off a truck. This particular grapple looked like it could lift a whole truckload of timber, Holly noted.

The machine slowed to a stop. Phil Montague stepped out of it and climbed down, his back toward them.

Raines pointed at him and yelled, "Hey, you. We want a word."

Montague turned, took one look at them and started running.

"Call it in, Holly," Raines yelled at her as he sprinted after Montague.

Holly yanked out her cellphone, hit the number for dispatch and told them to send backup. Looking up, she could see that Raines was gaining on Montague.

As she shoved her cellphone back in her pocket and sprinted after them. Searing pain flared in her side, but she kept moving, only to watch in horror as Montague picked up a heavy chain that looked like it was used to secure logs and started swinging it at Raines.

Raines tried to pull out his weapon, but the chain struck him across the arm and wrapped around his body. He lost his grip on his gun, and it skidded across the ground and slid under a shed.

Montague let go of the chain and started running towards the log yard. Behind the logs was nothing but forest all the way to Maine.

Raines shook off the chains and went after him, although he was moving a little more slowly now. He'd been hurt, Holly thought.

She slowed to a halt. There was no point trying to catch up with them on foot, but if she could somehow beat Montague around the other side of the yard and cut him off before he had a chance to reach the woods, maybe she could stop him.

Raines still had the keys to his SUV, but she spied the wheel loader Montague had just exited and ran over to it. She gave a silent prayer that the keys were still in it. Climbing up the steps was difficult because she had to stretch for the handles to hoist herself up, and the motion pulled on her wound. Ignoring the pain, she gamely hauled herself up into the cab and sat down in the driver's chair, where she quickly assessed the machine. In the center of the console was a steering wheel with a knob on it to help the operator move it. On the floor to the left of the steering column was a pedal that looked like a brake, and on the right side was the accelerator. There was a joystick that she assumed moved the jaws that lifted the logs. The layout was strikingly similar to the inside of a snowcat's cab, except there, the joystick moved the blade.

Holly had once dated a snowcat driver who worked at Hurricane Mountain. He had let her drive the resort's four-hundred-thousand-dollar machine up and down the mountain at night when he was grooming the trails. After they were done, they'd picnicked at the top of the mountain under the moon and stars. It had been one of the most romantic things she'd ever done with a man, she thought, then gave her head a quick shake. No time for fond memories now, she told herself. On with business.

The key was still in the ignition—luck was with her. She turned it, and a digital display lit up. Now, how to lift the grapple up off the ground? She pulled back on the joystick, and she watched it rise. Then she pressed down on the accelerator, but the enormous machine didn't move. *Damn.* She looked around the console, her brow furrowed in concentration. She remembered that the snowcat had had a parking switch, and sure enough, there was a red parking switch to her right. She pressed it, then pressed the accelerator again, and she was rolling.

She headed off in the direction she'd seen Raines and Montague running, and moments later, her heart almost stopped.

Montague was up on a log pile that was the size of a transport truck, and Raines was scrambling up on top of it, hot in pursuit. Montague was half-running, half-skipping, trying to cross the stack of raw timber instead of going around it. He struggled to keep his footing on the snow-covered trunks, slipping and stumbling in his haste to escape.

She swung her head around to Raines again—and her eyes widened in horror as she noticed the far end of the log pile start to roll to the left. Her stomach flipped.

"Raines," she yelled inside the cab, but he couldn't hear her over the rumble of the engine.

Slamming her foot down on the accelerator, she headed straight for the stack. Raines was on the right, and Montague was on her left. Out of the corner of her eye, she saw Montague sink and disappear into the pile of rolling logs. The whole stack was moving now, and she aimed to stop the stack from rolling over Raines and crushing him. She rammed the wheel loader into the pile.

The shock of it nearly threw her out of the cab, but she held onto the steering wheel and prayed.

Logs pushed her back like she was on a tidal wave, and the wheel loader bucked and rocked and almost toppled, but as she'd hoped it would, the grapple arm got caught up in the tree trunks. The machine stalled, but the logs piling up on the grapple steadied it.

The whole thing was over in seconds.

She scrambled out of the cab and spotted Montague's bloodied upper body, sprawled like a broken rag doll, among the timbers. He'd been crushed to death.

She couldn't see Raines. She started yelling but didn't get a response. An image of Melody's and Abbey's faces flashed into her mind. "Oh, God. Raines, where are you?"

She ran around to the other side of the wheel loader and spotted him. He was on the ground, on his back, and he wasn't moving. The grapple had deflected most of the logs to the other side of the wheel loader. A few had rolled the other way, but not on to Raines.

She ran over to him, not caring about the pain in her side, and dropped to her knees. He was bleeding from a gash near his temple. She felt for a pulse, but all she could feel was her own because it was pounding so hard. She almost sobbed in frustration as she tried to remember which finger to use to test for a pulse, but she couldn't think straight.

Instead, she put her hand near his mouth to check if he was breathing. She felt nothing. She placed her ear there instead to see if she could hear him breathing.

Then she felt arms wrap around her, and she turned her face back to his. He pulled her down on top of him, and his lips found hers. At first, his kiss was soft and gentle, but it became harder and more demanding. Holly had a flashback to the high school gym. As a teen, he'd been a great kisser. He'd been her first kiss, but this was out-of-this-world kissing. There was something desperate to it. A desperate need to grab at life. Her stomach flipped and her heart raced. And then she remembered Olivia.

She tried to push away from him, but Raines held her tight, as though he'd wrapped those logging chains around her, and then he rolled her over in the snow, in the middle of the log yard, and kissed her even harder. It took her at least a minute—could have been five, she mused later—before she had the wits to push at his chest, and this time mean it.

He lifted his mouth from hers, and breathed, "Holly…"

She saw blood run down his face. "You're bleeding. You have a head wound." Which, she thought, was probably why he'd lost his senses and kissed her in the first place.

She heard sirens blaring in the distance.

He got to his knees, then scooted back on his heels, giving her room to stand while he steadied himself for a moment before trying the same. Taking his hand in hers, Holly helped him to his feet.

He brushed at the blood and winced.

"Montague?" he asked.

"There's no chance to interview him. He's dead."

CHAPTER FORTY-SIX

The next morning, Holly was home, soaking in her bathtub with the hot water running. The bubble bath smelled of junipers. The scent and warmth smoothed her out. She found her thoughts drifting to Raines and that kiss. It had been sensational, and she hadn't wanted it to end. She flushed crimson and knew it wasn't from the heat of the water. But it was a pipedream. It would never work with him, she knew. Yesterday, after the paramedics had cleared him of having a concussion, she'd asked Angel to drive him home.

He'd looked bewildered at first, and then his face had hardened.

The phone rang, startling her out of her reverie.

It was the chief reporting that there had been an anonymous tip in the Justin Jarvis shooting. Lieutenant Gustafson and Lieutenant Hendricks had followed up on it and had found a weapon, and right at that moment, they were arresting Skip Johnson. The task force was due to convene in the chief's conference room in half an hour.

She rinsed off quickly in the shower, dressed carefully as the gunshot burn on her side still smarted like the dickens, then made her way through the deep snow on her driveway to her Jeep, and drove into work faster than she should have.

The Caxton PD buzzed like a giant beehive. Everyone had their tasks to do to keep the case moving forward to its conclusion.

Raines stood outside the conference room. She knew that he was waiting for her. Seeing his bruised and cut face, she faltered, and her heart fluttered.

"I need to talk to you, Holly," he whispered as she prepared to walk past him into the conference room.

She forced herself not to weaken. "No, Raines. It was a mistake."

He looked genuinely hurt by that. Was he crazy? He was the one dating Olivia while taking a timeout to kiss *her*. Obviously, he didn't consider that his rock and roll days were over if he wanted to date two women at the same time.

When Raines had left town and hit it big all those years ago, she'd read the tabloids like a junkie for news of him. There were reports of wild parties, lots of women, even proud photos of him with his arms wrapped around nearly-naked women who all looked like supermodels. There was a photo of him skinny-dipping in the Indian Ocean with several women at the same time. In the background, there had been a sleek, expensive, luxury yacht with a helicopter sitting on one of the decks. She'd marveled at that.

Then there was that exotic—no, erotic—photo of him on a motorcycle with a bikini-clad woman sitting in his lap. She was sprawled backward across the gas tank and was holding onto the handlebars in a wanton pose. Fleetingly, Holly imagined herself doing that with him, and felt a deep, guilty thrum of excitement.

His eyes glinted a gunmetal gray now. "Twice you've told me that you've made a mistake."

"And both times I've been right," she said, keeping her voice low so no one could hear them.

It had been a mistake to kiss him last night. Just as it had been a mistake to kiss him in high school. And she had told him so back then. He'd been in love with Sherry, but she'd dumped him to date his brother, and Holly knew he'd only kissed her that night in the high school gym because he couldn't have Sherry. She hadn't been prepared to play second fiddle back then, and she wouldn't be the other woman now. No way was she prepared to do anything that hurt Olivia, who'd been nothing but kind and supportive to his family. The woman was practically a saint in terms of how much she helped him with the girls. He should be ashamed of himself, she thought angrily. And besides that, there was Abbey, who would never be comfortable with Holly in their lives.

"Why?" he asked.

She struggled to find words that wouldn't make her sound jealous. "We're different people, Raines. Different values."

"Different *values*?" His voice was raw with emotion. "I see." Without another word, he turned and strode into the conference room.

She waited for a moment, trying to get her thoughts together. She had to focus on the case, instead of on Raines and how hurt he'd looked. On how bad she felt. She took a deep breath to steady herself and stepped into the room.

Around the conference table were Chief Finch, Bliss Jarvis, and Brady Coles from the FBI. Raines had taken a seat between Bliss and Brady. Holly chose the chair at the end of the table on the same side, so she couldn't see him unless she craned her neck.

The chief gave her a calculating look. He was the only one sitting on his side of the table. "I was about to play the recording of the anonymous tip." He waited for them to settle down before hitting the play button.

A creepy, computer-generated voice claimed that Skip Johnson had shot Justin Jarvis and the weapon was in his car. That was it. Nothing more, but it had been enough.

Bliss was telling them that she'd requested a trace on the phone when Lieutenant Gustafson marched into the conference room. He held up a rifle that was wrapped in plastic.

"I've got it!" he roared victoriously, as if he'd just defeated an army to get it. With great pride, he set it down on the conference table so they could all get a good look at his spoils of war. "We found this old 1903 Springfield on the floor behind the driver's seat, hidden under a blanket. Ballistics will match. I just know it."

Lieutenant Dennis Hendricks from the state police followed him in and took a seat opposite Holly.

"Is there a serial number?" Bliss asked.

"It's been filed down."

Brady Coles said, "I'll send it to our lab. They may be able to get a number."

"Let's dust it for prints first," Bliss suggested.

Gustafson sat down next to Hendricks. "It's a real shame, but the weapon looks like it was wiped down, and the rifle butt was wrapped in a silicone cloth."

"What else do we have on Johnson?" Bliss asked.

The chief placed his forearms on the table and leaned forward. "He didn't have an alibi for the shooting. He said he was upstairs looking for aspirin and then lay down in his room for a time."

"I saw him the following morning," Raines added, his voice calm now. "And he was a mess. Drinking heavily, and he appeared as if he had something serious weighing on his conscience."

Bliss looked at Hendricks and Gustafson. "Did he say anything when you brought him in?"

"He said he didn't do it," Gustafson responded. "And then he lawyered up."

"A jury likes a motive," she said. "Why would he kill Justin?"

Holly spoke up. "If we can connect the Stefan Lang homicide with Justin's death and assume that Skip Johnson and Phil Montague were working together, the motive is probably money."

Gustafson stared at Holly as if there was something wrong with her. She shifted uncomfortably in her seat but continued. "Thaddeus Blackthorn said the Johnsons couldn't afford to send their son to community college. When we asked him how the Johnsons could have paid for the expensive remodel of the inn, Thaddeus guessed that they used either Skip's winnings from sailing races or his winnings from gambling. Thaddeus said he was a good poker player."

"My team could look into his finances," Lieutenant Hendricks offered.

"Mark my words," the chief muttered. "It always comes down to either money or jealousy or a combination of the two."

"But what's his motive for killing Justin?" Bliss asked.

"Is it possible that Justin was in the forest near the clear-cut area and saw something?" Holly asked.

Bliss shook her head. "No. I've spoken with his supervisor. Justin was way up in the north, near the Canadian border, which ties in with what his mom told me."

They all looked at each other.

Brady Coles said, "You don't always find a motive. Justin could have overheard Skip Johnson and Phil Montague talking to each other the night of the auction. It could be that simple, but we'll never know if they don't want to tell us."

"A gun on the floor behind the driver's seat with the serial number filed down isn't enough," Bliss said. "We need more. We need a confession. The chief and I will take a run at Johnson when the lawyer gets here."

Gustafson raised an eyebrow. "With all due respect, is that wise? He's accused of shooting your nephew. Maybe Hendricks and I should take a run at him."

"Thank you for pointing that out." There was steel in her voice, but she took a moment to consider the consequences. "Okay. Dennis and the chief can do it, but we need a confession. The weapon alone isn't enough."

"He doesn't have an alibi," Brady Coles pointed out. "That helps the case."

"True, but we need more. And we need to confirm whether Justin's death is connected to the Stefan Lang and Frank Stanko homicides."

The chief scratched his belly. "It feels like a stretch connecting Stefan Lang with Justin and Frank Stanko. Stefan was killed two years ago with an ax. Justin was shot with a rifle, and Stanko was killed by a shotgun blast."

"Except," interjected Raines, "we do know that when Frank Stanko was shot, there were two people there—the shooter and the truck driver, who just happened to be towing a portable sawmill."

"That's if Kenny Fritz saw it right," Gustafson commented, not even bothering to look at Raines. "He was heading right for a tree."

Bliss folded her arms and leaned back in her seat. She was pale and looked like she hadn't slept since the shooting. "We need to connect Skip Johnson with Phil Montague. If they were working together, someone must have seen them together or know something. I want that missing link."

"We haven't interviewed Lilly Blackthorn yet," Holly said. "She's due back from Boston today. And Thaddeus may know something about a connection between Johnson and Montague. Before the tip came in pointing the finger at Skip Johnson, Raines and I were considering Thaddeus or Helga as possible accomplices to Stefan's murder. Both of them benefitted financially from his death."

Hendricks clicked the button on his pen distractedly. "The defense could use either one of them to create reasonable doubt."

Bliss nodded. "You're right, Dennis. We need to show that we've explored all leads and were able to rule them out." She paused for a moment. "I want Holly and Cal to finish the investigative trail they were on. We'll see where it leads. I also want to know who the tipster was, and how they knew there was a gun in Skip Johnson's vehicle. I'll let you run that down, Dennis."

"Sarah Mooney is a pain in the neck," Gustafson said. "She's a fruit-loop and calls in anything. It could have been her."

"What do you think, Holly?" the chief asked. "You've had the most contact with her."

"I don't think she would have disguised her voice. She would have just called us to report it."

Raines clasped his hands behind his head. "What I want to know is how did someone know it was a rifle if it was hidden under a blanket. Could you tell it was a rifle?"

"Yes," responded Gustafson.

At the same moment, Hendricks shook his head and said, "No. It wasn't easy to see on the floor. The rear windows are tinted, and the blanket was brown."

"Gus, will you follow up on the blanket?" Bliss asked. "See if you can find a matching one inside the inn."

Gustafson's eyes seemed to bulge at that request, and a vein throbbed on his forehead, but he said nothing, just nodded abruptly.

When the meeting ended, Holly followed the chief to his office, while Bliss waited in the conference room with Brady Coles until Skip Johnson's lawyer arrived.

"How's the side?" Finch asked, watching her face.

"It's fine."

He narrowed his eyes. "You sure? You don't look fine. You look about as uncomfortable as a short-tailed horse in fly season."

"Yep. I'm just peachy," she said, trying to sound convincing. Her side was still sore, but she didn't want to give him a chance to send her home and let Gustafson mess with her case.

"Then what do you want? You've got your assignment."

"I was wondering…"

"Oh, here it comes. You've got that look that makes me more nervous than a long-tailed cat in a room full of rocking chairs."

Holly didn't let his comment slow her down. "Raines was originally working the Justin Jarvis case, and now that Johnson has been arrested, seems like we don't need his help now. I can follow up with Helga and the Blackthorns. After all, he is with the sheriff's department."

The chief frowned. "Someone took a shot at you. Until I know who that was, you're not going anywhere on your own."

"Fine, but I could take Angel with me."

Chief Finch screwed up his face in concentration, which didn't bode well for her. "You and Raines make a good team, and these investigations are part of a joint effort. I want us to look like we're cooperating with other jurisdictions. I want you to work with Raines and try to tie up the loose ends. Dig around for motive. If Skip Johnson doesn't confess, and there are no fingerprints on the rifle, we're going to need more to prosecute him. Talk to Lilly and Thaddeus Blackthorn. See what more they know about Skip Johnson. See if you can find someone who can put Montague together with Johnson."

Great. How was she going to sit next to Raines in the car? It was going to be awkward as hell. She could tell by the way he'd refused to look at her, that she'd done serious damage to their friendship. Well, she couldn't help that. She'd made the right decision for everyone involved.

As she turned to leave the chief's office, she almost bumped into Raines, who was leaning against the doorframe. His furrowed brows and cold stare told her he'd heard every word.

Heat seared her cheeks, but she walked past him with her head held high. She wasn't the one dating someone else.

She walked out to the parking lot and said over her shoulder, "I'll drive."

Raines walked away from her towards his SUV. "I'll meet you over there. I have something to do later and need to get home as soon as we wrap things up."

CHAPTER FORTY-SEVEN

Raines had arrived at the Blackthorns' place at the same time as Holly even though she'd taken a short cut. They didn't speak as they waited on the doorstep. Holly recognized the woman who opened the door as Lilly Blackthorn, Thaddeus's wife, who had been at the inn the night of the auction. Her skin was luminescent and slightly tanned. She wore a subtle shade of beige lipstick, and her eyebrows had been meticulously sculpted into an elegant arch. She probably spent a fortune on skincare, Holly thought.

Lilly's eyes widened slightly as she looked up at Raines. There was a hardness to his face and a coldness in his eyes that gave him a dangerous quality, but there was a magnetism to him that made it difficult to look away from him.

Holly made the introductions, as Raines didn't seem to want to talk. It was going to be a long day, she thought, and silently cursed the chief for making her work with him.

"Thaddeus is not here. He was in a vile mood this morning, not fit to be around. Fortunately, he left early," Lilly told them, still staring up into Raines's eyes as if mesmerized.

Holly spotted a pulse at the base of her throat. "We'd like to talk to you."

"I'm having coffee in the sunroom. Why don't you join me?"

"We'd be delighted," Raines said with a sexy rasp.

Holly could have sworn that the pulse in Lilly's throat sped up.

They followed her through the house. Warm oak panels lined the lower half of the walls. Paintings of the mountains in winter and trees in fall hung above the paneling. The kitchen, which featured a stunning view of the town's snow-covered golf course and cross-country trails beyond, was modern with a dining area at one end and a large red couch under the window. The cabinets were white, and there were marble countertops and a marble backsplash.

Holly compared it to her tiny cottage kitchen—or tried to. There was no comparison. Lilly lived in a different world, one that Raines fitted into with ease. Regardless, she wouldn't trade her sweet little kitchen for this one. It was beautiful but too big, and Holly knew the white cabinets would be a nightmare to keep clean. It wasn't as if she could afford a housecleaner on her detective's salary.

Lilly took down two mugs from a cabinet, and they followed her out to a four-seasons porch that overlooked the trees and a yard. White wicker furniture, overstuffed with big floral cushions, filled the space. Potted indoor ferns and palms added more color to the room. Now, this room, Holly decided, she would love.

Lilly sat down and poured two cups of coffee from a carafe, then topped up her own. "Are you here about that trifle with Zack? It's all sorted. I've spoken with Helga, and she assures me that she will not press charges for trespassing."

"You know Helga?"

Lilly nodded her perfectly groomed head of sleek brown hair. "My husband and Helga's husband are related; same grandfather."

Holly frowned. This wasn't news, but she was surprised that the women were on friendly terms. "I didn't think Thaddeus and Stefan got on. Did they socialize, then? Is that how you met Helga?"

"Oh, no. You're quite right about that. Thaddeus couldn't stand Stefan. In fact, he was quite envious of the dear man. It's so sad what happened to him. Helga is devastated, naturally."

Holly was intrigued. "You liked Stefan?"

Another bob of her silky mane. "Very much so. Delightful man, and so handsome." She gave Raines a coy glance as if to say Stefan wasn't the only handsome man she'd met.

She had to be ten years older than Raines, Holly assessed, noting the fine lines around her eyes and mouth, which the bright sunlight in the room emphasized. "How did you get to know him if your husband wasn't friends with him?"

"Helga and I knew each other long before we came to North Caxton. Helga is Swedish, but we met at university in Switzerland. We had a lot in common. We'd both been educated in English boarding schools. We both love to ski, and our families vacationed in the same areas: St. Moritz and Aspen in winter, and summers in Monaco, St. Barts, Nice, and Fiji."

"Is that how you met your husband and came to live here? Through Helga?"

"In a roundabout way, yes. I met Thaddeus when he fell in love with Helga."

Holly hadn't expected that. "Helga?"

"Oh, yes. I thought it was love at first sight, we all did, but now I know him better, I think it was love at first sight of her checkbook. Helga is the sole heiress to the Lindholm fortune. We met him in Monaco. Helga and I were there with our parents.

"Thaddeus is a gambler like his grandfather and his father. He was a high roller back then, and so smooth and sophisticated. My parents had heard of the Blackthorns because they're in investment banking, and he cashed in on that timber fame. It seemed like a match made in heaven, until he brought Helga back here to the White Mountains to meet his parents, which was not his smartest move." She paused to take a dainty sip of her coffee.

She had Holly right on the edge of her seat. "What happened?"

"It was a disaster. Thaddeus didn't have the wealth he'd pretended to have. Helga is not the kind of person who would have held his lack of funds against him, but the problem was, he was living a lie, and Helga is a straightforward, honest person. His parents had a lovely home, but it was much smaller than he'd described, and of course, there was his father. He was an alcoholic. I believe things got a little wild over there one night."

She took the time to refresh Raines's cup. "Helga liked to get up early and go for long hikes, which she continued to do here because she wanted to get out of the house as much as she could. Early one morning, she met Stefan Lang at the top of a mountain. He shared his coffee and breakfast with her, and within an hour, it was all over for Thaddeus. Thaddeus never forgave Stefan for stealing Helga. He likened it to how his grandfather must have felt losing the business to Helmut Lang."

Holly wondered whether she realized that she'd just given her husband plenty of motive for killing Stefan.

"Are you aware of the Blackthorn family history?" Lilly inquired.

"We know a little," Raines said. "We know that Helmut Lang was a prisoner of war, married the boss's daughter and ended up with the Blackthorn fortune."

Lilly laughed at that. It was a delicate and coquettish sound, and she gave Raines a sly glance. "You are awful, Detective. You make it sound all so vulgar."

Holly realized that he'd not relayed what she'd actually learned when she'd paid Karl Hoffman a visit at his sausage shop.

"You don't appear to have all of the details," Lilly went on. "Thaddeus Blackthorn left part of his estate to his son Thaddeus the Third—my husband's grandfather—and the rest of it to his daughter Patience, who did indeed marry the German POW, Helmut Lang. It caused quite a stir here, and Patience lost most of her friends because so many of them had lost brothers, sons, and husbands in the war. Patience was a lovely lady, and she worshipped Helmut. Now that was a real love match."

"Did you know her?"

"I met her through Helga and Stefan. Helmut was already dead by then. It was before I married Thaddeus. I used to come here and stay with them. Such happy times. It was a real loss to the family when she died." She crossed her fabulously long legs. One of her pumps dangled from her foot. She had small, narrow feet that Holly couldn't help but notice.

Lilly continued, "Helmut was an extraordinarily hard worker. Patience's brother was not. He was lazy, and a gambler, and Patience believed he'd shot himself in the foot to avoid the draft. There had been another brother, who died in the war. Quite the hero, I believe. The family split over the inheritance, and Patience's brother gambled his share away while Helmut worked hard and grew the business."

"So, Christine Johnson didn't have any money either?" Holly asked.

"No."

Raines placed his empty cup on the table and asked, "Do you know if Skip sold his yacht to pay for the remodel of the Witch Cross Inn?"

"Good heavens, no. Skip didn't have a penny, although none of us knew that when Christine met him. I took her sailing with us to Cannes on my father's yacht. We threw a party on board, and Skip was moored near us. We invited him over. He was so dashing, and he swept little Christine off her dumpy feet."

She stopped to pour herself another cup of coffee from the thermos. "Christine was looking to marry into money, just like her brother had, and she'd seen Skip sailing his yacht. I have to say, he was rather dashing at the helm of that yacht. Masculine and capable. She adored him and his glamorous lifestyle. It wasn't until after she'd married him that she discovered he was actually only the captain of the yacht. He'd been sailing it from one port to another for the owner."

"What about his winnings? Thaddeus told us he won a lot of races," Raines said.

She rolled her eyes. "In yacht racing, you spend money to race. You don't win it. Thaddeus has no idea about sailing or the races. Why does he even bother to offer his opinion on something he knows so little about? There are plenty of trophies and cups in yacht racing, but very little in the way of winnings.

"There hasn't been any real money on their side of the family since my husband's grandfather gambled it away. Thaddeus lets everyone think that he has money, but it's mine, and that's why, after Helga left him for Stefan, he settled for me. I'm not as rich as Helga, but I was plenty rich enough for Thaddeus and fool enough to fall for his charm."

Raines came to her defense. "He hardly had to settle."

She bestowed a grateful smile on him. "That's why Thaddeus was so excited when he found out that he actually owned a piece of land that had some value to it. He told me that Stefan had offered to buy it, but then something happened, and Stefan left for Germany. Only now we know Stefan didn't actually leave."

Holly leaned forward. "Who told you Stefan had left for Germany?"

"I'm not sure. I suppose it must have been Thaddeus. Or Helga. I bumped into her on the chairlift one day, and we discussed it, but that could have been after Thaddeus told me."

They sat there for a moment while Holly sipped at her coffee. She wanted to give Lilly time to tell them more. She'd been a great source of information, and Holly wondered at her motives.

"The Blackthorn history is so tragic," Lilly went on. "It's as if they are cursed. Their grandfather drank himself to death after losing nearly everything because he was no match for Helmut Lang. Then their father, Eaton, shot himself when he lost what was left of the money and had managed to plow his way through his wife's inheritance."

"Thaddeus's father shot himself?" Holly asked, raising her eyebrows.

"Yes. Terrible, isn't it? He did it at a hotel in Boston."

"How old were Thaddeus and Christine?"

"It was soon after Helga broke up with Thaddeus. So, he was twenty-one, and Christine was seventeen. Since then, they have been trying to reclaim the stature in the community ever since. I mean, have you seen the Witch Cross Inn? All of those tedious trophies and medals on display. And the photos of Skip sailing a yacht that didn't even belong to him. It's embarrassing. They act like they have all the money in the world, when in fact they are flat broke. It's my money that keeps Thaddeus afloat." She stood and started to collect the cups, setting them on the tray that held the carafe.

Holly had one more question for her. "We understand that the night Justin Jarvis was shot, you had to take Zack to the hospital, and Thaddeus remained here."

"That's correct, and that is what I said in my statement."

"Did you see your husband when you returned?"

She placed a red-painted index finger on her bottom lip and thought about it. "No. We have separate bedrooms and sitting rooms. I don't believe I saw him, but I think he checked in on Zack later that night."

At the door, Raines shook her hand. "Thank you for the coffee."

"My pleasure," she purred.

"By any chance, do you know if Skip Johnson and Phil Montague knew each other?" he asked.

"Why, I have no idea. Is it important?"

"We're not sure, but it could be."

"Then come back later and ask my husband. He knows them both."

CHAPTER FORTY-EIGHT

Raines and Holly stood beside her Jeep. Raines was looking up at the sky. He'd lost the relaxed composure that, only moments ago, had been evident while they'd been sitting with Lilly in the sunroom. His face was taut and showed signs of strain, and there was a remoteness to him that she'd never felt around him before. In the light, she could see the hairline scar on his lip, which was always more pronounced when he was angry.

Forcing her eyes from his face, she looked across the street at a tree. "That's one bad relationship the Blackthorns are in," she pointed out needlessly. "Why on earth would Lilly marry him knowing that he was after her money?"

Raines shrugged. "I've reached a point in my life when I realize my ability to understand a person's actions is limited at best."

Was that a dig at *her*? She wasn't the one in the wrong. It shouldn't take too much understanding to realize she was thinking of Olivia and Abbey when she'd broken off the kiss. Surely, he got that? He was a detective after all. But now wasn't the time to discuss what had happened. "Lilly certainly gave Thaddeus plenty of motive for wanting to get rid of Stefan. Perhaps Thaddeus set Skip up."

Raines glanced at her then. "You don't think Skip did it?"

"I don't know, but it sure was convenient that someone knew there was a long gun in the back of Skip's car, especially when it was hidden under a blanket. Let's go talk to Helga. We need to push her. I want to know why she didn't mention her relationship with Thaddeus."

When they found Helga at home, it looked like someone had already pushed her all the way to hell and back. She looked shattered. Her hair wasn't brushed, and she wore no makeup. Her nose was red, and her eyes were puffy. Her skin had that papery-thin, blue-veined appearance Holly associated with a much older woman. Her shoulders were hunched, and her hands fluttered nervously as she showed them into the living room. She told them to sit, but she stood, then began pacing before the fireplace that hadn't been lit. The vast house felt cold and barren, like a mausoleum.

From the state of her, Holly wondered if she was involved in her husband's death. "You've heard about Phil Montague?" she asked.

"Yes. Late last night. Chief Finch came here to tell me that he believes Phil may have killed Stefan, but Phil is dead and can't confirm it. It's come as such a shock. I can't believe Phil would do such a terrible thing." She put her white, shaky hands to the sides of her face and whispered, "I didn't think it was him."

Holly didn't like it that she had to look up at Helga from her seat on the couch. She wanted to be able to read her expressions better, so she stood and moved to position herself with the window and sunlight behind her. "Who did you think it was?"

Helga placed a hand on the top of her head and looked down at the floor. She didn't answer right away.

"Who was it?" Holly persisted, but her voice was gentle, coaxing. "You'll feel better if you tell us. We can see that you're suffering right now."

At last Helga looked up at Holly. Anxiety had caused her pupils to dilate.

"We need to know the truth, Helga, and you need to tell us."

"I thought it was Thaddeus Blackthorn." Her words came out in a rush and were heavily accented in Swedish.

Raines remained seated on the couch with his legs stretched out before him. His presence was calm again and relaxed. "Why do you believe that?" he asked, his voice full of compassion.

Holly couldn't tell if it was genuine or an interviewing tactic.

"Because he's very angry with me."

"Why?" came Raines's soft prodding.

"A long time ago, I dated Thaddeus briefly. And then I met Stefan. All of a sudden, it was as if the sun had come out, and I'd been living in the dark all of my life without realizing it. I'd never believed in love at first sight until I met Stefan. I was drawn to him, couldn't bear to be parted from him, not even for an hour. I met him when I was searching for a way to end it with Thaddeus without hurting him. Of course, I failed miserably at that and always felt guilty that I'd hurt him. And Thaddeus is extremely good at making you feel guilty. I'd tried to explain that even if I had never met Stefan, the relationship was over. This, however, did little to comfort Thaddeus."

She drew in a ragged breath while Holly held hers. They were getting closer to solving the case. She had the feeling that Helga was the key now.

"Eighteen months after Stefan and I met, he had to go to Germany on business, and there was a party. You don't know how much I wish I hadn't gone to *that* party. I drank too much, and Thaddeus showed up. I tried to leave, but he was in a real state over my relationship with Stefan. I spent time with him, trying to earn his forgiveness, and we drank and kept on drinking. I'm not sure how it happened, but I ended up sleeping with him. I shouldn't have done it, and I've lived with the guilt of it for all these years."

Holly watched her start to twist her wedding ring.

"Stefan and I married soon after he returned from Germany. We were so happy, except there was always this ugly secret I somehow managed to lock away in my heart. Soon we discovered we were pregnant, though, and all of that seemed to fade away."

She wandered over to the windows, closer to Holly, and watched several skiers whiz past on the slopes.

Holly turned to face her profile. "What happened?"

"Thaddeus came here two years ago. He was looking for Stefan and he was furious, which I now realize must have had something to do with the land Stefan had refused to buy. He yelled at me and swore that if I didn't convince Stefan to buy the land at a reasonable price as he'd promised, then he would tell Stefan that Andreas was his son. I was so shocked. Not once had I considered Thaddeus to be the father, but when I thought about it, it was possible. I didn't know what to do. It was awful.

"As I waited for Stefan to come home from work that day, I kept trying to think of a way to explain it to him." She placed a palm on the window glass as if reaching out to a memory of him. "But he never came home, and I never saw him again."

She turned to face Holly, who gave her an encouraging nod.

"The reason I didn't try to contact my husband was that I was terrified that Thaddeus had told him what had happened, and he would say something to Andreas. I thought if Stefan had enough time, then maybe, just maybe, he'd come home and forgive me."

Holly noticed that her accent was more pronounced now. The "j" in "just" sounded more like a "y."

"But he never came home," she whispered.

Had Thaddeus, not Montague, killed Stefan? Holly wondered. But then why had Montague run when he spotted them at the mill? He wasn't going to risk his life over illegal logging. Or had Thaddeus and Montague been in it together? Didn't that scenario fit better than Skip and Montague? And who better than Thaddeus to plant the gun and frame Skip? He had access.

Helga continued, "Thaddeus came over this morning after Andreas left for school. He'd been drinking and was in a terrible state. He told me that if I don't buy the land and pay him for the trees that have been stolen, he'll tell Andreas that he's his father. He said it's all my fault. He blamed me for everything. And on some level, he's right. He wants a million dollars after taxes. The land is not worth it, but I've made some calls to move money over and written a check for him. It's on my desk right now, but I don't know what to do. I have to protect my son."

Raines asked, "Do you know where he went after he left here?"

"No."

Raines continued. "Who told you that Stefan had left for Germany two years ago?"

"Thaddeus. He came over here to gloat shortly after Stefan left. He said Stefan must have found out about Andreas, and that's why he went to Germany. He told me he wanted the money for the land, but I said that was between him and Stefan. He threw a chair across the room and threatened to wring my neck, but he left without either taking the money or hurting me."

Holly held her gaze. "I'm sorry that I have to ask you this, but it's a necessary part of our investigation. Are you, or were you, having an affair with Thaddeus when Stefan disappeared?"

"*Gode Gud!*" she blurted in Swedish, clearly horrified. "No. Absolutely not. Since I found out about Stefan's death, I've been living in fear that he's dead because of *me*. It was a nightmare thinking he'd left me because I slept with Thaddeus that *one* time and got pregnant, but it's even worse to think he's dead because of what I had done."

"And that's why you thought Thaddeus killed him?" Raines asked.

"I didn't want to believe it, but as each day passed, I couldn't come up with anyone else who would want him dead. But now Chief Finch thinks Phil did it. I'm so confused. I'm just terrified that Thaddeus is going to tell Andreas about... what happened."

Holly watched as she sank down in the armchair, exhausted and drained of her nervous energy now. "I can arrange for a paternity DNA test, if you'd like. I could use your son's hairbrush and get the results in a couple of days. Andreas would not need to know."

"What don't I need to know?" Andreas asked as he strolled into the living room.

Helga made nervous, fluttering motions with her hands. "I thought you were at school."

"I was, but I thought I'd come home for lunch. See how you're doing. What's this about DNA?"

The struggle was there on Helga's face for all to see. The need to lie. The need to protect her son from the truth. The desire to protect herself from the aftermath.

"There's no easy way to tell you this, my love, but something happened a long time ago, and I have to tell you about it." And she did. All of it.

Why Helga hadn't waited for them to leave before telling him the truth would always be a mystery to Holly. Had she needed their support? Or had she feared that once they'd gone, she'd be tempted to lie? Whatever her reasons, Holly felt sick with dread for her.

For a moment, it felt like the whole world had stopped, and they were hanging in limbo while they waited for the fallout. Then Andreas took a few shaky steps backward, instinctively holding up his hands as if he could protect himself from the news. "That's not possible." His voice cracked. "My dad *is* my dad. Look at the photos." He pointed to a painting hanging over the fireplace. It was a family portrait.

And it was obvious to Holly that not only did Andreas resemble his mother and the Swedish side of the family, rather than Stefan, he bore no resemblance to Thaddeus either.

And then, more quietly, he whispered, "It's like he's died all over again. You should have told me two years ago when this happened."

"I was scared. I lost my husband—your father. I didn't want to lose you, too."

"That wasn't your decision to make, Mom. I had a right to know." He turned to Holly. "I want to do the test."

"I'll need to come back with the kit," she told him.

Andreas nodded and walked over to his mother. He placed a hand on her shoulder and said, "Don't worry, Mom. I know Dad is my biological father."

Tears started to stream down Helga's face.

Raines stood up. "When we were here the last time, Andreas, you told us that your father was having an affair with someone he met in Germany."

He nodded. "That's what I heard."

"They were ugly rumors," Helga interrupted.

Raines ignored her. "Who told you about it?"

"It was Zack."

"How did he know?"

"His dad told him."

Helga gasped. "You never said it was Zack."

"I didn't want to hurt you. Better for you to believe that it was just rumors."

"What a mess," Helga muttered. "What a terrible mess."

Raines frowned and looked at Helga. "I'm sorry to have to ask you one last question, but do you know if Phil Montague had any contact with Skip Johnson?"

She looked puzzled. "Skip Johnson is married to Thaddeus's sister, Christine. I met her years ago when I first came over here with Thaddeus, but we haven't had any real contact since then. Of course, I've seen them around town, but I don't know Skip well at all, and I don't ever recall Phil mentioning it. All I know is that Phil went to the auction the other night at his inn, but that's it. Why?"

"Skip Johnson was arrested for the Justin Jarvis homicide earlier this morning," Raines explained.

She shivered. "That's awful. But why would you want to know if he's connected to Phil?"

"It's just part of our investigation. We have to explore all of the angles."

"Phil was at the Witch Cross Inn the other night because he told me he wanted to bid on Mr. Raines's guitar for me," Andreas said. "But there was another time I saw him there."

Interested, Raines asked, "When was that?"

He scrunched up his face. "It had to have been over a year ago, I think. Maybe not quite a year. I spotted his pickup in the parking lot one night when I was dropping Luke off after football practice."

CHAPTER FORTY-NINE

The sun was out when they walked out of Helga's home, and it had warmed up to a balmy forty-two degrees, melting some of the snow. But the atmosphere around Raines felt as chilly as Siberia. He said nothing to Holly as they walked to their cars. Ignoring her, he pulled out his phone and placed a call to Lilly Blackthorn.

While Raines talked on the phone, Holly mulled over the case, which had seesawed wildly from one suspect to the other and back again. At first, Thaddeus had been right at the top of her list of suspects. His claim that Stefan had stolen his land was a great motive. Then she'd learned that he hadn't actually spoken to Stefan. It was Montague who'd told Thaddeus that Stefan had changed his mind about buying it. Also, Montague had access to the machinery as well as having the skills necessary to clear-cut the land. Given those facts, Montague topped the list. Supporting his position as the prime suspect, she further ruminated, was the fact that if he hadn't killed Stefan, why had he run off when he saw them? He must have known the risks of running across a stack of unsecured logs. Would he have taken his chances of escaping over those tree trunks if he had only been guilty of timber theft? Not likely.

But now, after what Lilly and Helga had told them about his relationship with Helga, Thaddeus had plenty of motive to kill Stefan. Plus, they had only his word that it was Montague who'd told him that Stefan had planned to renege on their agreement. That could have been a lie. And Montague was conveniently dead so he couldn't refute it. But, given Stubby's account of the shooting at the mill, they knew that there were at least two people involved. It made sense that Thaddeus was in it with Montague, and he'd framed Skip Johnson. He would be familiar with his car. It wouldn't be difficult for him to visit his sister, take Skip's keys, place the gun in the back, return the keys to where he'd found them, then call in the anonymous tip.

Raines interrupted her silent deliberations to recap his phone call with Lilly. "I asked if she knew where her husband was. She didn't, but she gave me his phone number, which I just tried but didn't get an answer. Lilly suggested that we look for him either at the Hemlock Inn, which is just down the road from her house, or The Downslope Grill in North Caxton. They are his preferred places to eat lunch. There's no point in us following each other to both of the restaurants, so why don't you check out one while I do the other?" he suggested.

"Fine," she said. "I'll take the Hemlock Inn."

With a sharp nod, he turned and walked over to his vehicle, leaving Holly there without another word. She'd never known him to be this cold before, and it was unsettling. Still, if that was how he wanted to play it, that was fine with her.

She headed north, back to Liberty. It didn't take her long to check the Hemlock Inn. The staff knew Blackthorn well and hadn't seen him that morning. After that, she went over to the cross-country skiing center. Nobody had seen him there, either, but she was told that sometimes he simply skied from the back of his house across the golf course to the trails. Next, she revisited Lilly Blackthorn, who confirmed that he hadn't returned, and he wasn't answering her calls either. Holly asked if she would check to see if his cross-country skis were there. She walked to the window and pointed outside to them. They were leaning against the shed.

She was sitting in her Jeep with the engine running, contemplating calling Raines to see if he'd had any luck, when her phone rang. It wasn't Raines. It was Chief Finch.

"What's up, Chief?" she asked.

"Someone just took a shot at Stubby as he was leaving the hospital."

She slipped her Wrangler into drive. "Is he all right?"

"Yeah. He got lucky. They think the shooter was using a handgun at long range, and his ride had parked close to the building. Gus thinks someone was hiding in the woods. You know how much cover there is back there. Gus is there with him now, but Stubby is asking for you. I'm on my way over now."

"I'll be there in less than ten minutes, Chief."

She beat him there. Gustafson frowned at her when she walked over to them, but he didn't say a word. He was too busy coordinating the search effort.

Holly found Stubby in the back of Fennis Cooper's cruiser. Fennis was nowhere in sight, and she suspected that Gustafson had commandeered him to aid in the search.

Stubby smiled sadly when he spotted her and got out of the car. "I'm giving up Bigfoot hunting for good. It's way too dangerous for me, and it was Sticks who was really into it anyway. I'd rather run the comic store and take it easy for a while."

The bruises on his face were really pronounced now, and he sounded slightly nasal from his broken nose. "That sounds like a great idea," she told him. "The chief said you wanted to talk to me. Have you remembered something?"

He looked bashfully down at his feet and shook his head. "Nah. I just wanted to let you know that if you're ever over in the Lancaster area, you could stop in and pick up a free comic if you'd like. There are some great series with kickass female heroes."

"That's really nice of you, Stubby. If I'm ever over that way, I'll be sure to drop in and say hi."

He nodded and smiled his big grin. "Well. I'd better get moving. My mom and dad are waiting to drive me home."

"We're going to need a formal statement before you leave town. Could your parents drive you to the station? I'll have someone meet you over there."

"Sure, Detective. Anything to help."

She watched him walk over to a brown Chevy sedan as she called Angel to request that he take Stubby's statement. Disconnecting, she saw the chief pull in, followed by Bliss Jarvis, who was driving an Audi. The two of them parked and walked toward her. Bliss was wearing a black winter puffer coat, black pants tucked into black boots, gray suede gloves, and a pale lavender scarf wrapped snugly around her neck and tucked into her coat. She looked well prepared for an afternoon on the hunt for the shooter.

They congregated around Gustafson's command post, which, for now, was the hood of his brand-new Ford Police Interceptor. Holly listened as the chief and Gustafson filled Bliss in. Then Holly briefed her on what she'd learned from Lilly and Helga, closing with her opinion on Thaddeus Blackthorn's involvement and the possibility that he was the shooter.

The chief whistled. "That's one hell of a tangled mess."

"And you can't find Blackthorn?" Bliss asked.

"No, but Raines was checking the Downslope Grill."

Bliss raised her eyebrows in concern. "You haven't heard from him?"

"No."

"Call him. Let's make sure he didn't run into Blackthorn."

A stab of panic knifed through Holly at the thought of Raines facing him on his own, and she pulled out her phone and punched in his number. He must have heard the relief in her voice when he answered because he asked her what the matter was. She filled him in quickly, and Raines told her that no one had seen Blackthorn at the Downslope Grill, but the bartender had suggested a couple of other places. He'd checked those, too, but had come up empty.

After Holly relayed the information, Bliss patted her hands together absently. "We know Skip Johnson can't have been the shooter today because he's in custody. Nor, for that matter, could it be Phil Montague. What do you think about Thaddeus Blackthorn, Fred?" she said, turning to Chief Finch. "Could he be our guy?"

"Right now, he's our strongest lead. That's for sure."

Gustafson nodded along with the chief's words.

"I agree," Bliss said. "We need to put out an APB on him."

"His sister, Christine, may know where we can find him," Holly suggested.

Gustafson shook his head. "She was furious when we arrested her husband. I don't think she'll want to help unless we let Skip go."

"I'm not willing to do that," Bliss told him. "He didn't do the shooting today, but we found the rifle in his car, and we can't rule out that he shot Justin. Let's keep him locked up as long as we can. Okay." She rubbed her hands together. "This is the plan for now. Gus, you hold down the investigation here while the chief and I head back to the office. Holly, go talk to Christine. See if you can coax anything out of her."

"Will do."

As Holly hurried over to her Jeep, the chief called out to her. She waited for him to catch up.

His color was up, and she knew it wasn't the cold that was giving him his ruddy complexion. "I told you to work with Raines because you need backup. Why aren't you with him?"

She shrugged. "We had a couple of places to check. It made sense to split up. It was faster."

He gave her one of those looks that told him he didn't buy it for a minute. "Someone is out there taking potshots, and I'm not having any of my people out there without backup. You either work it with Raines, or I have Hendricks take over here when he arrives and have Gus go with you."

Holly looked over at Gustafson. Oh God, she thought. Would she really have to partner with him because Raines didn't want to be in the same car as her? She'd rather ride in the car with a rabid wolverine.

The chief frowned. "What's going on with the two of you, anyways?"

"Nothing."

"That's a pile of BS, and you know it. You've been friends with Raines for a long time, and although you may not want to hear this, you make a good team."

"We were friends when we were young, and then there was a big chunk of time when we went our separate ways. It's not like we kept in touch. People change."

"They don't change that much. You know another thing I like about the two of you working together?"

"No."

"I don't have to pay his salary. The sheriff is more than happy to loan him out to us because it's good for his reelection campaign. He's counting on Raines to help him come up with a big win."

"He certainly has the star power to pull it off," she muttered.

The chief didn't crack a smile. "What's it going to be? Raines or Gustafson?"

She pursed her lips, deciding on which was the lesser of two evils.

"I'll call Raines on the way over to the Witch Cross Inn," she agreed reluctantly.

"No. I'll call him. I don't want to hear later how you got a busy signal."

CHAPTER FIFTY

As Holly pulled into the Witch Cross Inn, Raines called to let her know that he was on his way, but he was going to be at least half an hour. He was north of town, over at Wildcat, searching for Thaddeus. Lilly had called him after she'd checked the closet and discovered that Thaddeus had taken his downhill skis with him when he'd left that morning. They had season passes to Wildcat, she'd told him. Raines had just finished checking the lots for the Blackthorns' silver Mercedes, but he hadn't spotted it.

As Holly sat listening to him, she stared at the inn. Something nagged at her, some connection she needed to make, something she'd missed. What was it? But the thought was elusive, and her conscious mind couldn't grasp it.

Why had Justin Jarvis died here? Was it merely a coincidence he had been staying in a bedroom with a secret passage? The question didn't bring her any closer to what it was she'd missed. The more she struggled with it, the further it slipped away.

The inn was deserted and looked forlorn in that way empty businesses can. Holly was surprised that they hadn't reopened, but then again, Skip had been arrested, and Christine probably couldn't run it without him. It was a shame because she'd done such a fantastic job restoring the inn, and this was always a busy time in ski country with everyone seeking a white Christmas. Holly wondered if she'd be able to afford to keep going without Skip. A rush of sympathy for Christine washed over her; she knew what it was like to have your dreams fall apart, to be helpless to prevent it.

She climbed out of her Jeep and locked it; she had her laptop with her, as well as her skis and boots, which were usually in her vehicle so she could get in a few runs either before work or after.

Justin's blood had been thoroughly cleaned away, and the walkway was clear, but Holly made sure to avoid the area where he'd died. Walking up to the front door, she rubbed her finger over the hex mark etched into the door handle. It had been a great idea to base the business around it. Still, it certainly hadn't been a lucky talisman for the family living there.

Holly opened the door, stepped inside and called out. Nobody answered. It was as quiet as a funeral parlor, she thought, and then corrected herself. Funeral homes weren't usually this quiet. They played a steady stream of atmospheric background music to help comfort the grieving.

Brittle shards of sunlight sliced through the windows, seeming to gouge patterns into the foyer's carpet. Holly noticed an old-fashioned bell on the counter near the stairs. She walked over and rang it. The shrillness of it pierced the quiet.

Seconds later, a flustered Christine scurried into the foyer. She stopped short when she saw Holly standing there.

Her hair was pulled back into what had once been an elegant knot at the nape of her neck, but wiry strands had escaped and were corkscrewing in all directions. Her plump cheeks were flushed, her eyes sunken, and her lips chapped. She looked precisely like a woman whose life had suddenly taken a turn for the worst.

"What's happened now?" she asked, sounding a little breathless.

"I'm just here to ask you a few questions."

"I don't know anything, which I already told them when they came to take my husband away." She twisted her rumpled apron around in her dimpled hands. "Is he coming home?"

"Not yet. How's Luke?"

"As you might expect, he's upset. This will hurt him academically. I know it."

"Where is he?"

"He's with Zack. They had a project due and are at the library working on it."

Holly doubted that and wondered if he'd gone back to the mill.

Christine drifted over to the dining room window and peered out. "Is anyone with you?"

"No."

"Not the press?"

"No."

"They've been here, taking photos, trying to get me to say something about Skip. They don't care that they're ruining my business. It's terrible what they can get away with writing."

The dining room smelled of dead flowers and stagnant water. Everything that had been delivered for the auction was still on the tables.

Christine sat down, and Holly joined her. She looked around the room again as that nagging feeling surfaced. The fireplace was behind her, concealing the entrance to the secret passage. Holly didn't like sitting with her back to it. It creeped her out, so she scooted her chair around a little. What side of the fireplace had Raines said it was on? The left? She eyed the wall. Was Thaddeus hiding in there?

Christine continued, seemingly unaware of Holly's efforts to move her chair and avoid sitting with her back to the fireplace. "It's all wasted. All of the work I've done to rebuild this beautiful family home is for nothing."

"You'll be able to carry on. You have Luke. He's a smart boy."

She shook her head and held her hands against her pudgy belly like she was protecting an unborn baby. "He has no interest in staying here. He wants to go to college, which is his right, as a Blackthorn." She sighed wearily. "Skip ruined everything. Again."

"He's done this before?" Holly asked. Did Christine mean he was the one who'd killed Stefan as well as Justin?

"When I met Skip, he led me to believe he had money. He had a beautiful sailboat and lived an exciting life. I imagined returning home to North Caxton with him to build a home my father would have been proud of, one worthy of the Blackthorns, but it turned out he had nothing. Not a penny. My mother had to help us, but it wasn't enough to build a dream home."

"How did you afford to buy the inn and remodel it, then?"

"We had just enough money. My mother gave us some, and Skip hit it big in Vegas for once. A place like this up here in the mountains wasn't as expensive as you might think."

"But your son told us he feels like he needed to drum up business for you."

Embarrassed, she glanced away for a moment. Holly hated having to humiliate her. She gave her time to collect herself before she resumed her questions and glanced over at the wall again, trying to see how the secret door opened. The grooves and curved edging in the oak paneling made it impossible to see it from where she sat.

"Things have been slow," Christine continued. "I'm not sure people really warmed to Skip. He's so pompous and insists on wearing that ridiculous sailing hat. People laughed at him behind his back. I know they did, but he didn't care; he just drank and didn't worry about anything. He left it all up to me."

"Do you know why Skip would want to shoot Justin?"

"I have no idea. Skip has a lawyer now, and he advised us not to talk to the police."

Holly gave her an unconcerned look and a careless shrug, downplaying the advice. "If you have nothing to hide, it shouldn't be a problem."

Christine gave a harsh bellow of laughter. "Problems are all I have right now, thanks to Skip."

"Did Skip know Phil Montague?" Holly asked.

That startled her. She raised a shaky hand to her mouth. "Phil? Oh. That was so tragic how he died. I heard a stack of logs fell on him. I can't imagine. Such a terrible way to die. Awful."

"You knew him, then?"

"Yes. He came here."

"You mean the night of the auction?"

"No. Phil would come here to play cards with Skip. They would have a drink and play cards."

"How long had they been friends?"

"I'm not sure. I never really paid attention. I was too busy getting the inn ready. I upholstered these chairs. Did you know that?" She waved a hand around the room.

Holly looked around, admiring her work. The striped red and beige fabric was smooth, and the upholstering looked professional. "You did a good job."

"Yes." She stared at one of the chairs for a long moment, and Holly felt she was losing her.

"Do you know where your brother is?"

"Thaddeus? No. Why?"

Holly glanced back at the wall, half expecting him to jump out at her. "I was wondering if your brother came here on Monday?"

Christine's face creased in agitation. "On Monday? That's the night Skip was arrested."

"That's right. The night they found the gun in his car."

"It's such a blur. Thaddeus was here the night of the auction, but after that, the days are all jumbled up."

Holly nodded. "Would Thaddeus know where Skip kept his car keys?"

Flustered again, Christine stood up. "Thaddeus would never want to drive Skip's car. Have you seen the Mercedes my brother drives? Now, I need some coffee. I haven't been sleeping since this happened. Would you like one?"

Holly nodded.

"I'll be back."

Holly watched her hurry toward the back of the dining room, push through a door and disappear down a corridor. Holly got up and went to examine the wall, looking for the secret door. Once she was up close, it didn't take her long to figure it out. She pushed on the section of wall where the crack was disguised as a groove in the paneling, but it didn't open.

She drifted over to the window to see if Raines had arrived and passed the glass cabinet full of trophies, right where she'd stood the night of the auction. An image of Raines and Olivia flashed into her mind. Then that nagging feeling hit her again. Her heart beat a little faster, and she stared into the cabinet.

She heard footsteps on the wooden floor near the foyer and turned to see Luke stroll in. His mouth gaped open when he saw her there.

"Hi, Luke."

"What's going on? Is Dad home?"

"No. Not yet."

He struggled unsuccessfully to keep the sadness from his face.

Then she turned back to the cabinet as if drawn to it. What am I missing, she thought? There's nothing but family keepsakes in there. Tennis trophies, sailing cups, photos… She opened the glass cabinet door to retrieve the biggest silver trophy, which was mounted on a marble stand. It was one of the marksman's trophies. She read the plaque on its base.

"Hey, Luke," she called out as he turned to leave the room. "Who was Cricket Blackthorn?"

"Why?"

"I was just admiring all of your family trophies. There are so many of them, and these shooting trophies are impressive."

"Cricket was my mom's nickname when she was a kid. No one calls her that anymore, though."

CHAPTER FIFTY-ONE

That was what had been nagging at her. The trophy for marksmanship. It had taken quite a shot to hit Justin from the woods in the dark while he was walking with the TV. Her thoughts whirled through her brain. If only the trophy had been titled "markswomanship" or Christine's name had been on it, she might have prevented Sticks's death.

Her mind continued to reel. So, did the rifle they'd found in Skip's car belong to Christine? Had she shot Justin, or had her husband done it? And how did Montague fit? Why shoot Sticks? Were Christine, Skip and Montague in it together for the money? How did Thaddeus fit? Had the brother and sister framed Skip, and were they in on it together? They were both obsessed with the Blackthorn name and money.

Luke was staring at her as she stood there studying the trophy. Concern creased his face. "What is it? What's wrong?"

"Stay here, Luke."

"Mom!" he yelled.

Holly shouted at him to stay where he was.

Had Christine really gone to make coffee? Of course not, Holly thought. She's probably running, and if she was trying to get away, she could leave through the kitchen door and take Raines unawares in the parking lot. Gustafson had found the rifle, but someone had taken a shot at Stubby that morning with a handgun, and Sticks had taken a shotgun blast to his head. Raines was in danger, she knew, and fear sliced through her.

She sprinted to the door that led to the kitchen, automatically checking for her weapon. It was right there on her hip. She drew it while she felt in her left pocket for her phone. It wasn't there. *Fool*, she cursed herself. She'd left it in the Jeep. She'd been talking to Raines on speaker while it charged, and she'd forgotten it.

The corridor was dark with oak paneling. Picture frames displayed antique maps and the old buildings of North Caxton. Holly slowed. She could smell the kitchen. It stank of rotting chicken. She wrinkled her nose and slowed her pace. Light spilled out into the hallway.

She kept her back to the wall and crept closer, straining to hear if Christine was in there. She heard nothing.

She glanced quickly into the room and pulled back. Nothing except commercial-grade stainless-steel appliances.

Then she heard gravel crunching. Was that Raines or Christine fleeing?

She slowly inched her way into the kitchen. She heard the sounds of someone running. Who was outside? Moving further into the room, she quickly surveyed it. No one was there.

Out of the corner of her eye, she glimpsed Luke through the kitchen window. It had been him running, not his mother. Not Raines. She barely had enough time to wonder where Christine was, when the woman stepped out from behind a bulky refrigerator with her gun aimed at Holly.

As Christine's finger moved to the trigger, Luke yanked open the outer door and yelled, "Mom!"

A bullet whizzed past Holly's head and hit the wall behind her with a solid thud.

Luke pulled on his mother's arm, but she shook him off.

Holly couldn't return fire because Luke was too close to his mother.

As Christine swung the gun back in Holly's direction, Holly quickly switched her gun into her left hand and the trophy to her right and hurled it with all her force at Christine. The marble base had plenty of heft to it, and it sailed through the air, hitting Christine right on the side of the head as she tried to duck. Christine jerked backward and then lost her balance and fell, the momentum forcing her to squeeze the trigger again.

CHAPTER FIFTY-TWO

Raines had just crossed the threshold of the inn when he heard gunfire, followed by a loud crashing. Fear ripped through him. Holly was on her own. Had Thaddeus been here all the time?

Drawing his weapon from his shoulder holster, he headed in the direction of the sounds. Entering the dining room, he heard someone yelling—a male voice—and he ran to the door that led to the kitchen.

As the door opened, he heard a low murmur of another voice. Was that Holly? *Please*, he prayed, let it be Holly.

As he neared the kitchen, he heard her. She was telling someone to calm down and drop the weapon.

Relief flooded through him. Reaching the open door, he whispered softly, so as not to startle her. "I'm right behind you."

She nodded almost imperceptibly.

Looking over her shoulder, he spotted Christine on the floor. She was out cold. Luke stood near his mom and had a handgun pointed at Holly. Holly had her Glock trained on him. Her hands were steady. His were not.

"You shot my mom."

"No, Luke," Holly said, far more calmly than she must have felt. "I didn't shoot her. It was your mom's gun that fired, not mine. I threw the trophy at her and hit her. That's why she fell."

His hands shook even more, and his finger twitched on the trigger. Raines held his breath.

Luke's chin started to tremble. "I don't know what's going on. Why did Mom shoot at you?"

"If you put the gun down, we can start to figure that out and get help for your mom."

"Am I going to go to prison like my dad?"

"Your dad is in jail right now. He will only go to prison if he's found guilty of a crime at a trial, or he pleads guilty to a crime."

"What about me?"

"Have you done anything wrong?"

"I'm pointing a gun at you."

"Is that it?"

"I *was* trespassing at the mill, but that's it. I swear it. Oh! And the Bigfoot thing. But we didn't mean for anything bad to happen. We were just goofing around."

"If you give me the gun right now, it's all going to be fine. Okay?"

He nodded slowly, then placed the weapon with a clatter on the immaculately clean counter and gently pushed it toward her.

Christine started moaning, and he dropped to his knees beside his mom. Picking up her hand, he patted it awkwardly, just like any teenage boy would.

As Holly secured the weapon, Raines called for an ambulance and then rang Chief Finch to let him know what had happened.

After Christine regained consciousness, Raines helped her to her feet and took her arm, gently guiding her over to a kitchen chair. Christine resisted, shaking free with considerable force and spinning away from him to reach out for a butcher's knife that had been left on the counter.

Holly moved fast to block her. Christine tried shoving Holly out of the way. Although the older woman probably outweighed Holly by forty pounds, Holly had strength in her legs from years of skiing and height on her side. She stood her ground and grabbed Christine by her chubby wrists while Raines pulled out his handcuffs to restrain her.

As Raines started to cuff her hands behind her back, Christine cried out and complained of shoulder pain. Luke started to cry and pleaded with him not to cuff his mom. Raines compromised, restraining her hands in front of her instead of behind her back. Then, with a firmer grip on her arm this time, he escorted her over to the kitchen chair. Christine sat and rested her hands demurely in her lap as if she were attending a ladies' church social.

With tears glistening on his cheeks, Luke sat beside her, wiped his nose on the sleeve of his sweatshirt, and stared down blankly at his mom's handcuffed hands as if he couldn't comprehend what was happening.

Raines read Christine her rights and then asked her, "Why did you shoot at Holly?"

Holly leaned against the counter, listening. Other than appearing a little pale, she was unharmed, her face impassive.

Christine raised her handcuffed hands to her face and struggled to brush a stray strand off her cheek.

Raines could tell that she was playing for time. He crossed his arms and gave her an intimidating look. During his music career, he'd developed a reputation for being tough and blunt. That reputation wasn't just a rumor. Dealing with all of the hangers-on and parasites, who'd either wanted to bask in his fame or get a free ride, had hardened him.

Christine swallowed. "I came in here to make coffee and heard someone hurrying down the corridor. I thought I was in danger... That I was going to die. I started to panic. I didn't know where to hide. Then I found that I couldn't catch my breath. I've been under a lot of stress lately, you know, with everything that's happened, and I've been unable to sleep, which has affected my mental health. I remember feeling really dizzy. I didn't realize what I was doing. It was dark by the kitchen door, and when I heard someone there, I thought it was the killer coming to get me. I've been terrified of staying here, especially after Skip was arrested."

Holly said matter-of-factly, "You knew it was me. I was just talking to you in the dining room."

Christine stiffened and clasped her fingers together tightly. "Guests aren't allowed back here." She sounded overwrought.

"I'm not a guest."

She glanced up at Holly and gave her a look of wide-eyed innocence that was so clearly feigned it would have been laughable at any other time. "I was confused, Detective. You have to believe me. It's all been so stressful, and as I've already mentioned, I haven't been sleeping well because I've been terrified someone would sneak in at night and kill me."

"And what about your attempt to grab the knife just now?"

With a quick shake of her head, Christine raised her clenched hands to her chest as if in prayer. "I lost my balance. It was the blow to my head. I was simply reaching for the counter for support."

Holly studied her for a moment as Christine continued to stare up at her with hands still clasped together and her eyes still wide open. "Why don't you tell us about the shooting trophies you won," Holly told her. Her voice was cold.

This was news to Raines. How had Holly found out about that?

Christine shrugged and looked away. "That was something I did when I was a child."

"But you must have been quite a shot to have won all of those trophies."

Christine's lips thinned. She didn't respond.

"What weapon did you use to win those trophies? It wasn't an old Springfield, was it?"

Raines looked over at Holly, who nodded to a trophy on the floor.

"And 'Cricket.' That's an unusual nickname. When I first noticed the trophies the night of the auction, I thought it was a boy's name, but I was wrong. Cricket is a nickname for Christine as well as for Christopher, isn't it?"

Christine slowly turned her head in Holly's direction, her eyes narrowed into slits. "I've done nothing. Skip shot that man. Not me, and not my brother. And you can't prove otherwise."

Beside her, Luke covered his face with his hands and began to sob.

CHAPTER FIFTY-THREE

After the paramedics had checked Christine for signs of concussion and cleared her, Angel Natale transported her to the Caxton PD for processing. Lieutenant Gustafson and Bliss Jarvis were there, preparing to question her formally. Chief Finch and Lieutenant Hendricks were now at the inn, waiting for the state police's crime scene team to arrive.

Luke had called his cousin, and Zack drove over to pick him up, informing the detectives that Luke could stay with him and his mom for as long as he needed to.

Once the teens had left, Raines had opened the door to the secret passage and staircase, and they'd checked it and all of the rooms for Thaddeus. He wasn't there. The inn was empty.

They were all seated in the dining room now. Holly filled them in on what had happened, going into greater detail about Christine's nickname and her history of youth shooting competitions. The chief nodded his approval and clapped her on the back, but only after he'd grumbled at her for not waiting for Raines before questioning Christine.

Hendricks said, "Christine has quite the story. It's not going to be easy to prosecute either her or Skip. They're going to blame each other for the shootings and create reasonable doubt. They could both walk unless we get something more." Hendricks had a high and tight military haircut, a furrowed brow and a square chin, and he ran the state police's major crimes team with the efficiency of an army unit.

"Do you really think Christine could have shot Justin? I mean, the kid was only a few years older than her son," the chief said.

"At the time of the shooting, Christine was in the kitchen," Holly told them. "When we were outside, people saw her walking into the dining room with a tray of food, which she dropped when she heard there had been a shooting."

Raines added, "Which was a clever way to make sure everyone noticed that she was there, but the kitchen is at the back of the inn, and the door opens onto the rear parking lot. The shooter was in the woods at the back of the parking lot. She could have had time to shoot Justin, get back to the kitchen, pick up the food and walk into the dining room if she really hustled."

The chief nodded in agreement. "She had plenty of time, when you think about it: she was already heading back in as we were heading for the front door."

"But," Raines interjected, "she ran a risk of being seen. Although there are trees around back that are close to the inn and would provide cover, there's an open area she'd have to cross to reach the door. If someone were parking back there, they'd have seen her."

"And we can't forget," Hendricks pointed out, "that Skip wasn't seen downstairs at all during this period."

"But why would she kill Justin?" the chief pushed. "Was he sneaking around the place using that secret passage and overheard something?"

"It's possible," Hendricks acknowledged. "But why wouldn't he have called his boss? Or, at the very least, mentioned something to his aunt or uncle? It's not as if he didn't have major contacts in law enforcement."

Raines leaned forward. "The night of the auction, Christine came over to me with a tray of drinks while I was talking to Justin. We were discussing the rosewood fretboard on the guitar I was donating. During that conversation, we touched on illegal logging." He closed his eyes for a moment, replaying the incident. "Yes. She walked over right when we were discussing it. If she's involved in illegally logging Thaddeus's land, she could have worried that Justin was somehow on to her."

"And there are huge penalties associated with it," muttered the chief.

Raines added, "When we came over here to question Luke about being at the mill, Christine was more concerned about her son being there than the fact that he'd been drinking. That struck me as odd for a parent."

Hendricks spoke up. "She seems cold to me, and there's something…" He paused, searching for the correct word. "… creepy about her. The way her eyes shifted all around the room before settling on you. And did you see her hands? Even with the handcuffs on, her hands weren't still. Her fingers kept twitching like she was planning something. She should have called this place The Witch Inn. There's no way I'd want to stay here."

"The only problem with her involvement in illegal logging is that she would actually be stealing her brother's lumber," Holly pointed out. "And I'm not sure she'd do that. She's extremely loyal to the Blackthorn family."

The chief shifted his weight on one of Christine's upholstered chairs. "Her brother could be in on it with her. He wanted his timber. That was one way to get it."

"That works for me," Hendricks said.

Holly was about to agree when she had another one of those fleeting, nagging sensations that she'd missed something else.

"What is it, Holly?" Raines asked.

"Did Lilly say anything to you about Thaddeus skiing at Hurricane Mountain?"

"No. She said that he had a season pass to Wildcat. Why?"

"There's a trail that goes right past Helga Lang's chalet, and I bet Helga doesn't keep the back door locked. Thaddeus could have taken his skis so he could get at Helga. She wouldn't see him coming from that direction, and if he had a helmet on, nobody would know it was him."

CHAPTER FIFTY-FOUR

They left Hendricks at the inn to coordinate with the crime scene techs. As they ran toward their vehicles, the chief called for all available units to head to Helga's house, while Holly called Helga and instructed her to lock the doors until they arrived. Helga reported that she hadn't seen Thaddeus since earlier that morning. That was when he'd showed up drunk, demanded money and threatened to tell Andreas that he was his father if she didn't pay. In a small voice shaky with fear, she asked Holly if she thought he would do something to Andreas.

"I can't answer that, but better to be safe. Keep all the doors locked and stay away from the windows until we get there," Holly told her. "You'll hear us coming."

Raines, the chief and Holly reached their cars. Chief Finch was out of breath as he yelled to them that he'd take his own vehicle. Raines got into Holly's Jeep with her.

As Holly sped towards Helga's home, she wondered if Thaddeus was out for revenge. He was angry with Helga, and if he was involved in the homicides, the noose was tightening around his neck. The killer, or killers, had been seemingly indiscriminate in murdering Sticks.

It was six o'clock and dark out, but Hurricane Mountain had night skiing. Thaddeus would have the cover of darkness to sneak up on Helga from an angle she wasn't expecting.

She pressed her accelerator to the floor.

A few minutes later, she pulled into Helga's driveway and parked under the drive-through portico. Finch pulled in behind them. As she climbed out of her Jeep, Chief Finch hurried over and asked her if she had her skis. She confirmed that she did.

"Bring them. Fennis just called. He's in the parking lot at the base of Hurricane Mountain. Blackthorn's silver Mercedes is there. The parking attendant said he hasn't been here long. He was probably waiting for it to get dark before he made his move."

She grabbed her skis and poles while Raines carried the bag that held her boots, gloves, and goggles, and they hurried up to Helga's front door and knocked. Helga opened it immediately; Andreas stood beside her. Both looked uneasy but seemed to be doing well at controlling their nerves. Helga stepped aside and motioned them into the front hall, then quickly locked the door behind them.

They all trooped into the living room, where the chief quickly explained what had been going on. Holly noted with satisfaction that the blinds had been drawn so Thaddeus would not be able to see them.

There was the crunch of tires on snow, and the chief moved silently back to the front door. A moment later, he unlocked it and stepped outside, and they heard him talking with Angel, who had dropped Christine off at the station and then hurried to join them. Finch posted him out front, and then came back into the house.

Telling Helga and Andreas to sit tight, Finch, Raines, and Holly went out onto the back patio that overlooked the trail. There was a bench in the snow a couple of feet from the patio, where family and friends could sit to put on their gear. Holly sat down on the bench, pulled off her winter boots and slipped on her ski boots, tucking the cuffs of her jeans into the tops. It was the first time she'd ever worn jeans skiing, and the material felt bulky in her boots. She decided not to wear her helmet because she needed to be able to hear, but she slipped on her goggles and gloves. She laid out her skis, then put the toe of her left boot into the front of her binding and stepped down hard, locking the heel of her boot in place. She did the same with her right boot, picked up her poles, and skated toward the trail. The chief and Raines followed her on foot. They went as far as the tree line, then stood in the shelter of the trees and waited, looking up the mountain.

A few skiers whooshed past them, but none of them were Thaddeus.

Five minutes passed. Chief Finch blew on his hands and stomped his feet. Raines had his hands thrust deep into his pockets. His black hair had grown out a little, and Holly watched the breeze play with it.

"This case is a nightmare," the chief said. "I can't believe that Montague, the Johnsons and Blackthorn are all involved, but they all connect somehow to at least one of the killings. Christine, Skip and Thaddeus don't have an alibi for Justin's shooting. Any one of them could have killed Stefan and taken a shot at you, Holly, but only Christine and Thaddeus had the opportunity to fire that shot at Stubby."

"Someone's coming," Holly interrupted quietly.

They glanced up the slope and watched someone ski slowly toward them.

They stepped back further into the cover of the trees and waited.

"He's not a beginner," Holly observed as she watched the man make big, slow sweeping S's in the snow. The closer he came, the more convinced she was that it was Thaddeus. "I think it's him. The body type is right."

They continued to watch as he slowed down even more and moved his ski poles into one hand so he could pull something from his jacket.

"Damn it!" the chief muttered. "What does he have in his hand?"

"I can't tell from here," Raines said.

Both Raines and Chief Finch unholstered their weapons and drew them.

Holly, who had the advantage of goggles, which cut down on the glare from the trail lights, said, "I think it's a gun."

"You're sure?" the chief questioned.

The man slowed some more. He was close now.

She held a hand up to the side of her goggles to cut even more of the glare. "No. It's too dark to know for sure, but it's him," Holly hissed.

The chief stepped out from under the cover of the trees and raised his weapon. "Police! Stop!" he yelled. Raines walked out into view a few feet from Finch, and Holly popped out a little further down the trail from him.

Thaddeus almost lost his balance, but he kept heading for them, picking up speed as he drew closer.

"It's a gun, Chief," Holly yelled out just as Thaddeus raised his arm and fired wildly into the trees.

All three of them dropped to the snow. There was no cover on the trail, just snow groomed flat and smooth. Thaddeus flew past them. The chief and Raines spun around on the ground, positioning their bodies so they could return fire at him. Neither had a clear shot, though. Two skiers had just entered the trail from a house further down the slope.

Holly had hit the ground with her skis still on. They hadn't snapped free from the bindings, because they were set to release when a greater force was applied to them, primarily if she wiped out while racing at high speed. Grabbing her poles, she used them to raise herself off the ground without having to remove her skis to stand. This would have slowed her down. Once up, she slipped her hands through the straps and pushed hard on her poles.

Thaddeus was really moving now, letting his skis rip.

Holly pointed her skis downhill and pushed out with her feet, power skating to build up speed. Once she was cranking, she crouched down into an aerodynamic tuck, with her hands out in front of her and her racing poles held tightly at her sides. The poles were curved, so they wrapped around her body. Both her position and her poles were designed to reduce drag.

"She'll never catch him," the chief said.

"Have you ever seen her ski? They're heading straight for the lodge," Raines yelled as he started running for his truck.

Holly kept her focus ahead of her and increased her speed. She noted that Thaddeus was using both poles. She didn't know if he'd dropped the weapon or still had it on him, but she wasn't going to give him time to slow down and draw it. She closed in on him and grinned, reveling in the chase. She was going to nail him.

As she pulled even with him on his left side, she stood up, slowing down to keep pace with him. Suddenly, she noticed his shoulder twitch, and then he swung his pole at her.

She released her own pole so it could dangle from the strap and yanked at the one he'd swung at her. He lost his balance and, wobbling, was forced to let go so he could re-center his weight back over his skis.

She noted that he was athletic and had probably been skiing most of his life. But that wasn't going to save him now, she thought, as she reached out to jam his pole right between his legs at a sharp angle.

He cried out in pain, and she knew she'd hit her target. His right ski hit the pole, and he lost control.

Holly veered to the left to avoid a collision and slowed, even more, waiting for him to wipe out. They'd been skiing fast enough that he hit the ground with force. His legs twisted, and his skis dug into the snow. The force caused his boots to pop out of the bindings, and the skis slid away. His goggles went flying and so did his other pole. He continued to slide downhill headfirst until he hit a pile of loose snow.

It was a yard sale of epic proportions, she decided as she skied down to him. She pulled even with him, removed her Glock from its snug holster at her side and waited for him to look up at her.

He rolled over and glared at her. "You could have killed me."

"Where's your gun?" she demanded, standing over him

"I dropped it up the trail. I'm going to sue you for police brutality."

She responded by reading him his rights.

"I haven't done anything," he snarled bitterly.

"You just fired a weapon at three police officers. How's that for starters? And then you struck me with your ski pole."

"I wasn't shooting at you. You startled me. It was a reflex."

She motioned for him to get to his feet, then walked behind him, keeping the gun trained on him, while he retrieved his poles, skis and goggles. He put everything back on, and they skied back down to the bottom of the mountain. By the time they got into the lodge, Chief Finch and Raines were running in.

She grinned at them, and they shook their heads at her.

Thaddeus claimed he hadn't done anything wrong and had fired his weapon out of fear when he jumped out of the woods. The chief wasn't buying it, but when Thaddeus said that perhaps he should call his lawyer, Finch suggested they all sit down, have a cup a coffee, and try to sort out what was going on; otherwise, he was going to have to lock Thaddeus up in the cell overnight.

Thaddeus didn't take long to think it over. He sat down and waited while the chief bought coffees for the men and a hot chocolate for Holly. It was a Tuesday night, and the lodge wasn't busy. They sat at a table by the windows that overlooked the slopes.

"So, what do you want to know?" Thaddeus asked.

"First, why did you have a gun?"

"It's not against the law to own a weapon."

"No, but it is to fire it at us," the chief responded.

"I keep telling you that I wasn't shooting at you."

"Then why had you pulled your weapon? It was in your hand before you even saw us," Chief Finch pushed back.

Thaddeus gave a weary sigh as if the weight of the world rested on his shoulders. "Helga and Andreas stole those trees from me and are preventing me from reaching my land. I'm desperate. I don't know what I was thinking. I just thought I would fire a warning shot in the air. That's it. I need the money from either the sale of the trees or the sale of the land."

"Why? You seem to be extremely well off," Holly observed.

He jerked his head back in frustration. "I think my wife wants a divorce, and it's her money, which is inconveniently tied up in a trust. I'll get nothing. Not a penny. I need that money."

"And that's why you threatened Helga this morning?" Holly asked.

"It wasn't a threat."

She gave him a skeptical look.

"Okay," he conceded. "I can see how she would think that. But I loved her at one time, and she betrayed me, and she's done it again."

Holly wrapped her hands around the cup of hot chocolate. "Helga and Andreas didn't steal your land. They knew nothing about it or your squabble with Stefan. They thought that he was in Germany for the last two years and were devastated to learn that he's been dead all this time. We don't believe Stefan reneged on his agreement with you either."

Thaddeus eyed her askance, clearly not buying it.

"Who told you Stefan had left for Germany?" Raines asked him.

"It was Phil Montague. He said that he found him sleeping in the office with his bags packed for Germany." Then his eyes widened in one of those Aha! moments. "And it was Phil Montague who told me that Stefan had no intention of buying either the land or trees from me." He looked at them sheepishly. "So, it was Phil Montague all the time? You think he killed Stefan and lied to me?"

Neither confirming nor denying it, the chief stirred a couple of packs of sugar into his coffee. "What about the 1903 Springfield that we found in Skip Johnson's car? Whose is that?"

Thaddeus looked perplexed. "Is that a rifle?"

"Yes. An old one, possibly from World War Two."

"That probably belonged to my grandfather's brother. It was up in the attic with all the other junk Christine wanted to use to decorate the inn. None of it was of any value, so I gave it all to her. I didn't have any use for any of it."

CHAPTER FIFTY-FIVE

Holly woke to a bright morning. It was December 22, and she hadn't done a single thing to get ready for Christmas. Not that she had to do much. Her parents didn't celebrate the holidays, and she was the last person they'd want to see anyway. She usually bought the chief a bottle of Jack Daniels and small gifts for Angel and his family, whom she joined for their big, noisy Christmas dinner. But she did enjoy selecting a small tree and decorating it even though she'd be on her own.

The gunshot burn felt tight and stiff, so she rolled slowly over on to her other side. Snuggling under her comforter, Holly stared at the black bears and fir trees adorning the curtains. She thumped her pillow under her head and thought about whether it was Christine, Skip Johnson, or both of them who were in on it with Montague.

During her interview, Christine had refused to answer any questions. All she'd told Bliss Jarvis and Gustafson was that when she'd fired the weapon at Holly, she'd been confused and terrified. She'd concluded the interview by stating that she now believed Skip had shot Justin because the rifle had been found in his car.

Skip Johnson had refused to talk, and his lawyer wouldn't even consider a plea. He knew as well as Bliss did that it would be difficult to get a conviction for any of the homicides if Christine and Skip blamed each other at trial.

And there was even more bad news. The bullet from Stubby's shooting had been found, but it had been destroyed on impact, and they couldn't match it to the handgun Christine had used to shoot at Holly.

Holly dozed for a few minutes before suddenly jerking wide awake. Hadn't Sarah Mooney once called in a report of seeing a man lurking at the Witch Cross Inn? Now that could be something, she decided.

The chief had told her not to work the case alone, but Sarah Mooney wasn't dangerous. More to the point, although Raines seemed to have warmed up to her somewhat by the time they'd all headed home the night before, she didn't relish calling him.

Flinging the flannel sheets and comforter back, she hopped out of bed. She needed to talk to Sarah Mooney. She showered, dressed and didn't even take time to make coffee before she was pointing the Jeep in the direction of Sarah Mooney's house.

Sarah was pleased to see her, and so was Pickles, who scrabbled at her leg with his tiny paws until she bent down to stroke him.

Sarah invited her into the kitchen. She was still in her pajamas and had just made a pot of coffee. Christmas music played softly on the radio. She told Holly to sit down at the table and asked her if she'd had breakfast yet.

Holly shook her head.

Sarah placed cream and sugar on the table with the coffee pot, spoons, and a mug and told Holly to help herself. The breakfast table overlooked the backyard where Holly had first met Sticks and Stubby. She felt a pang of loss. Sticks had been a real character, and Stubby would be lost without him.

Pickles jumped up on her lap and curled up like he was a cat. She poured herself a cup of coffee. While Sarah bustled around the kitchen, obviously happy to have some company, Holly stroked the little dog.

Sarah whisked milk, egg, and cinnamon together. From the cabinet next to the refrigerator, she took out a tin of Panettone and cut four thick slices.

Holly couldn't believe her luck. The Italian Christmas bread was a personal favorite of hers.

Next, Sarah melted butter in a large frying pan, soaked the slices of bread in the egg mixture and cooked them in hot butter until they were golden brown. She sprinkled them with confectioner's sugar and retrieved a jug of maple syrup. It was from The Sugar Shack on Hurricane Mountain, which was another personal favorite.

Holly's mouth was watering by the time Sarah placed the plate in front of her. She scooped up Pickles and put him on his bed in the corner of the room, picked up her own plate and joined Holly at the table.

"I hope you like Panettone French toast."

Holly nodded and poured syrup all over the fabulous concoction.

They ate in companionable silence for a time, with Holly praising the breakfast several times. After a few minutes, Sarah put her fork down and asked why she was there. Holly explained that she was following up on the time she'd reported seeing a man lurking at the Witch Cross Inn.

"Oh, that? That turned out to be nothing more than a mistake on my part," Sarah said, and picked up her fork again.

"What happened?"

"The first time I saw the man was nearly two years ago before the inn opened. I saw him running across the parking lot to the inn. I was scared and called the police station, but I didn't hear anything more about it," she said, taking a sip of very creamy coffee. "Then, maybe eight months ago, almost the same thing happened. I was out late one night, walking Pickles. He had a bad stomach, poor boy. I saw a pickup pull over near the inn, but not in the parking lot. A man got out, closed the door quietly, and ran across the parking lot to the kitchen door, which I thought was odd if he were a guest. I was worried because none of the inn's lights were on. I thought he was breaking in, but I didn't want to call the police in case I was wrong."

She paused to eat another mouthful of French toast before continuing. "I knew it wasn't Skip, because he would have driven into the parking lot, so I waited for the man to go inside, and then I walked over to the dining room windows and peered in. I was so surprised to see Christine greet him. She wrapped her arms around his waist and kissed him. Then they turned and walked to the wall beside the big fireplace in the dining room. Christine fiddled with the paneling, and all of a sudden, a hidden door opened in the wall. Then they disappeared. I was so shocked—can you believe that?"

Playing along, Holly shook her head in disbelief.

"Well, not long after that, Christine had refurbished the furniture, made new curtains and matching comforters, and she invited some of us over to show off her new work. I'd had a friend stay there, and I think it was a smart way for her to market the inn to local residents who had families from out of town. Anyway, we were able to look around some of the rooms, and I remembered the secret passage. It took me a while to figure it out, but when they showed me one of the bedrooms upstairs, it all clicked into place. There's a bedroom above the dining room that has beadboard on the wall, and the passage connects the two rooms."

She glanced at Holly, and Holly again feigned surprise.

"If you weren't looking for a secret door, you would miss it," Sarah said, "but I didn't. It was the perfect setup for a secret rendezvous. I felt sorry for Skip, but it wasn't any of my business."

"Did you recognize the man?"

"No."

Holly was disappointed, but asked, "How about his pickup? Were there any distinguishing features?"

Sarah's eyes widened in surprise. "You are such a good detective, Ms. Jakes."

"It's Holly."

She gave her a delighted smile. "And I'm Sarah."

"So, what did you notice?"

"There was a decal on the door. It said Blackthorn Timber."

CHAPTER FIFTY-SIX

Holly left Sarah's place feeling very full and extremely excited. She backed out of the driveway and drove slowly down the road where Sarah had told her she'd walked Pickles. As she rolled past the inn, she noticed a man shoveling the walkway at the side of the building. It was Skip Johnson. He must have made bail, she thought.

She slowed to a stop and sat thinking for a moment. Skip must have heard the engine because he turned and looked over at her, standing with his arms resting on the shovel. His face looked red, even from where she sat in the middle of the road. He lifted his sailor's cap and wiped his balding head with his sleeve.

Skip looked like he could do with a break before he had a heart attack, Holly thought. She decided to try her luck again for a second time that morning, so she pulled into the parking lot, came to a stop beside Skip and rolled down her window.

Sweat ran down his face. "What do you want?"

"I know you don't want to talk to me, Mr. Johnson, but I'd like to tell you what Christine has told us, and then you can decide what you want to do."

He said nothing.

"Christine blamed you for the shootings and for all the problems she's been having."

He rolled his eyes. "They told me that last night. But you're trying to trick me into saying something incriminating. My wife wouldn't do that. Not Christine. She loves me."

He looked serious, and Holly felt a wave of uncertainty as she realized that everything she knew about Skip Johnson she'd heard from other people.

"Where did you meet your wife?"

"Sailing in the Mediterranean. I was captaining a sailboat for a family. I met her at a party, and we fell in love."

"And you ended up here, landlocked. That must be difficult."

"Sometimes it is, especially now, but I have Christine and Luke, and they make up for it."

"Do you enjoy running the inn?"

He glanced over his shoulder at the old Colonial and frowned as though it were bearing down on him. His face had started to return to a normal color, and he was sweating less. "It wasn't a calling, but it makes Christine happy. Only now... After what happened to Justin Jarvis, I don't think I can bear to be here anymore. It's all closing in on me. I need the open sea and the smell of salt water, but Christine refuses to leave here."

"Your wife told me you were friends with Phil Montague and played cards together."

"We played once after she introduced us. He was an okay guy, but I didn't have anything in common with him. Sailing's my thing. We sometimes get sailors staying at the inn. They sail in the summer and ski in the winter. Quite a life."

"There's no easy way to tell you this, Mr. Johnson, but I have a witness who saw Christine kiss Phil Montague and sneak him upstairs through the secret passage door in the dining room."

Skip's mouth dropped open, and he stood motionless, staring at her in shock. "Who said that?" he asked at last, his voice husky.

"I can't tell you, but I believe the witness."

He shook his head. "Christine can't have done that to me," he said, almost as if he were talking to himself.

Holly pressed on, hating herself for compounding the man's distress. "I believe she was using the bedroom connected to the secret passage to meet Phil Montague at night."

He placed both hands on the shovel handle and bowed his head.

"Do you need to sit down?" she asked, unbuckling her seat belt. The chief would kill her if a suspect died while she was questioning him, especially when his lawyer had clearly stated for the record that they were not to question him without representation.

He looked back up at her. "No, I'm fine." He swallowed. "No wonder she was upset when I rented that room out. She told me she wanted to keep it to use as a sewing room, but I told her that was a waste of money. I moved her sewing machine and her box of fabrics out of there and rented it. She was not happy with me, but I told her it was just for the holidays, then I'd put everything back. Now I know why."

Holly gave him a moment to process the news before she hit him with more unpleasant questions. "Why was the rifle in your car?"

"Someone is framing me."

"Who would want to do that?"

"I don't know."

"Had you ever seen the rifle before?"

"No."

"Were you aware that Christine was a top shot when she was younger?"

"Sure. She has the trophies, but that was just a kids' competition."

"I don't think it was, Mr. Johnson," Holly said, then changed tack again. "Where did the money come from to pay for the house and remodel?"

"From her mother."

"Did her mother have a lot of money?"

"Not by the time Christine's father gambled his way through it."

"Do you gamble?"

"No."

"Christine told me you hit it big in Vegas, and that's where the money came from for the remodel."

"My only vice, Detective, is single malt whiskey."

CHAPTER FIFTY-SEVEN

On the way to the Caxton PD, Holly contemplated calling Raines to update him. She planned to interrogate Christine to see if she could get her to confess. They needed a confession. Otherwise, her lawyer was going to parade Skip in front of a jury and label him the killer. The jury would take one look at Christine, who was short, plump and the definition of motherly, and conclude the more likely suspect *was* her husband. But Holly had looked her in the eyes when she'd aimed the gun at her. She was as ruthless as they came.

As Holly drove past Sweet Cakes Bakery, she considered stopping for a chocolate croissant to celebrate what she'd just learned from Sarah and Skip. In view of the fact that she'd just wolfed down a plate of the most amazing French toast she'd ever had, she refrained.

She was just about to drive on when she spotted the jet-black 1947 Ford pickup crouched in the parking lot. Its grille of big chrome teeth glinted in the sunlight. Holly wasn't an expert on antique vehicles, but she knew this one well. It belonged to Cal Raines. When a man with enough money to buy a dealership full of cars decides to keep and restore the beat-up wreck he drove in high school, that says a lot about the guy.

In her teens, Holly had spent many hours cruising the mountain roads in that truck with him. Although there had been many fun times, there was one night in particular, her prom night, that she didn't want to think about. That damn kiss! It had been awkward—and still felt awkward every time she thought about it—for several reasons. Most notably, it was because they were not dating, had never dated, and had no plans to date. Second, she'd broken her leg in a skiing accident at the Olympics and had been wearing a full-length cast on it. She'd been about as nimble as a pig on ice. Not only had Raines coped with her sloppy kiss with grace, but he'd also somehow managed to get her, and her bulky plaster cast, into that very same pickup and drive her home. His efforts had not gone unrewarded. She'd whacked him in the privates with the rock-hard cast as he'd struggled to lift her into the cab. She felt the familiar heat of humiliation as she remembered falling backward onto the Ford's seat and laughing at his groan of pain.

Oh, to hell with it, she thought. On the spur of the moment, she made a U-turn and headed back to Sweet Cakes. Why not invite him to join her in Christine's interrogation? After all, she thought with a grin, it was Christmas. What better present could you give a detective who has everything than the chance to outwit a suspect and get them to confess to a murder? He was so lucky.

She pulled into the back of the lot and was about to hop out of her vehicle when common sense reeled her in: she needed to make sure he wasn't with Abbey. She didn't want to ruin her morning if they were together. Shading her eyes with her hand, she scanned the bakery windows, and then her shoulders slumped. The good news was that he wasn't with either of his nieces. The bad news was that he was with Olivia. They sat in the window seat, looking like they'd just stepped off a romantic movie set. They were deep in conversation and were leaning into each other.

Holly hesitated. Should she interrupt their cozy tête-à-tête? On the 'yes' side, he'd worked the case with her, and it was only fair he got to finish it. But on the 'no' side, he'd been pretty pissed off with her; and she wondered if he'd even answer her call. She set her jaw and pulled out her phone. In for a penny, in for a pound, she decided. If he didn't answer, she wouldn't have to feel guilty for shutting him out.

She saw Raines look down at the phone, checking the caller ID, and then he answered it.

"What's up?" His voice sounded deep and rich and had lost the coldness from the day before.

"Are you busy?" she asked, as she watched him cover the phone and mouth something to Olivia. It looked like 'Holly,' but she couldn't tell for sure.

"No. I'm just finishing breakfast."

"I've had a break in the case and wondered if you wanted to take a stab at getting Christine to confess her sins."

"That sounds like the perfect way to spend a morning. I'm in town. I can be there in a couple of minutes. Are you at the station?"

She smiled. "No, but I'll meet you there." Feeling slightly like a stalker, she watched him stand up, place some money on the table, say something to Olivia, and leave without giving her so much as a peck on her cheek. Could there be trouble in paradise? Or was he so eager to finish the case he'd forgotten his manners? And how would Olivia get home? She must have come in her own car.

As Raines strolled over to his pickup, Holly ducked down and waited for him to drive off. His powers of observation could do with some work, she noted, smiling to herself as she put the Jeep into drive and followed him.

CHAPTER FIFTY-EIGHT

The chief called Bliss Jarvis after hearing Holly's report. They both agreed that Holly and Raines could interview Christine if she were willing, and then began to discuss strategy. Bliss knew it was going to be challenging to get a confession because Christine had already said she hadn't done it and pinned the blame on her husband. If Holly could unsettle her by confronting her with the new evidence, however, they might have a chance. Raines would observe and only take the lead if Christine were resistant to Holly.

The interview room had been designed according to specifications established by John E. Reid & Associates. It was small, about eight feet by ten, and windowless. It was painted a soft, pale blue, with the observation glass set high enough that suspects couldn't look at themselves in the mirror. There were three plastic chairs, one with a hinged writing desk attached to it for the investigator. A beige carpet further softened the room and muted noises. There was a photo of Mount Washington on the wall behind where the suspect sat. The room resembled an office more than it did a police interview room, which helped relax the suspect. Also, it played well with a jury if the confession was viewed in court as not having taken place in an intimidating environment.

Christine looked like a giant pumpkin in her orange jumpsuit. Her hair hadn't been brushed, and it was matted at the back of her head. There was a noticeable lump on her forehead where Holly had hit her with the trophy, and it had begun to bruise.

"I've already told the Attorney General that Skip did it," she said, jutting her jaw out, "so I hope you are here to release me."

"Didn't your lawyer tell you that Skip has been released?" Holly told her, carefully omitting that Skip had been released on bail.

Christine's eyes widened. "But he's guilty."

"We now know that's not true, Christine, and so do you."

"He did it. You found the rifle in his car."

Acting far more relaxed than she felt, Holly stretched her long legs out in front of her and crossed her ankles. "I've just had an interesting conversation with someone this morning, Christine, that casts doubt on your accusation. Detective Raines and I thought you'd like to hear all about it."

"What is it?" Her initial bluster had evaporated now, and her voice was hesitant.

"There's a witness who saw a man entering your inn late at night. This person watched while you greeted him like he was your long-lost lover, then saw you escort him up your secret passageway." Holly raised a suggestive eyebrow at this.

Christine blushed at the double entendre. Holly didn't know which of the meanings had embarrassed her, but she now knew she was on to something.

"It wasn't Luke, was it?" Christine asked, concern furrowing her brow.

Holly didn't answer that. "If this goes to court, all of the Blackthorns' dirty laundry will be aired—your father's gambling, alcoholism, and suicide."

Christine gasped.

Holly continued. "It will come out that you pretended to have money, and that you married Skip for his money when he had none. People will talk about that, but it's your sordid affair with Phil Montague that will make headlines. There will be a crime scene video showing the secret passage and love nest. Everyone is going to believe the witness."

Christine pressed her lips together and bowed her head.

Holly forged on relentlessly. "The Blackthorn name will become synonymous with the lowest of the low. And then there's Luke. The last of your line. People will say cruel things to him. He'll hear all about how you fawned over Phil Montague, and he'll be ostracized."

Christine glanced at Raines. "I remember the reporters at your brother's trial. Those poor girls."

Raines frowned. "Yes. It was a difficult time. I wouldn't want that for Luke."

She bit her lip and looked away.

Holly sat up and leaned forward. She placed a hand over Christine's. "No reputable college will want him if his name is tarnished. The admissions people will be able to read everything that is said in the trial. Any prominent family he wants to marry into will steer their daughters away from him, just as you would if the situation were reversed."

"Luke has to carry on the family name," Christine said urgently. "Zack isn't up to the job. However—"

Holly didn't give her time to finish her thought. "If you plead guilty, it will be over for him. You know the press. It will be news for a day, and then they'll be on to the next hot item. But a long, drawn-out court case involving a Blackthorn..." She raised her eyebrows and shook her head. "Well, I don't need to explain how sensational that will be. However, you could plead guilty and tell them how Phil Montague led you astray. Get it over fast."

She nodded at that. "Phil was so convincing when he wanted something."

"I did wonder about that when I met him," Holly confided.

Christine sat up straighter, shook her head and raised her chin. "My father killed himself out of shame. His father had lost everything to the Langs. He'd planned to rebuild and restore us to our rightful position in town. We're descendants of the first Americans."

Not exactly, Holly corrected silently, but let her keep rolling.

"It's not right how the Langs took everything—even our name—and left us with nothing. My grandfather never recovered, but I was going to change everything when I met Skip. I thought we'd be able to restore the family honor, and then I found out he had even less money than I had. Then one day I saw that the Witch Cross Inn was for sale. I knew it had belonged to Verity Caxton. Can you imagine? We're descendants of *the Caxtons*, yet we lived like paupers. And that's when I got the idea of restoring the inn and reclaiming the Blackthorn family name for ourselves."

She smoothed down the rumpled jumpsuit, straightened her shoulders and raised her head regally, as if she were waiting to be acknowledged.

"That must have been a challenging time," Holly commented dutifully.

"It was. The biggest hurdle, though, was that I needed the money to do it. I'd already met Phil Montague quite by chance at a consignment shop. It's the same place I found the chairs I reupholstered."

"They were good chairs," Holly said.

"And so cheap," Christine added.

Holly looked impressed. "They didn't look it by the time you'd finished with them."

Christine gave a slight nod in appreciation of the compliment. "When I found out that Phil worked for the Langs, I knew it was meant to be. I discovered that he was in debt, but he didn't try to hide it like Skip had."

"And he was in debt because..." Holly prompted, making it sound as if she already knew the answer.

"It was the trouble he'd had with his tree service business before he worked for the Langs. It had been expensive to start because he had to buy all of the equipment, and then that man fell to his death, and his family sued Phil because he didn't have insurance."

Holly sat back in her chair and let her talk.

"The men who'd worked for him at his company needed money, so Phil decided to start logging Stefan's land to help them out and also pay off his debt. Stefan Lang had so much land, which had once been Blackthorn land before Helmut Lang married into the family. It was fairly easy for Phil to do it because he ran the operations for Stefan."

Holly interrupted her. "So, you didn't start out by logging Thaddeus's land?"

"No. That came later, when Thaddeus discovered he owned a piece of land with valuable trees on it. After that, Stefan became interested in forest preservation and started to visit the land he owned where he believed there could be pockets of old trees. That's when he discovered Phil had been illegally logging his land for several years. They had a fight, and Phil hit him with an ax. It was over in seconds."

"I don't understand why you clear-cut your brother's land."

"That was Phil's idea. He decided to do it because Thaddeus couldn't reach it, and they were valuable trees. I didn't want to do it at first because it was my brother's land, but Phil convinced me that we would use actual Blackthorn trees to restore the Blackthorn family name. It was perfect. And that land shouldn't have just gone to Thaddeus anyway. I am just as much a Blackthorn as he is. Phil used the same men who'd worked for his tree business, and they set up a temporary mill out in Verity Falls. And then someone found the skull, and everything started to fall apart."

So far, Christine had incriminated Montague in killing Stefan, but Holly needed her to confess to killing Justin. "But Phil didn't kill Justin because he was with us at the time of the shooting."

"I heard Justin talking to you," she nodded to Raines, "about illegal logging."

"I was actually talking to Justin about a guitar," Raines commented.

"A guitar? That doesn't make any sense. I thought he'd found the passage in his room and had overheard Phil talking to me downstairs about how Stefan's skull had been found. I told Skip not to rent out that room. If he'd listened to me, nothing would have happened to Justin. I thought he'd snuck downstairs and spied on us."

So, Justin probably hadn't found the passage after all, Holly thought. The footprints had been from Christine and Montague. They had just assumed he'd found it.

Christine was still explaining. "I talked it over with Phil right in the middle of the auction, and we quickly hatched a plan. He'd stay in the room with everyone, while I'd go to the kitchen and pretend to be preparing more hors d'oeuvres. It was the perfect alibi. I had the rifle in a small office off the kitchen." She sounded proud.

"And the rifle you used to shoot him? It was passed down through your family, wasn't it?"

"Yes. It's a family heirloom. My brother gave it to me with more family treasures he didn't want." She sighed. "It was a beautiful rifle."

"And the incident at Verity Falls?" Holly nearly had it all.

"When Phil realized one of the Bigfoot hunters had survived, he thought it was only a matter of time before you came to arrest him. They'd got a good look at him because he was driving the truck right at them, and he knew they could identify him because they'd bumped into him the night of the auction. When Phil died, I realized I needed to do something to stop you from looking for me. I decided it was the one thing Skip could do for me that would be useful. I hid the rifle in the car and called in the tip."

Raines interjected, "Skip acted suspiciously after the shooting. Why was that? He wasn't involved."

"He was worried that Luke had something to do with it. I told him he hadn't, but he'd seen Luke sneaking around, acting suspiciously. Of course, we didn't know at the time that he was putting that Bigfoot outfit on and sneaking out."

"And you shot Frank Stanko as Phil was driving the portable sawmill away from Verity Falls?" Holly asked.

"I had to do that. They'd seen us."

"And you took the shot at Kenny Fritz when he left the hospital?"

She looked Holly straight in the eyes and said as calmly as if Holly had asked her to pass the salt, "Yes."

Christine hadn't shed a single tear. She stood then and held her flabby chin high in the air. "We Blackthorns do what we must to protect our family honor."

The hair stood up on the back of Holly's neck.

After Christine had been returned to lockup, Raines and Holly stood in the conference room with Finch.

The chief shook his head. "The irony, of course," he said, "is that the witches' cross was used to ward off evil, when in fact, all the while, the evil was right inside."

CHAPTER FIFTY-NINE

On the way home, Holly decided to call in at Helga's. She had the DNA kit for Andreas and wanted to let her know what had happened. The chalet was a blaze of lights as she parked under the portico. Helga opened the door and invited her in. Andreas wasn't there. He and Zack had taken Luke snow tubing in the hopes that it would help cheer him up. Holly gave Helga the kit and explained how to collect the DNA from the inside of Andreas's cheek.

They walked together into the kitchen, where Helga warmed some apple cider with mulling spices. Carrying their mugs, they strolled out onto the patio. There was another fire roaring in the pit, and Holly sat under a blanket of stars, watching embers flit up into the night sky while she sipped the hot drink.

She told Helga as much as she could about Christine's confession without compromising the case, and Helga asked about Thaddeus, wanting to know of his involvement in Stefan's murder. Holly assured her that Thaddeus had nothing to do with his death. Holly went on to explain that he'd been charged with unlawful discharge of a weapon on private land, and that he'd been warned to leave her alone.

As the evening passed, Helga talked about the guilt she felt for betraying Stefan all those years ago, and for the pain she'd caused her son. Andreas had forgiven her, she said, her voice breaking. She pulled a tissue from her pocket and wiped her eyes, and Holly waited quietly for her to compose herself. Andreas didn't doubt for a moment that Stefan was his biological father, he'd told her. Because of his act of forgiveness, Helga, too, was convinced that he was his father's son. Stefan had been a loving and generous man.

She then told Holly how Andreas wanted to honor his father's memory by establishing a scholarship in his name for individuals who wanted to study forestry conservation and preservation.

Finally, she added that she'd contacted her lawyer earlier that morning to make a generous offer for Thaddeus's land. She'd also instructed her lawyer to buy the land adjacent to the high school so they could create a pollinator park in honor of Justin Jarvis.

CHAPTER SIXTY

The morning of December 23 dawned just as bright and beautiful as the day before. The chief had given Holly the day off in gratitude for her service to the department. But there had been a catch. And it was a major one.

Holly stood in the middle of North Caxton's square wearing the most ridiculous Santa's elf costume she'd ever had the misfortune to see. She wore a red and green hat with a big, fat white fluffy ball on the tip and a green dress with a red hem and red collar that resembled a 1950s jive dress. It was cut so high above her knees that she didn't dare sit down. If that weren't enough to humiliate her, the outfit came with red and white striped stockings and absurd black elf boots with long, curling toes capped by a fluffy white ball on each one.

She was collecting toy and food donations, and she'd been placed under the watchful eye of Santa himself, who was sitting in the bandstand cheerfully greeting the kids.

Angel had stopped by earlier to take photos and laugh at her and Fennis. Fennis had also been forced into service. He looked like an enormous weightlifting elf in an equally ridiculous costume— although his bordered on obscene because the tights he was wearing were a little too snug. Worse, he had to stand next to Santa and lift each of the little kiddies up onto Santa's lap.

Holly was just waiting to hear someone file an indecent exposure complaint.

Then, to her horror, she spotted Cal Raines striding in her direction.

She could tell that he hadn't recognized her yet, which probably had more to do with her ludicrous outfit than his observation abilities. She glanced around for a place to hide, but there was none. There was nothing she could do except tackle it head-on. If he dared to laugh, she'd kill him.

He was carrying bags filled with toys and food for the donation box, and as he drew within twenty feet of her, he spotted her.

He stopped dead in his tracks and tried to hide his surprise. Then he burst out laughing. People stopped to see what he was laughing at and looked over at her.

She put her fists on her hips and yelled, "Very funny, Raines."

Some of the parents looked nervously from her to Raines. Then they hurried their little ones off to see Santa before the sideshow got any more interesting.

He collected himself enough so that he could walk again and sauntered over to her. "If I'd have known Santa's helpers were so beautiful, I'd have been here every year," he said with a grin.

"You better watch it, or you'll be getting more than coal shoved down your chimney, Raines."

He laughed again. "You should take that act on the road. The wise-cracking, sexy elf armed with a Glock." He nodded to a bulge in her pocket. "Who convinced you to dress up in that ravishing outfit anyway?"

"The chief said it's my punishment."

"Oh, yeah? For what?"

"For giving him such a hard time about returning to duty."

Raines glanced around. "Where is he?"

She nodded to the bandstand. "He's Santa. He does it every year, and he's great at it. Takes it way too seriously, though. We'll be here all night."

They moved a little closer so they could hear what he was saying.

A little boy walked boldly up to Santa, and Fennis bent down and lifted the kid onto the chief's lap.

"Have you been good or bad, Bobby?"

"Good, Santa."

"What about the time you snapped the head off your sister's Barbie? Were you good or bad, then?"

Bobby looked up at him with saucer-round eyes and gulped. "You know about that, Santa?"

"Santa knows everything, Bobby."

"I guess I was half good and half bad. She ate all my Halloween candy."

The chief nodded like a wise old sage. "And I've spoken to her about that, but this is about your actions, Bobby. Two wrongs don't make a right. Can you remember that?"

The little boy nodded with gusto. "I sure can, Santa."

"So, do you still want that Masterblaster Robot?"

"How did you know I wanted that? I forgot to put it in my letter to you."

"Santa knows, Bobby. Now be a good boy for Mommy, and Santa will think about it."

"Okay, Santa. I promise."

Raines asked out of the corner of his mouth, "How did he know what dear little Bobby wanted?"

"He talks to all the parents beforehand and makes a list."

Raines grinned. "He's the real deal."

"Yup."

Two teenage girls came over to make a donation of ski coats, and Holly moved back to the box to take them. They giggled at her costume, and she scowled at them. One of them pulled out her phone and snapped a photo. They walked off, looking at it and laughing.

"That's just great," Holly groaned. "It's probably all over the internet already."

A mother holding a little boy's hand asked her where the bathroom was. Holly directed her to the train depot that was at the back of the bandstand.

When they'd left, Raines said, "Perhaps Santa's little helper could help me find the mistletoe."

"You're aware that mistletoe is a parasitic plant, Raines. It lives off its host, sucking water and nutrients."

"You've always been such a romantic, Jakes."

They fell silent.

She glanced around, feeling awkward. "You didn't bring the girls with you?"

He shook his head.

"Are you spending Christmas at Olivia's?"

Raines looked at her oddly. "We're not celebrating Christmas. It's too rough on the girls. Abbey will probably spend time over there with Jesse, but Olivia's probably seen enough of me."

"How's that?"

"She's been giving me a lot of free advice on how to talk to the girls."

Holly raised her eyebrows but said nothing.

"You're surprised she would help me?"

"No. It's not that."

Raines looked perplexed for a moment before it hit him. "You thought we were dating?"

She was about to reply when the chief called her up to the bandstand.

CHAPTER SIXTY-ONE

Raines had just returned from the ski shop, and he was wrapping a black and white sweater with a snowflake pattern on it when Melody knocked on his office door and walked in.

He tried, and failed, to hide the package under a folder.

Melody looked at the gift wrap, and her face fell.

He silently cursed himself for not wrapping it in his bedroom.

"It's for someone I know."

"Don't worry about it, Uncle Cal."

"I'm sorry, honey."

"It's okay, but you're doing a terrible job of the wrapping. Here—give it to me." She walked over to his desk and picked up the roll of Christmas gift wrap. It was red with polar bears on it. Melody smirked.

"What?" he asked, embarrassed.

"Nothing. It's cute paper." She picked up the sweater, refolded it and placed it on the paper. "Holly will love it."

"I didn't say it was for Holly."

"A lucky guess."

"I give all my partners presents," he said.

"I'll have to talk to Po and see what you got him when you worked with him in the DEA."

"Okay, wise guy."

She laughed.

God, how he'd missed that sound. Suddenly he was glad she'd caught him with the gift. She finished wrapping it and held it out to him.

"This looks amazing, honey," he said. It really did. "Why can't I do that?"

"It's this really mysterious thing."

"Oh, yeah. What's that?"

"You have to practice." She giggled and gave him a peck on the cheek. Then she perched on the edge of his desk and traced an imaginary pattern on the desktop with her index finger. It was obvious she wanted to tell him something, so he reminded himself to respond and not react and prayed it wasn't something worse than drinking at the mill.

"Olivia invited us over tonight," Melody told him.

"That's nice of her."

"Do you want to come?"

"I have something to do," he said, nodding at the gift.

"Is it okay if I go? Kayla will be there, and it's a tough time for her, too."

"Who's Kayla?"

"She's staying with Olivia for a while. She lost her mom, like me."

"How about I drop you off?"

She looked down at her feet. "Umm... I'm wondering if we can go somewhere first."

"You bet. Where do you need to go?"

Melody was silent for a minute. She looked at the floor and then up at him, her eyes bright and somehow shy. "I want to be with Mom," she said softly. "I don't want her to be on her own tonight."

He nodded, then turned and looked out the window as he thought about Sherry. Snow had started to fall, and it was dark out.

"It will be cold at the cemetery," he said, turning back to Melody. "You go wrap up warm, and I'll go get the truck out."

"Thanks, Uncle Cal," she said.

"You bet." He ruffled her hair as she hurried out of his office.

Raines parked the truck at the side of the cemetery drive, and he and Melody walked slowly over to Sherry's grave. The stars were bright overhead, and they could see their breath in the air. Melody knelt in the snow and placed a holly wreath against her mother's tombstone. It had the brightest red berries Raines ever remembered seeing. On the drive over, she'd told him she'd made it from clippings she'd taken in their yard.

"It's beautiful, honey. She would love it."

They stood in silence, and Raines looked up at the sky.

"What are you looking at, Uncle Cal?"

"I'm not looking, I'm listening to the snow fall."

Melody closed her eyes and listened, too. "I can't hear anything. It's so quiet."

"Exactly. We're listening to the sound of absorption. The tiny pockets of snow are absorbing sound. That's why it's so quiet when it snows."

"Kind of like the acoustic paneling in your recording studio."

"Exactly like that."

"Fascinating," she said, and giggled. "Is this what you talk about when you're on a date?"

"What date?"

"I can think of someone," she said, and gave him a pixie grin that melted his heart. For a brief moment, she'd almost looked like the kid from two years ago—almost.

"You know I love you, right?" he told her.

"I love you, too," she said, and slipped her hand through his. They stood there listening to the snow fall together, and then Melody started singing "Silent Night."

Raines was quiet for a moment as he blinked back tears, swallowing the lump in his throat. "You can do this, Raines," he thought. And then, as his voice joined hers, Melody looked up at him with such love that his voice caught anyway. He took her mittened hand in his and squeezed it.

Out of the corner of his eye, he saw movement. Then Jesse and Abbey appeared from under the trees, holding hands. Abbey hesitated for a moment, not wanting to disturb them, but Jesse tugged at her hand.

They walked up beside Melody and Raines, and Abbey slipped her hand into Raines's free hand.

He bent down and kissed the top of her head, and she squeezed his hand.

The four of them stood in the snow and sang together.

Silent night, holy night
All is calm, all is bright
'Round yon virgin Mother and Child
Holy infant so tender and mild
Sleep in heavenly peace
Sleep in heavenly peace

Until that moment, Raines hadn't realized how alone he'd felt. He gripped his nieces' hands in his and thought about Sherry, and how he wished she was there with them right now.

CHAPTER SIXTY-TWO

Holly looked at the small Christmas tree in her living room. She'd spied it lying off to one side of the tree lot; it had had a branch broken off it, and the owners had tossed it on to the discount pile. It had looked so forlorn, and she'd known she had to have it. A real Charlie Brown Christmas tree, she thought, as she poured water into the stand.

She'd managed to retrieve the ornaments and lights from her tiny attic, but her side was well and truly sore again now, thanks to all the recent activity, so it was time for a break. She decided to reheat the pizza she'd picked up when she'd been in town, eat that, and then decorate. Luckily, she'd already laid logs in the fireplace a few days before, so all she had to do was strike the match—no heavy lifting.

She was getting a plate out of the cabinet when she heard a soft knock on her back door. Puzzled, she set down the plate and walked over to it. It was Christmas Eve, and she wasn't expecting anyone. Angel would be with his family at church, and the chief was over at his sister's house with Fennis. She lifted the curtain, which had skiers printed on it, and found Scotty Pepper standing there grinning at her.

She opened the door. "Everything okay?" she asked, looking up and down the street.

Scotty held up a shovel. "Heard you got shot. Thought I could shovel your driveway, seeing as it's Christmas. I know how hard it is to do anything with one arm."

Holly didn't know exactly how many times Scotty had been wounded in the line of duty. He'd been in the Special Forces and didn't talk about his service, but she'd seen some of the scars and knew it wasn't idle talk.

"I didn't get shot in the arm," she told him.

"You sure? Heard you took a round in the arm, but someone else said it was your leg."

"I think I'd remember. It wasn't my arm or leg. The bullet grazed my ribs, but it didn't even bleed."

He held up a bottle of champagne. "Or we could celebrate how you wrestled Bigfoot to the ground. I'd love to hear all about that."

She laughed and opened the door wider so he could enter. He propped the shovel up against the house and walked in. The fire crackled in the hearth.

"Something smells real good."

"It's pizza from Rosario's. I'm reheating it. Are you hungry?"

"I'm always hungry."

Even though it was still snowing after he'd dropped off Melody, Raines decided to drive his '47 Ford over to Holly's. They'd spent so much time in it when they'd been teenagers that it didn't seem right to be heading over to see her without it.

As Raines drove, a bout of nerves started to plague him, which he found surprising. He was rarely nervous. And he'd faced far scarier situations than dropping off a Christmas gift for Holly. When he'd worked in the DEA, he'd confronted some pretty terrifying drug dealers. For that matter, singing in front of a hundred thousand people about his deepest, darkest feelings hadn't been a picnic, but there was something about Holly that was more daunting. He glanced down at the present on the seat and asked himself for the umpteenth time what he was doing.

Turning onto her street, he saw that her lights were on. Were his palms actually sweating?

Then he spotted a black Dodge Ram parked next to her Jeep. He recognized it immediately. It was Scotty Pepper's.

He braked hard, and the pickup slid on the snowy road. Wrestling the steering wheel, he continued to drive slowly past her house. As he did, he glanced into her window, hoping she wouldn't see him.

There was no need to worry. Scotty was helping her string Christmas lights on a tree, and they were laughing together. It was a warm and cozy scene.

Raines reached the end of Holly's street and pulled over. There were no other cars in sight; it was Christmas Eve, and everyone was home with their families. He closed his eyes and leaned his head back against the seat.

Then, with a sigh, he put the truck back into drive, pulled out onto the road and headed toward Olivia's home and his girls.

AUTHOR'S NOTE

North Caxton, New Hampshire is a fictional village that can only be found between the covers of this book. Kearsarge County is fictional, too, but they are both located in the heart of the very real White Mountains.

If you wish to visit a setting similar to North Caxton, then a trip to North Conway and the surrounding towns is recommended. This area is famous not only for its magnificent fall foliage, but also for its skiing, hiking and outlet shopping. It is the inspiration for the home of my detective series.

In the novel, I reference Stark, New Hampshire, which is an actual town in Coos County. It's home to a beautiful Paddleford truss covered bridge as well as the location of the only POW camp in the state during World War II. At the time, the camp held two-hundred and fifty German prisoners of war, who logged and worked for pulp and paper companies. Allen V. Koop wrote an interesting book on the subject called "Stark Decency: German Prisoners of War in a New Hampshire Village."

People often ask me where I get my ideas from. The idea for my title Witch Cross Inn came to me years ago after I had a lovely lunch at the Salem Cross Inn in their Hexmark Tavern. Located in West Brookfield, Massachusetts, the restaurant is well worth a visit, but check the times because they have a winter schedule and do close for a vacation.

ACKNOWLEDGMENTS

My husband is not only fast at producing sustaining cups of tea when I need it, but he's even speedier at offering up encouragement. Thank you, Joe, for everything you do for me.

I'm blessed to have friends and family who are always supportive and never fail to cheer me on—some of them are even brave enough to read my first drafts! A big thanks to all the special, loving people in my life.

I'm also extremely fortunate to have the skills and guidance of my wonderful and talented editor, Jennifer McIntyre. Thank you for helping make this book possible.

A LETTER FROM LESLEY

Dear Reader,

Thank you so much for taking the time to read Witch Cross Inn. I really appreciate it! This is the second story in the Jakes and Raines murder mystery series, and I hope you enjoyed reading it as much as I did writing it.

I grew up in England but now make New Hampshire my home. I've spent a lot of time in the White Mountains, skiing, camping and hiking. In the fall, there's leaf-peeping and outlet shopping. On a hot summer day, I love to paddle in the cool water of the Pemigewasset River or swim from the beach at Echo Lake in the heart of Franconia Notch. It's not surprising, then, that I found this area the perfect setting for my series.

Right now, I'm writing the next Jakes and Raines adventure. If you'd like to hear when it's released, please connect with me on my website or Facebook page, listed below. Finally, if you enjoyed spending time with Holly and Raines, please tell your mystery-loving friends about it, or write a review if you have the time. I would be grateful, and I'd love to hear from you.

Best wishes,
Lesley

www.lesleyappletonjones.com
www.facebook.com/lesleyappletonjones

CPSIA information can be obtained
at www.ICGtesting.com
Printed in the USA
BVHW042140220323
660993BV00004B/101